DOUBLEWIDE

DAVE + KAR—

ENJOY !

Jim T.

J I M   T I N D L E

ISBN: 153757129X
ISBN 13: 9781537571294
Library of Congress Control Number: 2016915285
CreateSpace Independent Publishing Platform
North Charleston, South Carolina

DOUBLEWIDE

Shibumi has to do with great refinement underlying common-place appearances. It is a statement so correct that it does not have to be bold, so poignant it does not have to be pretty, so true it does not have to be real. Shibumi is understanding, rather than knowledge. Articulate silence. In poetry, it is eloquent brevity. And in a man, it is...what is it? Authority without domination.

--------Trevanian, **Shibumi**

PROLOGUE

Cancun, Mexico...December 26th

The humid Cancun night was made bearable by the steady flow of margaritas. The Blue Turtle Bar was rocking. The pungent smell of marijuana filled the air. It followed you to the restroom and clung to your clothing like a starving *mendigo* from the barrio. The music was blaring, and the young crowd seemed even more raucous now that Christmas vacation was almost over.

Jenny Tanner was on her second drink of the evening and did not have a care in the world. She could feel the stares as she walked back to the table. Jenny's deep tan afforded an eye catching contrast to her white shorts and baby blue halter top. She wished she could stay eighteen forever. This was her last night in Mexico before returning to Dallas at noon tomorrow with her parents. One last semester of high school and then off to college.

Ruben handed Jenny her drink and proposed a toast as she sat down. Glasses held high, the four of them drank to world peace and Lady Gaga.

Ruben wasn't through. His play-on-words was indicative of his wit and charm. "Another toast to our new friend, Jenny Tanner." Pointing at his chest, he added, "Even though I'm *tanner* than she is!"

———

The car bounced along the pothole plagued street as its black exhaust mingled with the stench of garbage. It was near midnight and there was scarcely any traffic on Avenida Nizuc. The ten-minute trip from the Blue Turtle Bar remained right on schedule.

"Keep your hands on the wheel, asshole," Ruben ordered from the back seat as he exhaled a cloud of marijuana smoke.

"You got your hands all over that Tanner bitch," Hector growled as he removed his right hand from the breast of the Mexican girl who was slumped over next to him.

Ruben and Hector had been "brothers" for almost twenty-two years, having grown up together in the neighborhood they were now driving through. Ruben had always been the leader of this two-man pack, but Hector knew he was an important part of their new money making scheme. Estralita, the girl passed out in the front seat next to Hector, was part of the team, too, but she was in it only for the drugs.

Ruben sat up and spit out the open window, nervous, but looking forward to the evenings activities. "Park under the carport in back, this *chica* is not out of it the way she should be. *Tenemos que apurarnos…*we'll have to hurry."

Ruben's small, one story apartment was reasonably well kept. The door to the kitchen was about ten yards from the carport. Outside lights had been removed from both the pole next to the carport and over the kitchen door. Hector unlocked and opened the door while Ruben removed the limp bundle from the backseat of the car. The young Mexican girl remained passed out in the front seat.

The kitchen, with only a table and three chairs, was attached to a small living room that was sparsely furnished with a well used brown couch and a broad end table on which sat a lamp and a Dell laptop computer. A 20-inch TV/DVD player sat on the floor next to the end table. An oval shaped rug covered most of the living room area. A door in the living room connected to the hallway that led past several other apartments and terminated at an exit door.

Off the living room was a bedroom with a king size bed and a side table with a small CD player. Since the bed took up most of the room, it had been shoved against the far wall. Only about six feet separated the foot of the bed from the door to the closet and the door to the bathroom.

An abstract black velvet picture of a bull fighter covered the upper half of the closet door. Behind the picture, a six-inch square of the door had been removed creating an opening barely large enough for the Sony 1080i HD camcorder. A small flap had been cut in the bullfighter's crotch that covered the opening and could barely be seen in the dimly lit room.

Jenny could hear voices, but in her disoriented state could not process the words. She felt as if she were flying both in the air and underwater at the same time. Blackness would come and then a bright light. She wanted to open her eyes, but every time she tried, they slammed shut. She wanted to raise her head, but it refused to cooperate. Fear mixed with euphoria, consciousness with drowsiness and then more blackness.

———

"I wish he would hurry up and get here," Ruben mumbled as he buttoned his cotton pants. "We have to get her cleaned up, dressed and back to the hotel in forty-five minutes." He reached in the drawer of the side table for the syringe containing 0.2 mg of Flumazenil which his uncle had provided. Uncle Emilio had said this was the best known antidote for Rohypnol, his date rape drug of choice.

Hector emerged from the closet with a look of anticipation. "Yo *primero la proxima vez*...I get to share the next one."

She was floating again with a light numbness that seemed to be centered in the back of her head. Everything was okay, but nothing was right. Her clothes had dissolved in the thick, damp air and someone was stretching her hands above her head. Panic was just not possible when you were soaring through a giant white cloud. There was no explaining such a feeling of numbness and pain at the same time. This was a night that Jenny would not remember, but one she would never forget.

FIVE MONTHS LATER

CHAPTER 1

Ridgetop Mobile Estates...May 26th...Dallas, Texas
Boyd Tanner turned his dark blue Ford Focus left off of Shiloh Road just northwest of Dallas onto a gravel road that ran in front of the trailer park. A worn black and white sign indicated he had arrived at the Ridgetop Mobile Estates. He wondered if the person who started this venture was laughing to himself when he came up with the name.

The frontage road appeared to be about two hundred yards long. The Ford passed numerous lanes on the right that contained mobile homes of various sizes and colors. The trailers were situated at slight angles on both sides of each lane.

About half way down the road, a leasing office sign with an arrow that pointed nowhere in particular came into view. As Boyd turned right, he realized he had turned one lane too soon, but decided to proceed to the end of the gravel road. It was late afternoon and there was little activity to be seen. Apparently, few residents felt like braving the hot, humid day.

Driving slowly, Boyd counted twenty-two trailers on each side of the narrow lane, all spaced about fifteen feet apart. He had seen humanity packed in even smaller...much smaller...living spaces in Hong Kong and other cities in Southeast Asia. There was something about this place that seemed right, maybe perfect.

More noticeable than the scattered post oak and pine trees growing beside the lane, were the large chocolate brown trash containers placed at the corner of each trailer. White lettering proclaimed the plastic receptacles belonged to CleanKing, Inc. Bikes, tricycles and various types of toys littered the steps leading to the front doors of the metal homes. Pickup trucks, older model cars and motorcycles occupied the gravel parking spaces. It appeared almost all the residents had a charcoal grill either on their small decks or on the grass near the trailers.

Boyd tried to make a tight u-turn at the end of the gravel road, but had to backup and maneuver the leased Ford several times. Two pickup trucks on opposite sides of the lane made an easy turn impossible. It appeared the trash containers at each of the trailers barely outnumbered the pickups.

Finally arriving at the parking space in front of the narrow leasing office, Boyd unfolded his six foot three-inch frame out of the car and was immediately sucked into the grip of the sixty-percent humidity. His faded golf shirt hugged his solid upper torso.

A narrow community swimming pool, surrounded by a five-foot chain link fence, was situated next to the office. A sign next to the pool gate warned: **LITTER BUGS ME, DON'T DO IT!** Ironically, floating pine cones, leaves and debris from the nearby trees and a white paper cup floated about like a mine field. The pines, oaks and crepe myrtles seemed randomly placed and not well tended. The more he took in, the more he liked the Ridgetop Mobile Estates.

The office door opened almost before Boyd finished knocking. "Hi, I'm Boyd Tanner. I called you this morning about leasing one of your mobile homes." Unsure about the sensitivities in this type of neighborhood, Boyd was careful to use the term mobile home rather than trailer.

4

Squinting, and pressing his lips together as if trying to remember an important piece of information, the fifty-something manager, in an animated manner, hands and arms painting a picture on a canvas of thin air, muttered, "Oh yeah, I told you 'bout the doublewide for five hunert and twenty-five a month. That's all we got right now. Has three bedrooms, two toilets and two showers. One month up front and a hunert dollar deposit. Oh yeah, I'm Roscoe. Roscoe Ratliff. How many in your family?"

Wearing an olive green tank top and a pair of red, white and blue Bermuda shorts, his skinny arms looked spindly next to his ample beer belly. His scraggly, long brown pony-tail complemented his unshaven facial hair. His worn sneakers seemed somewhat embarrassed by the loose fitting, black calf-length socks.

As an old rock n' roll artist was screaming from a CD player on his desk, Roscoe offered his hand to Boyd and announced, "Sorry 'bout the sweat, but I've been in the back pumpin' iron."

"No wife and kids, just me," Boyd declared, with a straight face. "I'll be staying alone and plan to be here at least two months. You mentioned that a month-to-month lease is acceptable?"

Roscoe weighed this information like a seasoned diplomat and then drawled, "Suppose that works for me. Where you movin' from?"

Evasive, yet truthful, Boyd said, "I've lived in Dallas for a while, but I needed a change of scenery so I decided to move out here. As I said, I'll be here at least two months and maybe longer. Let me know if you get in a bind and I'll sign a longer-term lease."

The rusty wheels in Roscoe's head almost squeaked as they churned. Boyd had a distinct feeling that Roscoe would be "getting in a bind" well before the two months passed.

Looking askance, Roscoe asked, "Mind me askin' what type work you do?" Roscoe had a way of avoiding direct eye contact.

"Well, I'm in between jobs right now, but I used to work for a couple of companies in manufacturing operations. I have some money saved up, so that won't be a problem."

Boyd wasn't sure whether Roscoe suffered from some sort of floating eyeball syndrome or whether he was actually looking at something on the wall just to the left of where Boyd was standing.

Either out of questions or trying to remember the ones he had just asked, Roscoe said, "Okay, let's get some paperwork filled out and I'll take you over to see your new mansion."

———

Boyd followed Roscoe along the side of the community pool and past a mobile home that backed up to the office. Roscoe walked at a casual pace, carefully surveying his kingdom. As they reached the next gravel lane, he turned right, and then crossed over to the other side of the road.

Knowing the answer beforehand, Boyd innocently asked, "Do you own Ridgetop?"

"Hell no! I barely have a pot to piss in! Two brothers own Ridgetop and eight other trailer parks all the way from Florida to Arizona. They both have MBD's from Yale."

Boyd assumed he meant either MBA's or Ph.D.'s, but it didn't matter in Roscoe's case.

"These boys are heavy hitters. Shit, they got more money than the fuckin' Vatican. Plus, they do their own financing and sell ninety percent of the trailers. Easy to do in a tough economy. You were lucky to find a doublewide to rent."

Boyd quickly replied, "They sound like interesting guys." Gathering as many facts as possible, he added, "How long have you been managing here at Ridgetop?"

Roscoe drawled, "Been 'bout four years now, but seems more like twenty. Work my ass off seven days a week! Most of it 'cause of them damned teenagers and stuff. Got a few parolees that cause a lot of shit. Soma' my best friends are parole officers 'cause they're around here so much."

"What kind of problems do you have?" Boyd didn't think Roscoe would ever be a serious candidate for a Chamber of Commerce job in Dallas.

"Mostly vandalism and thefts. A few fights, now and then. Happens 'specially at the end of the month on paydays. Got so bad I had a security company put some surveillance cameras on top of my office trailer. The security guy was on top of the trailer working and an 'ole boy in a white pickup truck drove up and stole his ladder. Can you believe that shit? Stole his ladder right out from under him and just drove off. Then, 'bout a week later, someone stole the two security cameras off the top of the trailer. Just fuck me!"

"Well, guess I'd better keep my door locked," Boyd somehow said seriously without grinning.

"Used to be a couple of prostitutes that had a trailer here," Roscoe explained with a slight catch in his voice. "They was always on time with their rent...one way or another. Damn shame the day they got raided."

A cardboard **FOR LEASE** sign announced Boyd had arrived at his new home. The sun was beating down, and Boyd's close cropped brown hair was starting to feel damp, sweat now trickling down his back.

Roscoe continued, "Yeah, we have 'roun half or so Mexicans and another half or so whites living here and only one black family. Hell, most of the problems come from the goddamned whites. The Mexicans seem to be hardworking folks that just look out after their families."

"How many mobile homes do you have here?" This was exactly the kind of background information Boyd was seeking.

Roscoe tilted his head to the side and said in his best managerial tone, "Have a hunert and thirty-two trailers and no tellin' how many people. Reason is, some of the Mexicans have aunts and uncles and all sorts of relatives living with 'em. Hell, my maintenance man had seven people living in a two-bedroom trailer. I moved him up to a three-bedroom and he ended up with ten people livin' there. I just turn my other cheek to that kind of stuff."

The trailer was painted an off-white with mustard yellow trim and had a huge cottonwood tree growing near a small three-step deck that led to the front door. It appeared an addition had been added to the front portion of the trailer. Three small windows lined the side of the trailer facing Boyd and he could see a larger window, which was part of the addition, providing a view of the street. Boyd assumed this was a doublewide's answer to a picture window. A parking space with a rusted tin cover was located on the other side of the trailer.

As Roscoe pulled a key chain from his pocket and ascended the steps, he proudly proclaimed, "This here doublewide is twenty feet wide and 'bout ninety feet long. You're gettin' one of my best deals, cause a single wide is only twelve feet wide and 'round sixty feet long and they go for four-seventy-five a month. Plus, this here one is completely furnished. Now when I say completely, I don't mean a hook-up for TV. You'll have to get one of them sky things with a little dish antenna."

Boyd figured Roscoe was talking about either Direct TV or Dish, so again with a straight face, he replied, "Don't plan on watching much TV, no need for an antenna. By the way, I don't see a trash container for this…ah…mobile home. How do I get one?"

Roscoe replied, "Fuck me twice, I plum forgot to have you fill out the form to get one. I'll bring it down in the mornin' and get you to sign it. This damn heat must be affectin' my brain cells. Here's two keys for your new home. They both work in the locks on this door and the one under the carport that leads to the kitchen."

Boyd could hear the bass thumping and guitar screeching of very hard rock music getting louder and louder as a teenage boy with his Dallas Cowboys ball cap turned backwards and his baggy pants at half mast walked by. He held a smart phone in one hand and a small wireless cone-shaped speaker in the other. Technology meets the trailer park. His feet made crunching noises in the gravel as he bobbed and weaved in perfect timing to the music. He stared at Roscoe and Boyd as they entered the doublewide. Boyd stared back and thought, *Yep, this feels right.*

CHAPTER 2

Cancun, Mexico...May 26th

The Blue Turtle's outdoor bar was unusually busy for 7:30p.m. Ruben and Hector had been drinking for over an hour since Ruben didn't have to work on his "booze cruise" boat this particular Wednesday evening. The cruise had been cancelled because of mechanical problems with one of the boat's engines. Hector worked at a meat packing plant on the northwest side of Cancun.

Ruben Repeza was a charmer, charisma dripped from his shoes. His bronzed skin, smooth facial features and neat swept back hair made him look more like a movie star than a waiter on Cancun's six evenings a week Devilfish Party Cruz. He was proud of his mesomorphic body build, especially his muscular shoulders and well-formed pectorals. Since his booze cruise uniform consisted of going shirtless along with a pair of blue cotton pants and sandals, he had lots of hot-eyed female attention. His perfect white teeth completed the swashbuckling lady's man image....and he knew it.

Hector Acosta, on the other hand, looked more like a stereotyped Hollywood bad boy. His mustache and too-long goatee, for some reason, clashed with his shaved head and seemed at odds with his short, stout frame. With crossed bandoliers and a rifle, he would favor Pancho

Villa. He was about two inches shorter than Ruben and at least twenty IQ points in arrears. The "opposites attract" theory had been validated by Hector and Ruben.

However, in Ruben's mind, Hector had three outstanding traits…he was useful, loyal and most importantly, without conscience. Hector had demonstrated all three traits on more than one occasion.

Ruben drank half of the beer in one gulp and put down his bottle of Tecate on the bar. Tecate had been his good luck beer since his first bottle at the age of twelve. His Uncle Emilio, who at the time lived in the Northern Mexico city of Tecate where the beer was brewed, had started Ruben at an early age.

"See those two girls sitting at the table next to the juke box?" Ruben spoke to Hector without moving his eyes from his targets. "They aren't with anyone and they look bored."

"Been watching. Let's work 'em. Suppose you want to stick me with the heifer on the right!"

Ruben looked at this friend. "We may both get the cow if things go according to plan. The blonde could be worth three-thousand big ones if Uncle Emilio can hook us up with one of his friends."

Uncle Emilio was the key member of the newly formed scheme and the one member with client connections and ready access to drugs. He had moved to Cancun ten years ago from Tecate where he had been a pharmacist. Rumors circulated within the Repeza family as to why he returned to Cancun, but no one really cared. His *farmacia* business in Cancun was successful and Emilio provided everything and more than his wife and five daughters could possibly need.

"Be cool," Ruben whispered as they approached the girls' table. Hector frowned and wet his lips in anticipation.

The blonde appeared to be in her mid-twenties and her large brown eyes seemed to sparkle as she looked up at Ruben and Hector. She was wearing yellow shorts and a white tee-shirt with a red Canadian Maple Leaf symbol on the front. The Maple Leaf fit snugly between her ample breasts.

Ruben locked eyes with the blonde and with his best smile said, "Hi, I'm Javier and this is my friend, Jose." Ruben had learned that on a one night touch-and-go it was best to not use his real name. "Could we buy you a drink and tell you about our wonderful city?"

The blonde was first to reply. "Certainly. I'm Emma and this is Olivia," she said as she nodded toward her friend. "We arrived from Calgary last week and have been hanging out on the beach and at a few places close to our hotel." Her arms were sunburned and almost matched the red Maple Leaf on her tee.

Hector extended his hand to Olivia and sat down next to her. Olivia had dark brown hair and wore a pair of Sarah Palin look-alike glasses. Even though she was sitting down, Hector could tell that she was short and overweight. He wondered if she were wearing a bra under her *I Love Cancun* tank top. Chances were…he would find out.

"I see that you *senoritas* are drinking Tequila Sunrises," Ruben expertly noted with a hand gesture. "You may be interested to know that tequila was the first distilled spirit on the North American continent and is only produced in certain regions of Mexico. Almost all of Mexico's tequila producers are located in a one hundred-mile radius of the town of Tequila in Jalisco State."

Both Emma and Olivia seemed genuinely impressed by Ruben's knowledge of his country's most famous export. Or was it his dreamy smile. Or was it the three Tequila Sunrises they had each consumed in the past hour and a half. In any case it wasn't the usual pick up line.

Ruben continued with his verbal tour of Cancun and the majesty of Mexico, while the four of them discussed the pros and cons of the various hotels in the Hotel Zone. Emma and Olivia were staying at the Imperial Las Perlas, a moderately priced three-star hotel on Boulevard Kukulcan which was only five minutes away from the Blue Turtle and about ten minutes from Ruben's apartment.

A waitress appeared and took their orders. The girls stayed with Tequila Sunrises, and both Ruben and Hector ordered beer.

Ruben put his hand on Emma's arm and said, "Excuse me for a minute. I will be right back to propose a toast."

Hector continued to tell the girls about his wonderful city by the sea while staring squarely at Olivia's breasts.

As Ruben neared the men's restroom, he pulled his cell phone from his pocket and used the speed dial to call Uncle Emilio.

"It's my favorite nephew. Where are you this fine evening?" Emilio asked.

"We're at the Blue Turtle and I'll have a beautiful blonde on the bed by 10:00p.m. this evening. Can you get one of your clients on short notice?" Ruben was careful and meticulous in his calculations. He knew the importance of timing in his new business venture and he didn't plan on making any mistakes.

"I'll call you back in a few minutes, but first give me a description of this goddess so I can arouse my client's most intense desires."

"Her hair is golden, her lips are full and sexy and she has wonderfully large tits. Really, she's very beautiful and she's worth every bit of the three-thousand-dollar fee."

Ruben and Emilio had determined three thousand dollars was a fair asking price for Emilio's clients. Ruben and his two associates received two thousand and Uncle Emilio got the remainder. After all, Ruben was taking all the risks and it was his looks and flawless execution of the business plan that made all this possible. Ruben felt a little like Hugh Hefner or Larry Flynt and was certain that someday soon he would be just as rich and powerful as these two pioneering entrepreneurs. Besides, the three-thousand-dollar sex fee was only the beginning. Uncle Emilio didn't need to know about the entire plan.

Ruben went into the restroom and spent a few minutes admiring himself in the mirror and then went outside and stood beside the bar. He answered his phone on the first ring.

"Yes, Uncle," he whispered.

"Senor Salazar will meet you at your apartment precisely at 10:00p.m."

Salazar had spent nine thousand dollars in the past three months in the pursuit of diversity. He was becoming a valued client because of his seemingly endless supply of cash and his need to constantly gratify his senses. Also, he complied with the rules.

"*Gracias,*" Ruben said as he returned to the table and sat with his new friends.

————

By 9:00p.m., the small dance floor on the beach side of the outdoor bar was packed with sweating revelers in various stages of intoxication. A black musician was sitting behind a Yamaha MO8 88 synthesizer howling out the lyrics to an old blues song.

Hector's initial impression of Olivia had proven correct. She was about five feet two and weighed in the neighborhood of a hundred and fifty pounds. As she danced, the movement of her heavy breasts caused the lettering on her tee shirt to become almost unreadable. Hector twirled Olivia around and pulled her close to his chest.

As the song ended, Ruben motioned for Hector to follow him and Emma back to their table. On cue, a different waitress appeared and mimed "four more" with her fingers. Ruben responded with a two-handed thumbs up causing a knowing glance in Estralita's eyes. She had the two tiny bottles of clear liquid in her short's pocket.

Both Ruben and Hector acted as if they had never seen her before, even though the three of them had been drinking tequila and smoking marijuana the previous evening. Estralita was the fourth leg of this four-person business venture.

Looking at Ruben, Emma said, "Tell me, what kind of work you do in Cancun." She was having some trouble speaking, reeling from the drinks, the amount of sun she had absorbed during the day and the dreamy hunk of manhood sitting next to her.

"I'm a stock broker and my friend here is in the meat packing business."

Hector could barely keep from laughing out loud. The meat packing line was one he and Ruben joked about constantly. This was Hector's term for what he thought was his exceptional love making ability.

With a seductive look and as sultry a voice as she could muster, Olivia made her contribution to the conversation, "Do you have any hot tips!"

Hector muttered, "I have one."

Trying to get the conversation back on track, Ruben elaborated, "Well the stock market is doing better, so I would recommend a reputable mutual fund." Ruben decided not to go further with this conversation since he didn't know the difference between a mutual fund and a mutual friend.

Estralita returned with the drinks and Ruben made a toast to Canada and international trade.

This was the part of the process that fascinated Ruben. He could almost predict the moment the girls would start getting glassy-eyed and tongue-tied. It usually took five minutes or so and Ruben became aroused just thinking about it.

"What do you girls do in Calgary?" Ruben asked, not really caring. He had no clue as to where Calgary was located in Canada. He was only vaguely aware of where Canada was located relative to the United States.

It had only been a few minutes since the drinks arrived, and Emma was having trouble keeping her head still. She reminded Ruben of the little plastic birds you can buy that dip back and forth into a container of water. Some of them can even pick up toothpicks.

Emma finally replied by saying, "Hair."

The drink was also affecting Olivia. She seemed to agree with the *hair* statement, but could only shake her head since no words were forming on her lips.

After five minutes of blank stares at the table, both girls started slumping. Ruben and Hector helped them from the chairs and then assisted their stumbling prey across the crowded dance floor and through the parking lot to Ruben's 2007 Ford Explorer.

They were right on schedule and Ruben was already mentally counting the money.

CHAPTER 3

Ridgetop Mobile Estates...May 26th...Dallas, Texas
Boyd returned to his new doublewide home late the same afternoon he had leased it and unpacked his two suitcases. He made several trips to his car and brought in boxes containing kitchen supplies, his laptop computer, sheets, pillow-cases and bathroom necessities. He had also bought three sacks of groceries at Jake's All-In-One, a combination food mart and gas station in the nearby strip shopping center adjacent to the trailer park. One of the sacks contained two six-packs of beer which he immediately placed in the undersized refrigerator in the undersized kitchen. He continued to unpack a carton of milk, a package of turkey lunch meat, four cans of sardines, a jar of mustard, a loaf of bread, a box of raisin bran, a jar of peach jelly, a can of Folgers, a box of plastic eating utensils, paper plates and a roll of paper towels.

Boyd understood why Roscoe had given him such a good deal on the trailer. The front door opened into the living room that had been enlarged by about four feet in length and six feet in width. A red couch, a standing lamp, a wobbly coffee table and two lawn chairs completed the furnishings in the living area. The kitchen was connected to the living room by a low wall with a small built-in table-top and two stools. A door in the kitchen opened to the covered parking space next to the trailer. A narrow hallway led past the kitchen to the bedrooms in the back.

It had three bedrooms as advertised; however, two of the bedrooms were exactly seven feet long and about eight feet wide, barely enough room for a twin bed. The "master bedroom" was a spacious nine feet by eight feet and contained a bed, a short wooden pole mounted across one corner of the room containing wire clothes hangers, a lawn chair in the other corner and a door to the bathroom. The bathroom consisted of a toilet snugged up to a sink and a shower door that could not be opened if someone happened to be seated on the toilet.

A soft roar emanated from two window unit air conditioners located on the far wall of the living room and in the main bedroom.

Boyd retrieved a six pack of beer from the refrigerator, a lawn chair from the living room and parked himself under the cottonwood tree beside the front steps of his new home. It was 7:30p.m. and the sun was just starting to slip below the western horizon. The mosquitoes were buzzing.

A Calico cat suddenly appeared from the shadow of the trailer and rubbed against Boyd's leg.

"You look hungry," Boyd observed. "Hang in there and I'll get you something to eat after I finish this beer."

The sounds of the trailer community reminded Boyd of his early childhood in Canyon, a small West Texas town with a population of twelve thousand. Boyd remembered Canyon as a town of hard working families where there were no rich, no poor, and no class distinctions.

Boyd was a good student and graduated from high school as the valedictorian. He earned a combined twelve letters in football, basketball and track, was an All State quarterback his junior and senior years and had never played in a losing football game from the eighth grade through high school. He was one of the most highly recruited football players in the state during his final year.

This type of success can affect a person's personality in different ways. It had no effect on Boyd. He was driven, but not obsessed; confident, but not cocky; and most of all, he believed that a person would be ultimately rewarded...or penalized for his actions.

Boyd's fifty-two game winning streak ended in his third game as a freshman at Vanderbilt University. He suffered a hyperflexion injury to his knee causing his patellar tendon to rupture. This led to an early retirement from football and a degree in finance and a MBA.

The smell of various types of food being prepared on the rusty outdoor grills was appealing and the sound of kids playing in the street was comforting. The fluorescent streetlights on the metal poles lining the street began making a shrill humming noise hinting at the coming illumination.

A tall, angular young man emerged from the trailer directly across the street and walked toward Boyd. As he approached, it was apparent he was Hispanic and in his mid to late twenties. His thick, black hair was cut short in front and it gave him a classy, masculine look. He was wearing jeans and a white tee shirt with cut off sleeves that accentuated his well defined arms. He was carrying a beer and a can of Off mosquito spray in one hand, a metal folding chair in the other.

He unfolded the chair and extended his other hand to Boyd. "Hi, I'm Jamie Rodriguez. I was talking to Roscoe this afternoon and he mentioned I had a new neighbor. Need any help with the dive bombers?"

Grinning, Boyd said, "Good idea. I'm getting tired of throwing beer bottles at them. I'm Boyd Tanner and I've lived here about five hours. How about you?"

"Been here one year this month. Moved in on my birthday last May. It's not the worst place on the planet to live, once you get used to the noise. After a while you'll be able to tune out all the TVs, radios and CD players blaring. Too bad they aren't all on the same station or the same song."

There was something unique in Jamie's voice and facial expressions. He had a quiet enthusiasm about him and there seemed to be a sparkle of mischief in his eyes.

Jamie said, "I'm a nurse at Parkland Hospital, male nurse of course." Looking at the cat by Boyd's leg he smiled. "What do you do, raise cats?"

There are some people you meet and immediately like, and Jamie was one of them. After a brief hesitation and a long swig from his bottle of beer, Boyd made a decision to be fairly straight forward. "I sort of re-tired and decided to write a book. The story takes place in a mobile home setting and I'm doing some research." The statement was accurate, but only one-half of the reason Boyd was currently living in a trailer park.

"Seriously! You aren't old enough to retire. I'll be twenty-seven in two days and you don't look much older than I am," Jamie stated.

Speaking slowly with an exaggerated West Texas drawl, Boyd said, "Wish that were true, but I'm through the gate and half way across the pasture. I'll be forty-two in September. I've just had a few lucky breaks."

The lucky breaks were brought about by sixty-hour work weeks for the past twelve years and stock options from two successful start-up, high-technology companies. With almost eleven million dollars and a few prudent investments, it's not that difficult to take a few months off to research a book.

"Where did you work? Was it here in Dallas?" There was an element of excitement in Jamie's voice. This was not the type of person you typically have as a neighbor at Ridgetop.

"I worked for two venture capital funded start-up companies here in the Dallas area. One of them went public and the other was acquired by a larger company. Total luck on my part. I have a home near Hillcrest and Beltline Road, but as I mentioned, the novel I'm working on takes place in a trailer park, so here I am."

Boyd took another drink of beer and probed, "How long have you been in the medical profession? Do you specialize in any particular field?"

Jamie finished his beer and dropped it on the grass beside his chair. "Well, after high school, I got a degree in chemistry from the University of Texas at El Paso and then joined the Army. I served for two years, returned to El Paso, and completed a sixteen-month Basic Entry Option in nursing. I've been working at Parkland Hospital here in Dallas for the past year. My current title is Anesthesia Technician, and someday, if I can find time to continue my education, I'll work my way up to a higher position. That's probably more than you ever wanted to know about the nursing profession!"

"Interesting."

With a slight tilting of his head Jamie added, "I spent around eight months after the Army in another line of work, but that's another story. Hey...tell me about your book. Why did you choose a trailer park for the story?"

Handing Jamie another beer, Boyd explained, "Well, there was an author back in the late sixties and early seventies by the name of Arthur Hailey. Two of his books, *Hotel* and *Airport*, were bestsellers and were made into movies. He would spend a year or so researching his books and then another eighteen months writing them. In the case of Hotel, he researched every aspect of a large hotel chain including the front desk, housekeeping, security, maintenance and so forth. He then came up with a good story of human conflict and mystery. That's probably more than you ever wanted to know about Mr. Hailey."

Jamie reacted with mock surprise in his voice. "So you're going to do research here at the beautiful Ridgetop Mobile Estates and have your book made into a movie!"

Smiling, Boyd teased, "You got it. And I'll get you tickets to the movie premier in Los Angeles!"

"I'll give you all kinds of assistance on your research. I've had a couple of run-ins with some of the local bad boys and a few of the other characters that reside here. Hey, I'll introduce you to Trixi and Heather. They operate the Oasis Massage Center located in a trailer two rows from here. There's no sign in front of their trailer and it actually doesn't have a name, but if you ever go inside, you'll see why it's the Oasis."

Chuckling, Boyd joked, "Sounds interesting. I'll be sure and put your name in the Acknowledgements section of the book."

Jamie continued with a verbal guided tour of the Ridgetop Mobile Estates. He discussed the types of people that lived there...the construction workers, maids, gardeners, brick layers and the unemployed. People trying to reach their dreams, however modest. The ones who had already given up, the parolees, the suspected small time dope dealers and the trouble makers. The typical makeup of the lower income segment of every city in the country. The good, the bad and the very ugly.

Draining his second beer, Jamie summed up his feelings about the state of Ridgetop and the world in general. "I'm not sure these people should be referred to as lower income…maybe they should be called the desperate class."

Boyd slowly nodded in agreement. "The current economy is causing a lot of people to be desperate. Hopefully, things will improve over the next year or so."

"Coming from big business, you must be a staunch Republican." Jamie had no problem delving into areas some people considered to be rather private.

Boyd immediately replied, "Actually no. I'm about as independent as a person could possibly be. You could characterize me as being socially liberal and fiscally conservative. I'm both disappointed and frustrated with our two political parties right now. All of the finger pointing and name calling reminds me of junior high school…no it reminds me of grade school. If our congress was a football team, six of them would be trying to run the ball and the other five would be trying to pass. That kind of team seldom wins a game."

Laughing, Jamie quipped, "Yeah, it seems like the typical congressman is only interested in two things…getting reelected and bashing the other party. Maybe we need a more mature third party."

Boyd took a long swallow of beer and continued, "Not sure that will ever happen. I've traveled on business in the U.K., Europe and all over Southeast Asia and have returned from each and every trip with the feeling there is no place like the United States. However, the worst thing we can do is stick our heads in the sand and pretend that things are perfect here. I try to look at politics from thirty-thousand feet. Seems like most of our electorate looks at things from about three inches. You know, voting for candidates based on their looks rather than their core beliefs. There's still work to be done. What about you? Are you into politics?"

Jamie thought for a couple of seconds and answered, "I voted for the Democrats the last two elections, but I'm not exactly into politics. I took a basic economics class as one of my electives in college and that does interest me. You know, Adam Smith and John Maynard Keynes and all the various economic approaches. Right now, I'm focusing on saving as much money as possible in order to continue my education."

"Keep at it." Boyd was impressed with Jamie's maturity and insight. He was also surprised that he had been living in a trailer park for one day and was having a discussion about politics and economic theory.

Boyd added, "Oh by the way, please don't tell anyone here that I'm retired. I would like to blend in while I'm doing my research."

Lifting himself from the lawn chair, Jamie said, "No problem. Speaking of research, would you like to walk over to Christina's and have dinner. We can celebrate my birthday and your new book."

"Is Christina's the Mexican restaurant in the shopping strip?"

"Yes indeed. Excellent food and service."

Boyd stood and stretched. "I've driven by and seen the sign, but never eaten there. Sounds like a good idea. But first, let me get this cat some sardines."

CHAPTER 4

Cancun, Mexico...May 26th

At 9:45p.m., Hector parked the Ford Explorer under the carport in back of the apartment. Ruben opened the back door and pulled Emma into a semi standing position. He lifted her into his arms and struggled to the back steps. The night was warm and sticky and Ruben could already feel beads of sweat forming on his neck. Hector had unlocked the apartment door and was waiting to turn on the lights after Ruben was inside.

The window unit air conditioner in the kitchen had been running all day creating three separate climates in the apartment. It was extremely cold in the kitchen, moderately cold in the small living room and somewhat cool in the bedroom. A damp, musty smell enveloped all three rooms.

Ruben continued to the bedroom and laid Emma on top of the new bedspread. His description of her to Uncle Emilio was not an exaggeration and his first impulse was to remove her yellow shorts. Instead, he said in a loud whisper, "Hector, what the fuck are you doing? You need to be in the closet setting up the camera before Senor Salazar gets here. We only have fifteen minutes."

Hector whispered back, his eyes cold and vacant, "I'm going out to the Explorer and make sure that Olivia is still out. Be back in a second."

Olivia was still unconscious and slumped over in the front seat. Hector opened the door and placed his hands under her arms and drug her out of the car. Next, he opened the back door and maneuvered her into the back seat. As he slipped his hand under her shorts, he saw car lights approaching at the far end of the parking lot. He hurriedly closed the door and pushed the auto lock on the key as he ran for the back door of the apartment.

Standing in the living room, Hector announced, "I think Salazar is coming. I'll get things ready as spaghetti." Hector had a habit of trying to come up with clever sayings and phrases.

He walked into the bedroom and as he was about to enter the closet with the video equipment he glanced at Emma on the bed. "Fuck these tight schedules, I'm tired of jerking off in the closet." And he closed and locked the door from the inside.

———

Senor Salazar quietly knocked on the back door of the apartment and Ruben opened it almost instantly. He did not want his prized client to have to wait. Overall, this was the ninth "business" appointment Ruben had arranged in the past six months for his clients, not counting the complementary encounter for Uncle Emilio. Technically, they were Emilio's clients, but Ruben liked to think of them as his own. Emilio had excellent connections, including wealthy businessmen and Francisco Salazar, Cancun's Chief of Police.

"Senor Salazar, a pleasure to see you again," Ruben said flashing his best smile. "Tonight, we are pleased to offer you the best of the best. She's perfect in every detail. Men dream about such fine feminine qualities as this young lady possesses."

Salazar was obnoxious in every way. He was fat, balding, and wore thick, black framed glasses. His nose was too big and his eyes too small for his pock-marked face. Skipping all pleasantries, he demanded, "Show me the bitch. I don't have all night."

Ruben put up with Salazar's surly personality and disrespect, not because of the three thousand dollar "entry fee" that he and Hector joked about, but because sooner or later, the DVDs from the camera in the bedroom closet would provide a retirement fund for Ruben and his small team.

The police chief walked into the bedroom and closed the door. The music from the CD player on the side table and the camera in the closet simultaneously hummed a haunting melody.

———

Ruben sat outside on the back step next to the kitchen door of the apartment. He had at least thirty minutes before Salazar would be finished. He lowered his head and gently ran both hands through the smoothness of his hair. He lifted himself off the step and walked the short distance to the Explorer. Even though there was little light under the carport, he could see Olivia lying in the backseat. His first impulse was to get in the car and do some exploring of his own. Then he remembered that Hector had driven and probably had the keys with him in the closet.

"Shit," he uttered under his breath. Oh well, maybe if Salazar finished early, he could have a run at Emma.

As he returned to the back door steps, he quickly gained his composure and thought about how well his new business venture was progressing. Decisions had to be made and he was the one to make them. Tourist activity was starting to slow somewhat with the onset of summer and that would enter into his decision. The small stack of DVDs in the bedroom closet would be his springboard to a better life. He would take Hector with him. Screw Estralita.

Ruben reveled in the hero-worship he felt in Hector's presence. It was nothing specific Hector had ever said, it was just there, he could see it in his eyes. It was the same look women had for him. He was certain he had a superior aura about him, along with his good looks and charm.

He remembered the incident in Houston two years ago. He had applied to The University of Houston and he and Hector went on a trip to visit the campus. The first night in the city, they went bar hopping near the campus and met two young ladies at Etta's Lounge. Ruben told them he and Hector were from Mexico City and were opening an office in Houston for their import/export business.

As closing time approached, Ruben took the girl he had been chatting up out to his rental car in the parking lot. Ruben immediately became overly aggressive with her and she slapped him hard on the face. Ruben shoved her head against the window and she started screaming and became hysterical. Hector had given up on his chances for the evening and headed for the car hoping Ruben might share his good fortune with him. As he approached the car, he heard the girl screaming and saw her trying to exit the rear door. He pulled the door completely open and then slammed it on her head. She tumbled onto the pavement and Hector kicked her twice in the face.

Ruben and Hector left the next afternoon on the flight back to Cancun.

As Ruben reminisced, it was apparent to him that he was indeed special. He led a charmed life and the women idolized him. He was handsome, intelligent and on track to be very wealthy. Nothing could go wrong.

———

Senior Salazar stopped before leaving the apartment and turned around to face Ruben. Salazar had an odd look on his face as he spoke. "I want a younger one next time."

Ruben responded in his customary obsequious manner and offered, "There are many high school girls that come to Cancun un-chaperoned. I'm sure we can find a lovely eighteen-year-old for you."

The police chief's small black eyes seemed to shine behind his glasses. "*Doce*," he said and then walked out the door without bothering to close it.

Ruben walked into the bedroom and said urgently, "Come on, Hector, let's move!" Emma was lying nude, face down on the bed.

As Hector emerged from the closest, Ruben said, "Did you hear Salazar's request?"

"No, what in the fuck does our police chief want now?"

Ruben glanced at Emma's still form on the bed and then looked back at Hector and whispered, "He wants a child...a twelve-year-old!"

Hector smiled and said, "*No problema*. You remember the orphanage on the north side of the city...La Casita? It's full of urchins and cast-offs, I've fished in those waters before. I'll make it happen."

"Good idea," Ruben reasoned, "this one will be worth more than our usual fee. We can plan it for later this week. Now, we need to clean up this one and get her and her friend back to the parking lot at the Blue Turtle. Go check on the fat chick in the car, I'll get started on this one."

Ruben had a contented look on his face. It felt good to be so smart, so organized, so much in control. Yes, that was it, he was totally in control.

CHAPTER 5

Ridgetop Mobile Estates…May 26th…Dallas, Texas

Christina's was packed seven days a week and tonight was no exception. The Mexican food restaurant had a broad customer base and individuals from every walk of life came to enjoy the food and ambiance. The restaurant shared a small strip shopping center at the intersection of Shiloh Road and Highway 1171. Boyd had passed by here many times and had filled his BMW 750Li Sedan with gasoline at Jake's All-In-One which was only two doors down from Christina's. A real estate office, a drycleaner, a tack shop, a State Farm insurance agency and a one room gym rounded out the tenants, but Christina's was the big draw. A small, weather beaten, wooden church building hovered about fifty yards from the gym and didn't appear to be part of the strip center, although it shared the far end of the parking area. The trailer park backed up to the shopping center and was only a few minutes walk from Boyd's doublewide.

The two new friends drew casual looks as they walked through the restaurant door. Jamie was almost as tall as Boyd and it was obvious they both solidly filled out their jeans and tee-shirts. Both of them had well muscled arms that women noticed and men envied.

The young lady at the reception stand recognized Jamie, and after putting his name on the waiting list, pointed them toward the bar at the back of the restaurant. The room was separated from the restaurant seating area by a half wall and contained a thirty-foot bar inlaid with back-lighted, translucent glass tiles, a foot rail and four tables. The tables were all occupied, so Boyd and Jamie squeezed up to the bar and ordered drinks.

Boyd responded to the bartenders question by saying, "I'll have a George Dickel on the rocks."

Jamie ordered a beer and cocking his head, looked at Boyd, "What the hell is a George Dickel?"

"George Dickel is the smoothest Tennessee sipping whisky ever made," Boyd said. "Only real men drink George," he said smiling. "By the way, you mentioned that you spent eight months after the Army in a different line of work. What did you do, rob 7- Elevens?"

Smiling, Jamie explained, "I got involved in mixed martial arts, you know, like cage fighting. It started with the Golden Gloves in high school and then some kick boxing tournaments in the Army. I continued after being discharged and spent a lot of time training in Brazilian jiu-jitsu and wrestling and competed in several local competitions in El Paso. I finally got discovered by the UFC and received a thirty-five thousand dollar signing bonus."

Boyd nodded his head a couple of times and said, "Now I get it. You became a male nurse so you could fight at night and sew yourself up during the day!"

Laughing over the noise in the bar, Jamie went on, "The good news is I received the thirty-five thousand bonus, the bad news is I gave it back two months later."

"What happened?"

"Well, my UFC career, that's the Ultimate Fighting Championship, only lasted a total of fifty-two seconds."

"You have to be kidding me!"

"And that consisted of three fights. I knocked out my opponent in the first fight in twelve seconds and knocked out the guy in the second fight in twenty-two seconds. I thought I was pretty hot stuff about then. However, eighteen seconds into the third fight I got kicked squarely on the side of my head and was out for about fifteen minutes. I met with my manager the day after the fight and arranged for him to give the thirty-five grand back to the UFC and I started nursing school the very next week. Kind of a rags-to-riches-to-rags story, huh?"

The bartender placed the whisky and the beer on the bar and said, "That'll be seven dollars, gents."

Boyd handed him a ten-dollar bill and told him to keep the change. Looking at Jamie, he raised his glass and said, "Happy birthday neighbor. I expect us to be back here in September for mine."

The noise level in the bar had steadily increased and after fifteen minutes they still had not been notified of an available table. Jamie leaned closer to Boyd and said, "What do you think about ordering some bar food? I think we got here a little late to eat at a table. If it's okay with you, I'll go tell the girl at the front desk to scratch our names off the list."

Boyd nodded his approval and as Jamie tried to move his bar stool back, he brushed against the person sitting directly behind him, causing him to spill part of his drink. The burly young man stood up and hollered over the din of the bar, "What the fuck!"

As they stood nose to nose, the angry patron appeared to be a few inches taller that Jamie. It was hard to tell his height due to the size of the Stetson hat he was wearing. He wore a pair of tight Levis with a large belt buckle that was reflecting light from the red and blue Fat Tire neon beer sign hanging over the bar.

"I'm sorry, man. Let me buy you another drink," Jamie urged.

Trying to impress the two women and the other cowboy sitting at his table, the man with the big hat, who was obviously drunk, barked, "Watch where the fuck you're going!"

Boyd watched as Jamie apologized again and made his way out of the bar to the reception desk.

The cowboy half-turned toward Boyd and with an enlightened look on his face said in a loud voice, "That goddamned beaner almost got his ass kicked! And I'm thinkin, you two guys are a couple of queers. I seen how close together you been sittin' and leanin' against one another." His grin could barely be seen through his thick black mustache and goatee.

The cowboy's woman said in a sing-song, high-pitched voice, "Well, if the one at the bar with the broad shoulders will give up the beaner for one night, I could show him how us straights do it."

The other three at the table thought this was hilarious and showed their approval by raising their glasses in a toast.

Boyd remained calm, but highly irritated, his grey-green eyes reflecting a relaxed intensity. After thinking about the situation for a couple of seconds, he concluded that alcohol mixed with a large dose of ignorance was the reason for the current scene. He finished his drink and asked the bartender for two bar menus, another beer for Jamie and another George Dickel for himself.

As Jamie returned and sat down at the bar, Boyd said with a big grin, "Watch it, you almost knocked over my George!"

"Guess I'm getting too old to hold my liquor, or maybe I'm still too young, as opposed to you mature dudes," Jamie said with a laugh.

———

By 9:30p.m. the bar was beginning to become less crowded. During dinner, the two new friends had discussed Boyd's business successes and Jamie's fighting and nursing careers.

With a slight tilt of his head, Jamie asked, "So tell me, have you ever been married? Any family around here?"

Looking intently into his glass, Boyd hesitated and then said, "I'm married and have a daughter who just finished her senior year of high school. My wife and I are living apart for now. Trying to sort out a few issues."

Jamie finished his beer and set the bottle on the bar. "How long have you been married?"

"Twenty years. Almost as long as you've been alive."

"Damn, just can't believe you have that many miles on you." Then, almost apologetically, Jamie asked, "It's absolutely none of my business, but do you think things will work out with you and your wife? Just tell me to shut up if you want to."

Boyd enjoyed talking to Jamie and felt comfortable and somewhat relieved to talk about this particular situation.

"My wife and I met in college. Married my senior year. We had Jenny, our daughter, two years later. We've had a great marriage with the usual self-inflicted road bumps…most of which I caused. Guess I can narrow it down to the fact I spent an inordinate amount of time at work and traveling on business. My wife, Sally, gave up a potential career in order to raise our daughter and take care of all the household business. You know, taxes, insurance and generally running the household. It left me free to concentrate on my own career."

Jamie nodded and said, "Sounds like a good partnership."

Boyd thought for a second and continued, "I was the kind of Dad that came home after a long day at the office and couldn't say no to any request our daughter made. Don't get me wrong, she's a really good kid, but she had me wrapped around her little finger. Bottom line, that's why I'm now renting this doublewide."

"What do you mean?" Jamie asked.

Boyd stared at his drink. The combination of George Dickel, Jamie's engaging personality and the stress building up for months caused Boyd to make a split decision to be completely honest.

Locking eyes with Jamie, he said, "The three of us were in Cancun for a family vacation this past December. The last night there, we went on an evening cruise. It was called the Whiskey Cruise or some such thing. Our waiter charmed all three of us. He told us about how he was going to college the following summer and fed us a long line of shit. Very believable. He asked our daughter to go out dancing with him and his friends when we docked. My wife was not in favor of the idea, but Jenny begged to go and I convinced Sally to let her have a good time on the last night of our vacation."

A pained expression clouded Boyd's face and he finally continued. "Jenny got raped that night, but didn't tell us about it for almost two months."

Closing his eyes and slowly shaking his head, Jamie murmured, "Oh jeez."

Still looking at his empty glass, Boyd said, "She was scared and confused and was trying to decide whether or not to tell us about what happened. Then one day on her way home from school she had a miscarriage. That's how we found out. Her mother blamed me for letting her go out with that asshole and one thing led to another and now we're separated."

"What about the waiter guy on the boat? What happened to him?" Jamie asked.

With a distant look in his eyes, Boyd said, "I told you I was here to write a book, and that's true. However, I'm also going to use this trailer park as my base of operations for another little project. I need to be out of touch with family and friends for a while. I've got to set this whole thing right between me and the waiter."

Jamie opened the palms of his hands and shrugged. "Didn't you notify the police or somebody about what happened?"

Boyd said, "I went to great lengths to get the authorities involved. I called the Cancun Police, the American Embassy in Mexico City and a local FBI friend of mine in Dallas. The Cancun Police immediately wanted proof of a rape and implied that female tourists typically go to Cancun to get laid. The American Embassy essentially told me to fuck off and my FBI friend was cordial, but couldn't offer any encouragement or advice due to the circumstances."

"You mean because of the time that had passed?"

The darkness came back into Boyd's eyes. "Yes, the timing and also the question they all seemed to have regarding rape versus consensual sex."

Shaking his head, Jamie said, "I'm sure you have no doubt."

"Absolutely none. Jenny evidently was drugged. She only remembers bits and pieces of what happened that night." Hesitating, Boyd, lowered his voice. "She thinks it may have been more than one person that raped her."

Sitting straight up on the bar stool, eyes wide, Jamie said, "So what exactly are you going to do? Are you going to kill him?" The pitch in Jamie's voice rose an octave.

Boyd calmly replied, "No, but it's not going to be the best day of his life. I'm going to tattoo a four letter word on his chest and cut off a portion of his most private part."

"Holy shit, you're going to cut off his hooter!"

Staying calm and trying to decide whether to continue, Boyd finally said, "Not the whole thing, only about an eighth of an inch or so off the tip. I guess it will depend on my state of mind when it happens. Just want to leave him a couple of permanent reminders."

"Are you sure about this?" Jamie slowly twisted his empty beer bottle, knowing the answer before the question passed his lips.

Hesitating for a moment, Boyd said, "I honestly never thought about revenge or getting even with anyone before this Cancun thing occurred. Something inside me just won't let it go. I've been consumed with it for several months. And the scary part is… I'm glad the son-of-a-bitch wasn't arrested. I want to carry out the sentence myself. No compassion, no remorse. That's how it's going to be."

Slowly shaking his head, Jamie said, "Well, mess with the bull, get the horn where it really hurts. This puts a whole new meaning on a waiter losing a big tip!"

Boyd continued. "This type of thing is not such a rare occurrence in vacation spots such as Mexico, Hawaii and the Caribbean. Remember the missing Holloway girl in Aruba? My FBI friend told me there have already been twenty-five cases of rape reported in Cancun since the first of the year. He says four or five times as many go unreported."

Leaning forward in his chair, Jamie asked, "Need any help with this little project?"

"No. I need to do this by myself. I'm working on a plan."

"How can you carry this out by yourself! What are you going to do, hold him down with one hand and slice and dice with the other!"

"I'll figure something out. I have some ideas. Come on, let's head back to the trailer park."

———

They left Christina's and proceeded down the walkway in front of Jake's All-In-One. The two cowboys from the bar and their giggling women were just leaving Jake's as Boyd and Jamie walked past.

The loudmouthed cowboy with the big Stetson hat was carrying a six pack of beer. "Lookie here at the lovers! The beaner and his dad." He handed the beer to his friend and briskly walked up behind Boyd and Jamie.

What happened next would be talked about by the cowboy's friends for months to come. Boyd turned around and in one lightning motion hit the cowboy on the side of the head with an open hand. It appeared to have started with a whipping motion from his hips to his shoulder and then to the heel of his hand. The thud of hand-on-face could be heard all the way back to Christina's. As the cowboy crumbled to the sidewalk and his hat rolled over the curb, his friends involuntarily took several steps back and looked on in amazement. The two women were shocked into immediate sobriety and could only stand and stare with open mouths.

The cowboy tried to raise himself to his knees, but dropped back down on the sidewalk, his belt buckle making a scraping noise as he made his second trip to the cool concrete.

Jamie's eyes popped as big as saucers as he looked at Boyd and said, "Holy shit! You cold-cocked the motherfucker! Maybe we should mosey back home before the police arrive."

As they walked back to the Ridgetop Mobile Estates, Jamie had one last comment. "You know, that guy's belt buckle was as big as a clock radio. Hope he didn't scratch it."

Boyd simply nodded, and a solid, enduring friendship was born.

CHAPTER 6

Cancun, Mexico...May 27th

La Casita Orphanage looked like it belonged where it was on the run-down northern edge of Cancun. It was three o'clock in the afternoon, and the forty-five-minute drive for Hector and Estralita had not been without incident. Estralita was driving her 1989 Pontiac since Hector only owned a used, recently purchased motorcycle. Hector had made several attempts to caress her breasts during the trip, and as a result she'd made one wrong turn and had veered off the road on another occasion. Estralita was in a bad mood. She would rather have been substituting as a waitress at the Blue Turtle Bar where she worked as a temporary employee on a tips only basis.

Estralita was an orphan and had lived with a poor, foster family until the age of fourteen. For the next three years, she'd worked at numerous menial jobs before meeting Hector several years ago at a disco in downtown Cancun. She had always been attracted to bad boy types, and Hector certainly fit the mold. Although Estralita was street smart, she sometimes wondered why she continued to hang-out with Hector and Ruben, because she knew they loved to take advantage of her. The easy supply of drugs and the new money-making scheme, however, gave her the incentive to put up with their crap.

"You're stupid for buying that motorcycle. What are you going to do when it rains! You'll always be hot and sweaty! Jesus!" Estralita's mood was not improving.

Hector enjoyed annoying Estralita. He liked her company, but he took great pleasure in irritating her every chance he got.

"Thanks for comparing me to Jesus, but don't call it a motorcycle, call it a Harley. You know, like I'm your Harley Man!"

"You can't even afford a bike. What'd you do…steal it!"

"Nope. It's a vintage 1995 Harley Super Glide and it only cost four thousand, nine hundred and ninety-nine dollars." He prided himself in being precise. "I paid five hundred down, and in sixty months, it'll be all mine."

"How much are the payments?" Maybe she had underestimated his business skills.

"A mere seventy-four dollars and ninety-eight cents a month. The salesman told me it'll probably be worth twice as much as I paid for it within five years."

Rolling her eyes, Estralita ended the conversation with, "Yeah, right."

The orphanage was surrounded by a high, cinder-block wall. Three, two-story buildings rose above the height of the wall. A sprawling one-story apartment complex was visible on one side of the orphanage and a vacant building on the other. At Hector's direction, Estralita drove slowly past the orphanage, both noticing a metal gate at the far end of the wall.

It was her time to get back at him and sarcasm dripped as she asked, "What exactly are we going to do…crash through the gate and scoop up a little girl!"

Hector was deep in thought. "Let me think. Let me think."

Making a u-turn in front of the vacant building, they again drove past the gate and parked in an empty lot across from the orphanage. Estralita turned off the engine and lowered the driver's side window. The temperature was in the low nineties and the humidity was almost palpable. It could have been raining and no one would have noticed.

Turning and reaching across the seat, Hector lifted the lid of a Styrofoam cooler, placing his hand on the cool neck of a Tecate.

"Want one?" he asked.

"I need some white powder," Estralita said with a whiney groan.

"If we can pull this thing off, we can party tonight. Understand, bitch?"

"Fuck you and your little dick."

A dilapidated white school bus screeched to a stop at the intersection just beyond the vacant lot. As the bus was unloading, most of the kids headed in the direction of the apartment complex. And then, three boys and a group of girls stepped off the bus, crossed the street, and began walking the hundred yards toward the metal gate of the orphanage. A teenage boy grabbed a cloth bag from one of the girls and began running down the dirt path to the gate. The other boys were laughing and began running as well. Exaggerated screams erupted from several of the girls.

Hector's eyes widened, "Quick! Let's go! Park on the street just before the gate. I'll grab a *niña* and get in the back seat. Then you just boot it!"

Estralita quickly started the car and turned back into the street. She passed the girls and parked about ten yards in front of the orphanage gate. Hector got out of the car and pretended to be inspecting the back, right tire.

As the girls approached, he raised his head and said with a frustrated expression on his face, "Look at this tire. I need a new one."

The girls slowed their pace as Hector surveyed the group. They all appeared to be between ten and fifteen. Since Hector couldn't tell their exact ages, he firmly grabbed the arm of the nearest girl with his right hand and reached for the back door handle of the Pontiac with the other.

The other girls immediately started screaming again, but no one seemed to notice. The school bus was approaching from behind, but the driver didn't appear concerned.

Throwing the struggling young girl over the beer cooler and between the seats, Hector yelled, "Move it! Get the fuck out of here!"

As the girl kicked and screamed from the back seat, Estralita accelerated the Pontiac past the orphanage and turned left at the next street.

She was turning the corner and trying to raise her window at the same time. The edge of her front fender struck a garbage can and sent it flying into the back of a parked car she barely missed.

Hector was thrown forward and then against the door while the girl continued to kick and scream. Regaining his balance, he glared at the small passenger before hitting the side of her head with his fist. Her long black hair seemed to swarm about her face as she continued to scream. Hector hit her one more time. And then there was only the whump of the car bouncing over the pot-holes in the narrow street.

———

Hector continued drinking beer during the short trip. Pulling his cell phone from his pocket, he punched-in Ruben's speed dial number and took a long drink of the *cerveza*. The girl raised herself from the floor-board into a half-leaning, half-sitting position on the back seat.

Ruben was expecting the call and said excitedly, "How did it go? Did you find a young one?"

"Do I ever let you down, my brother?" he said smugly. "Call Senor Salazar and make an appointment. Tell him she's young, pretty and has long shiny hair and smooth skin. We'll be there in a few minutes."

"Good work. We'll be handsomely rewarded for this one."

Estralita braked sharply at the busy intersection of Kabah and Xcaret. Hector was attempting to put his cell phone back into his pocket as he balanced the beer bottle between his legs.

"Goddamn it, bitch. Watch what you're doing!"

The little girl sat upright in the seat and looked out the window. In one fluid motion, she raised the door lock and jerked on the door handle. She tumbled out of the Pontiac, quickly scampering to the back of the car parked in the next lane. Immediately a cacophony of blaring car horns filled the quiet afternoon. Stunned drivers looked on wide eyed. Two lanes of traffic were waiting to make a left turn onto Xcaret, but the traffic light was red.

Hector dropped his half-empty bottle while lifting his leg over the beer cooler. His toe dug into the Styrofoam causing the lid to join the bottle and the foam in the floorboard. Crawling over the seat, he freed himself and managed to step onto the pavement just as the left turn arrow appeared. The girl was nowhere to be seen as the cars started to move. A car drove slowly by with the passenger window down. An old man leaned out with a rolled up newspaper, swatting Hector on the side of the head.

"*Asno!*" the old man hollered.

The girl was gone.

CHAPTER 7

Ridgetop Mobile Estates...May 27th...Dallas, Texas
Boyd started a pot of coffee with the Keurig he'd brought from home. The constant roar of the air conditioner, the uncomfortable bed, and the altercation with the cowboy all contributed to a not-so-great-night's sleep. Not much could be done about the air conditioner and the bed, and even though the cowboy got what he deserved, it was troubling.

To heck with it. A man only has so much patience.

Boyd missed having a TV, but most of all he missed having a newspaper delivered to his door. He wasn't sure he would be able to digest his Raisin Bran without having a paper to read. His iphone could deliver all the news he ever needed, but it just wasn't the same. He'd forgotten to bring a toaster in his box of kitchen supplies from home. It wouldn't be the breakfast of champions, but he could make do with cereal, and bread with peach jelly. What he needed was a newspaper.

He slipped on a pair of shorts, sandals and a grey Vanderbilt tee-shirt with the gold V star in front. The coffee could wait; he needed the newspaper and reasoned Jake's All-In-One, where the scuffle had taken place last night, would be open at this hour. Hopefully, the cowboy had gotten up from the sidewalk and was sleeping it off at home by now.

He unlocked the door leading to the front side of the trailer, and sitting on the top step of the small deck was the Calico cat.

"Hey cat, are you back for more sardines?" Boyd had a soft spot for animals, especially cats.

This Calico appeared to be in excellent condition for a stray. Or, maybe it belonged to some little kid and just liked to vary its dining routine.

"I'll see if I can find you some dry cat food. Wait here, I'll be back in a few minutes."

Boyd liked the feel of the early morning humidity and the warm temperature. It gently wrapped its arms around him as he walked down the gravel lane leading to the frontage road. Several pickup trucks and cars slowly passed him and made their way toward the frontage road, another day of sweat and toil. The two lane highway in front of the trailer park was already busy with traffic.

The red OPEN sign in the window of Jake's All-In-One shone brightly as Boyd walked through the door. He immediately saw a stack of newspapers on the counter. Addressing the rotund lady behind the counter, Boyd asked, "Do you, by chance, have any dry cat food?"

The clerk nodded, dyed red hair swaying across her face, and without saying anything, pointed toward the back of the store.

Boyd returned the nod and walked in the direction the lady had pointed. Sure enough, several bags of Purina Cat Chow, along with Purina Dog Chow, were stacked next to the wall. He picked up a bag of cat chow and walked down two more aisles until he found what appeared to be children's school supplies, even though school had been out for at least a week. He settled for a small box of ball-point pens and a Big Chief writing tablet.

Returning to the counter, he picked up a copy of the Dallas Morning News and placed the cat food and writing material next to the cash register.

The heavyset clerk, probably in her mid-forties, had found her voice and asked crisply, "You live here at Ridgetop?"

Boyd reached in his wallet and produced a twenty-dollar bill. "Yep. I've been here one full day."

"Me and Lefty been livin' here at the Ridge three years. I like walkin' to work." She handed Boyd his change and said in a flat tone, "I guess you met Roscoe, the manager of the park."

Boyd figured it was either a factual statement or a rhetorical question and replied, "Yes, Roscoe leased me a doublewide yesterday. Seems like a nice enough guy."

The clerk tilted her head to the right and squinted at Boyd through her left eye. "He's a goddamn ex-con. Him and my husband served together at Huntsville. You know, the state prison. I swear he's goin' to get Lefty locked up again for doin' drugs."

Searching for an answer, Boyd finally said, "Well, let's hope not."

Continuing her story without any prompting, the clerk added, "They both got out on the same day, but Lefty had already been in for fourteen years. Armed robbery, ya know. Damned ole Roscoe only served three years for some drug dealing charge. Selling to minors, I think. And he's still at it."

"Sounds like he's not one of your favorite people."

"The cocksucker couldn't hit the ground if he fell twice." Extending her hand, she calmed down and continued, "My name's Gloria, what's yours?"

With a slight smile, Boyd shook her hand and replied, "Boyd. Nice to meet you."

Boyd decided to make a short detour as he left the All-In-One. He turned right and made his way down the cracked concrete walkway fronting Christina's and the other businesses in the shopping strip. The last storefront was Rusty's Weight Room. A dirt parking area extended around the end of the building where a weather beaten, wooden church was located.

Peering through the tinted window of the weight room, he could see several racks of free weights, a squat rack, three stationery bicycles and a couple of punching bags. Several people were in the gym using the equipment. The sign on the door was interesting:

$5 A VISIT or $700 MONTHLY DUES
Open 24 Hours
(Except from 6:00pm to 8:00am Mondays thru Sundays)

Rusty must have a sense of humor...or else he failed fifth grade math.

————

The Calico was still lying on the deck when Boyd returned to the trailer. As he opened the door, the cat ran between his legs and into the trailer, plopping down in the middle of the living room.

"Humm, guess you've adopted me," Boyd mumbled. "How about we call you Rosie instead of cat from now on? Your color scheme of orange, black, and white defies any logical name. Rosie will do."

Boyd opened the sack of cat chow, poured a small amount in one of his cereal bowls, and then placed it on the cracked, kitchen linoleum. Time for breakfast and the newspaper.

The air conditioners hummed as he ate the Raisin Bran and the two pieces of bread and jelly. This was the first time in months he could remember being completely relaxed.

Finishing breakfast and the newspaper, Boyd poured another cup of coffee, picked up one of the lawn chairs in the living room and walked toward the door. The cat followed.

It was only 8:00 in the morning and almost too warm to sit outside and drink anything hot.

Got to have some caffeine! This will make a bad night into a good morning.

Boyd placed the back of his lawn chair near the trunk of the cottonwood tree and sat down, careful not to spill the coffee. The distinctive noises of the Ridgetop Mobile Estates were gradually emerging. Cars and pickups were crunching down the gravel lanes, dogs were barking, doors opening and closing, an occasional loud voice.

Boyd noticed that Jamie's SUV was not parked next to his trailer across the street.

The young man must work long hours at the hospital.

He was surprised he'd known Jamie for less than a day and had already shared a few details of his personal life with him. This did not fit into his main objective for being at the trailer park. However, Jamie's charisma and his straight forward, enthusiastic personality made him easy to like and easy to confide in.

Boyd had worked closely with some very talented, driven executives over the past twelve years, but never considered any of them close personal friends. It wasn't that he didn't like them or enjoy interfacing with them in a business environment, but they never socialized to any great extent in their spare time. Probably because they were all too stressed and tired after a long day in a start-up company. Actually, upon further reflection, Boyd realized he hadn't had a close personal friend, a buddy, since high school. Well, maybe his wife was an exception, but now, even she was at least temporarily out of the picture.

Two young boys came into sight from the rear of Boyd's Ford Focus. The crunching of gravel on gravel announced their arrival. The younger of the two, maybe about ten years old, was intermittently sobbing and wiping his nose. He had a rather large bruise below his right eye and a reddish looking scrape above it. Both boys were wearing worn jeans, tank tops and Nike shoes that had seen better days.

The older boy was the first to speak. "Hey mister, you seen an orange Mongoose? We think somebody stole it!"

Taken by surprise, Boyd raised himself from the lawn chair and said, "Did you lose your pet?"

Maybe this is Rosie's owner.

"No man, it's his freestyle twenty-incher. My mom bought it for my brother last week." The boy seemed perplexed that Boyd didn't know a bicycle from an animal.

"Oh, a bicycle! Sorry son, but I haven't seen it. What's your name, young man?"

"My real name is Richard, but my friends call me Richie."

"Nice to meet you, Richie. Sorry about the bike."

The younger boy sobbed, "I'm goin' to get whipped again by Earl for not locking it up with that chain. Best bike I ever had."

Looking at his brother, Richie chimed in, "Yeah, Darell, Earl is going to kick your butt again and maybe mine too." Lowering his voice, he turned his head back toward Boyd. "Earl is our step-dad. He's okay, but he means business."

"Where do you boys live? I'll let you know if I see any stray bicycles."

The older brother pointed back toward the end of the gravel lane and sighed, "Down yonder on the end. Come on, Darell, let's keep lookin' for it."

Boyd seated himself in the lawn chair and thought about the conversation with the boys. He had a sinking feeling in his stomach as he surmised their station in life. He recalled his own childhood and the constant feeling of love and security he received from his parents. He could vividly remember walking hand-in-hand with his dad down the street or in the park or in a shopping mall. His dad's hand seemed enormous. It brought about a feeling of stability, security, love. Nothing bad could happen as long as his dad held his hand. Wonder how Darell got that bruise on his eye?

Boyd listened to the sounds of the trailer park, felt the humidity rising like heat in a steam room, and started to reflect about both reasons he was living in a trailer park at this particular point in his life. Some thought had been given to his book writing project, but he couldn't find the inspiration to get started. It was this other thing on his mind. He'd always considered himself a master at multi-tasking...until the past couple of months.

He leaned back in his lawn chair and placed his hands behind his head, elbows pointing toward the sky. The sky was a deep blue with only one long peculiar cloud formation visible at this early hour.

Boyd studied the slowly moving, ever changing cloud and tried to visualize some shape or form. Was it the face of an old man, a bird with only one wing or perhaps a mountain lake. The left side of the cloud had the most mass, while the right side seemed to be separating and forming the number seven. A narrow line of whiteness curved from the bottom right and joined the mass again at the top.

Blinking his eyes and slowly shaking his head, Boyd uttered, "No way." He was looking at a sky map of the Yucatan Peninsula with Cancun and the Hotel Zone standing out prominently.

He knew he needed closure on the events in Cancun or it wouldn't be long before he saw a picture of the Virgin Mary in a piece of toast. This was the reason he was living in a doublewide instead of his comfortable home which was only thirty minutes away. It was as if a moody passenger had been riding with him for the past several months. He did intend to write a book, but it became crystal clear that his Cancun obsession was the real reason he was here.

A couple of nagging thoughts had come to him intermittently over the past few days. His first concern regarded his motivation for what he was about to do. Was he motivated by a sense of justice or was it pure revenge? Maybe both. But who was he trying to seek justice…or revenge for? His daughter, Jenny, or himself.

He could vividly remember the night of the Cancun cruise and how the waiter had initiated a conversation during dinner. He'd introduced the waiter to his wife and daughter, and all three of them had been completely taken in by his charm and bullshit. Boyd was the one who, over his wife's objections, had allowed his daughter to leave the boat with the waiter. Was he ashamed and embarrassed he'd been played like the proverbial fiddle or was he consumed with the blistering hate directed at the waiter for raping his daughter? Again, maybe both.

Boyd knew the second source of his mental agitation had to do with something researchers referred to as the "revenge paradox". If he carried out his plan, and assuming there were no complications, would he feel better or worse afterward? Would retribution bring peace of mind?

As he listened to the sounds of the trailer park, he made a final decision…payback time! Time to quit vacillating and get on with it.

"*Senor.*" A woman's voice came from the other side of the cotton-wood tree.

With a start, Boyd leaned forward in his lawn chair, turned around and replied, "Yes, hello." He was looking at a short Hispanic lady in her late twenties or early thirties. She held a small child in one arm and a covered plate in her other hand.

"You know Jamie Rodriguez, yes? I see you sitting here yesterday."

Boyd stood and answered, "Yes. I met Jamie yesterday right after I moved in. Is he a friend of yours?"

The baby squirmed in the lady's arm and grabbed at her nose. "My husband and Jamie work on their cars together. Good boy."

"Yes, he seems like a nice young man."

"My name is Aurelia and my husband's name is Arturo." Nodding her head at the trailer next to Boyd's, she noted, "We live there." She extended her hand with the covered plate and said politely, "Maybe you would like to have some chorizo?" Handing the plate to Boyd, she added, "It's sausage with my special sauce."

Taken with the generosity, Boyd reached for the plate and said, "Thank you so much. I'm not much of a cook and I'm sure this will be delicious. I look forward to meeting your husband."

As Aurelia turned to leave, Boyd said, "Thanks again. I'll bring the plate over later." He figured this was something that could be included in his book.

With his coffee cup in one hand and the plate of chorizo in the other he walked up the steps of the deck.

The cat was lying by the door and got up as Boyd approached. "Sorry Rosie, you can come in, but I don't share sausage with anyone."

Here I am…seeing pictures in clouds and talking to a cat.

CHAPTER 8

Cancun, Mexico...May 27th

It was 11:30p.m. when Ruben arrived at the Blue Turtle Bar. He had worked for the past six hours at his waiter's job on the Devilfish Party Cruze. The Devilfish had docked at the nearby Playa Langosta pier after an uneventful Thursday night. For some unexplainable reason, the weekends were much more exciting in a city in which every day was a holiday. Hector had been waiting for him as requested.

This was Ruben's favorite bar in Cancun, or anywhere for that matter. He thought of it as a middle-of-the-road type bar. The Turtle often had a DJ serving up the music, occasionally a small band of some type. The huge, oblong bar served dance floors both outside and inside. The bar area where Ruben and Hector were sitting, overlooked the patio dance floor and the garden surrounding it. The inside bar and dance floor were occupied primarily during inclement weather, or by tourists trying to escape the heat. There were other more cosmopolitan bars and clubs in Cancun, such as Coco Bongo or Dady'O, but the Blue Turtle better served Ruben's dark purposes.

Ruben and Hector were sitting on bar stools, with their backs to the bar. Ruben was looking straight ahead at the gathering crowd, his eyes starting to adjust to the outdoor lighting. The dance floor was crowded with revelers from the local hotels, as well as numerous individuals

Ruben recognized from the recent Devilfish cruise. The loud music contributed to the crowd's adrenaline.

Hector asked submissively, "My friend, when are we going to…," he paused briefly, "do this thing?" It was more a pleading statement than a question, but his impatience was obvious.

Ruben replied, his tone even and unemotional, "Well, if you hadn't fouled up your assignment with the little girl for Salazar, we would have a video worth a lot of *dinero*." Ruben kept his eyes on the crowd.

"Yeah, but what about the other DVDs? We have videos of Salazar and the other clients with their pants down!"

"We need at least one more good show with Salazar as the star. The big cash potential is from him. We can always get something from the rest of them, but Salazar is the key to our wealth. His job as Police Chief has made him a fortune in bribes and drug dealings. I'm still trying to figure out how we can pull this thing, as you call it, off."

Not hiding his eagerness, Hector continued his pleading, "Why can't we just mail him a couple of the DVDs and tell him where to drop the money?"

Barely whispering over the noise of the crowd, Ruben turned to face Hector and spoke, his tone pedantic, "My good friend, do you know what will happen to us if this goes wrong? Salazar and his goons would cut us open and let us watch our insides spill out. Then he would remove our eyes, and chop off our heads. That would hurt…a lot!"

"So, what are we going to do? I thought we were going to make a lot of money and relocate to San Diego or someplace cool. I can't take working at the goddamned meat packing plant no more!"

Hector had worked at the packing plant for over two years and hated every minute of it. The misery of the animals had nothing to do with his loathing of the place, it was the stench of the entire building, the steamy smell that exuded for two blocks in every direction from the building. He'd started in a janitorial position...janitorial position was a much better sounding phrase than the actual work. He basically swept up innards from cows, and mopped up buckets of blood for ten hours a day. Due to his compact body and physical strength, he was later given the job of Head Stunner. A medium sized sledge-hammer and a thick apron were his only items of company issued equipment.

"Don't worry, my brother, it'll happen. We just have to be careful...very, very careful. The timing has to be perfect." Contemplating his next statement for a few seconds, Ruben continued, "I don't think Estralita fits into our future plans."

"Huh! She's been excellent at getting the drugs in the bitches' drinks."

"Listen to me. I've spent a lot of time thinking about this. So far we have three DVDs of Salazar slobbering over some unconscious girls. Plus, we have some juicy videos of each of the three clients Uncle Emilio provided. I figure we can get a hundred thousand dollars from Salazar and thirty-five thousand a piece from each of the others. That's over two hundred thousand for the two of us. Why split it three ways?"

"What do we do with her?"

"We don't have to do anything with her. As far as she knows, we are going to San Diego. I'm thinking about Costa Rica. We can buy a bar there, have a lower cost of living, lots of Costa Rican babes and live happily ever after. Maybe relocate to the U.S. in a few years after all this shit has blown over. She can stay here and be happy at being a drugged-out slut."

Hector had to think about this development. Ruben was the smart one and had never let him down. He liked the idea about owning a bar with Ruben, but it bothered him to leave Estralita behind…but not that much. "Let's do it. Just tell me when."

"Look, I told Salazar I would get him a tourist girl for free tomorrow night, since we screwed up on getting him a twelve-year-old. One way or the other, we have to pull this off. That will be four DVDs of him raping innocent, drugged out Americans and should be worth a hundred thousand big ones."

"How exactly do we get the money from these guys?" Hector was pressing forward.

"I'm still thinking about the details. Don't worry about it. I figure we can move forward within a week or so."

As they smiled and touched beer bottles, Hector said eagerly, "Well, speaking of Estralita, let's get her over to your apartment for a threesome. She's serving drinks here, but she can leave whenever she wants."

"Go get her and I'll meet you at my place. I'm too tired to work this crowd."

The bar was filled to capacity with enthusiastic, inebriated revelers who had forgotten that Thursday was not as exciting as the weekend.

———

It was near 1:00a.m. when Ruben arrived at his apartment. Hector was following on his motorcycle and Estralita in her Pontiac. The air conditioner in the kitchen was going full blast as usual, and Ruben wondered when it was going to conk out or just blow up. He walked over to the counter and poured himself a shot of tequila. He'd been thinking about Estralita as he drove from the bar to his apartment, and all of a sudden he was looking forward to the next couple of hours. This would not be the first time the three of them had been entangled in his bed. He had some type of sexual attraction to Estralita, but keeping her share of the money from their new business venture was more enticing than utilizing her other talents.

Hector and Estralita walked into the kitchen holding hands. Estralita's eyes appeared to be glazed, so Ruben surmised that she was either drunk or had ingested something on the way over from the bar.

Whatever. She'll be ready to have a good time.

Hector seemed quiet and subdued. Ruben knew he was still processing the news about Estralita being shuffled aside when they leave town.

Hector's programmable. He'll be okay in time.

Ruben spoke first. "I've got an idea. I haven't seen the video of Salazar and the Canadian chick yet. Want to look at it?"

Without waiting for an answer, Ruben went to the bedroom closet containing the video camera and the box of DVDs. He returned to the living room, where Hector and Estralita were sprawled on the couch, and proceeded to put the disc in the DVD player. He slid between Hector and Estralita, draping an arm around each of them.

The immediate image of Chief Salazar removing his clothes was disgusting to Ruben. Salazar was a disrespectful slob and he would soon be put in his proper place...reaching into his pocket for a hundred thousand dollars.

The next ten minutes was nothing more than hardcore porn, which could be found easily on the Internet. This porn show, however, was going to add to Ruben's cash account and help fund his entrepreneurial dreams.

Ruben decided to get this show on the road. "Anybody in favor of a little fun?"

Hector raised his hand, but Estralita had already started unbuttoning her blouse and unsteadily raised herself from the couch. Ruben and Hector looked at each other and without saying a word, followed the young lady into the bedroom.

CHAPTER 9

Ridgetop Mobile Estates…May 27th…Dallas, Texas
A late afternoon shower was well underway as Boyd parked under the dilapidated tin roof of his parking space. The sky was filled with giant grey pillows being thrown around in slow motion, and the roof was leaking like a colander. The round trip to his Dallas home had taken about an hour and a half.

He entered the trailer through the kitchen door, wiped the water from his shoulders, and placed a suitcase packed with clothes and shoes on the floor. No doubt about it, the cramped doublewide was a far cry from his home in Northwood Hills, an upscale neighborhood in North Dallas.

During the trip, his thoughts had drifted from his marital situation to the events in Cancun and finally to his planned course of action. He knew he could not let this sleeping dog lie. Time was not on his side, he needed to get moving.

After unpacking the suitcase, Boyd used the remainder of the hanging space on the wooden pole mounted in the corner of the small bedroom. He walked into his kitchen with food on his mind. He determined he had three dining options…the chorizo that the lady next door had given him this morning, sardines packed in tomato sauce, or maybe a turkey sandwich. A knock on the door saved him from the excruciating decision process.

Jamie was standing in the rain at the front door holding a paper sack over his head with one hand and a fifth of George Dickel in the other.

"George and I saw a light in your window and thought we would come over and say hello," Jamie said with a grin.

"Well, since you brought my friend George with you, come on in. I'm glad to see you've picked up a little culture since our last outing."

Jamie dropped his rain-soaked paper sack next to the door and looked around the living room containing the sparse furnishings with the two lawn chairs. "Jeez, man, who decorated this place? Your gardener!"

With a grin, Boyd said, "Once you get used to them, these designer chairs are very comfortable. Roscoe Ratliff told me I got the deal of a lifetime with this doublewide."

Jamie said dryly, "I think our boy, Roscoe, has been standing too close to his microwave. His momma should have hit him in the head when he was a baby and sold the milk!"

Laughing, Boyd walked into the kitchen to get glasses and ice. As he was removing ice cubes from a tray, he said loudly, "Do you want to drink your George on the rocks, or should I bring you some soda pop or maybe some red Kool-Aid so you can mix it?"

Jamie calmly assured him, "If you don't hurry up, I'll start drinking it out of the bottle."

Boyd returned with the drinks and looked at Jamie. "Sorry about the episode with the cowboy last night. As you know, I've been more than a little stressed lately. I don't usually get completely out of control like that. And by the way, thanks for listening to my problems. Guess I needed to unload."

"Hey man, no problem. I only wish there was something I could do to help."

Boyd raised his glass, nodded and then commented, "I met the clerk at the All-In-One this morning, a red haired lady named Gloria. Know her?"

"Oh yeah, kind of a character."

"She made an off-hand comment about Roscoe. She indicated he'd been in the big house for dealing drugs and was still in the business here at Ridgetop."

"I'm telling you, Roscoe is not wired properly. Sooner or later he'll go down again."

Pointing in the direction of the front door, Boyd continued, "On a positive note, I met the lady next door...I believe her name is Aurelia... and she spoke highly of you. Said you and her husband work on your cars together."

"Very nice family. Her husband, Arturo, is a mechanic at Lothar's Auto Service. Knows everything there is to know about U.S. and foreign cars."

Sitting in the living room lawn chairs sipping whiskey, the new friends rehashed their dinner at Christina's and the events that followed. Jamie talked about the high points of his day at the hospital and they both expressed their amazement at the noise the rain was making on the tin roof of the trailer.

Boyd turned his head toward the door and said quietly, "Do you hear that? Don't tell me it's my new friend."

"You must have some fine tuned ears, because I don't hear anything."

Boyd set his glass on the coffee table and walked to the door and opened it. The calico cat calmly walked into the doublewide and quickly shook the water from her fur.

Jamie smiled and using his best TV commentator voice said, "Well, aren't you just the greatest cat whisperer Ridgetop has ever known!"

Boyd quickly said, "Did you know that most, if not all Calico cats are female?"

"Well aren't you Mr. Encyclopedia. I'll bet you don't know the state capital of Vermont!"

The new friendship, the sound of water on tin and the predictable effect of the Tennessee sipping whiskey created a light hearted atmosphere in the doublewide.

Without hesitating, Boyd said, "Montpellier. Bet you don't know the capital of South Dakota."

Thinking for a few seconds, Jamie ventured a guess, "Fargo? No wait, that's North Dakota. Okay, I give up, professor. What is it?"

"Pierre."

"Okay, bet you don't know what a rear naked choke is."

"Sounds like something a pervert would do."

Laughing, Jamie said, "It's a mixed martial arts term. You basically get the opponent from the back and put, let's say, your right arm around his neck with his trachea at the crook of your elbow. Then, you grasp your right tricep with your left hand and squeeze like hell. It restricts blood flow to the brain via the carotid arteries. You can cause someone to pass out in a few seconds."

Boyd couldn't pass on a tongue-in-cheek reply, "You know, not knowing exactly how to perform that move has been haunting me for some time."

"Wiseacre!"

"Here's the last one." Boyd was not finished. "You hear people throwing around the term nanosecond. You know, describing how fast they did something."

Jamie smiled and chuckled, "Hear it all the time."

"Do you have any idea how fast a nanosecond actually is?"

"Tell me. I'm dying to know."

"Let me put it in perspective. There are as many nanoseconds in a second as there are minutes in thirty years. Chew on that for a while."

"You old guys know a lot of stuff!" Taking another sip, Jamie didn't retreat. "Okay, here's another factoid for you. My name is not Jamie, it's Diego."

"I figured you were running from the law."

Unaffected by the comment, Jamie continued. "Actually, Jamie is a nickname a couple of my Army buddies gave me. They thought it was funny that Spanish speakers, including myself at the time, have difficulty pronouncing the letter j. You know, it comes out sounding like an h in Spanish, such as jalapeno or Jose. My given name is Diego, but they told everyone it was Jamie and it stuck. It didn't take me long to get on board and get the pronunciation correct. My parents are the only people on the planet that still call me Diego."

"You're just full of surprises."

"Okay, we're even. What's next? Arm wrestling?"

"I'll pass. Don't want you taking me to Parkland to get it re-attached."

The pitter patter of rain on the doublewide suddenly subsided and a subtle silence gripped the living room. The clinking of ice in Boyd's glass broke the silence followed by a knock on the door.

"Wonder who that could be?" Boyd walked across the small room, taking the final drink from his glass, and opened the door.

"Sorry I'm a short bit late bringing you the trashcan paperwork." Roscoe was wearing a floppy brimmed golf hat that had seen better days. Water rolled off the back of the hat onto the porch as he raised his head and looked up. Pulling a sheet of paper and a pen from inside his yellow raincoat, he handed it to Boyd. "Sign on the bottom line."

Boyd scanned the agreement, signed it and asked, "Where will they put the trash container, next to the parking area?"

"Yeah, I think so. You can put it anywhere you want it, just so it's facin' the street. Hey there Jamie, how you be?"

In a flat tone, Jamie said, "Doing fine, Roscoe. Doing fine."

"Okay, see you boys. Got a ton of things to do."

After Roscoe left, Jamie shook his head and rolled his eyes. "The old boy is just not fully functional. And right now, if I don't get some sleep, I won't be functional. Had a hard day and I'm beat. Want to go someplace for dinner tomorrow evening? It'll have to be an early evening, 'cause I have to work Saturday morning."

"Fine by me. Any ideas where to go? We may have worn out our welcome at Christina's. As I recall, you kept spilling people's drinks."

Jamie slowly got up from his lawn chair. "Have you ever had a hamburger at the Greenville Avenue Bar and Grill in Dallas? You know, down on Lower Greenville. One of my squeezes is going to be working there tomorrow evening."

"One of your squeezes, huh. Just how many squeezes do you have?" Boyd asked, emphasizing the word squeezes.

With his characteristic smile, Jamie raised his hand showing one finger. "Okay, I was bragging. With my work schedule, I'm lucky to have one babe as fine as this one."

Shaking his head, Boyd offered, "Okay, let's meet under my cottonwood tree tomorrow around six and we'll have a drink before we leave. And since you'll have had a couple of Dickels, I'll drive. Getting knocked out in a candy-ass cage fight is nothing like George busting your chops. You can show me the way to the Greenville Avenue Roadhouse."

"Catch up old man, it's the Greenville Avenue Bar and Grill!"

CHAPTER 10

Cancun, Mexico...May 28th

Ruben arrived at the Playa Langosta pier at 5:15p.m. on this warm, breezy spring afternoon. He parked his Explorer in a lot near the pier and headed for the boat. The Devilfish Party Cruze had been in business for three years, and by all accounts was very successful. According to the brochure, one had to be at least twenty-one years of age before they could sign-up for this cruise. However, it was widely known that if a guest had a driver's license, valid or not, getting on this cruise was not a problem. It had become one of the most popular cruises for the single, college crowd.

Ruben was wearing his blue cotton pants with a white rope belt and a pair of sandals. He would take off the loose fitting white beach shirt later in the evening. He often thought he should charge the tourists a viewing fee for the privilege of seeing his spectacular body.

Friday was his favorite work day of the week. An "anything goes" attitude prevailed and Ruben had experienced some wild and exciting events on this particular cruise. The Devilfish would leave the dock at 6:00p.m. and arrive at a private beach on Isla Mujeres about forty minutes later. A dinner buffet and entertainment would follow.

Ruben was not satisfied with his paltry salary, but felt lucky to have been hired as a waiter on this boat. Four months ago he had been fired from his position on the Caribbean Vacation Booze Cruise because of a complaint filed by one of the guests. All he'd done was to slip his hand under her midriff blouse and fondle her firm breasts. Besides, anyone who would wear a belly shirt was just asking for someone to grab skin. Ruben was an expert on women and knew what they wanted. If he'd known where she was staying, he would have instructed Hector to kick the shit out of her. She deserved it.

Uncle Emilio obtained the job for Ruben on the Devilfish. It was rumored the Devilfish was financed, and maybe even owned, by one of the Mexican drug cartels. Ruben didn't care if the devil himself owned the boat, it provided income and opportunities to meet beautiful women.

Ruben's initial responsibility was to hand out the complimentary drinks at the top of the gangplank for the hundred or so partiers that would soon be arriving. He was aware of the minimal amount of rum and tequila the specialty drinks actually contained. He equated this lack of liquor with his lack of salary. The customers seemed to drink enough of the pink and blue crap to eventually get drunk anyway. Actually, the customers purchased most of their drinks at the two cash bars located on the first two decks of the Devilfish. Ruben couldn't care less where the liquor came from…only where it ended up. Tonight, he would be on the prowl.

The sun was reflecting on the side of the Devilfish as Ruben walked up the gangplank. The tri-level catamaran was pearl white, one hundred feet in length, with bright red letters splashed across the side, spelling out the boat's name. The lower level included a two thousand square foot dance floor with disco lights and an oval shaped bar. The DJ was already on board, cranking up music to compete with the slap of the waves against the side of the boat.

The Devilfish advertised seating capacity for one hundred fifteen guests, but could carry up to two hundred people if necessary. Ruben wasn't sure if there were regulations regarding the maximum occupancy for the boat, but what the heck, surely they could swim if anything went wrong. Americans were only good for one thing anyway…fucking.

And tonight there would be plenty of that.

Ruben caught an earful from both Senor Salazar and Uncle Emilio due to Hector's screw-up with the orphanage girl. He promised Salazar a freebie tonight to make up for the inconvenience. According to Uncle Emilio, Salazar's wife was out of town for the weekend and Salazar was seeking an American companion. The easy way.

Salazar would be at the apartment tonight at 12:30a.m. and Ruben was under considerable pressure to deliver. It wouldn't be a twelve-year old, so he would have to give Salazar something special. Fortunately, Friday nights were full of opportunity on the Devilfish.

The bar was located in the center of the lower deck. Several female bartenders were busy mixing the colored drinks and placing them in carrying-trays containing sixteen drinks each. Ruben's immediate job was to place four of these containers on a table at the top of the gang-plank before the guests arrived.

Ruben approached the bar and spoke to Carmen, one of the bartenders, who was in the process of mixing the pink Tequila Sunrise concoctions. "Hey blender bitch, when are you going to give-up on that short little slob you call your boyfriend and go out with me?"

"My boyfriend will be kicking your pansy-ass if he ever hears you talking like that!" Carmen had heard stories about Ruben and didn't like him. She narrowed her dark eyes and disgustedly pointed to one of the containers. "Take these over to the table, pretty boy."

Ruben leaned his upper torso closer to the bar and countered, "Your tight little ass will be mine one of these days. Count on it." He gave Carmen one of his brightest smiles and picked up the container of drinks.

After placing the drinks on the table adjoining the gangplank, Ruben observed the moving line of young men and women coming toward him. At first glance, it appeared to be a multi-colored river gently flowing up-hill with splashes of every color in the rainbow. One of the scantily dressed girls stopped in the middle of the gangplank and focused her camera on the red, white, and green Mexican flag gently waving in the breeze on the second deck of the catamaran.

Most of the boarders were already swaying to the loud disco music blaring from the eighteen speakers on the first two decks. It was difficult to tell if the music was being sung in Spanish or English, but no one cared. The second deck was seventy-five feet long, and like the lower deck, had tables and chairs situated around the deck railing. Jose Padilla, the captain of the Devilfish, operated from the third deck, which was only about fifty feet long. Wide ladders made the second and third decks easily accessible. Another employee was collecting the seventy-nine dollar tickets as the guests boarded the boat. His million dollar smile evident, Ruben stood next to the drink table while nodding his head toward the pink and blue drinks.

The gangplank was now packed with the excited visitors eager for an evening of debauchery, and there appeared to be more skin than clothes visible on most of them. A few of the women sported sundresses, but most were wearing shorts and skimpy tops. As Ruben observed the laughing, bubbling stream of party-goers, he estimated about half of them to be females.

He continued his calculations with a simple thought: *A third of them are as ugly as a jar of raisins, another third okay for at least a quickie and the remaining third hot as hell!*

They seemed to travel in either pairs or threesomes. In his experience, it had been easier to latch on to someone in a group of three when he was working alone. He was on a tight schedule and Hector would be of little assistance until later that night. Hector was working at his job at the meat packing plant on the outskirts of Cancun and planned to meet Ruben at the Blue Turtle at 11:30p.m.

Fucking Hector! This was all his fault because of the screw-up at the orphanage.

The young men in the line, as usual, were loud and generally obnoxious, trying to get attention or trying to get up the nerve to say something clever to a woman. As Ruben expected, an inordinate number of the guys had earrings or were wearing some sort of necklace. Almost all of them were wearing shorts and sandals. The ones that had been doing sit-ups for the past three months had their shirts completely unbuttoned and the rest of them had tee-shirts with various college names, cute sayings or pictures of beers on them. Ruben didn't care how cool they thought they were...none could compete with his charm and good looks. Bring on Clooney and Pitt, he could kick their asses with no problem. This was like fishing in a stocked pond.

Two females in their early twenties approached the drink table, and Ruben slowly waved his hands, palms up, over the table of drinks. "Ladies, what's your pleasure?" He knew his smile and that particular phrase would make them both wet.

"I'll have a blue one," the first one said as she flashed her eyelashes at Ruben. She had a mouth full of shiny braces which appeared to be the only thing on her head not sunburned.

The second young lady was slightly better looking, but didn't even make eye contact with Ruben as she picked up one of the watered down drinks and moved forward.

The males tended to pick up their complimentary drinks without slowing down as they passed by the table. Ruben thought they looked like marathon runners grabbing cups of water at the twenty-mile mark. Most of them didn't even look at him and instead were surveying the possibilities ahead.

Several couples passed the table, followed by a group of six women. Ruben guessed they were sorority sisters since four of them had the same Greek letters on their tee-shirts. They were all nice looking, but the possibility of separating one of them from the herd was not good. Ruben knew women and he knew the pick-up odds.

Two black ladies in their early twenties stopped at the table and smiled at Ruben. The first to speak asked, "What's in the pink one, rum?" Her hair was cut short and her firm body was evident in the white shorts and tight, white tee shirt.

Ruben smiled back and said slyly, "Indeed it is and try not to spill it on your lovely top." He raised his eyebrows and stared at her chest as he spoke the word *top*. Ruben was pleased with his mastery of the double entendre.

As she picked up the drink, she pursed her lips and gave a throaty reply, "Stay on it." Her friend also selected a Tequila Sunrise, and they both waved as they made their way to a table.

Several more couples boarded, followed by another pair of young ladies. One had long, raven black hair and the other was a blonde. They both were noticeably overweight and already drunk with excitement. As they picked up their drinks, the blonde put her hand on Ruben's arm and asked, "Is it true that the women on this cruise are encouraged to put their hotel names and room numbers on their panties? You know, just in case we get too drunk to find our way back."

Ruben looked at the blonde's nose ring and the two rings in her lower lip and responded with a smile, "I will personally ensure you make it back to the hotel zone." Then laughing, he continued, "Or I can help you write your hotel number on any...ahh... place that seems appropriate."

Both girls giggled and hurried toward the tables lining the deck.

Ruben was beginning to wonder about his ability to make good on his promise to Senor Salazar. And then he saw her. She was approaching the top of the gangplank...alone. Ruben quickly scanned the individuals walking near this goddess and none of them seemed to be accompanying her. She was about five-feet-five, shoulder length light brown hair hanging in swirls around her neck, and as she came nearer he could see her dark brown eyes and perfect legs. Her full figure was evident under the white tank top and the short, flowered skirt. A small white handbag dangled from her left hand.

Completely ignoring the other people in line, he flashed his dazzling smile and made direct eye contact with this most beautiful woman. She was probably in her late twenties or maybe even early thirties, but Ruben didn't care. He knew she was the one.

"Senorita, may I offer you some refreshment?" He was stunned by her beauty and unassuming manner.

She reached for one of the blue coconut concoctions and replied in a low sultry Southern accent, "This is just what I need. It's been really hot standing in line."

"It'll cool down when we get closer to Isla Mujeres. Perhaps I could treat you to a more pleasing drink during the trip to the island."

She returned his smile and said politely, "Looking forward to it."

Extending his hand, Ruben widened his smile. "I'm Ruben, and you are..."

"Beth."

Ruben's heart was racing. He could feel his night coming together.

CHAPTER 11

Greenville Avenue Bar and Grill...May 28th...Dallas, Texas
The rain had stopped. Lower Greenville was alive with the typical Friday night crowd. The street was filled with college students from nearby SMU, young professionals, teenagers with fake ID's and the older generation trying to be young again. Parking was scarce, so Boyd parked in a private lot next to Terilli's, a well known Dallas restaurant located near the Greenville Avenue Bar and Grill.

Arriving at the bar with Jamie, Boyd noticed a chalkboard next to the front door. Elvis T. Busboy and the Texas Blues Butchers would be playing at 8:00.

How could anyone write so neatly with three different colors of chalk?

As they entered the front door, Jamie stopped at the hostess-stand and began talking to a petite, young blonde wearing an Elvis T. Busboy tee-shirt.

The interior of the establishment was deep, with a long bar on the right, and booths lining the left side of the room. The seats at the bar appeared to be completely occupied. Tables were scattered throughout the center area, with a stage and dance floor at the far end of the bar. Most of the tables near the dance floor were already taken. A staircase on the left side of the stage led to an upstairs loft containing several more booths and a pool table.

There was something about the atmosphere that caused Boyd to take a deep breath. It could have been the dim lights and the constant hum of voices. It could have been a memory flash of his own college days at Vanderbilt. It could be the past or it could be the uncertainty about the future. Whatever it was, Boyd was enjoying the present.

"Hi, I'm Amber." The blonde extended her hand to Boyd. "Jamie speaks very highly of you."

"Pleasure to meet you," Boyd said with a smile. "I guess he's just too young to be a good judge of character."

Placing her hand on her chin, a slight smile on her pouty lips, Amber replied, "You two could be dangerous together."

Jamie chimed in with mock seriousness, "With my maturity and good judgment, we'll be A-okay. Right now we're in desperate need of something to eat. Send one of your best looking waitresses upstairs to take care of us."

Not skipping a beat, Amber fired back, "Why don't I send up Guido and the boys to take care of you properly!"

After giving Amber a light kiss on the cheek, he led Boyd past the bar and up the stairs to the loft area. Two of the five booths were unoccupied, so Jamie chose the one farthest from the pool table.

Looking at the surroundings, Boyd said thoughtfully, "I like your little Lower Greenville hangout. Also, your girlfriend is very cute."

Leaning back in the booth and crossing his arms, Jamie grinned. "Yeah, darned tough having to select from all these beautiful Dallas chicks! There are some seriously beautiful women in this town. So much beauty and so little time."

"Well, enjoy it while you can, big boy. Sooner or later one of them is going to get you domesticated and then your picking and choosing days are over!" Changing the subject, Boyd inquired, "What was it like growing up in El Paso? I've only been there a couple of times, both short business trips."

"El Paso is an interesting place, full of contrasts. It's a college town, an army town and a border town. The University of Texas at El Paso, Fort Bliss and Juarez all blend together and make up the city's personality.

"What's the population of the city?"

Thinking for a second, Jamie replied, "El Paso's population is around 750,000, but Juarez, on the other side of the Rio Grande, has a population of over three million. So take your pick."

"Does your family still live in El Paso?"

"Yes. My parents own a small grocery store and my two older sisters are married with kids. I'm an uncle three times over. I helped out my folks in the store from the time I was eight years old. You know, stocking, cleaning, things like that. Wonderful people, my parents. They encouraged me to join the Army after high school and then to go on to college or a trade school."

"Sounds like a good family."

Continuing the personal small talk, Jamie said, "You've never told me about your wife. Tell me about her."

"She grew up in Memphis, and as I mentioned, we met in college. She has a degree in Finance. Right now, she and her best friend, who's divorced, are on a trip to Europe. I hope we can work out our differences when she returns." Boyd returned to his reflective mood.

"Did you say your daughter just finished high school?"

"Yes, she'll be a freshman at Vanderbilt in the fall. She's currently visiting her aunt, my sister, who lives in Boston and will be back at about the same time my wife returns from her trip...in three weeks or so."

Leaning forward with his elbows on the table, Jamie said firmly, "I've been thinking about our conversation last night. As a matter of fact, I've been thinking a lot. I can be of great assistance on your Cancun project."

"How's that?" Boyd responded with a slight frown.

"First of all, I can get a couple of doses of secobarbital sodium. One injection will put a grown man out of touch for two to three hours. I know how to administer the shots."

Shaking his head, Boyd disagreed, "You could get into serious trouble for lifting that kind of drug out of a hospital."

"It wouldn't be out of the hospital. I have a friend who works in pharmaceutical sales. Believe me...no problem for such a small amount. Absolutely not an issue."

"How would you safely get the drug through customs in Cancun?" Boyd was still frowning.

"I've already thought about that. All I would have to do is put it in a diabetes travel kit, which costs less than fifty dollars, and put the kit in my carry-on bag." Jamie persisted, "Really, you can't just pound-in someone's head and perform the little operation you mentioned! He'll need to be out. Totally out."

Boyd was quiet for a few seconds. "Several things could go seriously wrong with this project, as you call it, and I don't need any collateral damage. You being the collateral."

Trying to control the excitement in his voice, Jamie quickly replied, "What about the chest tattoo? That's going to take a while. What's the plan...go to tattoo school!"

"I can probably find all the information I need on the Internet."

Jamie was relentless. "Man, you need me and you know it! Come on, let's do this. I've been thinking about a lot of things. I think you cold-cocked the cowboy with the big belt buckle because he called me a beaner. Not because he called you an old man, or my Dad, or whatever else it was he said. Oh yeah, I also speak Spanish which could definitely come in handy in Cancun. And, I have an updated passport. Hold on, here comes a mouth-watering waitress."

Boyd watched as the waitress approached the table. She appeared to be in her mid-twenties and at first glance, Boyd immediately thought of Halle Berry. She was extremely attractive, and like Amber, was wearing a white Elvis T. Busboy tee-shirt which accentuated her light ebony skin.

She smiled at Boyd and spoke to both of them, "I understand you want the best looking waitress in the house. Well, here I am."

She and Jamie both broke out laughing as Jamie stood and gave her a hug.

"This is my friend Boyd. Boyd, this is Kara, with a K."

"Hi Kara, nice to meet you."

"And what would you gentlemen like to order?" Despite the dim light, Kara's eyes seemed to sparkle.

Jamie ordered a pitcher of beer and a hamburger with curly fries. A sign on the wall next to the booth claimed the house burger was world famous.

Pointing at the sign, Boyd said, "Well, if it's world famous, I'll have the exact same thing."

"Good choice, boys." Kara's smile was captivating.

As Kara walked to the stairs, Boyd looked at Jamie and commented, "You do know some lovely women!"

"Amber and Kara are best friends. They met last year at SMU and share an apartment near the campus. Amber will be getting a degree in Marketing at the end of the summer and Kara recently completed an M.S. in Biology and will be going to medical school next fall. Amber says Kara is one of the most intelligent individuals she's ever met. I think she's dating a local doctor."

The unrecognizable song playing on the bar's sound system, along with the welter of discordant noise from the lower level, was somehow soothing to Boyd. A steady stream of patrons filled the booths in the loft, and the pool table was occupied by four young Minnesota Fats wannabes.

A waiter, also wearing an Elvis T. Busboy tee-shirt, appeared with a pitcher of beer and two mugs.

Jamie, looking surprised, said, "Wow, that was fast! Were you standing on the stairs when Kara walked by!"

Laughing, the waiter remarked, "Kara said to take good care of you guys. You must be some special dudes."

Jamie smiled. "I'm a poor boy, but my friend here is a big tipper."

The waiter made his way to the next booth as Jamie poured the beer. "Okay, where were we? Oh yeah, you were about to tell me I could be part of the Cancun project. Right or wrong, Boyd?"

Boyd studied the glass of beer as if it were a crystal ball. "Right or wrong is probably the question I should be asking myself about this whole thing. Let me try to articulate my logic...such as it is."

Placing his elbow on the table and his thumb on his chin, Boyd continued, "Back when, I mean way back, there was nothing to interfere with anyone's actions other than someone else's actions or response. Primal desires ruled. Over a period of time, more civilized ways have replaced those primal desires due to religion, rules, laws and so forth. However, if you look closely, even the most cultured in our society still have some primal DNA in their personalities. Look at sex for example. Ladies and gentlemen by day, animals at night. War, murder, crime, greed, envy and a host of other items could be listed and makes one wonder how far we've come as a society. Just contemplating this Cancun project makes me wonder about how far I've evolved. See what I'm getting at?"

"Sometimes you have to do what you have to do." Jamie was beginning to better understand his complex friend.

Four young ladies, all wearing tight jeans and halter tops, were now standing at the rail of the loft looking down at the dance floor. Although they were standing no more than fifteen feet away, their chatter and laughter could barely be heard over the noise of pool balls colliding with the music from the sound system. The hum of voices had become a not-so-quiet roar.

Boyd was still deep in thought. Finally, he looked up from his glass and commented, "So, you want to go to Mexico with me. I'll be leaving in one week. Thinking about Friday, June fourth, returning on Monday, the seventh. Can you make vacation plans with so little advanced notice?"

With a broad smile, Jamie quickly replied, "No problem, amigo. No problem at all. I've already been talking to my supervisor about taking some vacation the week after that. I can work a couple of extra shifts and get someone to cover for me a few days early."

Boyd forged ahead, "Actually, I initially was thinking about leaving a week later, but this thing has been eating at me and I need to get on with it. We shouldn't have any problem getting airline or hotel reservations since this is close to the end of the season in Cancun. I'll get you the information tomorrow and you can make your own reservations. Of course, I'll reimburse you for your plane tickets and the hotel. You'll be my guest."

Kara appeared at the top of the stairs carrying a platter of food in both hands. The quarter-pound burgers and fries were hanging over the plates.

With a slight nod of his head, Boyd quietly said, "Okay, let's do it. We can discuss the details later."

"Hi fellows, did you miss me?" Kara quipped as she placed the tray on the table.

Trying to look serious, Jamie wisecracked, "Well, we didn't miss you at all, but we're glad to see the food."

Kara laughed and looked at Boyd. "I hope you'll be able to teach this ingrate some manners."

"Don't count on it. That would be a twenty-four-hour job." Boyd couldn't help but notice Kara's flawless, smooth facial features and her engaging smile. Maybe it was the reflection of the dim light, but her skin seemed to have a faint glow. Maybe he had overdone the George Dickel and the beer for one evening.

Placing the plates on the table, Kara asked, "Ready for another pitcher?"

Jamie looked at Boyd and then back at Kara. "I have to work tomorrow, so I'll pass. Like we say at the hospital…I keep on tryin' to keep em' from dyin'. My Dad here may want something else though."

"I'm good. I have to drive the kid home." Boyd smiled at Kara and reached for the burger.

"I'd dump him by the side of the road!" They all laughed and Kara walked toward the stairs.

The two friends continued with small-talk about Boyd's college experiences and consumed the small mountain of food on their plates. The loft rail was lined with spectators who'd been waiting for the band to begin playing. The pool table was still busy and the booths in the loft were all taken.

A rocking blues song was being howled from below. The sound was a mix of Joe Cocker and an old Mississippi blues singer. Elvis T. Busboy was alive and well.

Boyd and Jamie each left twenty dollars on the table and walked toward the stairs.

————

The trip back to Ridgetop took a little over thirty minutes. Jamie tried to be calm and collected, but was excited at the prospect of assisting his new friend. As they neared the turnoff for the trailer park, he finally said, "You mentioned you were going to tattoo a four letter word on the waiter's chest. I assume the R-word is what you have in mind. You know, kind of like what the young lady did to the dude in *The Girl with the Dragon Tattoo.*"

"No. I have a different four letter word in mind. Using your one letter inference, I'm going to use the C-word, which is probably the most despicable word in the English language. More so than the F-bomb. Women hate the word and you don't hear many educated men use it. I want to humiliate this son-of-a-bitch. Sorry. I must sound like some kind of psycho."

"Not at all. I understand."

Thinking for a few seconds, Jamie continued, "Okay, what exactly is the plan? I'll get my vacation scheduled tomorrow, and get after the airline tickets and hotel reservations as soon as you get me the travel info. What if this guy you're looking for doesn't work on the cruise boat any longer? This could be like looking for a baked potato in a dark room!"

He thought of several more questions, but knew he was starting to sound too eager and didn't want Boyd to change his mind about letting him get involved.

Pulling into his parking space, Boyd turned off the car's air conditioner and then the ignition.

"There's another bit of information I haven't shared with you. As I mentioned, I called the Cancun police and the Mexican Embassy and essentially got blown off."

Shrugging, he explained, "In desperation I called the Security Director at the last company I worked for and asked him to assist me in finding a private investigator. I specifically asked him if he knew of a Spanish speaking PI I could meet. He made a few calls and sent me the name of a fellow by the name of Miguel Burbano who's been in the business for twenty years, and has an excellent reputation in Dallas. Long story short, I met with Miguel, liked him and sent him to Cancun to do a little background work."

"What did he turn up? Anything useful?" Jamie instantly knew his friend left no stone unturned when he faced a problem.

"My Security Director told me Miguel Burbano's nickname is *The Shadow*. And now I think I know why. He was in Cancun for a week and turned up the waiter's name, address and what kind of car he drives... license plate number, color and model. I also know he has an asshole buddy that hangs out with him at several of the bars in the Cancun hotel zone."

"Cool." Jamie was hyped. "I can see you're definitely working on a plan."

Still looking straight ahead, Boyd said, "My first boss had a small sign on the wall of his office that stuck with me all during my career. It basically said that a poor plan violently executed, is better than an excellent plan only moderately executed, and ten times better than no plan at all. I'm going to have an excellent plan and execute the hell out of it!"

"I believe you, my friend. No question." Jamie could sense Boyd's quiet confidence showing through his level of concern.

Boyd finished. "I want you to think hard about what we're about to do. If you have second thoughts, I'll completely understand. If you decide to go with me, I'll want you to stay in the background in the event of any negative fallout. Okay?"

Jamie looked at Boyd and nodded his understanding. "I'm pulling an early shift at the hospital tomorrow, so I'll see you sometime in the afternoon. I want to be on the team and you can count on me. Completely."

CHAPTER 12

Cancun, Mexico...May 28th

The twin 380 horsepower Cummins diesel engines roared to life as the Devilfish left the dock. It was 6:45p.m. rather than the scheduled departing time of 6:00, another example of the "Mexican minute" gone wrong. On the starboard side of the catamaran, the giant white towers of the *Zona Hotelera* reflected the bright shards of the setting sun.

This was Ruben's favorite part of the short trip to the Isla Mujeres. The heavy beat of the music blaring from the speakers provided a background for the sounds of partying revelry coming from the boat. The laughter, the loud voices, and the thrum of the catamaran's engines accelerated Ruben's heart rate. Even though he had a few minutes of downtime before beginning his responsibilities as a waiter, it was hard to relax as he contemplated his seduction of the beautiful brunette who had just boarded his boat.

The sun was low on the horizon, but there was still another twenty minutes or so of daylight. Ruben emerged from his reverie and scanned the tables by the railing for Beth, the sensuous lady with the Southern accent. She was sitting at a table near the bow with a young couple.

Ruben removed his shirt and placed it under the bar, knowing all the women would be staring at his low slung blue cotton trousers and shirtless torso. As he flexed his shoulder muscles and slowly walked toward

Beth's table, he could see the young couple pushing back their chairs, attracted by the writhing mass on the crowded dance floor.

"Senor and Senoritas, may I get you some liquid refreshment?" Ruben had to raise his voice over the din. He flashed his smile and tried nonchalantly to flex his pectoral muscles.

The girl, who appeared to be barely eighteen, pulled on her partner's hand and said, "Not yet, it's boogie time. Be back in a few."

As the couple walked away, Ruben maintained his broad smile. "And you, Miss Beth, could I get you the complimentary beverage I promised?"

With a slight tilt of her head and a sultry look, even her throaty response was sexy. "I'm flattered you remembered my name. Sure, I'll have a rum and Coke."

"I'll return immediately with the best rum and Coke in the Caribbean."

Ruben hurried to the bar and placed his order with Carmen, his bartender nemesis. As he picked up the drink and was preparing to return to the table, Carmen stated dryly, "Got a hot one in your sights, pretty boy?"

Ruben leaned into the bar and silently mouthed, "Fuck you."

He'd regained his composure as he returned to the table. Beth was looking westward toward the setting sun.

"For you, *Senorita*." With a slight bow of his head, Ruben handed the drink to Beth.

"Thank you. You're so kind."

"Where are you staying during your vacation in our wonderful city?" Ruben enunciated. He was back to his charming self.

"I've been at the Cancun Oasis since last Monday. It's a very nice hotel, right on the beach."

"How long are you staying?"

"Unfortunately, I have to return to Memphis in a couple of days. Wish I could stay a month. I've been involved in a lengthy divorce and it was finalized week before last. This is a vacation I desperately needed."

Ruben took this to be a positive sign; a good looking woman volunteering a little tid-bit of information about her divorce, and lamenting having to return home so soon. Time to put the extraordinary Ruben Repeza charm into overdrive!

"Do you work?"

"Yes, I own and manage three hair salons in the Memphis area. My ex-husband tried to take them from me, but it didn't work out for the lazy bum. Anyway, I don't want to talk about my unhappy past. What about you? How long have you worked on this cruise boat?"

"Oh, this is temporary. I'll go back to work on my Master's degree at San Diego State in the fall." This was one of Ruben's favorite lines. And like any good con man, he'd actually visited several college campuses and read the curriculums for degrees in business and in engineering.

"Really! That's outstanding! How long will it take to get your Masters?"

This was the exact response Ruben was expecting, so he continued his convincing college story. "I'll only have one year of course work remaining and then a few months to finish my thesis." He only had a vague idea of what a thesis was, but it sounded good. "Most of my coursework concentrates on finance, and I hope to move to either Chicago or New York after graduation."

Deciding to take the more direct approach, he sat down next to Beth and said, "Do you know the legend of the Green Flash?"

Thinking for a moment, Beth replied quizzingly, "The Green Flash? No, tell me about it."

Uncle Emilio first told Ruben about the Green Flash when he was a child. Emilio simply explained that a green flash occurred the instant the sun disappeared below the ocean's horizon.

He said it was magic, and only good little boys and girls could see it. Ruben had spent many evenings searching for signs of the flash, and actually thought he'd seen it once or twice.

A few years ago, Ruben looked up the Green Flash on Wikipedia and memorized much about the phenomenon in order to enhance his charm with the women.

Placing his thumb on his chin, he explained, "Green Flashes are optical phenomena occurring at sunset when a green spot is visible, usually for no more than a second or two, above the sun." Ruben spoke as if he had done the research himself.

He clarified. "The reason for a green flash lies in refraction of light, as in a prism, in the atmosphere." He didn't know what refraction meant and didn't know a prism from a pot, but it was impressive to the ladies, especially after a few drinks. He lowered his voice and adlibbed, "It's rumored that only lovers can see the flash over the ocean horizon."

Beth was taken with the new information and asked, "Do we have time to look for it now?"

Evening sunset in the Caribbean is a beautiful experience under any circumstances. Salt water spray, background music and the humming of twin diesels can be intoxicating, even with watered-down rum drinks. The water was shining and smooth and the soothing movement of the catamaran created an eighty-proof atmosphere.

"Yes, look closely as the sun drops below the horizon. Darn! Those clouds may hamper the flash." Ruben placed his hand on Beth's arm and pointed toward the west.

In a few seconds, the sun disappeared below the line of clouds and left only a warm, red glow. No green flash tonight.

"Ruben kept his hand on Beth's arm and with a sad smile said, "There will be other nights and other flashes. Could I buy you another drink when we arrive at Isla Mujeres?"

"I'd love it."

Ruben gave himself a mental pat on the back as he returned to the bar area. He would do as little work as possible during the remaining twenty minutes of the trip to the private beach.

————

The somewhat drunk, moderately drunk, and totally drunk members of the crowd disembarked from the Devilfish when they reached Isla

Mujeres. Palm trees, decorated with tiny white lights, were scattered along the beach. A large dance floor, surrounded by picnic tables and chairs, peeked through the swaying coconut palms. The voice coming from the speakers on the Devilfish repeatedly informed the passengers about the party about to take place on their new island paradise. Tables on both sides of the dance floor overflowed with a lavish buffet. The world famous Mexican DJ...Jivin' Juan Ramiro, who was cranking out the dance music, made two announcements... happy-hour drink prices all evening, and the Devilfish would be leaving for Cancun at 10:00p.m.

The temperature was still in the mid eighties, and the humidity was gripping Ruben's upper torso tighter than the shirt he left on the catamaran. He was feeling light headed due to his stroke of good luck. Well, it wasn't all luck. His inherent charm and good looks actually made possible the coming events with Beth. Tonight he would mend fences with Salazar, the disgusting police chief, and perhaps if there was time, a quick hit on Beth for himself.

Some of the crowd made it to the dance floor, but most were lined up at the buffet tables which were stacked with platters of fish, chicken and beef. A variety of rice and pastas, fresh baked bread and a complete salad bar and dessert bar rounded out the fare. Mixed drinks and beer were available from three bars located just beyond the dance floor.

Let the party begin.

———

A small stage had been set up next to the dance floor. Five ladies giggled with false modesty as two young men poured cups of water on their chests. All inhibitions had been checked at the dock, it was easy to melt into the party scene on this sultry night. The licentious crowd screamed with delight as the clear outline of breasts and cleavage became visible through the tight, wet bikini tops and tee shirts. Whistles and cat calls rose above the music blaring from the speakers.

Jivin' Juan assumed the job of MC, and stood in front of each of the girls. He held out both hands, palms up, toward their breasts and asked the crowd for a response. A cute young lady barely five feet tall drew the most noise and received a free drink ticket for her effort.

The limbo contest started off the evening entertainment and ended in a tie between two college students. According to their tee shirts, they attended Texas Tech and the University of Oklahoma respectively. Spectators threw beer on the other competitors as they were eliminated.

Next came the "motor-boating" spectacle which drew screams and groans from both the audience and the participants. The music was temporarily turned off and four of the more inebriated couples lined-up on the stage, the women all wearing bikinis. The males took turns pouring beer on their female partners' chests followed by pressing their mouths to the exposed cleavage and making a blowing sound. The MC held his microphone close to the action so that the resulting "motorboat" sound reverberated through the speakers and could be heard all the way back to the Devilfish.

Ruben kept his eyes on Beth and intermittently flirted with her in-between his waiter duties. He worked his way toward Beth as the MC was explaining the "Pass the Olive" game about to take place. Ruben stood next to her and with and unctuous smile whispered, "I can get you a drink... or pass you an olive. Tell me what would satisfy you the most."

Beth slyly smiled and said, "Another Tequila Sunrise would be wonderful...for now."

97

Ruben placed his hand on Beth's forearm and gently squeezed. "I'll be right back."

"Passing the Olive" began with several of the staff randomly giving members of the crowd large green olives. The MC explained how olives brought good luck and should be passed around without use of the hands. Besides, this was a good way to get to know everyone at the party. Most of the patrons passed the olives mouth-to-mouth, lips-to-lips. Some of them placed their olive in the nearest available cleavage, and then it was passed on.

The music continued and the dance floor was packed with gyrating, slithering, sweaty bodies. A newcomer would swear that some sort of fertility rite was taking place. No worries, no concerns. It was Friday night in paradise and tomorrow would just have to take care of itself.

After taking care of additional drink requests from several thirsty couples, Ruben returned with the Tequila drink and an olive he held gently between his teeth. As he handed the drink to her, he leaned forward and Beth took the olive, their lips gently brushing together.

"Here's to good luck." Ruben flashed another of his radiant smiles.

Beth whispered, "Indeed." Her mouth only inches from Ruben's ear.

The MC, who had achieved his purpose of whipping the crowd into a frenzied state, announced the Devilfish would be boarding for the return trip in fifteen minutes. He also mentioned the one-per-person free drink tickets being distributed at the top of the gangplank, the tickets redeemable at the Blue Turtle Bar. The Blue Turtle, located about five minutes from the Playa Langosta pier, had some type of revenue sharing program with the owners of the Devilfish. The MC, who sounded inebriated, continued with his announcement by yelling into the microphone, "Throw up and get another drink!"

The Devilfish left Isla Mujeres at 10:15p.m. with all revelers present and accounted for, several of whom were hanging over the railing, swearing they would never drink again.

Beth and Ruben arranged to meet at the end of the pier after the passengers disembarked. Part of Ruben's job description was to say his "goodbyes" to anyone sober enough to listen. Beth was having an exceptionally good time…not knowing this would be her final Caribbean cruise.

CHAPTER 13

Ridgetop Mobile Estates…May 29th…Dallas, Texas
Boyd slowly opened his eyes, momentarily wondering where he was. The light filtering through the flimsy window covering was his first clue, the musty smell of the doublewide's bedroom removing all further doubt. Thanks to the giant hamburger and fries he'd consumed at the Greenville Avenue Bar and Grill, his night had been filled with random dreams that made absolutely no sense.

After dressing, Boyd walked into the living room and stood for a few seconds looking at the sparse furnishings. The air conditioning unit in the living area was alternately humming and rattling, but he hardly noticed. He was vaguely aware of the sound of crunching gravel as a vehicle slowly drove down the street. The scratching noise at the front door was feline and familiar.

It was 8:00a.m. when Boyd, having finished a light breakfast, leaned back on his couch, feet resting on the unsteady coffee table. Rosie effortlessly jumped up next to him looking for an ideal place to lie down. The cat finally stretched out next to Boyd's briefcase, its orange, black and white fur clashing with the red couch.

Boyd was surprised at the unfolding of events during the past four days. He'd moved into a trailer park, met a new friend, and was about to embark on a questionable, if not dangerous, adventure. Jamie would provide a huge assist to the whole operation; but what if something went wrong? He would need to ensure Jamie did not get too close to the fault line.

As Boyd took a sip from his second cup of coffee, he wondered why he was not more concerned about the situation with his wife. It was as if his mind was on a short vacation and not even cognizant of their marital issues. How could all of his thoughts and focus be on the low-life waiter in Cancun, when the central part of his life was now in jeopardy?

Their relationship had been showing signs of stress for the past couple of years, primarily due to the amount of time he spent at work and work related travel. In hindsight, he was aware of the mood swings caused by the small day-to-day conflicts due to his work schedule. Some days he just wanted to go home and kick the furniture. Success is sweet, but Boyd knew it came with a price. Oh sure, she wasn't perfect either, but at least she seemed to understand the pressures of working in a young, growing company. She was better at dealing with his moods than he was at preventing them.

Were they still in love? Could they kiss, make up and move on with their lives when she returned from Europe? He'd been able to master the art of multi-tasking in his professional life, but he knew this Cancun cancer must be removed before he could concentrate on anything else.

Maybe this weird plan of revenge, or justice as he called it, would clear his mind and put the world back in balance.

Picking up the writing tablet and one of the ballpoint pens, Boyd sat and stared at the coffee table for a few seconds.

Time to get serious, no more delays. Time to work out a detailed plan. Time to get this obsession out of my mind.

He needed to have a working plan on paper before he met with Jamie this afternoon.

The various pieces of the plan were swirling in his mind, waiting to be organized into some meaningful, sensible order. He began to randomly jot down his thoughts. He would prioritize them later.

He needed to make the airline reservations and then decide on an appropriate hotel. Leave next Friday, the fourth of June, and return on Monday, the seventh. Should be plenty of hotel options. Might be prudent for him and Jamie to travel on separate days and check into the hotel at separate times. Reimburse Jamie for both the airline and hotel costs. Jamie needs to make his own reservations. No need to have their names connected unnecessarily.

How many days will this take? Wife will be back from Europe June twentieth. Daughter will return about the same time. What if the waiter is not there this particular week?

Tattoo equipment. Where to buy it? How to use it? How to get it to Cancun? FedEx it or pack it in a bag? What about Jamie's drug with the big knockout punch? Syringes? Make sure he has a diabetic travel bag to put it in.

Rental car in Cancun or just use taxis? After some thought...definitely a rental car.

And then the big question. Where to find the waiter and how to carry out the central part of the plan? Miguel Burbano, the private investigator, said his name was Ruben something or the other. Name in the report. He and a friend hang out at two different bars for the most part, the names of the bars also in the report. What nights does the waiter work on the cruise boat? The name of the boat is in the report.

The address of the waiter's apartment is in the report. Need to thoroughly study the report.

What else? Nothing can be left to chance. Have to have an excellent plan, and as the sign on the boss's wall indicated...needs to be violently executed. No problem with that part.

Boyd removed the folder with the private investigator's report from his briefcase, and then reached over and put his hand on the cat and gently stroked its neck. For a stray, Rosie's fur was as soft as baking flour. The cat rolled over on its back, looking Boyd in the eyes.

Boyd continued petting the cat and said in a subdued voice, "If only I could be as laid back as you, Rosie."

The report was surprisingly detailed, given that the PI was only in Cancun for a week. Boyd continued with his random thoughts, and as he reread the report, he wrote down the waiter's name, address, car description, license plate number, name of the cruise boat, the cruise boat's web address and dock, days the waiter worked and the names of the two bars he frequented. The name of the waiter's friend was not listed, but a thorough description of the individual was included.

The report also indicated that during the week of Burbano's surveillance, the waiter didn't have any female companions at his apartment.

Burbano had included one other item of interest...the name and phone number of a person in Cancun, who, if circumstance dictated, could drive Boyd from Cancun to Matamoros, a Mexican city on the Texas border. According to the PI, the drive was about fourteen hundred miles and would take two or three intensive travel days. Boyd doubted he would need a backup plan this extensive, but as an afterthought, he wrote down the information and put it in his wallet.

Carefully tearing the top sheet off the writing pad, Boyd placed it on the coffee table and referred to it as he began preparing a preliminary plan:

1. Make roundtrip airline reservations on the Internet leaving Friday, June 4th and returning Monday, June 7th. Have Jamie make reservations on a different airline to leave and return on the same dates, if possible.

2. Make rental car reservations in Cancun.

3. Select a hotel in the Cancun Hotel Zone near the docking area of the waiter's boat and make reservations. Get information on the Internet.

4. Find information about tattoo equipment on the Internet. Find equipment for sale in the Dallas area, if possible.

5. Determine the best method of getting tattoo equipment to Cancun: checked luggage, carry-on luggage, or FedEx from Dallas to FedEx location in Cancun. Call FedEx.

6. Purchase latex gloves, duct tape and shaving equipment (either straight razor or razor blades). Should be able to find these supplies in a Cancun supermarket or drug store.

7. Double check with Jamie regarding a diabetic travel bag for the syringes and the knock out drug.

8. The waiter, Ruben Repeza, doesn't work on Monday. Alternative locations to approach him:
   a. Saturday night or Sunday night after he returns from the cruise.
   b. Saturday morning at his apartment.
   c. Sunday morning at his apartment.
   d. Sunday night at one of his bar hangouts.
   e. Early Monday morning.

9. Discuss details and complete plan with Jamie. Ideally, conduct the main portion of the operation in the privacy of Ruben's apartment.

It was almost 9:00a.m. and Boyd was restless. He got up from the couch and began a stretching routine. After a few minutes, he started his daily dose of fifty push-ups and fifty sit-ups. The cat stretched out beside him as he finished the sit-ups.

"You're more like a dog than a cat." Boyd liked the attention...so did the cat.

He continued to lie on the floor and thought about the gym in the shopping strip. The gym could add some local color for the book he had completely ignored so far.

Okay, back to the plan.

Boyd got up and retrieved his laptop from under his bed and returned to the living room. The laptop would be easier to use than his iPhone for this particular research. After attaching the wireless adapter to the computer, he turned it on and waited for it to boot up. He had a lot of research to conduct before Jamie returned this afternoon. He had a warm feeling. This entire, crazy idea was starting to materialize.

———

It was 12:30p.m. when Boyd finished with his computer and phone calls. He'd made online reservations with American Airlines and jotted down the flight times for Jamie to take on Delta. Their flights departed the Dallas/Fort Worth Airport at about the same time, but Boyd arrived in Cancun at 3:55p.m. which was three and a half hours earlier than Jamie, since Delta connected to Cancun through Atlanta. Both flights left Cancun on Monday afternoon at about the same time. Since it was near the end of the tourist season, there were plenty of vacant seats on both the American and Delta flights.

Boyd called the toll free Avis number, and after winding his way through several voice commands, talked to an international rental agent and reserved a car for four days. He was surprised the rate was only forty-six dollars a day with unlimited mileage. He would get the rental car, check himself into the hotel, and Jamie could follow later in a taxi. They needed to keep their movements as separate as possible.

Next, Boyd used the toll free number of the Casa Maya Hotel he'd researched, and made reservations for himself. He wrote down the phone number for Jamie. According to the hotel website, it was located near Playa Langosta, the home port for the Devilfish, Ruben Repeza's employer.

Oddly enough, the easiest part of his Internet research was locating tattoo equipment. The second ad listed under *Used Tattoo Equipment* was located on Harry Hines Boulevard, a seedy area on the west side of Dallas. The person answering the phone at Anarchy and Ink indicated he had a used professional tattoo kit consisting of two tattoo guns, a power supply, foot switch, twenty needles, six bottles of ink, compact carrying case and an instructional video. The individual seemed proud to announce the everyday low price of ninety-nine dollars for about ten pounds of quality equipment. Boyd made an appointment to meet with the tattoo artist at 9:00 the following morning.

Boyd decided he didn't want to risk taking the tattoo kit through Cancun customs, so his last call was to a FedEx store in North Dallas. He got a quote of one hundred ninety-seven dollars to ship a twelve to fifteen-pound box from a Dallas FedEx store to another FedEx store in Cancun, near the hotel zone, with a guaranteed two business day delivery. This seemed like a reasonable way to get the tattoo equipment into Mexico with a minimum of scrutiny.

Even though it was early afternoon, Boyd was not overly hungry. A low-level of excitement had removed food and discomfort from his conscious mind. He looked at the cat still lying on the floor and said, "You've been asleep for about three hours and haven't even moved. What did you do all night? Let's eat some more sardines."

And they did.

CHAPTER 14

Cancun, Mexico...May 28th

It was 11:20p.m. when Ruben finished his duties on the Devilfish, and walked toward Beth at the end of the Playa Langosta pier. He quickly dialed Hector's cell number and hesitated for a few seconds before proceeding.

Hector answered on the second ring and said with a deadpan tone, "What's up, boss?"

"I'll be at the Blue Turtle in fifteen minutes. Tell Estralita to put a little extra of the magic potion in my chick's first drink. We have to have her at the apartment a little before 12:30 and I want her out for a while. We'll be cutting it close."

"No prob. Over and out."

Uncle Emilio coordinated this particular assignment, and told Ruben to "make it happen". Ruben had guaranteed the honorable police chief he would have a hot one ready for him at 12:30a.m. This was Salazar's second *event* in two days even though he was married and had a large family.

How does Salazar manage to stay out so late? Guess they're accustomed to his late hours since crime never takes a day off. Those low life criminals must be busy twenty-four hours a day! As long as he shows up with cash, who gives a shit about his personal life.

Beth was standing with her arms casually crossed, pressing her white tank top to her impressive breasts, her flowered skirt highlighting her tanned legs. As Ruben approached, he was struck by the simple beauty of her face, the long brown hair with eyes to match, and the most alluring lips he'd ever seen. If it was anyone but Salazar, he would have kept this one entirely for himself. He wouldn't have needed drugs, videos or Hector. He knew he could deliver a night of love and tenderness if he put his mind to it. Ruben had viewed the videos of Salazar performing. Not impressed.

Oh well, she'll be just fine after Salazar does his thing with his limp dick. Beth is on vacation alone, so she can stay out late tonight…whether she's aware of it or not.

Ruben smiled as he walked up to Beth, his white teeth reflecting an overhead-light on the pier.

"I had to call the owner of the Devilfish and let him know we arrived safely back in port." Ruben had never seen or met the owner and figured safety was the last thing on his mind.

He took Beth's hand and said gently, "Let's walk over to the parking lot and take my car to the Blue Turtle Bar. That's where most everyone on the boat will be going. They have a great band and the drinks are fantastic. It's hard to beat a Turtle party."

"Turtle party. That's cute. Let's do it." She smiled seductively and pressed against Ruben's arm as they walked up the ramp to the parking lot.

———

The short ride to the Blue Turtle was filled with mutual small talk. The parking lot was packed, but Ruben confirmed that his luck was legendary when a car loaded with screaming, drunken youngsters pulled out of a parking space in the second row.

Beth took Ruben's arm in hers and they started the short descent down a curving cement pathway surrounded on both sides by vegetation. A feverish mix of music and crowd noise seemed to shake a small palm tree they passed.

Small, but dense Peccary Wood trees were prominent in the man-made jungle snuggled next to the walkway. Forsythia plants with their thumbnail sized yellow flowers and narrow soft leaves, Bay cedar bushes and Mangrove vines with white, yellow throated flowers reached out for anyone trying to reach the Turtle. Spider Lilys with their clusters of long, slender white blossoms stood guard next to the handrail. As the path neared the bar, Flowering Baybeans, a sand stabilizing plant, and its coarse stems, scrambled across the sand.

Ruben had tried to memorize the names of some of the indigenous Yucatan plant life, but to no avail. Besides, the babes were more interested in the history of local beers and shoulder muscles that glistened in the sun. Flowers were for wimps.

Hector was sitting at a table on the patio bar near the cement pathway. Estralita was standing next to him taking his drink order.

Acting surprised, Hector blurted, "Well, look who's here! You're in luck. This may be the only available table at the Turtle. I'm waiting for my girlfriend, who should be here in about thirty minutes." Hector picked up his line of bullshit from Ruben over the years.

Estralita chimed in, "Let me know what you want and I'll hurry back with your drinks."

Beth ordered a Captain Morgan rum and Coke and Ruben and Hector each asked for two shots of tequila. A gentle breeze joined the threesome and brushed back the wool blanket of humidity lingering in the thick foliage next to the patio.

"Beth, this is Hector, my good friend from earlier school days." Ruben decided to use Hector's real name in this instance. Hector knew that Ruben had to use his actual name when he met women on the Devilfish since other members of the staff might address him at the bar.

Hector reached across the table and shook Beth's hand. He was on a roll, so he looked at Ruben and continued, "Say man, when are you going to start your MBA." Hector didn't know if Ruben had already given her the MBA line, but it made for good conversation.

"I was telling Beth I'll be going back to San Diego State in the fall."

Beth, a little tipsy from the four drinks she'd consumed on the Devilfish, smiled at Hector and inquired, "Do you both go to San Diego State?"

Hector glanced at Ruben for guidance and then answered with their standard story, "No, we only went to high school together. I own a meat packing plant on the other side of the city. I've been really lucky."

The electronic clamor emanating from near the dance floor stopped and an announcement barely audible over the din of the crowd proclaimed something about fifteen minutes of a Northern Mexico sound. The sweaty crush of humanity never slowed down as the music changed its rhythm. A group on the other side of the patio began shaking to the *Norteno* beat.

Estralita returned with Beth's drink and the tequila shots. Ruben placed several bills in her hand and told her to keep the change.

As was custom in many Cancun bars, Estralita played the interactive waitress and held up one of the shot glasses in a toast. Ruben and Hector joined in the toast and Beth followed suit, taking a large sip of her drink. The tequila disappeared from the small glasses as easy as rain sliding down a window pane, the rum followed.

Ruben looked at his watch and raised the second shot glass. Estralita watched as Beth drained over half of her remaining rum and Coke. Hector smiled and tossed his drink down like a Western cowboy. Ruben did the same.

It was ten past midnight and Ruben felt a small rush of anxiety as he looked closely at Beth's eyes. He could tell she was having trouble focusing, and her posture was a definite deviation from vertical. Her head started to sag as she leaned slightly forward on the table.

Beth felt light as a feather. She didn't feel sick, only weightless. She knew she was at a table with other people, why didn't they have faces? Was that music surrounding her or was it the wind?

"Beth, do you feel okay? Maybe I should take you back to your hotel."

Thank God for Uncle Emilio.

Ruben nodded at Hector and they stood and each took one of Beth's arms. Estralita helped guide them to the walkway leading to the parking lot. The casual observer would assume it was another drunk tourist on her way to a major hangover.

"Let's haul ass." Ruben got behind the wheel after they deposited the limp body in the back seat.

Hector climbed in the passenger seat and said, "Okay, boss. We'll make it with time to spare."

———

The Ford Explorer pulled into the carport at exactly 12:25a.m. The shadows cast by the lights from the other carports resulted in a sinister grayish-black pall that seemed to foretell events to come.

Ruben's cell phone rang just as he put the Ford in park. "Oh shit, what now!" He didn't work well under pressure, he liked the more laid back, totally in charge atmosphere.

"Good to hear from you, Senor Salazar." Slight pause. "Yes, we just arrived at the apartment and she'll be ready for you shortly. This will be the most outstanding one you have ever seen!" Always the salesman. Another slight pause. "No problem. We will be waiting for you."

Ruben removed the keys from the ignition and exhaled with a sigh of relief. "Salazar will be here in fifteen minutes. He's a hard man to figure. He sounded calm, and believe it or not, friendly. What does he do...stay up all night!"

"Well, I know his boner doesn't stay up all night." Hector snickered at his own quick wit. "Maybe we have time for a quickie with Miss Beth before Salazar arrives. Okay?"

Ruben shook his head no.

Ruben opened the driver's side door and looked back at Hector. "My friend, I put in a lot of effort on this one. No offense, but I plan on spending the rest of the night with her after Salazar leaves. In the morning, I'll tell her she passed out and then take her back to her hotel. Why don't you go see Estralita."

"Fuck! I deserve some of the good stuff you turn up. I thought I was an equal partner! I do my part of the job."

"Don't worry, we have a lifetime ahead of the really, really good stuff. And it won't be long before our good times begin. Come on, let's get her in the apartment."

Hector easily lifted Beth from the backseat and carried her to the back door as Ruben unlocked it. He continued through the apartment and gently laid Beth on the bed, the damp smell of mildew and the three distinct climates ever present. Ruben turned on the bedside CD player and instructed Hector to get in the closet and prepare the video camera for the coming event. It was a satisfying feeling to be back in total control due to raw intelligence and superior planning. He walked back into the kitchen and placed his left palm on his right bicep and flexed. The only way to get ahead in this world is with brain power and good looks... and a line of bullshit that could stop a train.

A light knock on the door and Salazar let himself in as usual. He was smiling, but he barked in short, direct sentences, "So this is the *numero uno* of all women, huh? I'll be the judge. I'm going to take my time. I don't have to be home tonight. Make sure I'm not interrupted."

Salazar hurried into the bedroom and quietly shut the door.

CHAPTER 15

Ridgetop Mobile Estates...May 29th...Dallas, Texas
Boyd felt as if a giant cobweb had been removed from his thought process. He'd tortured himself for what happened in Cancun, and now, just maybe, the nightmare was nearing an end. He was still conflicted about justice versus revenge, right versus wrong and other morally binding customs and attitudes instilled in him since childhood, but he kept coming back to the same primal conclusion...the Cancun asshole has to pay.

After cleaning the kitchen counter and letting the cat out, Boyd looked at his watch. It was nearing 2:00p.m. and it would be at least three hours before Jamie returned from work. He had a growing level of excitement about the preliminary plan, and looked forward to discussing it with his new partner. The more he thought about it, the better he felt about Jamie becoming involved. This was going to work out fine.

Thoughts of his wife popped into the periphery of Boyd's consciousness.

Maybe I should try to call her. No, give it more time. Don't rush it. It's only been a few days since she left on her trip.

Perhaps the book project should get more attention. Boyd, for some unexplained reason, had always wanted to write a novel. He'd always approached life and business in a logical, structured manner, and writing a purely fictional story, making it up on the fly, inventing characters and situations, seemed like the ultimate respite from the real world. The real world of hard work, reason, and sensibilities had taken a toll on him and his marriage over the past years. Could the Cancun project and the writing of a novel free him from himself?

He was set to meet with the tattoo artist at 9:00 tomorrow morning. It struck Boyd as odd that this type of business would be open on Sunday.

Oh well, anything to help the economy along.

He decided to jog over to the gym in the shopping center and pump iron for a while at…what was it called?…Rusty's Weight Room. He knew he needed all the information he could gather about the trailer park and the surrounding area to add a bit of realism to his book. The more local color, the better.

Dressed in workout shorts, a Vanderbilt t-shirt and basketball shoes, he descended the steps of the doublewide and began a slow jog to the strip center. The sky was mostly cloudy, making the temperature somewhat cooler than it had been in the previous several days. The slight breeze in Boyd's face felt soothing as he passed several rows of trailers. The residents of Ridgetop were out-and-about on this Saturday afternoon and the aroma from the outdoor grills filled Boyd's senses. The typical Saturday noise of loud music, children laughing and the low hum of traffic on the road out front rounded out the Ridgetop experience. A long-haired, brown dog joined in the jog and ran silently beside Boyd for about thirty yards before giving up.

What's with me and the animals all of a sudden!

The parking area in front of the strip shopping center appeared to be completely filled. Christina's, the Mexican food restaurant, was still conducting a booming lunch business at this late hour.

Boyd glanced at the sign on the door of Rusty's Weight Room and grinned at Rusty's sense of humor. As he entered, he was surprised at the amount of space in the gym. The room was large, probably about two thousand square feet. Windows were located on two of the walls, with restrooms in the back corner. Two large fans on each end of the room, along with the open windows, served as the air conditioning system. The stale, sweaty smell of the gym brought back memories of high school and college. Three other men were on the far side of the room rattling around the weight equipment.

On the edge of a desk, wearing reading glasses as he thumbed through a golf magazine, was an imposing looking man of about sixty. He had thinning reddish hair, with a graying mustache and goatee, and appeared to weigh in the neighborhood of two hundred-thirty pounds. He was wearing long workout shorts and a tank top with **BITE ME** lettered on the front.

"Afternoon," he uttered.

"Have any more of those seven hundred dollar-a-month memberships available?" Boyd asked the question with a straight face.

Rusty lowered his head slightly and peered over his reading glasses. "You're shittin' me, aren't you?"

Smiling, Boyd replied, "Yeah, guess I'll settle for a five-dollar one-time fee."

"Well, come on in. The iron is all yours." Rusty seemed to appreciate Boyd's attempt at humor.

Boyd pulled a five from his pocket and handed the money to Rusty. As he turned and started toward the stationery bicycles, Rusty asked, "You live around here?"

"Staying over at the trailer park for a couple of months." Since Rusty appeared to be able to supply some of the local color, Boyd continued, "I'm writing a book and plan on doing some local research."

"What kind of book, if you don't mind me asking?"

"Oh, you know, just a trashy cloak and dagger novel with a little murder and sex thrown in." For some reason, Boyd figured that Rusty could shed some light on those kinds of topics.

"Man, I can be a consultant for you! I've lived at Ridgetop for five years, and I know all the wild stuff that goes on." Rusty pointed toward the door. "Come out here and let me show you something."

Boyd followed him out the door to the parking lot at the end of the building.

Rusty nodded toward the old wooden church structure and said, "See those three pickup trucks over there at the church. Well, that's not exactly a church. Some ole boys are getting their ashes hauled in there as we speak. That's the best little whore-house at Ridgetop! I, myself, have never been in there, for church or any other purpose, but I have several customers that come over here to pump iron before going over there to pump some of the little chickies. I hear they're fairly young ones from China or some such place."

"Interesting."

"You probably met Roscoe, the trailer park manager. I hear he's actively involved in the operation. I guess we could call it... Screwing for the Lord." Rusty chuckled at his own cleverness.

"Well, who knows. This could be just the kind of material I can use. I'll be back over later in the week and we can talk about some of your Ridgetop experiences."

Boyd went directly to one of the stationery bicycles and warmed up for fifteen minutes. He then walked over to the dumbbell rack where he picked up a set of forty-pound weights, sat on a bench and began bicep-curl exercises. As he was finishing, one of the other guys in the weight room approached him.

"Hey, man, ain't you the fellow that smacked the shit out of Earl the other night?"

Rising slowly from the bench, Boyd processed the questionable grammar and the essence of the question and his face stoic, said, "I didn't know his name was Earl."

"Well I was the fellow with him..."

"I know," Boyd interrupted.

"And I'm sorry about Earl's behavior. He'd been drinking too much and was just tryn' to impress his girlfriend. He's not all that bad a guy and I think he learned his lesson."

"He's lucky it was me that went after him rather than my friend who he referred to as a beaner. Otherwise, we'd be down at the hospital having this conversation."

Extending his hand toward Boyd, the young man said, "Anyway, I'm sorry 'bout the whole thing."

Boyd shook his hand and with a slight grin said, "*No problema.*" He wasn't sure if Earl's friend got the message or not.

The rest of the workout lasted about forty-five minutes. As Boyd was leaving, Rusty mentioned again that he had more Ridgetop stories and details.

———

It was three-thirty in the afternoon and the humidity seemed to be taking a day off as Boyd headed home. The cat was waiting in the small shaded area next to the steps.

"Had enough of the great outdoors? Let's go in and cool off."

As Boyd opened the door and let the cat inside, he heard the crunching of gravel. He turned and saw the brother of the young kid who had lost his bicycle.

"Hey son, did you ever find your little brother's bicycle? I believe you said it was a Mongoose."

"Heck no, it never showed up. My step-dad says it's in some pawn shop in Dallas by now. Darell sure as heck will be walking this summer!"

"What was it, a twenty-incher?"

"Yep...orange twenty-incher. I'll bet if Darell ever gets another one, he'll keep it locked up. I got one, but it's got a flat. We ain't got much luck with bikes."

The boy continued down the gravel street with both hands in his pockets.

Boyd managed a shower in the undersized bathroom and changed back into his standard shorts and a clean Vanderbilt tee-shirt. He sat on the couch with his writing pad and cat. The process of writing a book was more difficult than he had imagined, nothing like preparing an operations report for his boss or an annual plan for the Board of Directors. He decided to begin by jotting down random notes about his Ridgetop experience...the endless conglomeration of trailers, Jamie and his unique personality, the nature and mix of the residents according to Jamie and Roscoe, Roscoe himself, the Mexican lady next door who had brought him the chorizo, the lady at the All-In-One, Rusty's Weight Room, the wooden church, and of course, the altercation at Christina's with the drunk cowboy.

He sat for a few minutes staring at his brief notes, trying at least to come up with a title. Anything to get started. He had an idea, but needed to put more thought into it. Now, only about a hundred-thousand or so words short of a great novel!

Okay, what's the general subject matter. A CIA operation headquartered in a trailer park? No. Missing kids at a trailer park? No, too creepy. Or a drug and prostitution ring operated out of an old wooden church building next to a trailer park?

Something to work with. There seemed to be an endless supply of characters to develop and incorporate into the book.

It had taken about twenty exhausting minutes to get this far with the book plan. Boyd propped his feet on the shaky coffee table, leaned back and immediately fell asleep.

Boyd's unconscious mind was not in overdrive for the first time in several months. He awoke and looked at his watch… he'd been asleep a little over an hour. The cat was sitting on the couch looking at him.

"Sorry to ignore you, but I needed the time off. How about some cat chow?"

After feeding Rosie, Boyd got a beer out of the refrigerator, and took a lawn chair outside. The shade of the cottonwood tree made the afternoon heat bearable. He leaned back and listened to the Saturday sounds of tires-on-gravel, children's high-pitched voices and music of all types blending into one incoherent, harmonic movement.

Boyd could see Jamie's SUV coming slowly down the street. Jamie waved as he turned into his parking space.

Walking toward Boyd, Jamie spoke loudly, asking, "What's going on?"

"As little as possible," Boyd drawled. "Did Doctor J have any important medical breakthroughs today?"

Smiling, Jamie said, "No, but it would be a breakthrough if you got me a beer."

"Just a minute. I'll get you not only a beer, but also one of IKEA's best lawn chairs."

Returning with two beers, his note book and the lawn chair, Boyd touched bottles with Jamie and sat down.

Boyd took a long drink, and said enthusiastically, "I'm feeling good about our Cancun project. Very good!"

Jamie listened intently as Boyd went over the general outline he'd prepared. He could tell that Boyd was meticulous in his thinking and planning. He could also sense that he would carry out this plan come hell or high water.

Boyd finished, put the notebook in his lap and looked at Jamie. "What do you think? Still want to be part of this crazy scheme? It's not without potential pit-falls."

"Absolutely! I'm good to go. Got my vacation approved for one week starting on June fourth. Plus, I made arrangements for the secobarbital sodium. No problem at all. My friend will have it for me later this week."

"Good. Just don't take any chances. None at all."

"Don't worry, I'll be careful."

"I made arrangements to buy some used tattoo equipment tomorrow, down on Harry Hines."

"Will they show you how to use it?" Jamie's voice contained a small amount of skepticism.

"I'll only need some basic instructions. Don't plan on ending up in the Tattoo Hall of Fame for my work." Finishing the beer and rubbing his thumb across his lips, Boyd added, "The key element of the plan will be in determining how we approach the waiter, and get him alone in his apartment."

Jamie took a last drink from his bottle. "Let me put some thought into that. I'm meeting Amber this evening and need to shower and get dressed. We can go over more of the details tomorrow afternoon when I get off work. I'll be home by 5:00." Looking Boyd in the eye, he added, "I'm excited about this little adventure. And, by the way, I'll tell Amber we're going to Cancun to research your book. She'll be good with that."

"Glad you're on board. Tell Amber hello." Taking a piece of paper from his wallet, Boyd said, "Oh, by the way, here are the flight times. You'll need to make your own plane and hotel reservations. You can call Delta directly or go through a travel agency. The name of the hotel, the Casa Maya, is also on here and the toll free number. As I mentioned, this is on me, so just bring me the receipts and I'll give you the cash. Okay?"

"Done deal."

CHAPTER 16

Cancun, Mexico...May 29th

Salazar's lips quivered and he became partially erect as he looked at the unconscious young lady on the bed. She exceeded even Ruben's simple-minded description. The light in the bedroom was dim, but he could see the outlines of her nipples through her white tank top. Salazar was a boob-man, and in his mind, the sexiest thing a woman could do was go braless. The blue and green floral patterns on her skirt were a pleasant contrast to her smooth, tanned legs. The skirt was designed to be short, and it bunched-up as Hector had laid Beth on the bed. The sight of her thighs caused Salazar to lick his lips repeatedly. The act of staring at a semi-nude, drugged-out woman, or even a fully clothed one, was as sensuous to Salazar as the sex act itself.

Salazar quickly dropped his clothes to the floor. He would prefer to hang his clothes in the closet, and had tried on one occasion, but the damned door was locked. His entire body trembled as he stood beside the bed and slowly moved his left hand under Beth's tank-top and began to fondle her breasts. Beth was breathing in uneven, short breaths and Salazar was amazed at how he could arouse a woman who was completely passed out. He pushed the tank-top up to Beth's neck and stared at her large, white breasts which were highlighted by the deep tan surrounding them. He continued to fondle both breasts and then placed his right hand on Beth's thigh and slowly moved it between her legs. This was the most sensuous part of Salazar's ritual. He was so hard that even he was surprised.

Hector was in his usual position in the small closet, sitting on the stool with his eyes glued to the tiny screen on the video camera, shorts unbuttoned at the top, zipper down. The camera was on the dim-light setting providing Hector with an unobstructed view of the show. He referred to it as the "Salazar Little Dick Extravaganza." He'd heard the word extravaganza used in a movie one time and was pretty sure he knew what it meant.

He chuckled to himself as he savored the moment. Here he was no more than four yards from one of the meanest, most disgusting characters in Cancun, watching him rape a total stranger. The shelf above Hector's head contained ten or so DVD's of Salazar and some of the other clients raping young women. And there were a few DVD's of himself and Ruben indulging in some of the fun. If Salazar knew what was going on...well, it would be worse than terrible.

Hector noticed Beth's rapid breathing. This was not something he'd seen before with his drugged-out clientele. It was almost as if she were in the throes of making love to a long-time lover, or maybe a fiancée, or even someone she'd been out with a couple of times. Not the ugly pig, Salazar!

Fuck! If Salazar can get her going like this, I can make her see shooting stars!

Hopefully, Salazar and his little dick would get tired and go home soon. He hoped Ruben would let him take a shot at Beth. He deserved some special privileges for being locked up in this damned hot closet.

The girl was still breathing unevenly when Salazar finished his sordid act. He stood up beside the bed and looked at her naked body and considered staying longer. He decided what he really needed was a nice, quiet meal. He'd built up an appetite with all this activity. Besides, the smell of this apartment was repugnant, and he was accustomed to the better things in life. Ruben did an excellent job and should be commended, even if he did screw up the little girl thing.

Salazar finished dressing and took one last look at the girl on the bed. He tried to tell himself that if he weren't so hungry, he would give her another go. No need to fool himself though. He knew full well his lack of sexual stamina would keep him in check for the next two or three days. Maybe Ruben could find him another beauty next week.

As usual, Ruben was sitting on the back steps as Salazar exited the apartment. The expression on Salazar's face indicated he was pleased by tonight's activities. Right on cue, he reached into his pocket and handed Ruben a wad of bills.

"This girl was a good one. Maybe we can do another one sometime next week. Okay?" It was a demand, not a question, but that was Salazar's style.

Ruben got to his feet and responded like the sycophant he was, "Yes sir, I aim to please." All the while thinking about the DVDs he had of Salazar and how much money they were going to bring him.

A crooked smile emerged on Salazar's face as he walked away. "Stay out of trouble."

Ruben's single thought was, *"Fuck you!"*

Hector turned off the video camera, zipped his pants and was exiting the closet when Ruben walked into the bedroom.

"Come on! Give me a chance to go first this time. It's hot as hell in the closet and I deserve a break!" Hector hated to beg, but Beth was one of the most sensuous women he'd seen in a long time.

Ruben gazed at Beth in all her naked beauty lying motionless on the bed. Cocking his head slightly, he stared intently at her face.

Hector repeated, "Really, let me go first!"

Raising his hand, as he would to quiet a child, Ruben walked next to the bed and leaned over close to Beth's face. He jerked his head back and then leaned over again and placed his index finger on her neck.

"Holy shit, I don't think she's breathing!"

Hector calmly walked to the side of the bed and lifted one of Beth's eyelids. "The bitch is dead."

"What the fuck happened?"

"Salazar didn't do anything different. Same old little dick stuff. She was breathing hard the entire time and I thought the fat loser had turned her on!"

"Did Salazar know she was dead?"

"Nope, he looked at her before he left and I thought he was thinking about staying longer. I'm sure he didn't know she was checking-out."

"Where's her purse!"

"Must still be in your Explorer. I didn't bring it in."

"Wait here...and don't touch her! I want to see what's in her purse. She had it with her all night."

After only a few minutes, Ruben returned to the bedroom with Beth's white handbag. The contents were minimal: her driver's license, a hair brush, a tube of lipstick, several twenty-dollar bills, two bottles of pills and her passport. He quickly walked into the kitchen and came back with a notepad and pencil.

He wrote the names of the medications...he assumed they were medications...on the notepad and murmured to himself, "I'll ask Uncle Emilio about these tomorrow. Too late tonight."

Ruben was silent for a few seconds and then turned his head slowly toward Hector. "What now?"

Hector shook his head and shrugged. "Why don't we just dump her on the outskirts of the city? That way we won't take a chance of someone seeing us."

Ruben took a deep breath and decided to start thinking like the genius he knew himself to be.

"No, it has to be near her hotel. She needs to be found. Soon. It will appear she died from an overdose or alcohol poisoning or some such shit. This could make the payoff from Salazar even larger than we thought. If a gringo girl shows up dead while on vacation in Cancun, and Salazar knows he was one of the last people to have seen her, he would have to be more than a little concerned. Right?"

Sullenly, Hector snorted, "Okay, but let's get going. It's late."

Ruben looked again at Beth. Her face was pale and her eyes were partially open and rolled back into her head. A clear, viscous substance was oozing from the corner of her mouth.

"Let's clean her up and get her clothes back on. I just can't believe this." Ruben was still shocked by the events and more than a little queasy being in the presence of a corpse, but he was starting to feel a slight glow of excitement as he thought about the big payday to come.

———

At this time of night, it didn't take long to drive to the Cancun Oasis Hotel where Beth had been staying. It was almost 2:00a.m. by the time they arrived. There was minimal traffic, and no activity could be seen near the main entrance to the hotel. Ruben drove by the hotel, made a u-turn and parked across the street next to a concrete bench. The hotel was about a hundred yards diagonally across the street, and the passenger side of the Explorer was next to the curb.

"Drag her out of the backseat and lay her on the bench. Hurry!" Ruben seemed unusually agitated as he barked out instructions to Hector. Ruben had nearly vomited as they dressed Beth in the apartment. It was one thing getting a woman out of her clothing, but struggling to dress a dead person was something Ruben did not intend to do again.

"Why don't I just put her under the bench?"

"Goddamn it, do what I say! Put her on the fucking bench and leave her purse on the ground. And by God, the eighty dollars and the pills had better still be in it! I don't want this to look like a robbery." Ruben was stressed.

"Okay, okay."

As the Explorer slowly drove away, a warm Caribbean breeze gently ruffled Beth's long, light brown hair.

CHAPTER 17

Ridgetop Mobile Estates…May 30th…Dallas, Texas
Boyd awakened at 6:00 Sunday morning, somewhat earlier than usual. For some reason, which no amount of logic could explain, he felt refreshed after another night in the doublewide. The air conditioning units hummed and rattled incessantly, and the mattress on the so-called bed was still too short. Maybe his first decent night's sleep, in what seemed like months, was the result of a plan actually being developed. There were details to be determined, but the plan was taking shape.

There seemed to be an absence of the familiar noise he'd become acquainted with over the past five days in the trailer park. There was still the occasional barking of the many dogs, but where was the crunch of the pickups and motorcycles on the gravel road, the clamor of early morning activity? Boyd finally realized this would be the first Sunday he'd spend at Ridgetop. For most of the residents, a day of rest before starting another week of the daily grind.

It was much too early in the morning for deep philosophical thoughts, but Boyd wondered just how much purpose these working class folks could muster. He'd always had purpose. Purpose was the motivation, the inspiration, the reason to get up each morning. He remembered looking forward to graduating from high school, graduating from college, getting his first job, getting married and numerous other goals he'd attained along the way. Do the people in this trailer park have purpose? What keeps them going? Maybe to not experience true purpose is to not miss it.

Hesitating for a moment in his early morning thought process, the light came on!

Sure these people have true "purpose"! Look at Jamie. Look at Arturo and Aurelia. They haven't lowered their expectations for the future. Maybe their goals are different, but their hopes and dreams are every bit as real as someone who lives in the more affluent neighborhoods in Dallas...or anywhere else. The desire to provide-for and protect one's family could be one of the strongest of motivational forces. Jamie hasn't given up on the world. He appears to be one of the most driven individuals I've ever known. Wake up!

These random thoughts came to Boyd as he put on a pair of jeans and sandals. He slipped on a tee shirt and went to the door of the trailer. Sure enough, the calico was sitting on the top step waiting for him to open the door.

"Hope you didn't have to wait too long." Boyd was getting used to talking to the cat. "Come on in, we have plenty of dry food, and I know your purpose in life is to eat! Guess I'll have some cereal while I wait for you to finish."

After checking for messages and taking care of some personal business, Boyd left for the tattoo parlor at 8:15. He figured the trip would take about twenty-five to thirty minutes and sure enough it did. Thirty minutes exactly. As he pulled into the strip shopping center, his first thought was the irony of a strip shopping center being located on Harry Hines Boulevard, which happened to be *the* place in Dallas for strip clubs. Boyd was feeling a mild level of excitement as a key milestone was about to be achieved at the tattoo parlor. He was on his way to partially relieving his mind of his five-month burden.

Anarchy and Ink was located between a liquor store and an adult book store. Typical Harry Hines. He was fifteen minutes early, but an *open* sign hung on the door. Boyd entered and was pleasantly surprised as he observed a brightly lit, spotlessly clean interior. A semi-circular counter on the right stood watch over four curtained booths lining the opposite side of the large room.

Since no one was in sight, Boyd walked over to the counter, leaned back and folded his arms across his chest. After only a few minutes, a young man emerged from the back of the room and waved as he walked toward the counter.

"Greetings. Are you the fellow that called yesterday about buying a tattoo kit?"

Boyd's expectations were met. The young man was in his mid-to-late twenties, dressed in shorts and a tank top, dark mustache and goatee, with tattoos covering his arms and legs. The tattoo of a snake with a red head circled his neck.

"Yep, I'm Boyd Tanner. You mentioned yesterday on the phone you had a used tattoo kit for around ninety-nine dollars."

"My name's Gus Davis, but my friends call me Harley. Get it… Harley Davis. And I don't even have a motorcycle!"

Reaching under the counter and removing a black, soft leather bag, he elaborated, "This is one fine deal. I think I told you about everything in the kit. It has everything you need…power supply, foot pedal, needles, ink and it works on a one-ten outlet. The power supply pulls two amps and can run from one, up to eighteen volts. I'm almost giving it away!"

"Could you plug it in and show me exactly how it works?"

Picking up the tattoo kit, Harley pointed to the back of the room and drawled, "Follow me to that empty booth and I'll give you a quick lesson. By the way, what are you going to do with this stuff?"

Boyd replied, "Well, I'm writing a book and one of the characters has been wronged and plans on tattooing the word *cunt* on a fellow's chest."

Chuckling, Harley began plugging in the power supply and setting up the kit. Pointing to the face of the power supply, he said, "See this little screen. It shows the voltage rate." He turned a dial near the screen and a humming noise became progressively louder. "The normal range I use is between five and ten volts, depending on the picture I'm working on. The higher the voltage, the deeper the needle goes into the skin."

"Is there much bleeding caused by the needle?"

"Oh yeah. You'll need a clean towel to keep it patted off. There'll be at least two layers of skin affected by the needle. The guy in your book may want to practice some before he gets after the bad boy's chest!"

"The guy in the book doesn't really care about the bad boy's chest. Is there any particular ink you would recommend for this type of job?"

"One bottle of ink that comes with the kit is Black Onyx. Hell, you use that ink and you won't be able to get it off someone's chest with a belt sander!"

"Perfect."

Getting back to his tutorial, Harley pointed out, "This is the tattoo tube and it holds the needle." He placed a needle, about six inches long, into the clear plastic holder and connected it to the machine. "See how only an eighth of an inch or so of the needle sticks out from the tube? The amount the needle oscillates from its connection in the tube depends on how high you set the voltage."

"Got it. How long do you think it would take to tattoo four letters that are about three inches high and a half inch wide into someone's chest."

"Depends on the type of quality you want."

"Quality is not in the equation. Only easy to read results."

"I'm guessing twenty to thirty minutes would get it done. I've completed tattoo work anywhere from ten minutes to eight hours, depending on the complexity of the tat."

Harley spent another fifteen minutes showing Boyd how the foot pedal worked and the basics of tattoo art. He packed the equipment into the leather bag and walked back to the counter.

Boyd reached into his wallet and handed Harley a hundred-dollar bill and two twenties. "I appreciate your time and the information. This is going to be a big help."

"Gee, thanks." Harley seemed surprised by the extra forty dollars. With a wry smile, as if he knew it was not going to be some book character that was getting ready to get his first tattoo, he said, "If you go too deep, there'll be a lot of scarring."

Boyd just nodded. Sometimes you say nothing and you've said everything.

As Boyd left the tattoo parlor, he hesitated and reached into his pocket for his iPhone. He dialed a number from his contacts and was immediately rewarded with an answer.

"Miguel here."

"Miguel, this is Boyd Tanner. Sorry to bother you on a Sunday."

"Not a problem my friend."

"Say, I've got another assignment for you, if you have the time. It's kind of spur of the moment, but I'll make it worth your while."

"Tell me about it."

————

After finishing his conversation with Miguel, Boyd got an address from his phone, got into his car and headed for Royal Lane which was only a few minutes away. His inquiry led him to a Bike Mart which was the size of a small city.

Boyd entered and was overwhelmed by the sheer number and styles of bicycles on the floor and hanging on the walls. The store must have been at least an acre.

"Can I help you." The clean cut salesman was no older than Boyd's daughter.

Thinking for a second, Boyd recalled the conversation with the two kids at Ridgetop. "Do you have a twenty-inch Mongoose in stock? Preferably an orange one."

"Follow me. That's one of our most popular models. Your son stepping up to a freestyler?"

"Something like that."

Leading Boyd two aisles away, the salesman pointed toward the ceiling. "Here we go. Just like you ordered! Do you want it boxed or already assembled? It's one-forty boxed or you can have this one assembled for one-sixty."

Suspended from the ceiling was an orange, twenty-inch Mongoose.

"I'll take this one. Also, I'll need a bicycle chain and lock."

"I've got a flexible chain and a lock with two keys. Add fifteen bucks and we're in business."

———

The traffic was substantially more congested as Boyd made his way back to Ridgetop. He and the salesman had positioned the bike in the trunk of the Ford and secured it with a piece of rope.

Boyd decided to wait until later tonight, and anonymously leave the bike on the steps of the boy's trailer.

Was his name Darell? Oh well, hopefully he will be forgiven by his mom and his step-dad.

This brought Boyd back to his present situation, the nagging worry constantly on his mind. Will he be forgiven by his wife? Will he feel better about himself after his trip to Cancun?

*Life is full of choices, but Cancun is not a choice...**it's a must.***

CHAPTER 18

Cancun, Mexico...May 29th

Ruben had been exhausted when he arrived back at his apartment after dumping Beth's body across the street from her hotel. He'd shuttered at the thought of sleeping in a bed that a dead person last occupied. Instead, he tossed and turned all night on the living room couch.

It was almost noon by the time he staggered into the bathroom. His stomach was a mess, and food was out of the question. His mental state was even worse. What he needed was a stimulant or medicine or something. He was still wearing his blue cotton pants and the white beach shirt from the night before. They were wrinkled and reeked of sweat. Ruben took them off, threw them on the bed and found a fresh set of essentially the same clothing. As he walked back into the kitchen to make coffee, he had a change of plans. Curiosity was sending him a strong message, an urge every bit as strong as his sex drive. He needed to know what was going on at the Cancun Oasis Hotel where he and Hector deposited the body only ten hours earlier.

Ruben checked the bedroom one last time to ensure there was no evidence left behind. Satisfied he and Hector had removed all traces of Beth's presence, he left the apartment, carefully making sure the back door was locked.

The Cancun Oasis was at least a four-star hotel. The huge open air lobby was unusual for anyone traveling from most parts of the United States or Canada. Expensive chairs, plants and statues adorned the lobby and paintings were hung on the half-walls and pillars. The check-in desk was on the right and several people were either checking in or out. Ruben couldn't discern which it was and didn't care. He needed something to bring him out of his present stupor.

A coffee and pastry bar was further into the lobby where Ruben found a table near the counter. He surreptitiously turned his head and noticed four other couples sitting at either tables or in comfortable stuffed lounge chairs.

"Could I get you something?" The young man's voice startled Ruben due to his fragile state.

"Coffee...black."

"Right away."

Ruben surveyed the lobby, looking at the four couples, the front desk and the wait staff. Nothing seemed out of order. He'd imagined people scurrying around talking in lowered voices and gasping at the news of a dead women being found close to the hotel. However, he knew how the Cancun police and local media sources typically cover-up and under-report whenever vile and unpleasant events occur in the *Zone Hotelera*. Tourism was king and had to be protected.

The waiter returned with the coffee and set it on the table.

Ruben nonchalantly asked, "Hey, did you have a good season?"

"I think we were at least ninety percent booked most of the time. It's starting to slow down a little."

"Any excitement? You know... arguments, fights or other gringo bullshit? I work on one of the booze cruises and we have shit going on all the time."

The waiter glanced around furtively and lowered his voice. "Well, the police were here this morning asking questions. Someone found the body of one of our guests across the street on a bench. She was dead as a doornail. Don't know what happened. Probably heroin. Stupid *gringos*."

"I'll keep it quiet."

As soon as the waiter departed, Ruben reached for his wallet and removed the information he'd jotted down from the pill bottles in Beth's purse. Next, he removed his cell phone from his pocket and speed dialed Uncle Emilio.

Before Emilio finished saying hello, Ruben stated hurriedly, "I have a question about some drugs."

"It's a little early in the day to be taking drugs. How about a salad instead?"

"No, no. Last night I overheard a couple of women talking about pills they take. I'm just curious."

"And what kind of pills were they talking about?" Emilio was beginning to think Ruben was a little on the slow side.

"I wrote them down. One is called Doxepin and the other is Klonopin." Ruben spelled out each letter of both drugs.

"Well, Doxepin is an antidepressant. There are a number of drugs of this type. Klonopin is used to control seizures, such as epilepsy. Was it a pink pill with a K in the center?"

"I didn't see them, only heard the women talking about them."

"I am beginning to wonder why a fine looking young man such as yourself, can't find a healthier specimen of the other sex."

"Oh, I was just sitting next to them at a bar. They were too old and fat for me."

"I've got a customer that needs attention. Stay out of trouble. And, by the way, don't forget my cut from our little side business. Nothing has come my way for several weeks."

"Don't worry. I have two payments to give you. Talk to you later."

Even though that was the second time in two days someone had told him to "stay out of trouble," the conversation eased Ruben's mind. Surely it was Beth's own fault, nothing he caused.

He sat back, took another sip of the black Mexican coffee and breathed a sigh of relief. Now he could focus on another idea swimming around in the back of his mind...Carmen. The blender bitch on the Devilfish continued to disrespect him, but more than that, she was a huge turn-on. Carmen was far and away the sexiest woman working on the boat. Ruben fantasized on numerous occasions about running his hands all over the bitch's firm looking body. Besides, he had seen her with the asshole she claimed was her boyfriend. There was no way the short little fucker could match Ruben in bed.

Even to himself, Ruben had always been an enigma. Just hours ago a dead woman's body was in his apartment. He was hung over, worried and tired from lack of sleep, but here he was thinking about having sex with a co-worker. On a few occasions, fleeting thoughts regarding his strange desires with the opposite sex had entered his mind...and then were dismissed. Reason and sound logic were not necessary for a person with his talents. At least in his mind this was the case.

He removed his cell phone from his pocket and decided to call Estralita first. As the phone rang, his lips formed into a smug grin.

Might as well use little Miss Estralita right up until we dump her.

She answered on the third ring and Ruben, without even identifying himself, asked in a lowered voice, "Hey, are you working at the Blue Turtle tomorrow night?"

Estralita usually worked at the Turtle on Friday, Saturday and Sunday nights. The Devilfish had an arrangement with the bar and referred its passengers there after each cruise. Ruben had seen Carmen and her boyfriend there most weekend nights with the rest of the crew.

"I'll be there. What's up?"

"You've heard me talk about the bar-bitch that works on the Devilfish, right?"

"You've pointed her out to me several times. Don't tell me you want to give her some of the shit!"

"Her time has come. She and her boyfriend...remember the short little dick she hangs with...will both be there."

"Are we going to hit them both?"

"Yes. How many doses do you have left?"

"Five or six. Six, I think."

143

"Okay. Hector will be with me. Make sure you wait on our table. Bring it with the first drink they order. Also, and listen carefully, when the girl starts to fade out, I want you to help her to the parking lot. No one will pay any attention to two women staggering out of the bar. I can't be seen with her. *Comprende?*"

"Got it, but what do I do when we get to the parking lot?"

"I'll arrive before the cruise and park my Explorer in the parking lot as close to the walkway as possible. The keys will be behind the front tire on the passenger side."

"No problem. Consider it done. Hey, why don't we juice 'em up to-night. I've seen them at the Turtle on Saturday nights."

"Can't do it tonight. I was up too late last night taking care of some other business. Tomorrow will be perfect. I'll call you as soon as the Devilfish docks and we'll go over it again. Okay?"

"You know you can count on me."

Estralita didn't even think to ask about the cute chick with the light brown hair...the one whose drink she'd doctored the previous evening. Her thought process was a little cloudy since graduating from marijuana to mostly crack cocaine.

Ruben's total concentration and thought process were now focused on his contempt and lust for Carmen. Her indifference toward him increased his desire for her body. Beth's death last night failed to occupy a single brain cell in Ruben's head. He was morally vacant and that made life much easier.

The next call was to Hector who bought-in to the idea, and indicated he would wait to hear from Ruben the following evening. Hector, as usual, asked if he could participate in the action with Carmen.

Ruben rolled his eyes and answered heatedly. "Be there!"

Taking the final sip of his coffee, Ruben leaned forward and placed his forehead in the palms of his hands. The beginning of a headache was coming on and knew he needed something in his stomach, and maybe a short nap before he reported for work on the Devilfish this afternoon. It was Saturday and the cruise would be packed with drunken gringos. It took such effort to be a successful entrepreneur and the ultimate ladies man. Very tiring, but rewarding.

Ruben figured it would be another week or so before he could unleash his big extortion plan on Salazar and Uncle Emilio's other clients. He had a modicum of guilt regarding Emilio, but all of the big time, powerful millionaires he'd ever heard of started out by screwing over someone. Guilt was something that caused other people to get bogged down...not Ruben. Besides, Emilio had lots of money and didn't seem to care one way or the other about his family. He could always make a clean start somewhere else.

Ruben would talk with Hector about the details of the plan, but he knew he would have to make all the big decisions. He'd looked at a map of Central America and pinpointed a couple of possible destinations. Limon, in Costa Rica, and Puerto Cabezas, in Nicaragua, were both located on the Caribbean coast side of their respective countries. He and Hector had passports, but he would have to look into visas, driving time and other minor items. The idea of owning a bar in a small beach city was hugely attractive.

Now...the big decision would be how to get the cash from Salazar and the boys.

Ruben would have to sleep on that one.

CHAPTER 19

Ridgetop Mobile Estates...May 30th...Dallas, Texas
It was almost 1:00p.m. when Boyd arrived back at the doublewide. He had made a quick stop at his home in Dallas to check the mail. An arrangement had been made with a teenage neighbor to bring in the mail each day and to leave it on a table just inside the front door. The Dallas Morning News had been cancelled for now.

Boyd parked the Ford under the dilapidated tin parking space and noticed the calico on the steps leading into the kitchen.

"How did you know I would be coming in this door?" Boyd was continually amazed by Rosie's instincts. "I've had employees that weren't as smart as you." He figured he had better quit talking to this darned cat; someone could hear and think he was nuts.

After removing the bike from the trunk, Boyd took it inside the trailer and leaned it on the living room wall.

Humm, this bicycle goes with the general décor.

He filled the cat's dish with dry food and then prepared himself a ham sandwich and opened a package of potato chips.

Nothing like a healthy meal to keep a man going at his full potential.

Jamie had said he'd be home about 5:00 this afternoon. Boyd was looking forward to telling him about his new tattoo kit and the tattooing instructions he'd received.

One issue, though, was in the back of Boyd's mind and had been bothering him since talking to Rusty at the gym and the clerk at the All-In-One...Gloria.

Sometimes in a flash of clarity a thought can appear for no definable reason...and Boyd had an idea.

It's been said that very few truly original ideas are generated by an individual in a lifetime. Most are derivative works or stale thoughts that people come up with. Shakespeare himself said one should avoid "unnecessary invention". Maybe this idea had come from some movie or television show Boyd had seen in his lifetime, but it seemed original.

It was cloudy and not as warm as usual during Boyd's relatively short walk to the All-In-One. He needed another loaf of bread and a package of lunch meat, but what he really wanted to do was talk to the clerk...Gloria.

Two men were standing at the counter as Gloria made change for their purchases. Boyd found the bread and was trying to decide between ham and bologna when he heard Gloria's voice.

"Finding everything you need?"

Walking to the counter with the bread and package of ham, he said, "Yep, got it right here."

"We been busy as bees all day. Sunday's are usually slower than this here one." Gloria had not taken any grammar classes since Boyd had last seen her.

"Things are pretty calm over at Ridgetop." And then as if he just thought of it, Boyd said innocently, "Say, you mentioned the other day that Roscoe might still be in the petty drug business. I just heard he's also involved in an illegal prostitution ring and its being run out of the old church building around the corner."

Gloria had a shocked look on her face as if the devil himself had walked into the All-In-One.

"That goddamned son-of-a-bitch. No wonder Lefty's been hanging around with him so much. And I thought they was smoking pot or something!"

"Well, it's a shame anyone would take advantage of young Asian girls that way."

"Young Asian girls!" The words came out of Gloria's mouth like the blast of a twelve-gauge shotgun.

"What I heard. Got to get back. Have a good day."

Boyd had a feeling Gloria would do her part in helping eradicate all of Roscoe's business ventures.

———

At 4:00p.m., Boyd took one of his lawn chairs, along with a beer, and sat down under the cottonwood tree. As he took a long drink, a bright red Volkswagen slowly drove by and parked in Jamie's driveway. Boyd watched as a flash of long legs became visible. Two ladies wearing shorts and sleeveless blouses emerged from the car. It was Amber, Jamie's girlfriend, and Kara, the waitress at the Greenville Avenue Bar and Grill.

With a slight wave of his hand, Boyd called out to them, "Good afternoon. I don't think Jamie will be back until about five or so."

Returning the wave and walking across the rocky street toward Boyd, Amber said cheerily, "Jamie called and said he was getting off work early and asked us to come out here for a cookout. He said he would ask if you could join us."

Before Boyd could reply, Jamie's SUV came crunching down the street and parked beside Amber's Volkswagen. Jamie walked around to the passenger side of the vehicle and removed a large paper sack of groceries.

"Hey girls...and you too, old man, get ready for some of the best steaks in North Texas!"

"Only if you do the cooking and you clean the dishes," Kara jested.

Looking at Boyd, Jamie suggested, "The girls have to be at work by seven, so I thought we could have an early dinner. You furnish the beer and the George Dickel, and the steaks are on me. Let's do the grilling under your cottonwood tree since you have a monopoly on shade. I'll go get my grill."

"Sounds too good to turn down."

"Get another of your IKEA lawn chairs and I'll bring two of mine." Jamie enjoyed chiding Boyd about the furnishings in the doublewide.

"Sure thing. Eating red meat outdoors on Scandinavian furniture is one of my favorite pastimes."

The breeze and the cloud cover kept the heat and humidity at bay. Boyd and Jamie had changed into shorts and tee shirts. All four were drinking beer, while Jamie was preparing the grill.

"So, Jamie tells me you are here to write a book." Amber seemed genuinely interested in Boyd's presence at Ridgetop.

Not knowing exactly how much Jamie had mentioned to Amber, he answered, "Yep, that's the plan. My wife and a friend of hers are in Europe for a few weeks and my daughter is spending part of the summer on the East Coast with her aunt, so I'm here doing some research."

As Boyd was talking, Rosie parked herself under Boyd's outstretched legs.

Both Amber and Kara had questions about the nature of the book and Boyd told them about the similar work by Arthur Haley and how he intended to proceed.

"Who are some of your favorite authors?" Kara appeared to be sincerely interested in understanding the process of writing a novel.

"There are several, but a few stand out for me: Dean Koontz, Nelson DeMille and a fellow who went by the pen name of Trevanian."

"What makes them special?" Kara pressed.

"Well, when we look to the west in the evening, we see the sun disappear below the horizon. When they look to the west, they don't see anything. Instead, they feel everything. The brilliance of the colors, the softness of the clouds, the magic of the moment. That's what makes them special."

Glancing at Jamie, Boyd continued. "I haven't prepared an outline on paper yet, but I'm thinking about having a couple of the characters in the book live in a trailer park in Texas. A couple of the other characters are from Mexico…let's say Cancun. I'm going to Cancun for additional research in a few days, depending on various circumstances."

Amber chimed in. "Jamie mentioned he might be going on a short trip with you. You'd both better behave!"

The activity had increased in the trailer park during the late afternoon hours. Several cars had driven by Boyd's doublewide and the foot traffic was steady on this Sunday afternoon.

Jamie nodded toward the gravel street and with a lowered voice said, "See those two guys leering at our girls? Now there are a couple of characters for your book. Lester and Frank. Lots of rumors about what they've supposedly done around here, plus they consider themselves real-life bad-asses."

The conversation continued as the steaks were being devoured. Boyd asked the visitors about their college experiences, Jamie was teased about his short MMA tenure and the girls quizzed Boyd about his executive career.

Boyd decided there would be no harm in commenting on his discussion with Rusty, the owner of the gym, regarding Roscoe and the alleged house of prostitution. This could be part of the embryonic storyline of his book. Even with his Cancun obsession blurring most everything else, Boyd had been storing away bits and pieces of his short five-day experience at Ridgetop for the novel…the overall feel of the trailer park, its residents and now the church of ill repute.

These thoughts flashed through Boyd's mind as he asked, "Jamie, have you ever been to the gym next door in the shopping strip?"

"Oh yeah. I know the owner pretty well, a guy named Rusty."

"I had a workout over there yesterday afternoon and met Rusty. He took me outside and pointed out the old church building at the end of the shopping area. He claims the place is being used for prostitution purposes and that our boy Roscoe, who gave me this great doublewide deal, is involved in the business."

"You're kidding!"

"I'm only reporting the news, not making it up."

"Roscoe spent too much time as a small child staring at the sun, but surely he's not that dumb. Erase that last statement...he's that dumb!"

Kara, only slightly serious, said, "I wonder what's more difficult... making it with a prostitute, or getting a stale package of chips out of a vending machine?"

With a slight frown, Amber looked at Jamie and added, "As soon as you save enough money, you need to move closer to the big city!"

Jamie shrugged. "Well, this isn't exactly the wealthiest neighborhood in the metroplex, but most of the people I've met here are pretty decent. Always seems to be a few bad apples no matter where you live. Sooner or later they just rot away."

Leaning over and touching her cheek to Jamie's, Amber teased, "Well, you'll never be a poet, but you're my good apple."

Kara stood and looked at Boyd and then at Jamie, "Give me a break, he's an unripe grapefruit at best. By the way, we need to get to work. There are hamburgers to be sold and tips to be earned."

———

As the girls drove away, Jamie was back to business. "Okay, I'm good to go. My vacation time was approved, and I made arrangements for the secobarbital sodium, which is no problem at all. My friend will have it for me tomorrow."

"Good. Just don't take any chances. None at all." Reaching down and stroking the calico's back, Boyd drawled, "Got time for a little George on the rocks?"

"Never thought you'd ask."

"Be right back."

Picking up a plastic garbage bag containing the paper plates and the last remnants of the cookout, Boyd walked around the corner of the doublewide and deposited it in the CleanKing trash receptacle.

The evening breeze held off the mosquito onslaught and kept the humidity to a surprisingly acceptable level. The symphony of Ridgetop was at full crescendo: barking dogs, a mix of various music types, crunching gravel and occasional laughter.

Returning with a bottle of George Dickel and two glasses filled with ice, Boyd quipped, "Okay sis, here's your dessert."

Jamie said, "I'll bet George here can cure polio, cancer and crooked teeth."

Clinking glasses, both men sat back and enjoyed the evening trailer park ambiance.

Jamie broke the short silence. "I've been thinking about how we nab the dick-head waiter in Cancun. Didn't you say you have the address of his apartment?"

"Yep, the private eye I sent over there has the address in his report."

"Like you said, the best place to take care of business would be at his apartment. We know the name of his boat, the nights he works and the bars where he hangs out, so I propose we follow him home. Since he's never seen me, I could nail his ass as he's unlocking the door. We'll have to scope out his apartment building and see what's possible."

Nodding his head in approval, Boyd's confidence in Jamie continued to grow. "That's generally what I had in mind. The report indicates this Ruben character parks his SUV near the back door and enters there. Depending on the circumstances, we can either be waiting for him in the parking lot or just knock on his door after he's entered."

Jamie continued, "Another thought is to follow him after his cruise boat docks. If he goes straight home we can do as you said, or if he goes to a bar, we can check out the scene and maybe leave before he does and be waiting for him in his apartment."

"Waiting in his apartment?"

"Hey, in El Paso, you learn how to get through doors, my friend. I'll bet I can get through the lock with a credit card." Jamie didn't appear to be joking. "Seriously, considering what you're going to do to him, breaking and entering will be the least of our worries!"

With a slight smile, Boyd said, "I can't argue with that."

Finishing his drink, Boyd told Jamie about his experience at the tattoo parlor, and as an after-thought mentioned the twenty-inch Mongoose bicycle.

"Man, that's one nice gesture. Those kids will be your friends for life! I don't know those folks, but I've seen them out and about. They live in the last trailer on the left."

Boyd, with a lowered voice, said, "Not sure how their step-dad will feel about a total stranger buying a bicycle for his kids. He'll probably think I'm some kind of stalker, or even more likely, he won't appreciate me interfering with his disciplinary process."

Laughing, Jamie said, "Yeah, in your case I'll have to go with the first scenario. Guess you'll have to ride it yourself." Getting immediately serious, he continued, "So, what are you going to do?"

"I'm thinking about taking the bike down there tonight and leaving it next to their door. Who knows, they may think it's the same bike and someone just brought it back."

"Not a bad idea. No matter what, it's a heck of a nice thing to do." In less than a week, Jamie had come to think of Boyd as not only a friend, but as one of the most unique individuals he had ever met.

After a few minutes Jamie spoke first. "I can't believe you're now a tattoo expert. Maybe we should get some of your venture capital friends and start a nationwide chain of tattoo parlors. I could be your V.P. of Marketing."

The George Dickel had kicked in.

Going along with the new conversation drift, Boyd quickly replied, "Yeah, we could name it Tattoos Are Us."

"I was thinking of something more professional, like Ink in a Blink or Blue Skin Blob.

"You certainly have the makings of a tattoo V.P."

Pausing for a second, Boyd remembered something Jamie had said earlier in the week. "What was the name of the massage business here in the trailer park you mentioned? This could be another area of research for the book. Plus, I have a few stresses and strains from my latest workout at Rusty's."

Gently rattling the ice cubes in the glass, Jamie thought for a moment and said, "It's, ahh, the Oasis Massage Center. A couple of Ridgetoppers by the name of Trixi and Heather run it. Here, I think I have their card in my wallet."

Removing a card from his wallet and handing it to Boyd, Jamie went on, "The trailer number is on the card." Pointing over his shoulder, he said, "It's two rows past my place. I've only been there once and the massage was pretty good. Oh, and you'll be amazed at the décor inside the trailer. And, you'll be amazed at Trixi's personality…all three or four of them. It'll be good material for your book. "

"Thanks. I'll check it out tomorrow or the next day."

"Speaking of tomorrow, I think I'll check out early this evening. I traded an early Monday shift for a couple of my vacation days. Plus, Amber and I are hooking up tomorrow evening."

"Sleep well my friend, I know I will."

CHAPTER 20

Cancun, Mexico...May 29th
Ruben left the Cancun Oasis Hotel early in the afternoon with the thought of taking a short nap. The steady drinking and late nights were taking their toll. However, when he arrived back in his apartment, the idea of leaving Cancun with lots of cash and the possibility of owning a beach front bar in Nicaragua or Costa Rica, completely revitalized his senses.

He was now researching Puerto Cabezas, a beach city on the Caribbean side of Nicaragua, and Limon, an even smaller town on the Caribbean coast of Costa Rica. Google assured him it was 1,250 miles to Puerto Cabezas and promised it would be at least a twenty-seven hour driving trip. From Cancun, he would cross Belize, Guatemala and Honduras before reaching Nicaragua. The more distance between himself and the Police Chief, the better. Costa Rica was another fifteen-hour trip from Puerto Cabezas.

Ruben figured he and Hector could spend the first night in Belize City which was about five hundred miles from Cancun. Over the next few days, they could leisurely make the next leg of the trip to Puerto Cabezas. No way Senor Salazar would be able to track them.

A nagging thought persisted somewhere in the back of Ruben's mind. He knew he should be focusing on how to get the payments from Salazar and the three other clients who had participated in his rape business. Or, at the very least, he should be thinking about the details of the trip...passports, visas, credit cards versus cash and currency differences in the four or five countries they would be crossing. Ruben, however, had been told by a previous Devilfish employee about the time he got laid in Puerto Cabezas. Best ever! Why worry about details when the end result was going to be booze and hot women. As a matter of fact, screw Costa Rica. It was too far from Puerto Cabezas and Ruben knew he would be sick and tired of being in a car after a twenty-seven-hour trip. Costa Rica would have to do without his charm and intelligence until another day.

Puerto Cabezas, Nicaragua, here we come!

————

Surprisingly, Ruben arrived at the Playa Langosta pier a few minutes earlier than usual. He parked in the lot next to the Blue Turtle Bar, which was about a hundred yards from the pier. His raging headache and his stomach were both trying to reject his body. The events last night with Beth left him generally unsettled, both mentally and physically.

Ruben usually looked forward to Saturday evenings on the Devilfish, but he knew tonight would be a struggle due to his weakened condition. Maybe some sexy gringo babes would bring him back to top form.

There was one thing he wanted to accomplish on this particular Saturday. He would make an effort to be nice to Carmen, the bar-douche, and get her set up for the following evening. Hector and Estralita would play a big part in pulling this one off. He started feeling better as he thought about drugging Carmen and slipping down her shorts. He even had a workable idea on how to handle her boyfriend who would be with her at the Blue Turtle tomorrow night.

Walking down the pier toward the Devilfish, Ruben removed his cell phone from his pocket and dialed Hector.

"Yo Ruben, what's up." Hector wasn't as gruff as usual.

"My man...are you busy busting open cow heads?"

"Cleaning up blood and brains. Can't wait to get out of this place."

"Soon, very soon. As a matter of fact, let's meet tonight at the Blue Turtle and talk about a few things."

"I thought you wanted to do the deed on Carmen tomorrow night?"

"Yes, but we need to check her out tonight. She'll be there with her boyfriend and we can see where they sit. I'll tell you about it tonight. Also, we can talk about how we're going to get the money from Salazar and the other clients. Okay?"

"Super urb." Hector felt he was getting fairly clever with cool sayings.

"The Devilfish will get back around 11:15 tonight and I'll call you from the pier. Be there early and get us a table on the edge of the patio so we can check out the activities."

"Got it. Any chance you can bring us a gringo bitch to mess with?"

Trying not to lose patience with his partner, Ruben replied evenly, "Hector, focus. We have a lot to discuss. Stay with me."

"Okay, okay, I'll wait for your call."

Thirty minutes early, Ruben made his way up the Devilfish gangplank. His first stop was at the bar where Carmen was mixing the colored drinks that would be served to the obnoxious gringos.

Ruben extended his hand and articulated every word. "Good afternoon, Carmen. I would like to say I am sorry for my previous behavior toward you. I will try to be a better person. Please try to forgive my rudeness."

Cocking her head and squinting, she questioned, "Are you drunk so early?"

With his hand still extended, he continued his apology. "I've been a dick and I'll do better."

Leaning over the bar and rapping Ruben's hand with a hard fist bump, Carmen said warily, "We'll see, bad boy."

Ruben handed out the colored, watered-down drinks to the arriving passengers, trying his best to be friendly and charming. Several sexy women stirred his interest, but his headache over-ruled his basic desires. Besides, it was the same mix of Saturday night hard-ons and silly, giggling bitches. Tonight he would focus on setting up Carmen. Ruben was proud of his long range scheming abilities, even if this one was only twenty-four hours in advance.

The big dilemma, on the not-so-distant horizon, was determining how to obtain the extortion money from the clients. He had a couple of ideas he would kick around with Hector tonight. He knew Hector wouldn't be able to come up with an original idea, other than some strange way to abuse a drugged-out chick, but it was always good to bounce ideas off him anyway. Sometimes he was inspired by just listening to his own ideas.

Soon after the Devilfish left the dock, Ruben was standing at the bar waiting for a drink when one of the more attractive females he had seen board approached him. She was wearing tight yellow shorts and a silk halter-top printed with curved abstract figures. Her dark brown hair almost matched her spray-on tan.

Touching Ruben's arm, her voice sultry, she asked, "Where would you recommend a lonely girl sit?"

Knowing Carmen was within earshot, Ruben pointed toward a table near the dance floor and replied in a very business-like manner, "There are three young ladies sitting at that table and there's a spare chair. I'm sure they would appreciate your company. If you would like, I could introduce you to them."

Without responding, the tanned brunette walked away. Ruben spotted her fifteen minutes later raising her silk top and letting a drunken college student pour beer on her exposed breasts.

Where do the damned gringos get the money and time to spend in my city?

———

The rest of the trip was uneventful by Ruben's standards. His headache was gone, but his stomach was still acting up. He would try to start eating better when he and Hector arrived in Nicaragua. Good food, cold beer and hot women were only a couple of weeks away.

The Devilfish docked a few minutes before 11:00p.m. and the crowd dissipated within the next fifteen minutes. Most were going to the Blue Turtle to cash in their free drink coupons.

It was 11:25p.m. when Ruben completed his clean-up duties and dialed Hector.

Hector answered on the first ring. "It's 'bout time. I've been sitting on my fist for forty-five minutes."

Ruben assumed Hector meant "sitting on my thumb," but didn't comment on the apparent misuse of the cliché.

"I'll be there in five minutes. Where are you sitting?" Ruben put emphasis on the word *sitting.*

"Where you told me to *sit.* On the edge of the patio. Out of the mainstream. Next to a goddamn plant. Okay!"

"Contain yourself. I'm on my way."

Ruben knew he would have to let Hector participate in tomorrow night's activities with Carmen. Even though Hector could be a pain, his strong-arm tactics were invaluable to Ruben's well-being.

Just have to live with it.

As Ruben walked down the curving pathway toward the patio bar of the Blue Turtle, a hard-rock clamor battered his eardrums. The already inebriated crowd was in total vacation mode.

He immediately spotted Hector sitting alone at a table on the edge of the patio. Hector waved and held up a shot glass filled with tequila.

"Sorry I'm a few minutes late. Had to help clean up. You're not the only one who has to clean up after animals. Most of the gringos are trash!"

"Yeah, I know."

"Has Carmen and her fat boyfriend showed up yet?"

163

"They're on the other side of the patio. I can see her from here."

Ruben turned around and looked in the direction Hector was pointing.

"Excellent. I'm pretty sure they plan to be here tomorrow night. I started sucking up to her this evening on the cruise and I'll keep it up tomorrow night. I'll propose that I buy her and her boyfriend a drink after the cruise. Surely she will accept."

Interjecting his brand of humor, Hector grinned and said, "You mean we are going to screw both of them!"

Totally ignoring him, Ruben pressed on. "I'll work the details with Estralita later, but bottom line, I plan on drugging both of them here at the Turtle after the cruise. Now listen carefully. I'm going to have Estralita assist Carmen from the table to my Explorer. She'll put a little extra juice in the boyfriend's drink and you'll help him out of the bar, up the sidewalk and dump him in that stand of small trees and bushes next to the parking lot. You'll need to make sure he's far enough away from the cars so he won't be seen."

"And?"

"You and I'll take Carmen back to my apartment and have our own private party. You'll be part of it."

"OooooKayyy Yeaaah!" Hector continued to coin more cool sounds and sayings.

"That's not all. After we finish with Carmen, we'll bring her back to the parking lot and put her in the bushes with her boyfriend. I'm thinking about putting them on a blanket and pulling his pants down to half-mast. They'll never be able to figure out what happened. I'll tell her that she and fat boy left the bar together and we didn't see them again."

Hector was involuntarily licking his top lip with the tip of his tongue. "I like it."

Ruben loved the admiration he received from his sidekick. It assured him of his brilliance and cunning. A force to be reckoned with.

"I've done some research and decided that Nicaragua is going to be our destination when we leave here."

Quickly responding, Hector said, "I thought you said something about Costa Rica."

"Too far. Puerto Cabezas, Nicaragua is on the coast. Looks like the right place."

"Whatever." They could be going to the moon and Hector wouldn't care. As long as there were babes, booze and no cows.

"Now, I've been thinking all day about how we're going to get the money from Salazar and the boys. We'll do it in four parts. First of all, we need to get three copies made of each video recording we're going to use. One to send to each of our clients, one set we'll keep for ourselves and Estralita will keep a set at her place for insurance."

Getting with the program, Hector agreed, "Good idea. I know where we can get copies made and no one will breathe a word about it."

"Next, we'll get a messenger to deliver each client a copy of their video to their office. A note will be with each video telling them how much they have to pay and how to do it."

"*Brilliante.*" Sometimes Hector resorted to Spanish when he couldn't come up with a clever English word. "So, how will they get the money to us?"

"The note will instruct them to have the thirty-five thousand ready in two days...hundred thousand in Salazar's case... and that a messenger will pick it up at their office. Oh yeah, they'll put the money in a manila envelope."

"Who will be the messenger?"

Somewhat irritated at Hector's focus on unnecessary details, Ruben replied, "I don't know who specifically the messenger will be! There are lots of messenger services in the city. We'll just select one."

"Where will this *messenger* take the money?"

"Well, I haven't thought that part out yet. Maybe the messenger takes the package to Estralita's apartment. I don't know. I'll work on the plan over the next few days. We just need to make it impossible for anyone to follow us."

Hector's mood brightened. "What about Estralita? Does it mean she's going with us to Nicaragua?"

"No, absolutely not! I told you we don't want to split the money three ways. We'll arrange the drop-offs on days when Estralita works. She can't be part of it."

"Seems like a shitty thing to do to Estralita."

"She'll be fine. She doesn't know anything about our big plan."

"What's the fourth part of the plan? You said there would be four parts."

"Are you paying fucking attention! I just told you all four parts!"

Considering the tequila shots, Hector was fairly rational. "You said we get copies made of the videos, send a messenger to the client's office and then another messenger takes the package to Estralita's apartment. Count them...one, two, three. What's the last one?"

Seriously irritated and physically exhausted from last night's activities, Ruben exclaimed, "The contents of the note, the envelope. Hell, maybe I should have said the plan has six or seven parts. What difference does it make!"

Trying to make amends with his friend, Hector said, "You're the boss. I'm with you all the way."

CHAPTER 21

Ridgetop Mobile Estates...May 31st...Dallas, Texas
Two decent night's sleep in a row. This was an all time record for Boyd, since maybe the seventh grade. He slept well despite the climate control in the doublewide being non-existent, the on-and-off rattling of the air conditioning units being unsettling, and the incessant barking of dogs being similar to the ringing of a phone, but not as consistent. Still...a refreshing feeling on this his sixth day at Ridgetop.

The first thing on his mind when he put his feet on the floor was his wife, and their current problems. The second item on his mind was the waiter in Cancun.

Last night, he'd placed the orange mongoose bicycle next to the steps of the trailer where the two boys lived. The streets had been deserted and there were no lights visible in the trailer. No problems. Minor deed, satisfied feeling.

Boyd finished breakfast, fed the cat and was on his second cup of coffee. He was satisfied with the preliminary thoughts he and Jamie had discussed last evening regarding the waiter on the Devilfish. However, he still felt the need to further fine tune the timing of the initial contact.

Sitting on the living room couch, Boyd went over the report again from the private investigator. He reviewed Ruben's full name, his home address, the name of his cruise boat and the days of the week he worked. On the nights he worked, Ruben usually frequented the Blue Turtle Bar after the cruise and was back at his apartment between midnight and 1:00a.m. Only on one occasion did the private eye observe Ruben take a female home with him.

It was critical for the initial confrontation with Ruben to go smoothly. The idea of accosting him at his apartment was fine, but the exact details needed to be worked out and executed without a flaw.

He and Jamie would be in Cancun for four days, Friday through Sunday, returning on Monday. They could conduct reconnaissance on Friday, their first night in Cancun, at both the bars Ruben frequented and at his apartment. Ruben worked on the cruise boat on Friday, Saturday and Sunday evenings, but had a day off on Monday.

It appeared to Boyd that Sunday would be ideal for the planned event; they would have from morning until night to catch Ruben alone at his apartment. Plus, he and Jamie would be leaving the next day. It would be awkward having to hang around the hotel district any longer than necessary after what he planned for Ruben. However, what if for one reason or another they couldn't make contact with Ruben on Sunday? If a more opportune time presented itself on Saturday, then so be it. Boyd was very familiar with the concept of the triple option in football, but Sunday would be the primary goal.

It was 7:30 when Boyd was on his second cup of coffee. He briefly reflected on his modest achievements during his short six-day stint at Ridgetop. The situation with his wife was on auto-pilot, but progress had been made on the Cancun project, largely due to having met Jamie. He was even formulating ideas about writing the book.

Boyd topped off his coffee cup, picked up one of his living room lawn chairs and opened the door for the cat. Following the cat outside, he seated himself in his usual spot under the cottonwood tree. It was already warm and there was not even a hint of a breeze. The humidity had made its early morning appearance with the promise of a sticky day.

Two pickup trucks and an older model car made their way past the doublewide, along with three teenagers on their way to the school bus stop at the main entrance to Ridgetop. Following the teenagers, Boyd saw the bicycle-brothers, Darell and Richie, approaching.

Holding up his coffee cup in greeting, Boyd said, "Good morning, boys."

The older brother waved, and the younger one named Darell quietly walked over to the lawn chair and wrapped his arms around Boyd's shoulders, giving him a tight, lingering hug. With a catch in his voice, he uttered, "Thank you, mister. That was the nicest thing anyone ever done for me."

Caught by surprise, Boyd could only stammer, "Well, ahh, yeah. Not a problem. You boys have a good day in school."

As the boys walked away, Boyd could hear Darell whisper, "I told you so."

Boyd leaned back in his chair and watched the two boys and several other kids meander toward the bus stop. As another car crunched by the doublewide, Boyd abruptly stood as he remembered the plate sitting beside the sink in his kitchen. He'd been meaning to return it to Aurelia, the lady who'd given him the chorizo several days ago.

Having to step over the cat on the top step both going and coming, Boyd retrieved the plate and walked over to the trailer where Aurelia and her husband lived.

Knocking on the door, Boyd expected Aurelia to answer. Instead, a man in his late thirties, holding a baby, opened the door with a simple, "Hello."

"Oh, hi. I'm Boyd Tanner. I live next door and I'm returning a plate your wife gave me a few days ago." Smiling, he added, "The best chorizo I've ever had."

"Yes, Aurelia told me she met you. You're friends with Jamie." Grinning and extending his free hand, he added, "I'm Arturo. Good to meet you. Any friend of Jamie's can be my friend. Very good boy."

Walking up behind her husband and taking the baby, Aurelia chimed in, "Yes, a good boy."

Laughing, Boyd said, "I'll keep it to myself. Jamie might get the big head if I told him how popular he is around here."

Walking outside and leaning against the side of the trailer, Arturo went into great detail regarding how he and Jamie had fixed several problems with Jamie's SUV.

"How long have you been in the auto mechanic business? Jamie speaks highly of your talents."

"Oh, I started working on cars when I was just a kid. Gradually learned all about fuel injection, and all the new electronic systems. I've worked on most American car models and just about all European and Asian cars. It's in my blood."

Deciding not to mention the BMW in his garage in Northwood Hills, Boyd said, "I envy your experience. I'm pretty good at opening the gas cap and filling her up."

Lowering his voice, Arturo said, "I got laid off from my job at Lothar's Auto Service yesterday. My boss, Lothar, has had trouble competing with the foreign car dealerships. I think he's going out of business."

"Sorry to hear that."

"I used to work at Sears Auto and a couple of other places, so I'll be checking with them. To make ends meet, I'm going to work part time with a friend of mine in his lawn and moving business. I start there tomorrow. Everything will be okay."

"I'm sure it will. I'll tell Jamie I met you."

Boyd walked back to his trailer and stood next to the large cottonwood tree. The last six days had been eye opening and it was becoming apparent to Boyd that he'd been living on a certain socioeconomic island occupied by very few. He was pleased with his success, but he was becoming more attuned to the status of others, who Jamie referred to as the "desperate class."

A muffled sound attracted Boyd's attention. It seemed to be from a small child or maybe an animal. It was difficult to determine whether it was close by or at some distance. Suddenly, a loud scratching noise accompanied the whining. Boyd walked around the corner of the doublewide and could see the CleanKing trash container shaking. Knowing immediately what the commotion was all about, Boyd lifted the lid and looked inside.

"How in the world did you get in there?" He leaned over the container and lifted Rosie into his arms.

Looking at the cat and then back at the trash bin, Boyd felt a surge of anger. The cat didn't get in that predicament by herself. Someone put her there.

Walking to the edge of the street and looking both directions, the early morning activity had mostly subsided. Putting the cat down, Boyd murmured, "How many times have I told you to stay away from strangers."

It was still early and Boyd decided to take his laundry to his home in Northwood Hills. He needed to get some replacement items, including a novel he'd purchased a month previously. There were a couple of things he wanted to accomplish at the trailer park today, one being another workout at Rusty's gym, and two, a visit to the Oasis Massage Trailer, or whatever it was called. The plan for the Cancun project was coming along nicely and the events of the past few days at Ridgetop had inspired him to get serious about writing a book. Also, there was a business card in a drawer at his home office with the phone number of the North Dallas BMW dealership.

―――

The sun was barely leaning toward the west when Boyd returned to Ridgetop. The pure white clouds were billowing high overhead and seemed to be slowly moving in a northerly direction. It didn't appear rain was imminent, but the air was thick and heavy.

Removing a box containing towels, wash cloths, underwear, tee shirts, more Cheerios and the novel, Boyd almost stepped on the Calico as he turned to walk up the steps to the back door of the doublewide.

"Glad to see me?"

The cat followed Boyd into the trailer and immediately jumped on the red couch and began cleaning her paws. Boyd took the box to the bedroom and changed into his workout shorts and Vanderbilt tee-shirt.

It was relatively busy on this early Monday afternoon at the strip shopping center. As he walked by the All-In-One, he could see red-headed Gloria talking to a customer. The parking area in front of Christina's was completely filled, primarily with pickups and SUVs. Three middle aged men wearing grease-stained work clothes and ball caps with various logos were sitting on a bench outside the front door waiting to be seated.

Entering the gym, Boyd was surprised to see ten or so individuals working on various pieces of equipment.

"Hey, glad you came back to sweat with us." Rusty smiled, and greeting Boyd like a long lost friend.

"Just walking over here caused me to sweat. Hope you have all your fans on."

Laughing, Rusty said, "Manly men don't need fans, but the water cooler works, so feel free to use it."

Boyd handed Rusty a five-dollar bill and made his way to the stationary bicycles to warm up for his workout.

Forty-five minutes into the free weight portion of the workout, Rusty briskly walked over to Boyd and exclaimed, "Hey, hey, hey! Remember me telling you about the goings-on over at the old church building?" Pointing toward the door, he encouraged Boyd to follow him.

The sight of flashing red and blue lights greeted them as they walked out the door and looked toward the church. Three police cars were parked facing the church and several uniformed police officers were standing by the double doors at the front of the building. After a few minutes, two men in handcuffs, followed by three other officers exited the building. Another officer followed the procession out the door with three young ladies in tow.

Barely able to contain his glee, Rusty blurted, "Damn, looks like the law is cleaning up Ridgetop and all of North Texas! The Lord is kicking ass!"

Boyd just grinned.

Gloria does make stuff happen. Don't mess with the red-head.

Rusty rambled on in an excited tone, "I don't think I recognize either of those two guys in handcuffs. I wonder if they'll give up Roscoe? This is pretty darned exciting, right? You'll have all kinds of stuff for your book."

"I'm taking mental notes. Think I'll head home and write them down."

One of the patrol cars passed Boyd on his way back to the trailer park. As he walked down his gravel street, he looked to the right toward Roscoe's office and saw the red and blue flashing lights once more.

Gloria strikes again.

———

It was late afternoon when Boyd finished showering following his work-out at the gym. The steam was stifling in the small bathroom and flowed into the bedroom and down the hall. After putting on a pair of beige casual shorts, a blue Vanderbilt tee shirt and a pair of Sebago docksiders, he retrieved the Oasis Massage Center card from his wallet. The card had the trailer number and the phone number printed in bright green letters.

Boyd dialed the number on his iPhone and wondered how late the "establishment" was open on a Monday afternoon.

"Oasis, this is Trixi," was the sultry answer.

"Oh, hi, this is Boyd Tanner. I live a couple of rows over from you and I wanted to know if it would be possible to get a massage this afternoon?"

"Honey, I'm so sorry, but I'm on my way over to my mother's to help her move from one apartment to another. I'll be spending the night with her, but I could see you tomorrow afternoon at 4:30." Her voice was lower than when she initially answered the phone.

"Not a problem. I'll see you at 4:30 tomorrow afternoon."

"You got it." It was throaty and a cross between a whisper and a purr.

It had been an eventful day, and since he was cleaned up and dressed, Boyd decided to get take-out Chinese food and to put some more thought into the outline for his novel. He also needed to jot down notes regarding this afternoon's activities at the old church building.

And more thought into the Cancun project.

Boyd exited through the kitchen door and was about to unlock his rental Ford, when Jamie pulled into his parking space across the street.

Boyd crossed the street, greeting Jamie as he got out of the SUV. "Hey young man, how'd it go today?"

Smiling, Jamie said, "I worked my tail off. Such task masters I work for! How was your day? You don't have to answer...I know how you old retirees just sit around all day sipping wine and eating carrots."

Laughing, Boyd nodded. "If you substituted Dickel for the wine, and doughnuts for the carrots, you'd be close. Actually, there was one interesting development today. I was at Rusty's gym this afternoon working out and saw the old church being raided by the police. They had a couple of guys in handcuffs."

"No kidding! Did they get Roscoe?"

"Not at the church, but I saw police lights flashing at Roscoe's trailer as I was walking back, so I assume he's up to his eyeballs in trouble."

"Well, he deserves whatever happens to him." Continuing in a lowered voice, Jamie said, "My friend came through as promised and gave me the secobarbital sodium this morning. He assured me there would be no problems on his end."

"Good work. We don't want him or you to have any repercussions."

"It's covered."

"Didn't you say you were meeting up with Amber this evening? You'd better get it in gear."

Going into a body-builder pose, Jamie bragged, "She'd be crazy not to wait for this!"

Shaking his head, Boyd turned to leave, but remembered, "Oh yeah, I forgot to tell you...some dickwad got Rosie and put her in my trash container. Can you believe that?"

"Is she okay?"

"She's fine. It's just hard to imagine anyone being that stupid. And, I have an appointment with the Oasis Massage Center tomorrow afternoon... based on your Yelp review."

"It'll be good material for your book. Really good!"

CHAPTER 22

Cancun, Mexico...May 30th

Ruben slept ten straight hours and felt reinvigorated. He had read that all great men sleep well because they knew how to eliminate distraction from their minds, relax and focus only on the important issues. And he was on his way to becoming one of those great men.

He'd awakened with only one thought on his mind...Carmen. The fact a dead woman had been in his bed less than two nights ago didn't bother him at all. Today he would focus on positive thoughts, and Carmen was the positive thought of the day. As he admired his naked body in the bathroom mirror, he felt a pang of sorrow for the other women in Cancun who would be missing out on this treat. Tonight was all about Carmen, the sexy bitch who dissed him in front of the other bartenders on the Devilfish. In addition, for the past two days he'd become aroused every time he thought about her. She was definitely the cream of the crop on the Devilfish, and it was time she was put in her place.

It was close to noon and Ruben was hungry. Food was only one of his hungers. It was all coming together, the big score from the police chief and the business men, and of course, Nicaragua. He would own a bar, and bitches would be crawling all over him.

Ruben dressed and decided a couple of giant tacos at the Blue Gecko Cantina would suit his hunger needs. The Gecko was only fifteen minutes from his apartment, across from the Grand Oasis Hotel on Boulevard Kukulcan. Beth's death and having to dispose of her body had affected his appetite somewhat, but now he was back on track.

He drove with all the windows down and took in the fresh, warm air. The parking lot at the Gecko was busy, but not impossible. The small structure rested on a concrete slab, the sign on the thatched roof displaying a blue gecko reclining on a beach with a mug of beer in its hand. Ruben didn't want or need a beer. He hesitated at the sign showing today's specials...*Fiery Fish Tacos, Fried Avocado Tacos and Spicy Salmon with Feta Cheese.*

He waited for the waitress while sitting at a wooden bar facing the street. There were no black ties or white table cloths at this establishment, only tacos and cold drinks of every description. There was a low hum of activity since it was only early afternoon, a welcome respite from the drunken din Ruben would be experiencing on the Devilfish.

"Good afternoon, what can I do for you?" A rather plain, plump waitress stood next to Ruben with a pencil in one hand and a pad in the other.

Ruben's first thought was: *What an ugly toad. My bar in Nicaragua is going to have beautiful waitresses wearing skimpy outfits, maybe topless. Yeah, topless.*

"Do you still make the green chili pork tacos?"

"Indeed, want one or two?"

"Two. And a glass of iced tea." *Need to save myself for Carmen tonight.*

After wolfing down the tacos, Ruben noticed there were no other customers at the bar, and several of the tables were now vacant. He decided to call Estralita and get her on-board for tonight's activities.

He was about to hang up when Estralita answered with a dull, "Hello."

"You sound like you're half asleep. Did I awaken you?"

"No. Feel fine."

"Are you ready for tonight?"

"Yeah, I'm going to juice what's-her-name's drink. Right?"

"And her boyfriend's drink. Are you okay!"

"Yes, I'm fine, just like I told you."

"Hector will get to the Turtle early and get us a table. I'll arrive before Carmen...that's what's-her-name. Christ, you've met her before! Make sure you're ready to wait on our table. Got it?"

"Yes, sir," came the sullen reply.

"Her boyfriend is a fat tub, so maybe you should give him a dose and a half."

"Will do, sir."

Goddamn it, I'm glad she's not going to Nicaragua with us.

"See you tonight."

———

The Devilfish was at total capacity with close to one-hundred seventy-five guests. The stated pricing for the Adult Party Cruz was seventy-nine dollars, but for some reason, a don't-miss-it special of fifty-nine dollars had been advertised for this Sunday's party. And a party it was!

Ruben had never seen so many X-rated tee shirts and string bikinis in his time on the 'Fish. One of the obnoxious gringo assholes was wearing a tee shirt with **If You Have Big Tits, Be My Girlfriend** printed on it. His girlfriend had a black string bikini that left nothing to the imagination. Ruben stared at them as they walked by.

Just as I thought, a *tattoo of an eagle just above her butt crack.*

Three young men reached the top of the gangplank and turned to the rest of the people in line to show off their sleeveless tees. One was printed **Hung Well,** the second sported **Big One** and the third claimed **Always Hard**. When several of the girls started chanting *Show Me, Show Me,* Ruben knew it was going to be a wild night. But not as wild for them as it would be for him.

The party on the island was ribald as usual. Two voluptuous blondes danced on the stage and then exchanged their two-piece string bikinis in full view of the crowd. The booze cruise "sensual overload" was making good progress as the evening wore on. An older woman passed out, and several of the inebriated college boys vomited without warning. One had barfed in his date's hair and another deposited his lunch on the dance floor. Some of the guys spent an inordinate amount of time on the stage sipping tequila from the navel of a blonde beauty.

The Devilfish left Isla Mujeres about thirty minutes early and was nearing the Playa Langosta pier. The DJ, perched in his raised chair near the dance floor, had the crowd in a frenzy. At one point, he shouted, "This is a sandbox for your inner child. Live it up!" It had been this way since the Devilfish had first left dock, continued on the island and was still going strong. An unbelievable display of stamina and determination. Every dance move known to mankind was on display. The gentle swaying of the boat enhanced the moves as well as the drunkenness.

Ruben had been tempted to put some of his patented moves on a couple of the more sensuous ladies, but he stuck to his plan...Carmen.

"Were you exceptionally busy tonight with this crowd?" He gave his most gracious smile as he leaned on the bar and addressed Carmen.

"It was busy, wasn't it," she said, lacking the usual animosity.

"Again, I'm truly sorry for being such a jerk the past couple of months. Could I make it up to you by buying you and your boyfriend a drink tonight at the Turtle?"

"Sure. That would be nice. You've met Paco before, haven't you?"

"Yes I have. Seems like a really nice guy. See you at the Turtle."

———

Ruben hurriedly completed his part of the boat clean-up. He was on his way down the pier when he decided to dial Hector's cell phone.

Hector uttered, "It's me."

"Where are you sitting? I'm almost there."

"Where am I sitting!" Hector gasped, annoyed. "Hell, I'm exactly where we were sitting last night. On the edge of the patio."

Ignoring Hector's response, Ruben was direct. "Everything is set. Carmen and her boyfriend will be joining us. Be on your best behavior." He didn't like being short, but lately he'd been losing his patience with Hector's constant complaining and demands. Ruben was the brains of the team and that was that.

"I'm ready for action."

Ruben hung up without saying goodbye. He was not thrilled with the idea of Hector participating tonight with Carmen, even though they'd shared other drugged women.

What the fuck. This is going to be a good night no matter what!

The bar was packed, and the crowd had not slowed down since the Devilfish docked. If anything, it appeared the loud music coming from the speakers spurred them to new heights of drunkenness. Ruben spotted Hector sitting alone at a table.

"I see Carmen and her boyfriend over there by the dance floor. Where's Estralita? Is she ready?" Ruben was revved and still talking in short, choppy sentences.

"Estralita's over there by the bar. Seems to me she's been acting kind of weird."

"Weird how?"

"Just fucked up, weird. That's all."

"Go tell her to get her shit together. They'll be here any minute."

"Okay boss," Hector said sarcastically.

Ruben raised his hand and waved to Carmen and Paco as Hector returned from his short stay at the bar.

Hector sat down and whispered, "Estralita's on the job. I see her coming this way now."

Standing and offering his hand to Paco, Ruben said cordially, "Glad you could join us. This is my friend Hector. Your girlfriend and I had a busy night on the Devilfish. Glad it's finally over. Right, Carmen?" Ruben was nervous and continued talking in an abbreviated manner.

Sitting down at the table, Carmen affably agreed, "It was a wild crowd, but fun."

Estralita arrived before all the chairs were pulled up to the table. With a strange, silly grin on her face, she asked, "What are you drinking tonight?"

The guys all ordered tequila shots to get started and Carmen, after hesitating, decided to join in.

"And what do you do, Hector." Carmen was first with the small talk, sensing Ruben was embarrassed to be in her company after his behavior over the past few months.

"I'm the General Manager at a meat packing plant on the other side of the city." Hector liked the title General Manager better than Owner, so tonight he was GM. "Me and Ruben went all through school together. Right, amigo?"

"Indeed we did." Trying to calm his nerves, Ruben addressed Carmen's boyfriend. "Paco, where do you work?"

"I run a boxing gym over on Oaxaca Street near the Universidad del Caribe." Paco was wearing a dark blue polo shirt and a pair of white shorts. His forearms were the size of small tree trunks. Even though he was thick through the torso and only about five-six in height, it appeared he didn't have an ounce of body fat.

Not how Ruben remembered him.

After a couple of involuntary blinks and before Ruben could reply, Estralita returned with the tequila shots. She looked carefully at the shot glasses on her tray before carefully placing them in front of each person at the table, with Ruben receiving the last one.

Ruben looked into Estralita's vacant eyes. *What the fuck is the matter with her!*

Hector, almost too enthusiastically, raised his glass and said, "Here's to peaceful men and the good earth."

Even though they didn't entirely understand Hector's toast, Paco and Carmen glanced at each other and tossed down their shots.

Shaking his head, Ruben raised his glass and swallowed the golden drink he loved so much. No salt, no lime, just the wonderful, biting tequila.

Still standing by the table, Estralita asked, "What now? You know, does anyone want another one?"

"I'll have a rum and Coke," Carmen said first.

"Another tequila shot for the boys, I'm buying," Ruben chimed in.

Estralita looked down at the table for a few seconds and then turned and weaved her way back toward the bar.

The temperature was ideal. The slight breeze made it difficult to tell whether it was warm or not. It was almost as if the concept of hot, warm or cool didn't exist. The music was loud and the crowd had no intention of settling down.

"That lung yady is strange." Carmen was struggling to speak and had a far-away look in her eyes. She appeared to be having trouble keeping her head upright.

Ruben thought, *That shit is working fast. How much juice did Estralita put in her drink?*

Hector's upper body was gently swaying in a circular motion and then with a sudden crash, his head hit the table, barely missing a glass with a lighted candle in it.

Carmen leaned forward and put her cheek on the table. She performed the move in a very precise, very smooth, drugged-out manner. Her long dark hair was in a neat pile around her head and face.

"What's going on!" Paco quickly got out of his chair and stood over Carmen's limp body. Glaring at Ruben, he growled, "I'm taking her home. Carmen, can you get up!" He effortlessly lifted her into his arms, walking the short distance to the curving path leading to the parking lot, and then out of sight.

Ruben was shocked. He looked at Hector's motionless body, which was taking up half of the table, and slowly shook his head. He knew immediately what had happened. Estralita must be on something and had totally screwed up the entire evening. He had told Hector to make sure she was up to the task, but instead, they both completely failed him. This was just not possible. It was totally unacceptable.

As Ruben sat and fumed, Estralita arrived with the second drink order. "What's wrong with Hector? Where are the other two?" She was still acting scattered.

In a loud whisper, Ruben said, "You dumb bitch, you gave Hector the wrong shot glass. Put the drinks down and help me with him. Let's get him to my car."

They both got Hector to his feet and put his arms around their shoulders. He was out like a light and the toes of his sandals dragged along the pave stones as they exited the bar. Arriving at Ruben's SUV, they managed to get Hector into the back seat.

"Get in!" Ruben barked. "We're taking him to my place."

"But I've got to work."

"You're too fucked up to work. Get in!"

Ruben figured Estralita would get the workout of her life tonight. He would set the video equipment on auto and Hector could watch it in the morning.

CHAPTER 23

Ridgetop Mobile Estates...June 1st...Dallas, Texas
The first day of June began with a thunderstorm and light rain. Rosie came running from under the steps when Boyd opened the front door. She immediately jumped onto the couch and started cleaning herself.

"How did you ever make it in this world before I came along?" Boyd slowly shook his head.

After breakfast and his initial cup of coffee, Boyd went into the bedroom and retrieved the novel by Nelson DeMille he'd brought from home. *The Gatehouse* had piqued Boyd's interest, not only the story line, but the structure and style of the author. He read six chapters last night and decided to read a few more this morning. Other than business related material, Boyd hadn't had much spare time for reading during his professional career. This was a pleasant change.

Boyd sat down on the couch with his feet resting on the coffee table. He placed the book between himself and the Calico and turned on the lamp next to the couch. The light was barely adequate due to the morning dullness of the overcast skies. The unique patter of rain on the roof created a feeling of melancholy.

Leaning back with his hands clasped behind his head, Boyd once again thought about his wife, his daughter and what the future held. He had been at Ridgetop for only a week and now there was no doubt about his priorities.

An extraneous thought entered Boyd's mind...essentially, he had not watched TV in a week, and really didn't miss it. He'd looked at news headlines on his iPhone, but no TV.

Maybe a new trend, a regeneration of intellectual structure. Maybe not.

Boyd opened the book with one hand and put the other on Rosie's back. He became completely absorbed in the story and didn't look up until almost 11:00. The author's style was interesting, giving Boyd ideas for his own approach to writing a novel.

The rain stopped and the familiar sounds of Ridgetop returned. Remembering the card with the contact information for the North Dallas BMW dealership, Boyd retrieved it from his wallet and dialed the number.

"North Dallas BMW."

"Hi, this is Boyd Tanner and I've been a customer there for several years. Could you connect me to the service manager? I think his name is Tom Gilmore."

"One moment please."

"Gilmore." The answer was brief, but not unpleasant.

"Tom, this is Boyd Tanner. Don't know if you remember me, but I've been a customer of yours for a number of years."

"Sure, I remember you. You drive a 750Li and we've serviced it a time or two. What can I do for you?"

"I have an acquaintance who's looking for a job as a maintenance technician. He has extensive experience with both foreign and domestic automobiles. I guess I have two questions: do you know if you guys are hiring mechanics and if so, whom should I talk to?"

"You're talking to him. The maintenance manager reports to me and he's currently on vacation. We're looking for two technicians right now, and I mean as soon as possible. Here, let me give you my cell number. Have this guy call me."

Boyd wrote down the name and number on the back of the card, thanked Tom, slipped on his shoes and walked to the door of the trailer. "Be right back. Don't go anywhere."

The cat simply stretched out its forepaws and yawned.

Walking down the steps and toward Arturo and Aurelia's trailer, the air felt rested; still heavy, but fresh. The grass was damp and the gravel on the lane glistened from the scattered light coming through the partially cloudy sky.

Aurelia answered the door and smiled at Boyd. "Arturo is working today with his friend. I think they are working on lawns or moving furniture."

"Yes, Arturo mentioned that yesterday." Handing her the card, he continued, "Tell Arturo to call this fellow at the BMW dealership in Dallas and to mention my name. They're looking for a couple of technicians. No guarantee, but it could be a good possibility for him."

"Oh, thank you very much. I am grateful and Arturo will be grateful."

"Hope it works out."

Even though it was not yet noon, Boyd was ready for an early lunch. He decided to walk over to the All-In-One since he was already out and pointed in that direction. Besides, he was curious as to what frame of mind Gloria might be in today.

The store was empty, except for the redhead, when he entered.

"Hey, I was hoping you would be coming in! Do you know what happened over at the old church?"

"No, what happened."

"They arrested those son-of-a-bitches! I didn't see it, but I heard the cops nabbed two guys at the church along with several prostitutes or sex slaves or whatever they were!" Gloria was on the verge of hyperventilating. "Fucking Roscoe got arrested too. They hauled 'em all off to jail!"

"No kidding! Fast times at Ridgetop!" Gloria didn't pick up on the vague movie reference. Boyd was enjoying her excitement.

"Remember me telling you about my husband, Lefty, who's been hanging around with Roscoe? Well, I nailed his ass to the floor last night. I mean I grilled him up one side and down the other and he swears he's never been to the old church building. I reckon he's telling the truth. If I ever find out different, he'll be wearing diapers the rest of his miserable life!"

Re-focusing on his hunger, Boyd said, "Have anything here you would recommend for lunch?"

"The spaghetti and meat balls back there in the frozen foods is darn good. We have it a couple of times a week. A big boy like you could probably eat two of 'em without any problem."

"I'm sold. Ring me up and I'll go get two."

———

Boyd returned to the trailer and micro-waved both frozen dinners. After eating, he reclined on the couch and opened his book by Nelson DeMille. He was almost half-way through the novel when he looked up at the time.

Since it was after 4:00, Boyd decided on a George Dickel on the rocks to get him prepared for the Oasis experience. He sat on the couch as he sipped the drink and reflected on his day.

Boyd started the short trip to the Oasis feeling relaxed and actually looking forward to a deep massage for his tired muscles and joints. He had a feeling this experience would make the short list of items to be included in his fledgling book project. Walking past Jamie's trailer, he saw his SUV in the parking space and assumed he had just returned from work. He crossed the next street and through a vacant space occupied by a concrete slab and a short, stubby mesquite tree. Pausing to look at the numbering sequence on two different trailers, he turned left and arrived at number seventy-seven. A small green sign above the door identified the **OASIS**, a doublewide with a three-step porch which was also painted green.

The door opened before Boyd's knuckles made contact.

Looking at Boyd and hesitating for a moment, the middle aged, peroxide blonde, dressed in a multi-colored v-neck muumuu, tilted her head and exclaimed, "Well, well, aren't you the perfect physical specimen. I'm not used to this! I'm Trixi." Her voice had gone up two octaves since the phone conversation. "Come on in!"

Entering, Boyd took in the sight and grinned. It was as if he had walked into the middle of a jungle. A jungle in Dallas!

Was it a jungle, or a jungle cavern, Boyd thought.

Green ferns, ivy and plants of every description and size filled most of the trailer's interior. Plants were hanging from the ceiling and the walls. Faux stalactites and stalagmites protruded from the ceiling and the floor, individually and in clusters. It was difficult to tell if they were made from paper mache or hardened mud. In one corner, water flowed from an opening in the rock-covered wall into a miniature pool. A massage table, covered in a mossy looking material, occupied the center of the room. The floor of the trailer was covered in green, extra-shaggy carpet.

"Put your shoes and clothes under the table and lay face down. There's a towel on the table... if you're inclined to be inhibited."

As she walked out of the room, Trixi touched a dimmer switch and the lights went down to a soft glow. Dim blue and red lights at floor level around the walls created deep shadows throughout the ersatz jungle.

Following instructions, Boyd removed his clothes, folded them and placed them on top of his sandals under the table. As he finished wrapping the towel around his waist, Trixi returned barefoot, wearing what appeared to be a short, black negligee. Even in the dimly lit room, Boyd could tell she had a shapely body and thought: *Jamie, what kind of book research is this!*

Boyd positioned himself on the table face first, adjusting his forehead just above the small opening. The climate in the room transported him to a jungle oasis with the gurgling of the water gently falling into the small pool adding to the atmosphere. Trixi stood near Boyd's head, beginning the massage by pressing her fingers into Boyd's scalp and carefully moving them over his head and the back of his neck.

"Would you prefer a deep massage or something a little more mild?" The softness in her voice belied her physical attributes. She appeared to be about five foot seven, and her hands on his neck felt like two vice grips.

"Deep will be just fine."

Boyd flinched slightly as she dug her fingers into his right shoulder.

Damn, I'll bet she could bend steel rods!

She continued by leaning over and working on his shoulder with the point of her elbow.

"You know, maybe medium rather than deep will get the job done." Boyd was raising the white flag.

This lady is strong!

"No problem. Sometimes I get carried away with a client who has a body like yours." Her voice was a low purr. "How long have you been living at Ridgetop?"

"Just a little over a week. How about you?"

"Couple of years. Moved here from Houston. What kind of work do you do?"

"I'm in between jobs, but I've been in manufacturing."

"Were you in one of those companies that sent jobs overseas? You know, outsourcing?"

Surprised that she knew about, or had an opinion on outsourcing, Boyd said, "I was in high-tech manufacturing and we had two plants here in the U.S. and two in Asia. The labor costs are much lower in Asia than here, so in order to be competitive in a global economy, we had to have foreign plants. We competed with companies from China, South Korea, Taiwan and India. It was either be competitive from a cost stand-point or go out of business. End of story."

Is this a massage or a job interview?

"Makes sense, if you put it that way."

Moving to the other side of the table, Trixi started on Boyd's left shoulder, using a little less pressure.

The waterfall continued its soothing sound and Boyd was starting to relax. His mind was starting to drift as Trixi moved from his shoulders to his lower back, her fingers and hands strong, but under control.

The hands on each of his calves were not nearly as strong as the ones working his back.

I don't think I'm dreaming, so what is this?

"Have you ever had a four handed massage?" Trixi voice was low and even.

"Ahh…no, I don't think so. I mean no, I actually haven't."

"Well, Heather is at one end and I'm at the other. Try it, you'll like it." Trixi's voice was barely audible.

Trying to justify all four hands in the name of research for the book, Boyd uttered through the opening in the massage table, "Okay, nice to meet you Heather."

"Likewise."

The two syllable word gave away her Southern drawl and even though Boyd couldn't see her at this stage of the massage, he visualized her to be younger than Trixi.

It's going to be very difficult to relax now.

After about thirty minutes, Trixi spoke softly, "Okay tiger, turn over on your back."

Boyd complied by rolling over while keeping the towel across his midsection.

What now?

Trixi started with his temples and moved slowly down to his chest. Heather was working on his right foot.

"You know, you need a lot of work on your feet." Heather didn't say much, but when she did, it was body part specific. She immediately shifted to his left foot.

Trixi started with his left bicep and forearm. All four hands seemed to be synced up.

"Wow, you have a couple of guns."

Boyd assumed Trixi was referring to his biceps, since the towel was still in place. Not knowing whether he should respond or not, he grunted, "Ummhuh."

Heather moved her attention from Boyd's feet to his knees and now to his upper quads. Trixi was slowly moving from his chest to his lower stomach region. The meditative feeling left the room, replaced by a relaxed tension.

"Okay big boy, your hour is about up, anything else you would be interested in?" Trixi's voice had gone from the more professional "outsourcing" tone to the soft purr.

Thinking for a second, Boyd replied, "No, that should do it. I have a meeting this afternoon I need to get to. That was a fantastic massage and I'll be back." A little white lie never hurt anyone, although he did enjoy all four of the hands.

The only sound that came from the other end of the table was a low, "Aww, heck."

After the masseuses left the room, Boyd dressed and took two fifty-dollar bills from his wallet. When Trixi returned, he said, as he handed her the bills, "That was really super. I'm sure I'll be seeing you again. Tell Heather thanks."

"Anytime, day or night. You've got my number."

The sky was still filled with clouds as Boyd crossed the vacant lot and walked across the street behind Jamie's trailer. He could see Jamie's SUV still parked in its space. As he approached, he could hear loud voices coming from across the street near his doublewide. The SUV was blocking his vision, but after a few more steps he could see the source of the noise.

Someone was sitting against the CleanKing trash container with a dazed look on his face, blood seeping from his nose and running into his mouth, his close-fitting, black knit cap still in place. Jamie was gripping another skin-head looking character by the throat, and had lifted him almost off the ground, the small swastika on the right side of his head clearly visible. It appeared the man's toes were barely touching the ground as Jamie screamed at him. Boyd immediately recognized the two men as the ones Jamie had pointed out two nights before during the cookout with the girls.

As Boyd crossed the street, Jamie yelled in the face of the individual he was holding by the neck, "Lester, you're nothing but a piece of shit! I don't ever want to see you on this street again. Do you read me?"

Lester's face was red and when he tried to respond, the toes of his shoes scraped the gravel under them.

Shoving Lester backward and on top of his friend, Jamie continued his barrage. "If anything happens to that cat, even if it dies of old age, I'm going to fuck you up! Understand? Now pick up your asshole buddy and get out of here!"

Lester did as told, assisting his friend as they stumbled across the gravel road. Richie, Darell and two of their friends who had been watching from down the street, approached the doublewide.

"Wow, you guys mean business. That's some cool stuff!" Richie was impressed.

Jamie was as calm as if he had just awakened from a nap. Looking at the boys, he said, "It's just not a good thing to pick on helpless animals, right?"

Smiling, Darell responded, "Not if the animal lives on this street!"

Richie chimed in, "Man, they're going to be calling you guys the Legends of Ridgetop."

Using his somewhat flawed Schwarzenegger impression, Jamie replied, "You boys better get out of here, or I put you all in the trash can."

Laughing, they wandered on down the street, kicking gravel as they walked.

Looking at Boyd, Jamie explained, "I looked out of my window and saw Lester and Frank doing something by your door. They'd picked up Rosie and were headed for the trash can. Frank was holding the cat and Lester was opening the top of the container when I yelled at them. About the time Frank dropped Rosie, my elbow said hello to his nose and then you saw the rest. Just can't believe those guys."

"Rosie and I both thank you."

"Don't worry about those guys, they won't be back around. They think they're really tough guys until someone stands up to them. You up for some more Mexican food at Christina's?" Jamie was ready to end the day with food and drink.

"I've already had one Dickel today, but maybe a couple more and some tacos will be just right. Besides, I need to fill you in on the Oasis

Massage Center. You know, this neighborhood is way more interesting than where I reside in North Dallas. Way!"

The Calico was sitting on the top step of the door leading into the kitchen. She was licking her paws and cleaning her face. Her expression was nonchalant. Just another day in the life of a cat.

CHAPTER 24

Cancun, Mexico...May 31st

It was late on Monday morning. This was Ruben's day off and he didn't have to work this evening on the Devilfish. And that was a good thing due to the fiasco at the Blue Turtle last night. Then he remembered how pissed he was with Hector and Estralita due to the fact he would never have another chance to abuse Carmen, the blender bitch. That train had pulled out of the station and was long gone.

Ruben occasionally thought about the irony of his situation. He was good looking, charming and had a way with women, yet he preferred to drug and rape them rather than spend the time to develop any type of relationship. In the far recesses of his mind, he knew this was perverted, but he also knew he was in charge and could treat people any way he wanted and get away with it. Big money and success were just around the corner.

He rolled over and started to get out of bed when he realized Estralita was completely nude and lying beside him. He had taken full advantage of Estralita's drugged out condition last night and had managed to video the entire two-person orgy. Well, it was really only a one-person orgy since Estralita didn't have a clue as to what was happening. He wondered if it was possible to sell this type video to an adult web site, but finally decided to put it on the back burner and file it as a potential future business venture.

Pushing her shoulder, Ruben growled, "Hey bitch, time to get up and go home." He was constantly amazed how anyone so pretty could be so dumb.

Mumbling some mostly incoherent sounds, she moved into a fetal position and completely tuned out the world. Ruben climbed over her smooth, bare body and thought about giving her a hard slap on the butt, but decided not to cause a scene this early in the day.

Ruben slipped on his blue boat pants and walked barefooted into the living room. Hector was still on the couch where he had been placed last night. He was lying face down, snoring loudly, with one arm hanging off the couch and touching the floor.

Ruben shook his head in disgust and went to the refrigerator. He took a long drink from a carton of orange juice and remembered a partial box of doughnuts on the shelf next to the sink. They were at least a week old, but he grabbed two of them and sat down at the kitchen table. Looking at Hector sprawled out on the couch, he was reminded of all the times, both good and not so good, they had spent together since childhood. Hector was a loyal follower and Ruben knew he just had to continue with his brilliant leadership. Although he hated to admit it, Hector was essential to Ruben's well being...both physically and mentally. He was a follower, but he always came through in delicate situations...except for last night.

As the decision maker, Ruben came to the conclusion they would pull the plug on Uncle Emilio's clients by the middle of next week and head for Nicaragua. He needed to finalize plans with Hector. They needed to pull off the extortion plan quickly and surgically. Their lives could be at stake if there was a screw-up like last night.

Not bothering to take a shower, Ruben finished dressing and went to the closet next to his bed. Getting on his hands and knees, he removed the cardboard boxes stacked in the corner and pulled back the piece of carpet with the plywood square tacked to the bottom of it. The metal box in the shallow space underneath contained over twelve thousand dollars he had made from his various sexual related endeavors. He counted three thousand dollars from his stash and put it in his pocket. This was Uncle Emilio's cut for arranging clients for the past three encounters. Standing, he took the small disk from last night's tryst out of the video camera and placed it in the box on the top shelf. The box contained videos of fourteen or fifteen rapes. Ruben couldn't remember exactly how many DVDs were in the box, but he knew there were ten videos of Uncle Emilio's clients, each labeled and dated in plastic holders. He also knew this was his start to financial independence.

A thought came to Ruben and he reached back into the video box and removed the DVD he had just placed there. He found a pen and piece of paper in the kitchen and wrote *Worst piece of Ass I Ever Had* on it. He put the note and DVD on the kitchen floor by the back door and quietly closed it so as not to awaken his guests.

———

The drive to Avenida Coba only took ten minutes in the early afternoon Monday traffic. Ruben called Uncle Emilio to tell him he was on his way to the *farmacia*. He had three reasons for seeing his uncle today. One, he needed to pay him for setting up his clients over the past few weeks and two, Ruben was curious if Uncle Emilio had heard anything from Police Chief Salazar regarding the recent death of an American tourist...Beth. The third purpose of the visit was to get several more doses of the rape drug from his uncle. Emilio indicated over the phone he would have several more vials ready when

Ruben arrived. Ruben planned to save most of them for the journey to Nicaragua.

Ruben was amused every time he arrived at Emilio's place of business, the full name on the sign over the one story building being *Farmacia del Barato.* The name implied savings could be had at this *farmacia,* but Ruben knew that Uncle Emilio marked most items, especially medications, up by at least ten percent more than other *farmacias. Drugstore* was prominent on the upper right side of the sign for any English speaking person who happened to be in the neighborhood. *24 Horas Farmacia* completed the red lettered sign.

The *farmacia* was located in a small strip center just off Avenida Coba. The most distinguishable feature of this business district was the iron bars over the doors and windows of the stores. A store selling women's clothing was on one side of the *farmacia* and an auto parts store on the other. Two parking spaces were unoccupied in front of the clothing store and Ruben took one of them.

Avenida Coba was packed with cars, trucks, motorcycles and bicycles. The exhaust fumes added to the already smoggy conditions in this section of the city. The noise pollution created by the traffic was so bad Ruben could barely hear the door of his SUV close.

The store was larger than it appeared from the outside. It contained the usual aisles of items found in most *farmacias* or drugstores: beauty supplies, dental needs, sleep aids, pain relievers, feminine products and snack foods. Uncle Emilio and a female assistant were chatting at the pharmacy counter when Ruben entered.

Uncle Emilio was the older brother of Ruben's father. Ruben figured he was around fifty years old and had always admired his premature gray hair and short cropped gray beard.

Standing close to his assistant, Emilio was talking in a sexy voice. "I don't always drink beer, but when I do, I prefer Coors Light."

They both broke out laughing at a joke Ruben didn't quite grasp.

"Well if it isn't my nephew." The greeting from Emilio had a less than cordial tone.

"Hello, Uncle."

Ruben didn't recall seeing this employee when previously visiting his uncle's place of business. She was wearing a white smock and appeared to be in her mid-thirties with long black hair and a strikingly beautiful face.

I'm sure my dear uncle is porking this one.

"Ruben, I'd like for you to meet Azahara, my new assistant."

"Nice to meet you, Azahara. Hope to see more of you." Ruben hoped she grasped the real meaning of his reply.

Emilio glanced at his assistant and she moved to the far end of the counter and began typing on a desktop computer.

Handing the wad of cash to Emilio, Ruben quietly said, "This should make us even for the time being."

"Thank you nephew, even though the payment is over three weeks late. When conducting business, you need to pay attention to details. Understand?" Reaching under the counter, Emilio handed Ruben a white paper bag. "Here are six more items you requested. Do you have any plans for assisting my clients in the near future?" Emilio's voice had become stern and his stare intense.

Ruben was taken aback by the tone of the conversation.

Dumping this old fool will be easier than I thought. How could he even think of lecturing me on business matters!

"I don't work today, but something is likely to turn up on tomorrow evening's cruise. As usual, I'll call you when the Devilfish docks if I'm able to find a lovely...ahh...specimen."

"I have a new client, Senor Diaz. He's the owner of Cancun Realty and his wife is out of town for several days and he's first in the queue. Could you try extra hard to accommodate him?"

"Tell him to be on stand-by tomorrow night and I'll do my best." A thought came into Ruben's mind and Estralita was at the forefront of the enlightenment.

Lowering his voice again, Ruben probed, "Police Chief Salazar had a five-star beauty a few days ago. She was prime time."

"Good. Did he seem to enjoy himself?"

"Oh yes. I talked briefly to him before he left. He was very pleased."

Glancing toward the young lady, Emilio said, "My assistant and I are going to a conference in Mexico City day after tomorrow and we'll be gone until late Friday night. Are you sure you can deliver the goods tomorrow night?"

"Yes, I'm pretty sure I can pull it off." Still thinking of Estralita, Ruben was absolutely sure he could guarantee the arrangement.

"Okay. Call me an hour or so prior to the meeting and I will ensure Senor Diaz meets you at your apartment. I have some business to attend to, so I'd better get after it." His lecherous smile left no doubt as to what kind of business he was referring.

"I'll call you tomorrow evening."

Ruben's brain was on overload as he was driving back to his apartment. He hoped Hector was still on the couch when he returned. There were a number of things they needed to discuss. One of them was drugging Estralita tomorrow night and collecting another three thousand dollars from the new client. Estralita was pretty, had a good body, and drugged-out could pass as a visitor from...Chicago or Boston. Maybe New York City. Yes...New York City.

If he drove fast, he could get there before Hector woke up. He needed to remove the note and the video of his depraved exploitation of Estralita. No need to complicate a good thing.

The traffic cooperated, taking Ruben only fifteen minutes to arrive back at the apartment. Remembering he had driven both Estralita and Hector to the apartment last night, he realized they would need a ride back to the Blue Turtle parking lot.

Ruben made as little noise as possible opening the back door. Estralita was standing at the sink drinking a glass of water. Glancing down, Ruben leaned over and picked up the disk and the note and placed them in his pocket. Hector was still spaced-out on the couch, still face down and still snoring.

"Good morning, hope you slept well last night." Ruben didn't care one way or the other what Estralita remembered, but he was curious.

"I've had better," was the short, ambiguous reply.

Ruben walked to the sink and filled the glass Estralita had used with water. He walked to the couch and slowly poured the water on the back of Hector's head.

Hector's arms started flailing as if he were nearing the finishing line of the fifty-meter free style. The first words out of his mouth were, "What the fuck!"

"Get up. Were you supposed to work today? You two screwed up the program last night." Ruben's irritation with his two cohorts was obvious.

"What the fuck happened?" Hector's vocabulary had not expanded since being awakened.

"Doesn't make any difference now. Get up. I'll take you both back to the Turtle parking lot. Okay!"

Estralita mumbled something inaudible and walked to the back door while Hector, with great effort, raised himself from the couch, rotating his shoulders and neck. Ruben gave him a slight shove toward the door, which Estralita had just exited.

There was dead silence in the SUV on the way to the Blue Turtle. There were more cars in the parking lot than Ruben had imagined, this being a Monday afternoon. He assumed since the Turtle opened for business at noon, the hard core drinkers must be gearing up for another week of excessive indulgence and sensual pleasures.

Ruben stopped at Estralita's Pontiac. She exited the SUV without saying a word, slamming the door shut.

"Stupid bitch," was Ruben's response as he drove a few spaces further and parked next to Hector's motorcycle.

"What happened last night?" Hector's brain seemed to be finally engaging. His voice sounded like a small boy trying to understand the ending of a complicated story.

In an even, unemotional tone Ruben said, "You didn't keep an eye on Estralita and she gave the spiked tequila shots to you and Carmen. I could tell she was high when she first came to our table. Didn't realize she was completely fucked-up!"

"She can get out of hand."

"Look, we've agreed she isn't going with us to Nicaragua. You're on board. Right?"

"Okay," was the half-hearted reply.

"I've got an idea for tomorrow night that will make us another three grand. We're going to give Estralita a dose of the stuff she gave you last night and arrange for one of Uncle Emilio's new clients to have a little fun. We won't have to split it with my dear uncle because we'll be heading out of town soon. What do you think?"

Hesitating, for a moment, Hector answered the question in a subdued manner. "I don't like the idea of giving Estralita the shaft, but when are we leaving?" His voice had an urgent sound to it.

"I need to get out of here."

"We'll discuss the final plan tomorrow, but I'm thinking we can clear out of here by the middle or maybe the end of next week. As I mentioned to you the other day, one thing is for sure…we're going to Nicaragua. Keep thinking about the bar we'll own together, the babes that'll be hanging all over us. Man, it's going to be fantastic!"

"Fine."

"In the meantime, I'm working on the details of how we'll collect the cash from the clients. I've got some new ideas since the last time we talked. This is critical and the really tricky one will be Salazar."

"Sooner the better." Hector was in his pouting mode.

"You okay to ride your motor bike?"

"It's a Harley, Goddamnit! How many times do I have to tell you!"

CHAPTER 25

Ridgetop Mobile Estates...June 1st...Dallas, Texas

The two friends had a lighthearted, early evening walk to Christina's. Jamie recounted "CatGate" and the "Catnapping at Ridgecrest" story to Boyd.

"What makes some people just plain mean?" Jamie was both irritated and puzzled by the actions of Frank and Lester. "Were they born that way? Are they bored? Or could they be seriously stupid!" Answering his own questions, his final guess was, "Probably all three."

Laughing, Boyd said, "You should change your profession from anesthesiology to psychotherapy. I think you nailed it, although I would put the emphasis on seriously stupid."

The large white stone exterior of Christina's set it apart from the other small businesses in the strip center. The red and blue sign identified the restaurant as having served fine Mexican food since 1989. The glass paned, double doors at the entry were open as if to show that the establishment was not as busy as it had been last week. The two compadres were immediately seated at a table in the center of the main dining room. The aroma of Tex-Mex cuisine invaded the senses, serving as an incentive to order more food than a normal person could possibly consume.

Setting a basket of tortilla chips, a small bowl of salsa and two menus on the table, an attractive young lady asked, "Would you like something to drink?"

Jamie quickly said, "George Dickel on the rocks and a glass of water."

"Same."

Boyd sat facing the bar, which he noticed was completely empty. His initial thought was: *Hope the cowboy with the big belt buckle doesn't show up.*

With his elbows on the red, white and green vinyl table cover, he surveyed the rest of the interior. He estimated only a third of the available tables were occupied, causing his business mind to wonder about the daily breakeven revenue for this type of business.

"Quiet Tuesday," he observed, more to himself than to Jamie.

"A heck of a lot quieter than last week when we were here." Dipping a tortilla chip into the sauce, Jamie asked, "Know what this is called?"

Thinking for a few seconds, Boyd tilted his head slightly and answered with another question, "Picante sauce?"

"Nope, it's salsa. Salsa refers to a sauce in which the ingredients have been chopped, while Picante represents a sauce that's been pureed, as in smoother. There's actually a third type of sauce called pico de gallo. It's chunky with extra peppers...chunky with heat."

"Jeeze, in addition to being our designated psychotherapist, you're also our culinary expert. Is there no end to your talents!" Boyd smiled and sat back as the waitress placed the drinks on the table.

"Now that was fast!" Jamie grinned and held his glass up to the waitress.

"The service is fast now, but it'll slow down when the rest of the crowd gets here. Still early." The waitress smiled at Jamie and walked away from the table.

"I think she's smitten with you." Boyd reached over the table and touched his glass to Jamie's.

"Can you blame her?" Jamie took a sip of his drink and sighed. "Thanks for introducing me to Mr. Dickel."

"I guess we're even. Dickel for an education on salsa."

Concentrating on their drinks and the warm, friendly atmosphere of the restaurant, the two friends enjoyed their drinks and studied the menus.

The waitress returned and asked, "Ready to order?"

Nodding at Jamie, Boyd said, "Go ahead."

"I'll have the *Carne Asada Y Enchilada*, medium on the steak."

Unsure of the exact Spanish pronunciation of *Pechuga Limon*, Boyd looked at the waitress, "Believe I'll have the grilled chicken breast with the lemon seasoning." Pointing to the menu, he asked, "What exactly are the *borracho* beans that come with it?"

Smiling, the young lady responded. "Well, you start with pinto beans and add diced tomatoes, cilantro and most importantly beer and then they have to be cooked for a couple of hours."

"Sounds good to me."

Grinning, Jamie added with polite sarcasm, "How are you ever going to remember all this new information that's being stuffed into your brain!"

"I think I am starting to get a headache."

"It's probably the George that's causing the headache!"

"Oh no, as we've discussed, George cures headaches."

The bar area and the main dining room had become more crowded in the short amount of time since Boyd and Jamie arrived. The two couples at the next table were in the process of ordering a pitcher of margaritas. One of the men was trying to convince the rest of the table as to the merits of Christina's margaritas when compared to any other in the Western Hemisphere. The other male at the table could be heard saying that he wished he had a dollar for every time he had heard someone say that such and such Mexican restaurant had the best margaritas in the world. The ladies at the table just rolled their eyes.

Their orders arrived. After a few bites, both men said almost simultaneously, "Delicious!"

"Okay, only two days to go before we leave. Are you sure you're up for this? It won't be a picnic." Boyd became serious. He knew the answer to his question before the last word left his lips.

"I'm ready to go, partner. As I mentioned, my friend got me the *stuff*, and I purchased a diabetes travel bag to put it in. Three vials, three needles and me, the sandman. No problems. Oh, also, I'll be picking up my plane tickets tomorrow morning. Made hotel reservations at the Casa Maya Hotel." Reaching into his pocket, Jamie removed his wallet and took out the receipt for the tickets. "Here's the airline receipt as you requested."

"Perfect. Let's get together Thursday evening to work out the final travel details. Basically, I arrive about three hours or so before you, so I'll get a rental car, you'll take a taxi to the hotel. We can talk more about it on Thursday. I have a few more odds and ends to work out."

The noise level in the restaurant had increased significantly and most of the tables were now filled. The waitress returned and asked if they would like to order another drink or dessert.

Looking at Jamie, Boyd said, "Nothing else to eat, but since you probably need the table, we'll go to the bar for another drink. What do you think Jamie, you need anything else?"

"Nope…can't eat another bite, but there are a couple of empty seats at the bar. Let's pay the check and head on over."

Placing the check on the table, the waitress smiled at Jamie and left.

Looking at the check, Jamie said, "Well, the total is thirty-nine-eighty. How about we both drop twenty-five dollars on the young lady?"

"Let's do it."

Three bar stools were open in the center portion of the long bar. The back-lighted onyx tiles that made up the bar top cast a warm glow to the otherwise dimly lit area.

The bartender recognized the two friends and immediately asked, "You gents be having another Dickel?"

Smiling, Boyd said, "You have a very good memory, and the answer is *yes* for me."

Jamie, without speaking, raised his index finger and wiggled it, then looked at Boyd and in a serious tone asked, "Tell me, what has been the secret to your success?"

Thinking for a few seconds, Boyd said, "Well, from a business success standpoint, there were several things. As I mentioned before, I've always set lofty goals for myself, some on the outskirts of reality. Whether in sports or in business, I've never been afraid to lose, but I was always afraid of not being prepared. Helped me focus on my goals."

Taking mental notes, Jamie nodded in understanding.

Boyd elaborated, "Another thing, which many people don't fully appreciate, is being satisfied or excited about your work. A few years ago I was asked by the dean of the business school at Vanderbilt to give a talk to the MBAs who would be graduating that year. The first slide in the presentation had two numbers on it: 86,950 and 116,983. I waited a few seconds and then asked if anyone knew what the numbers implied."

"Was it their starting salaries?" Jamie was interested in Boyd's story.

"Nope. I told them that the 86,950 represented the number of hours they would spend at work during their careers and the 116,983 number would be the number of waking hours they would spend at home. Of course, I explained how the numbers were calculated; i.e., hours sleeping, time traveling to work, forty-five-hour work week, vacations and holidays, retiring at age sixty-five, etcetera, but the point was to show the minimal difference between waking hours at home and the time spent at work. In other words, enjoy your work because over the course of a career, you're going to get a huge dose of it."

"Interesting."

Boyd had one more pearl of wisdom.

"There's one last thing. Do you remember when you achieved something noteworthy in your life? Winning the big game, getting the big contract, finishing the difficult project, the birth of your child...or maybe knocking someone out in twelve seconds of your first UFC fight! It's not so much about the high fives, the congratulations, popping the cork on the champagne...or even the adulation. It's all about the feeling you have that night when your head hits the pillow. It's a *feeling* that's hard to describe, and it applies to all accomplishments in one's life. I know this will sound awkward...almost as if I'm trying to define the indefinable... but it's a quiet hurricane of emotions, a silent celebration, a feeling of perfect calm. You just have to reach for that feeling."

Jamie uttered, "I'll remember that."

The two sat in silence for a few minutes after their drinks arrived.

"Oh, one other thing that's been bothering me." Looking at Jamie, Boyd pressed his lips together and after a pause said, "I don't want you to think I'm some sort of possessed psycho about this whole Cancun thing. The truth is, if that waiter from the cruise boat walked right up to this bar stool and looked me in the eye and said he was really, really sorry for drugging and raping my daughter...do you know what I would do?"

Jamie realized it was a rhetorical question and continued to listen.

"I'd dial my daughter's phone number, hand him the phone and tell him to apologize to her. Then I'd tell him to turn himself into the authorities before I did something drastic."

Jamie blinked twice, but remained silent.

"But you know what? That would never happen because he's a scumbag and Jenny is probably not the only one he's raped. There are probably plenty of other victims and apparently no one is going to do anything about it. I know it sounds all melodramatic and movie like, but this is something that is burning at my soul. So, I've got to do what I've got to do. Just wanted you to know."

Jamie nodded in complete understanding of his friend's ongoing conflict of conscience.

Trying to change the subject from himself to something regarding Jamie, Boyd said, "So...is Amber okay with your trip to Cancun?" It seemed appropriate for Boyd to ask.

"Oh yeah, no problem."

"If you don't mind me asking, are you two fairly serious?"

Looking at his drink, Jamie with a tentative tone to his voice muttered, "I'm probably more serious than she is, although we haven't openly discussed it one way or the other."

"I see. Didn't mean to pry."

"Actually, I'm glad you did ask. This is one of those things a person keeps bottled up. I'm sure you know what I mean."

"Yep."

"Amber comes from a fine family and will soon have a degree from SMU. We've only been dating about six months, but I must admit, I'm into the situation head over heels. We have a great time together and I know she likes me a lot, but I'm just not sure if she feels like I do. This must seem like kid stuff to you."

"Not at all. I'm going through something similar right now."

"It may be similar, but it's different. Just the fact of having a Hispanic surname puts me at somewhat of a disadvantage...at least in my mind. It's a thing you may not see on the surface, but it's always there, lurking somewhere in my head. Topping it off, Amber will soon have a four-year degree from a prestigious university and will be starting a career."

Without hesitating, Boyd offered encouragement, "Jamie, you're young, you're intelligent and you have something I can't fully describe that sets you apart from most people I know. I hear what you're saying, but I think there's a fine line between desire and reality, between wanting and obtaining, between staleness of thought and imagination. Some people have the ability to cross that line, and some don't. *You do.*"

"Thanks. I appreciate your comments. I guess nothing is impossible."

Raising his glass and taking the final drink, Boyd said, "My friend... to nothing impossible. Just reach for the feeling!"

CHAPTER 26

Cancun, Mexico...June 1st

It was late morning when Ruben crawled out of bed with a slight head-ache and an unusually strong urge for food. Since he didn't have to work, he'd spent the previous evening over-indulging on tequila and peanuts.

For some reason, he'd gone to the lobby bar in the Krystal Cancun Hotel and sat alone for over four hours drinking and thinking and more drinking. He'd even considered at one point trying to pick up one of the tourists, but they all seemed to be accompanied by husbands or boy-friends. The same phrase kept going through his mind every time he failed to make eye contact with one of them...*stupid bitches!*

The more alcohol he'd consumed, the more he dreaded seeing Carmen on the Devilfish. What would she say about the fiasco at the Blue Turtle two days ago? Did she know she'd been drugged? Would her animal-like boyfriend be looking for him? Ruben rationalized that small concerns such as these accompanied all successful men in their pursuit of greatness. In just a few days the trip to greatness would begin.

As he drank alone, his alcohol-fueled thought process had shifted to the blackmail scheme directed at Uncle Emilio's friends and the police chief. He needed a better plan than the one he had previously discussed with Hector. He'd borrowed a pen and piece of paper from one of the waiters and had written a first draft of the extortion note. The plan was finally materializing.

This morning the headache and the craving for food took backseat to his excitement about his great blackmail strategy. He wasn't sure if it was the alcohol last night or simply his brilliant mind, but the term *hiding in plain sight* popped into his head, and this is what his plan would be based on. He needed to meet with Hector immediately.

"Yeah," was Hector's answer on the other end of the call.

"How about we have lunch today?"

"Well, I'm at work and my lunch break starts in exactly thirty minutes. If you can get here, we can get something in the lunch room. It's five-star cuisine."

Ruben thought, *At least he's in a decent mood*, and then sighed, "Hector, my friend, I've been there before and you only have vending machines in your lunch room."

"They're five-star machines."

"Okay, I'll be there in thirty minutes. Wait for me if I'm a couple of minutes late. We need to talk about a few things, 'cause we're hauling-ass out of here sometime next week."

"Hurry."

Even though Ruben devoured a stale donut on the way to the slaughter house, he was still hungry. He wasn't looking forward to more stale food out of a machine, but the need to talk to Hector outweighed his hunger concerns.

Ruben made another decision as he continued to think about his newly finalized strategy. He and Hector needed to move rapidly, starting this afternoon.

The parking lot in front of the slaughterhouse was sloppy with mud and grime even though it had not rained in over a week. The building complex consisted of a series of one to three level connected structures, all with a rusted sheet exterior. On each side of the small lot were huge holding pens filled with cattle waiting for their end. Hector told Ruben he killed about two-hundred cows a day with a sledge hammer, but that it was better than sweeping up blood and guts as he had done in his previous job at the slaughterhouse.

Before he opened the door of his SUV, Ruben could smell the stench. He shook his head in disgust as he walked toward the door of the one story building and didn't bother to wipe the mud off his shoes as he entered. He had visited Hector here on one other occasion and nothing had changed: the smell, the inimitable sounds and the depressing feeling. No wonder Hector was in such a hurry to vacate this job.

Ruben walked down a dimly lit hallway with windowless doors on both sides. He assumed this was where the offices of the business were located. The last door on the left opened into the small, crowded lunch room. It appeared thirty to forty men were either sitting or milling around the vending machines on the far wall. Cigarette smoke was heavy in the air and the noise level consisting of loud chatter and laughing was deafening.

Hector was sitting near the door at a metal table with two folding chairs. He was wearing a half-length canvas apron covered with black and crimson stains.

Still shaking his head, Ruben sat down and complained, "Holy fuck, this is the biggest shit hole I've ever seen! How do you stand it!"

"Some of us have to sacrifice in order to feed the world."

He's definitely back to his normal obnoxious self.

Handing Hector a few dollars, Ruben directed, "Why don't you get us a couple of sandwiches and something to drink and I'll save the table. We have stuff to talk about. You know, getting you out of here. Soon."

"Be right back."

The odor was hard for Ruben to identify. It wasn't as strong or as vile as it was in the parking lot, but it seemed to have invaded every nook and cranny of the building. Maybe it had stuck to his shirt, or had been tracked in on shoes over some period of time. It was irritating to the nose and even seemed to make his eyes water. Ruben was starting to wonder why he came all the way out here. Wasn't he the boss of this operation?

Hector returned with two sandwiches wrapped in cellophane and two cans of orange drink. Sitting down, he said smugly, "Okay, here you go. Enjoy your meal."

"Keep the change."

"I already have." Hector was already unwrapping his sandwich.

"We have a couple of important things to discuss. As I mentioned yesterday, we're going to set up Estralita tonight with one of Uncle Emilio's new clients and we also need to talk through the details of how we're going to get the money from the other clients. Our biggest concern is how to get the asshole police chief's cash without getting ourselves killed."

"Sounds to me like we're going to discuss three things." Hector was back in his manic mode.

"Would you pay attention! This is important."

Slowly processing what Ruben said, Hector paused and then gave his two cents. "Estralita will not be happy about going to bed with one of these guys? Besides, she's helped us a lot!"

Ruben anticipated continued resistance from Hector on this issue and was prepared. "We've already decided that she's not going to Nicaragua with us, plus the fact she's become a goddamned drug addict. She proved that when she fucked-up the thing with Carmen the other night. Forget about whether or not she'll be happy, I have a fresh batch of knock-out juice from Uncle Emilio and that'll do the job on her. She'll probably never even know what happened. Come on, get on board, catch up!"

"Okay, okay. But I guarantee she'll freak out if she finds out one of our clients banged her!"

Talking with his mouth full of ham sandwich, Ruben answered with detailed instructions. "Hook up with Estralita and tell her we're meeting at my apartment tonight after I get back from the Devilfish cruise. Tell her I'm sorry for reacting the way I did about the Carmen thing. Have her there around 11:30 and promise her a night of coke and tequila shots. You know... a make-up party. I'll call Emilio and have his client meet us at exactly 12:30a.m. at my place. You and I'll keep the three thousand since we're dealing my dear uncle out of the game. Plus, this new client will bring in another thirty-five big ones for us."

Hector was considerably more loyal to money than to Estralita. "Right. I'll get it done and won't mess it up. Okay?"

"Good. I knew I could count on you. Now the good news. On the way over here, I decided that this is the last meal you'll ever have to eat in this shit-hole. I've got some things you need to do and then next week it's off to paradise."

"Huh?"

"You get paid on Monday's, don't you?"

"Yeah, I got paid yesterday for last week's work." Hector's voice had an excited tone to it.

"Forget whatever it is they owe you for yesterday and today, you'll make ten times as much with the payout we'll get tonight from the client. Okay?"

"*No problema*! You mean I just go in and quit right now?"

"Yes. Just as soon as I finish telling you how we're going to pull this off. We're pushing a lot of shit down the road here at the last minute, but we might as well make hay while we can."

"Pushing shit down the road?"

Completely ignoring Hector's smart-ass comment, Ruben continued, "First, you said the other day you knew someone who could make three copies of each of the client's DVDs. No questions asked."

"Absolutely."

"Good. We'll video the new client tonight, decide which of the other DVDs need to be copied and be good to go in the morning."

"It'll happen on schedule. It won't take long to get copies." Hector was back on track.

"Okay, your immediate responsibilities are to get Estralita to my apartment before midnight tonight and to get the DVD copies made in the morning. Got it?"

"Got it. Actually, I got both of 'em."

"There's one other thing. Can you get a messenger uniform, or at least a shirt with the name of some kind of messenger service on it?"

"Once again, *no problema*. I pass a uniform shop about two blocks from my apartment every day. What kind of name do you want on it?"

"Makes no difference. AA Messenger Service or something like that."

"Why do we need a messenger shirt?"

"I'll tell you in a minute. Now, the most important item to discuss is how we're going to get the money from all these guys. I've put some thought into it and I think I have the perfect plan."

Hector had finished his sandwich and was all ears. "Let's hear it."

The chatter in the lunch room had gradually subsided and was replaced by the scraping of chairs on the concrete floor. Even though most of the lunch crowd was gone, smoke still hung in the air.

Lowering his voice, Ruben said, "Okay, listen carefully. I know a guy that used to work on the Devilfish who now works for a messenger service near the Hotel Zone. I'll call the service and set up the delivery of the instructions and the DVDs to each of the clients at their offices. They'll be in sealed envelopes, so the delivery boy won't know what he's delivering. If you can get me copies of the DVDs by tomorrow, no later than noon, I'll have them delivered to their offices tomorrow before quitting time. The instructions will specify they have the thirty-five thousand in cash within two days. I'll include in the instruction letters the exact time the cash will be picked up on Friday. We'll pick up the four payments one right after the other during Friday afternoon rush hour."

Hector cocked his head and muttered, "The other day you said some bullshit about the money being dropped off at Estralita's apartment."

"I hadn't put enough thought into it, okay? This is the new plan and it'll work! The best part of the plan is the pickup. Guess who'll be picking up the cash payment?"

"Give up. Who?"

"You my friend. That's why you're getting the messenger shirt. The clients have never seen you, only me. Nothing can go wrong, because they'll think you're just some guy working for a messenger service. You'll pick up the money, get back on your motorcycle and get lost in the Friday afternoon traffic. We can meet at a bar and celebrate."

"I can dig that." But Hector wasn't through questioning the details of the new plan. "You said four payments. With the new guy tonight, that makes four of Emilio's business friends. What about the hundred thousand from Salazar?"

"I'm glad you finally asked a good question." Speaking in a slow, deliberate way, Ruben continued. "Today is Tuesday. We get the instructions to the four business men tomorrow and give them two days to get the cash together. You pick up the cash on Friday afternoon and the easy part of the operation is complete. I'll have the delivery service send the instructions and DVDs to Chief Salazar on Monday. I'll need to move out of my apartment sometime Monday morning, because I don't want to be where he can find me. He'll have two days to come up with the cash. He probably has it in one of his desk drawers...the corrupt bastard! That means you'll pick up his payment on Wednesday. How's that sound?"

"What makes you think he won't just kill me right there in his office? The other clients will have already told him about their letters."

"I know for a fact that none of the clients know one another. Uncle Emilio told me that. They sure don't know about Chief Salazar. Plus, my dear uncle is out of town until late Friday night. Not a problem, my friend. This plan is foolproof."

Pulling a piece of paper out of his pocket, Ruben said, "Here, look at the instructions these assholes will be getting. I'll type one for each of them on a computer at Kinkos."

Hector took the paper and studied it.

Dear_____,

Enclosed is a DVD of you raping a drugged out tourist girl. There are two more DVD copies of this horrendous act and they will be sent to your wife and to the Cancun News Journal unless you make a one-time payment of $35,000 this Friday afternoon at your office. A messenger service will pick up the payment between 2:00pm and 4:00pm. Be there! Wrap the cash in a sealed manila envelope with Repeza Enterprises written on it. The messenger will not know the contents of the envelope and will receive information about where to drop it after he leaves your office. Don't even think about following him. If the payment is not made or any interference occurs with the messenger or me, your wife and the News Journal will be given the DVDs by an independent third party. Also, you are not to communicate with anyone

about this letter! If you call Emilio, anyone at his farmacia, or the po-
lice, the DVDs will be given to your wife and the News Journal. Once
the money is delivered, the other two DVDs will be destroyed. This is
serious, so don't fuck it up!

Hector studied the note and after a few seconds said, "Cool. So you'll put their names in the blanks. And you'll put a hundred thousand in Salazar's letter and tell him the pickup is on Wednesday for him?"

"No, I'm only going to ask Salazar for fifteen dollars! Of course, Salazar is going to pay us a hundred thousand on Wednesday! Stay with me! I make no mistakes and starting right now, you don't either. Okay?"

"On top of it!" Hector's excitement level was growing. "I think it's funny that the letter tells Chief Salazar not to call the police. He would only have to holler from his office for the police to hear him, you know… since he is the police."

Slowly shaking his head, Ruben calmly replied, "I'll leave the word *police* out of his letter. Okay?"

CHAPTER 27

Ridgetop Mobile Estates...June 2nd...Dallas, Texas
Boyd spent the morning checking on his home in Dallas. The four-bedroom house was situated on a three-quarter acre lot with numerous live oak and giant post oak trees. The live oaks stayed green year round balancing out the deciduous nature of the post oaks. The entire neighborhood looked as if it had been created in a forest.

A sense of melancholy gripped Boyd as he walked through the front door into the foyer. After closing the door, he hesitated as he looked at the empty living area. You know when you're alone. You feel it when you're alone. Not a sound emanated from the kitchen or from the other rooms. Boyd felt a tightness in his stomach as he sat down in his favorite chair in the living room. His first thought was to pick up his cell phone and call his wife. He wanted to tell her he was sorry for the way things had turned out. He wanted to tell her to get on the next plane and come home. It had been just over a week since she left and it felt as if it had been months.

As Boyd sat in the quietness of the large room, he realized there was only one way around his mental despair. The main goal was to make amends with his wife and to get life back to normal on the home-front. That was the most important part of the problem, but to get there he needed to clear his mind and solve the rest of the equation...the issue in Cancun.

Walking into the bedroom, Boyd was again flooded with memories and regrets. The memories of his wife, her body next to his, the late night chats about nothing and everything, their daughter at a young age running into the bedroom late at night and jumping into bed with them.

He retrieved a medium-sized rolling suitcase from the closet, placed it on the bed and packed it with clothing items, shoes and toiletries required for the short trip. As he left the bedroom, he turned and looked at the bed one last time. He could only shake his head as he mentally compared this bed to the one in the doublewide.

After leaving his home, Boyd drove to a nearby FedEx store on Preston Road. The black bag containing the tattoo equipment was in a small cardboard box, which was left unsealed in the event it needed to be inspected before being shipped. The lady behind the desk assured Boyd it would be packed, sent out within a couple of hours, and guaranteed to arrive at the FedEx store on Avenida Uxmal in Cancun by Friday afternoon. He was instructed to pick up the package within three days of its arrival. The bag weighed exactly twelve pounds and cost Boyd one hundred ninety-seven dollars.

The drive back to Ridgetop was a challenge. The spring weather had taken a turn for the worse. Rain, strong winds and threatening clouds had arrived from the southwest causing treacherous driving conditions. The sky was dark, the look of bad dreams. Boyd thought of the term regarding trailer parks he'd heard since childhood...*tornado magnet*.

As he drove slowly down the gravel road in the trailer park, he noticed how the wind was testing the tall cottonwood tree next to his doublewide. A barrage of large leaves slapped against his windshield and held fast. He noticed Rosie's head protruding from under the back steps as he parked under the rattling, metal parking structure. She was on the top step and ready to go inside before Boyd could unlock the door.

The force of rain on the roof made the trailer sound like a giant popcorn popper. Boyd swiped the water from his sleeves and shoulders while the cat shook the wetness from her fur.

"There's something too simple about your life," Boyd muttered while filling a bowl with dry food.

The sound on the roof subsided as Boyd changed from his khakis and put on a pair of blue sweatpants and his usual tee shirt. He was always amazed at how the weather could change on a dime. He was considering a workout at Rusty's Gym when he heard a knock on the front door. It was Aurelia, the lady from the next trailer.

"Aurelia, what brings you out in this weather!"

"Senor Boyd, good news for us!" She was carrying a bowl and a partial bag of tortilla chips. "Arturo got the job this morning. He just called me!" She handed both items to Boyd. "This is chili for you. I just want to thank you."

"Thank you, Aurelia, this is very thoughtful of you. Your husband is very skilled and I'm sure the BMW dealership will be happy to have him."

Boyd couldn't tell if Aurelia had tears in her eyes or if it was just droplets of rain.

"You are very good to us. *Gracias, gracias.*"

"I'll bring the bowl back tonight or tomorrow and say hello to Arturo."

A simple favor. Really good feeling.

Rosie was still eating the dry food when Boyd walked into the kitchen. "Okay cat, I'll have lunch with you. Don't wait for me, I'll be ready in a couple of minutes."

Getting a glass of ice water, Boyd put his lunch on the coffee table and thought, *What would I do if suddenly I heard the tornado sirens? I wonder if this place even has sirens? Hide under the bed? Get in the car and try to outrun it?*

Rosie jumped up on the couch next to Boyd and casually looked at the bowl of chili on the coffee table.

"Don't even think about it, cat. I'm big enough to put you back in that trash container!"

The rain had completely stopped by the time he finished the chili and chips. A workout at Rusty's, even on a full stomach, seemed more enticing than hanging around the doublewide.

The familiar sound of his cell phone interrupted his decision process. Picking up the phone, he saw it was his daughter, Jenny, calling.

"Hey, kid, how's life in Boston?" A warm feeling came over Boyd. It was comforting to hear his daughter's voice.

"Hi Daddy, I'm having a great time. We've been to all the sights and had a lot of good seafood. We ate last night at a restaurant called Legal Seafood. It was really wonderful."

Boyd loved to hear Jenny call him Daddy. Even though she was almost nineteen, the word hit a tender spot.

"How's Aunt Sis?"

"She's so nice. This has been a good break. Is Mom still coming back on the twentieth?"

Before she left for Boston, Jenny was aware of her parents' unspoken tension.

"I believe so. And you'll be arriving about the same time?"

"I get there on Saturday, the nineteenth. Can you pick me up at DFW?"

"Absolutely. E-mail your itinerary and I'll be there."

"Okay, I'll send it to you tomorrow. Got to go now. Love you."

"Love you too, babe. Be careful."

A flood of conflicting emotions hit Boyd all at once. This was his daughter who had been violated, his daughter whom he was supposed to take care of and protect. The whole rotten episode had caused the rift with his wife. That son-of-a-bitch waiter had brought all this on. Even though his vacillation troubled him, Boyd was once again completely sold and satisfied with his Cancun decision.

The sunlight streamed through the windows of the doublewide as if the storm had never existed. Boyd opened the front door and walked out onto the steps. The clouds had moved eastward and the wind ceased to exist, not a leaf was moving on the cottonwood tree. Strange weather, even for this part of Texas.

"Hey, mister."

The high-pitched voice came from the gravel road. When Boyd turned to look, he smiled as he saw the young brothers, Darell and Ritchie.

"You fellows staying out of trouble?" The smile on Boyd's face assured them he was only teasing.

"My middle name *is* trouble." Darell was the first to respond.

The older brother Richie, quickly added, "You must've been driving in the rain, 'cause your car's a mess. Got mud and leaves all over it. We'll give you a half-price bargain if you'll let us wash it for you. We can do it right there under the carport."

Putting his hand on his chin and deliberating for a second, Boyd slowly replied, "Well, just how much would a first class, bargain car wash cost me?"

"Five bucks." Richie was firm. No negotiating.

"It's not a very big car, how about two bucks?" It was easy to tell that he wasn't serious.

Darell cocked his head and responded, "Just because we're good looking doesn't mean we're stupid."

"Okay, five bucks it is. Get after it, but I'm not paying until I see a first class job." The gleam in Boyd's eyes told the boys they would get paid, no matter what.

"We'll get the buckets and be right back."

"Hey, how come you boys aren't in school. Isn't this a school day?"

Darell shook his head and quipped, "Where've you been! We've been out of school for three days!"

"Guess I need to keep up."

As they turned to leave, Darell looked back at Boyd and said, "Hope your cat's doing all right. We'll help you keep an eye on him."

"I think Rosie is a she, but I appreciate any help you can provide." *What nice kids!*

Boyd went back inside and sat on the couch next to Rosie. Leaning back with his feet on the coffee table, he slowly stroked the cat's back. His thoughts turned once again to the master plan. The randomness of the initial approach and confrontation with the waiter was troubling. Boyd preferred a well thought out plan with a clear path to the objective. Some flexibility was always built into a plan, but in this particular case, not knowing where or when the initial encounter would occur caused Boyd to frown. Not a deep frown, but a frown nonetheless.

The wind calmed and not a sound could be heard on the metal roof of the trailer as Boyd continued to ponder the plan. He could hear the faint sound of splashing water as the two youngsters washed his car.

They were probably hoping it would rain again tomorrow so they could make another five bucks.

Boyd visualized the Cancun hotels and beaches. They would be leaving for Cancun in less than two days, arriving on Friday afternoon and leaving on Monday. He knew that Sunday would be the ideal time for the grand finale with Ruben, but that would be cutting it close since they were leaving the next day. What if they couldn't find Ruben on Sunday? What if he was with his friend the entire day? What if? What if?

Looking at the cat, Boyd expressed his thoughts out loud, "Well, Rosie, the target date is still Sunday. We'll gather data on Friday and Saturday and keep our options open, but Sunday would be ideal."

Satisfied with his latest decision, Boyd decided to have a short workout at Rusty's Weight Room. An inner tension was starting to build and maybe a little exercise would provide the calming influence he needed.

After changing into his workout clothes, Boyd went out to the carport where the boys were washing his car. They appeared to be almost finished as Boyd surveyed the final product.

Nodding his head in approval, he said, "You lads are real pros." Handing each of them a five-dollar bill, he continued, "I appreciate anyone that puts this much effort into their work."

Darell was the first to speak. "Gee, thanks, mister." Looking at Boyd's arms highlighted by the tee shirt, he added, "Good grief, how did you get your arms so big!"

Smiling, Boyd jokingly replied, "Washing cars and digging ditches. Keep up the good work and yours will be this size someday."

Richie, the older brother, chimed in, "Yeah, thanks a lot. Let us know if you have any other chores we can do."

"I'll keep it in mind."

Boyd walked around, over and through the puddles of water between his trailer and the gym. The parking lot in front of the All-In-One and Christina's was completely full as usual. As he entered the gym, Rusty was sitting at his desk, wearing a Texas Ranger baseball cap, working on a crossword puzzle.

Raising his head and smiling, Rusty greeted Boyd with his patented humor. "You know, we're going to have to quit meeting like this or people are going to talk."

"Especially when they see me giving you five dollars every time we're together." Boyd smiled as he handed Rusty the five-dollar bill. "It's hot and sticky out there today."

"Yeah, about a billion percent humidity. By the way, how's your book coming along? I have a tidbit for you. See that fellow over there doing curls. His name is Willy Gomert and he lives at Ridgetop. We were talking, and I ask him what he would do if he won the Texas lottery. You won't believe it, but he said he would buy a two-story doublewide! I told him there was no such thing. His answer was...*well, if you got the money, there're smart people out there that'll do the work.* I told him he was a total dumbass, and he didn't even respond!"

Chuckling, Boyd said, "Rusty, it's possible I'm going to have to hire you as a paid consultant. That juicy bit of information will be included in the book!"

"Glad to help out anyway I can. Be sure and get me tickets to the opening in L.A. when they make a movie out of it."

"Sure thing."

Rusty would be a fun guy to hang out with.

———

It was four in the afternoon when Boyd finished showering and putting on a pair of shorts. The steam from the shower had made its way down the short hall and was creeping into the living room. The air conditioners were going full blast, but only barely keeping up with the temperature in the trailer. Rosie was sleeping on the couch, unaffected by anything in her surroundings.

Boyd sat down and picked up the book he had been reading by Nelson DeMille. The novel was written in a concise, entertaining style, with a good dose of humor thrown in. Boyd appreciated DeMille's story-telling expertise. It would be difficult to write a novel even approaching one like this.

Oh well, just another of life's hurdles.

Rosie meowed, causing Boyd to look up from his book. She had walked to the front door and was staring at him.

"Cat, you're getting bossy."

As he opened the door, letting Rosie out, he saw Jamie's SUV pulling into his driveway across the street.

As Jamie exited the car, Boyd hollered, "Hey Doc, what's going on in the world of medicine?"

Walking toward Boyd, Jamie smiled and said, "We continue to make advances in everything but old age."

"Well, good. I'm glad you're at least trying."

"Want to have dinner this evening?" Lowering his voice, Jamie suggested, "We can discuss the trip."

"You bet. Where do you want to go?"

"Let's do something simple. How about I bring over my grill and put it under your cottonwood tree. I'll get some hamburger meat, buns and all the trimmings. You supply the beer and your Ikea lawn furniture. What do you think? About an hour?"

"Okay, Doctor, see you in one hour."

CHAPTER 28

Cancun, Mexico...June 1st
Ruben's stomach was churning as he drove out of the slaughter house parking lot. He wasn't sure if it was from the sandwich he ate at lunch or if it was because he still had to face Carmen this evening on the Devilfish.

He punched Uncle Emilio's cell number on his speed dial and waited for a response.

"Yes, nephew," was the short greeting.

"Uncle, I touched base with a young lady this afternoon," he lied, "and she will be on the Devilfish with me tonight. You can assure Senor Diaz he will have a beauty on the bed at 12:30a.m. Okay?"

"Diaz will be there promptly at 12:30 tonight."

Ruben was irritated at the abrupt tone of his uncle's voice.

Let's see how abrupt he is when he finds out I've left town with a ton of cash from his clients. Screw him!

Details of his plan skipped and danced through his mind as he made his way through the afternoon traffic.

Half thinking and half mumbling out loud Ruben debated with himself.

Since the four business clients will be getting the extortion letter tomorrow, maybe I should move out of my apartment right away. I could move in with Hector until we leave for Nicaragua. No... Hector lives like a pig and it would be unbearable to stay with him that long. Besides, Emilio's clients will be scared shitless when they get the letter and they'll be spending their time rounding up the thirty-five thousand. The letter specifically tells them not to contact Emilio or anyone else. Forget about them. They all seem like pussies anyway. Chief Salazar, the fifth and most important client, is the only threat. Definitely need to move out Monday morning before he gets his letter.

Ruben's destination was the Kinkos on Avenida Kabah, just a few blocks from Uncle Emilio's pharmacy. He'd been there a number of times before buying his own computer. There were several items he needed to accomplish this afternoon before leaving for work on the Devilfish. One, he would type each of the extortion letters and then use a Kinkos printer. Two, he could use the computer to find the business addresses of the four clients, including the one who would be with Estralita tonight. The address for police headquarters would be easy to find. And finally, he would purchase five envelopes.

Kinkos was located in a small shopping center and Ruben was able to park his SUV directly in front of the business. Even though he only walked about ten steps from his car to the door, the air conditioning in the store was refreshing.

There was a long counter on the right where a female clerk was assisting a customer. A male clerk, with thick glasses, was standing with his arms folded looking bored. A FedEx sign decorated the wall and several shelves of envelopes were adjacent to the counter. All four computer booths on the left side of the room were empty.

Approaching the clerk, Ruben asked, "How much to use a computer and printer?"

"Five dollars for every twenty minutes." The indifferent response was noticeable.

"Also, I'll need five eight-by-ten manila envelopes."

"Okay, I'll have them for you when you check out," he said, pointing toward the computer booths.

The clerk added, "Use the first booth."

It took ten minutes for Ruben to look up the addresses of the clients. He and Uncle Emilio had discussed the clients several times and Ruben was familiar with the businesses and the positions the clients held. One was a bank president, another owned a trucking firm, the third was a dentist, and the realtor would be at the apartment tonight with Estralita. Francisco Salazar's address was the easiest to find... One Police Headquarters, Cancun.

Placing his hand-written paper on the table beside the computer, Ruben carefully typed the extortion notes. He changed the thirty-five thousand number to one hundred thousand in Salazar's letter and left out the reference about calling the police. Double checking the letters, he printed two copies of each.

A clock on the wall showed the time to be almost 2:00p.m. He needed to keep moving.

The clerk was still leaning on the counter and still looked bored.

"How much?" Ruben asked the short, direct question. He had no tolerance for the little people.

"Twelve dollars." The clerk came back with a short, terse response.

"How do you figure that!"

"Seven dollars for the computer, plus five dollars for the envelopes. In other words, twelve-dollars total."

How did this four eyed piece of shit figure it right down to seven dollars for my time on the computer. Asshole!

Opening his wallet, Ruben gave the clerk a ten and two ones and walked to the door without further conversation.

The drive to the apartment was unsettling. The traffic was terrible, a thousand thoughts were racing through Ruben's mind and the showdown with Carmen was nearing. Would she know she had been drugged? Would she figure out why? And most importantly, would her muscled-up boyfriend be waiting to kill him on the Devilfish pier.

The first thing Ruben did when arriving at his apartment was to call the messenger service.

"Cancun Messenger," a male voice answered.

"Hi, this is Ruben Repeza. I need to have four envelopes delivered to various businesses in the city by 4:00 tomorrow afternoon. Can you handle that?" Ruben was blunt and to the point. He could feel the pressure building as he put his blackmail scheme in motion.

"Sure. You'll need to bring the items to our office tomorrow by noon. We're located at 12222 Avenue Tulum, near the hotel zone. Know where that is?"

"I've been there before. Now, I have an additional envelope that needs to be delivered on Monday. That's four tomorrow and one on Monday. Can you assure me all four envelopes will be delivered by four o'clock tomorrow afternoon as well as the one on Monday?"

"If you have them here by noon, we'll have them there by 4:00p.m. We're always on time."

Ruben was in no mood for slogans. "Will the same person be making the deliveries?"

"Yes. Bring the addresses in the morning and we'll do the rest. We're always on time."

Ruben had to pause a few seconds so that he didn't scream at the slogan-quoting asshole on the other end of the line. "I'll be there before noon."

After printing the addresses on all of the envelopes, Ruben decided to take a shower. He wasn't sure if he could ever rid himself of the slaughter-house stench.

———

Ruben parked his Ford Explorer and cautiously walked through the parking area toward the pier leading to the Devilfish. He fully expected Carmen's boyfriend to leap out from behind a car or a bush and beat the crap out of him. His nerves immediately started to calm as he reached the long pier leading to the boat.

A light ocean breeze tousled his hair as he walked down the pier. As the waves lazily teased the large pilings supporting the walkway, Ruben knew he was looking good in his blue cotton pants, white linen shirt and sandals. The fact he had not been accosted by Paco, or whatever his name was, restored his confidence somewhat. However, within a few minutes he would still have to face Carmen.

The temperature was in the high eighties, which was not unusual for this time of year, and Ruben could feel the sweat starting to run down his back and chest. He wasn't sure if it was the heat and humidity or the imminent meeting with Carmen that was causing his discomfort.

Walking up the gangplank, Ruben turned his head and was pleased to see that no one was following him. It would be another thirty minutes before the tourists would start the boarding process.

He approached the oblong bar and could see two bartenders already preparing the colored, watered down drinks. Carmen was not one of them.

Trying to be as nonchalant as possible, Ruben made eye contact with Rosa, one of the newer employees on the Devilfish, and casually asked, "Hey, where's Carmen. She's usually the first one here."

"Sick. Won't be able to make it tonight."

Ruben's eyes widened involuntarily, and his voice went up an octave. "Oh. Too bad. Let me know if I can help."

"We'll have the drinks ready before the gringos arrive. Come back in fifteen minutes or so."

Relief flooded over Ruben as he exhaled and said in a hushed tone, "Okay."

This was the most relaxed he had been in twenty-four hours. He assumed some stress must be associated with all great entrepreneurial activity, and he was on the verge of being part of that scene.

The sky, like the ocean, was a light blue and was punctuated by towering white, cumulus clouds. The eighteen speakers on the Devilfish were cranked to the limit and the music did not go unnoticed by the revelers starting to gather on the gangplank.

As usual, Ruben had his four containers of the pink and blue drinks on a table beside him. He flashed his smile to the ladies as they boarded and nodded to the young men. This was all familiar to him and so he had become somewhat immune to the actions of the obnoxious tourists.

Ruben was disgusted by the sameness of the people boarding the Devilfish. Everyone wanted to look and act cool and everyone wanted to get laid. Same skimpy clothing, same gold chains, same whitened teeth and same cocky attitudes. Why couldn't they be as naturally good looking, charming and intelligent as he was? Why was everyone else so phony? The world was full of mysteries that even Ruben couldn't fathom. However, he knew it would be impossible for most other individuals to have the personal charisma and talents that he possessed.

One young lady stood out from the crowd as she stopped to get one of Ruben's complimentary drinks. She had long auburn hair along with a beautiful face and perfect lips. The loose fitting white tee shirt still hinted at some voluptuous curves, and the pink shorts and shapely legs tended to confirm that. He handed her the blue drink and tried to give her his best, most seductive smile.

This is not the time to be fooling around...is it? Need to focus on arranging the meeting with Senor Diaz and Estralita tonight and the blackmail scheme tomorrow. The messenger and all that stuff. No time for pleasures with the gringo bitches.

"May I ask your name?" Continuing to show his white teeth, he added, "I'll bring you another drink on the house after we leave the dock." Ruben couldn't help himself. The feeling in his groin took over any logic and self-control he could muster.

Tilting her head and smirking, as if this wasn't the first time she had been offered a free drink, she said, "Oh, thank you. My name is Ginger. See you later."

Ruben knew he couldn't make any of his patented moves tonight on this Ginger chick, but perhaps he could put things in motion for tomorrow night or sometime before he left for Nicaragua.

A few seconds later, Ruben noticed a huge, black mountain coming up the gangplank. This guy stood out like no other man Ruben had ever laid eyes on. He was at least six-five and built like a tank. He was wearing calf-length white beach pants, not unlike the ones Ruben was wearing, but they must have been double stitched in order to contain this behemoth's lower-body muscle mass. The half tee shirt was grey with a blue star that nestled between his pectorals.

Ruben's first thought was, *This guy doesn't have a six pack...he's got an entire case of stomach muscles! He must be some type of pro athlete.*

The bald head, glistening with perspiration, was combined with a perfectly chiseled face and large brown eyes. He was wearing sandals that must have been size eighteens.

Ruben's second thought was, *If I was that big and that well built, I would make people pay to live!*

The big man stopped at Ruben's drink station and looking down at him said, "What have we here?"

"A tequila sunrise. Want one?"

Smiling, the big man extended his large hand. "Keep 'em coming all night."

Three more individuals made up the big man's posse, two black and one white. They all accepted the free drinks from Ruben and moved on.

When the line finally came to an end, Ruben made his way back to the bar with the empty drink containers. He was looking forward to taking Ginger the free drink he had promised. As the Devilfish left the dock, he leaned back on the bar and surveyed the crowd milling about on the main deck. The afternoon breeze had picked up and the high clouds had moved to a more comfortable position in the west. There was little chance Ruben could use his "green flash" line on Ginger or anyone else since the horizon was completely blocked out.

Walking along the right side of the boat, Ruben was aware of the smaller than usual crowd on the boat. It was late in the season and the Devilfish would cease operations for six weeks or so after this month.

Ginger was not difficult to locate. She was far and away the best looking woman on this cruise. The other reason she was easy to locate was because her hands were draped around the huge mountain-of-a-man's waist and she was gazing up at his face. Several young ladies were standing around the chick magnet vying for his attention.

250

"Shit," Ruben mumbled as he tossed the plastic container of watered-down liquid over the rail.

Total focus on the events of tonight and tomorrow. No more screwing around!

———

The Devilfish left Isla Mujeres at 10:00p.m., which was about fifteen minutes earlier than usual, and arrived back at the dock at 10:40. There was plenty of time for Ruben to finish his chores on the boat, return to the apartment, and get Estralita drugged and ready for the new client.

This had been the least enthusiastic cruise Ruben had ever experienced. The crowd was smaller, inebriation was less and tips had been at a minimum. Maybe the cool gringo dudes had been intimidated by the huge pro athlete, or whatever he was. The Ginger bitch never left the big man's side. Ruben was glad he'd not wasted his precious time on her.

Traffic was almost non-existent on the trip to the apartment. The lights were on and the back door was unlocked when Ruben arrived.

At least Hector hadn't fucked this one up.

Walking through the door, Ruben smiled and said, "My good friends, good to see both of you!"

Still smiling, he walked over to Estralita and hugged her. "I'm so sorry for being angry with you yesterday. You are very important to me and I love you dearly."

Having heard Ruben's line of bullshit many times before, Estralita's simple reply was, "Great."

Ruben poured himself a shot of tequila from the bottle on the cabinet, held it up in his hand and tossed it down. Sliding two more shot glasses from the back of the counter, he filled them and said, "Here, let's drink to the team."

As they finished the toast, Ruben pointed to the table. "Let's sit around the table and I'll tell you about my uneventful evening on the Devilfish."

As Hector and Estralita were moving toward the table, Ruben reached into his pants pocket and removed the small bottle of liquid he had recently received from Uncle Emilio and poured it into one of the shot glasses. He carefully refilled all three glasses and took two of them to the table, making sure Estralita got the correct one. He went back to the counter, got his glass and once again held it up and toasted, "Friends forever!"

It only took five minutes for Estralita to look blankly at Ruben and gently lower her head onto the table.

Hector looked accusingly at Ruben and spoke softly. "Well, this is what you wanted."

"Stick with me. This is money in our pockets."

"I guess so."

"Help me get her to the bed. Diaz will be here in twenty minutes. Uncle Emilio promised he would be here promptly at 12:30."

They each took an arm, lifted Estralita from the table and dragged her to the bedroom. The toes of her flip-flops skidded across the tile while her hair fell forward across her face.

Ruben took charge. "Lay her on her back and remove her blouse and shorts. Diaz can do the rest."

While Hector was begrudgingly doing as he was told, Ruben turned down the lights and turned on the CD player.

After returning to the kitchen, Ruben spoke first. "Did you quit your job at the feed lot?"

"Oh yeah, and they were pissed. They said I would be ineligible for rehire, like I give a shit."

"Good. I stopped at Kinko's after I left you and made copies of the clients' letters. Got the addresses for all of them and wrote them on some envelopes. I called Cancun Messenger and they assured me the envelopes will arrive at the addresses by 4:00 tomorrow afternoon. I need to get the envelopes to the messenger service by noon."

"It'll be done. After I video this Diaz guy tonight with Estralita, we can sort out the rest of the DVDs we need. I'll get the copies made and have them to you no later than 10:00 in the morning. Also, I'll get a messenger shirt tomorrow."

Ruben was impressed with the initiative Hector was displaying. Even after a few drinks, he was showing good judgment. He would be a good right-hand man for the empire Ruben was about to build.

Promptly at 12:30a.m., there was a soft knock on the back door.

Ruben glanced at Hector and said, "Get in the closet."

Ruben went to the door, opened it and was greeted by a slender, middle aged man wearing glasses and dressed in khakis and a flowered shirt.

"Welcome. You must be Senor Diaz."

"Yes," was the barely audible, furtive reply.

Ruben assumed Senor Diaz was either embarrassed, ashamed, scared or all three.

"Please come in. I guarantee you will have a completely confidential, wonderful evening." Ruben was trying to set the timid man at ease.

Pointing toward the bedroom, he continued, "The young beauty that awaits you is from New York City. I'm sure you will find her to your satisfaction. I'll be waiting on the steps outside, so take all the time you want."

Senor Diaz entered the bedroom and quietly closed the door. It was warm in the small room and the perspiration dotted and glistened on his forehead. The dim lighting and the soft music created a somewhat calming atmosphere, but he did not appear calm. Still fully clothed, he leaned over with his knees on the side of the bed and ran his hands over Estralita's breasts. As his gaze slid down her torso, he put his right hand on her stomach and gently moved it over her navel.

Estralita's eyes flickered and then opened wide. It could have been a weakened dose of Rohypnol that Uncle Emilio provided or it could have been that Estralita's body had developed a tolerance to chemicals in general due to her heavy drug use. Whatever the cause, she sat straight up in bed and screamed, "Cocksucker!"

Senor Diaz vaulted off the bed in a violent, backward motion, throwing his entire body against the wall. He put his hand over his heart and stood there for a few seconds before slinging open the bedroom door and racing across the kitchen, his glasses still in place.

His voice was raised for the first time as he ran past Ruben, who was still sitting on the back step. "You'll pay for this!"

Ruben silently mouthed, "No...actually you'll pay for this." And then out loud, "What the fuck happened!"

Hector and Estralita were screaming at each other when Ruben entered the bedroom.

"What did you do to me!" Estralita was standing, but having difficulty balancing.

"I didn't do anything!"

She slurred, "You and Ruben are assholes!"

"I'll explain everything. You'll make some extra money for tonight. Come on, I'll take you home." Hector had a pleading tone in his voice.

As Estralita unevenly stomped out the back door, Hector passed Ruben and said, "I'll take her home and then come back and get the DVDs that need to be copied. Have them ready. Okay?"

Ruben acknowledged the request by nodding his head.

This drug shit is getting out of hand!

CHAPTER 29

Ridgetop Mobile Estates...June 2nd...Dallas, Texas
Boyd folded the two lawn chairs in his living room and carried them outside to the top step of the doublewide. Hesitating, he looked out at his limited view. It was perfectly still, not a breath of air. The large cottonwood tree stood tall despite the recent rain and wind. It was somewhat cooler, but the humidity was thick. Large clouds in the west partially blocked the late afternoon sun. As Boyd unfolded the lawn chairs and placed them near the tree, he was surprised that the grass was barely damp after two days of early afternoon rain. The scattering of leaves on the ground was the only remaining evidence of the mild storm.

Noticing Jamie across the street cleaning his portable grill, Boyd called out, "Need any help?"

"Sure. I've got a couple of items you can bring over."

Boyd carried a sack containing the hamburger buns, mustard, onions and tomatoes in one hand and a bag of charcoal in the other. "I'll bring out my coffee table to set this on. I'll grab some beer, also."

"Sounds good to me," Jamie agreed. "I'll get the hamburger meat as soon as the coals heat up... already made the patties. Also have some hotdogs if you'd rather have one of those."

"Hamburger's my choice."

"Do you have any paper plates?"

"Of course I do. *Mine* is a well furnished doublewide!"

Boyd returned with the coffee table, a six-pack of beer and a package of paper plates. Jamie stood back as the lighter fluid blazed on the stack of charcoal.

The auditory impressions of the early evening could be heard as they skipped off the metal trailers. It was the usual jumble of children's voices and the mixed vibrations of music and dogs barking in the distance. The sounds and smells of Ridgetop were remarkably consistent.

Boyd and Jamie sat in the lawn chairs drinking beer without talking. Jamie finally broke the silence. "Two days from now we'll be in Cancun. Are you excited?"

After hesitating a few seconds, Boyd simply nodded. An almost imperceptible look of satisfaction appeared on his face as he gazed at the brightly lit coals in the grill.

A woman's voice drew his attention. "Senor Boyd." Aurelia and Arturo approached from their trailer.

"Hey, how're you folks doing?" Boyd had developed an affinity for this couple.

"I'm so grateful for your help," Arturo said quietly. "Your friend at the BMW dealership gave me the job and I started this morning. I just want to thank you."

Aurelia chimed in, "Yes, we both thank you with our hearts."

His grin broadening to a smile, Boyd said, "I'm really glad it worked out. Arturo, you must have a special talent and I wish you the best of luck."

257

Jamie toasted Arturo by holding up his bottle. "Hey, you guys want to have a hamburger with us? We've got plenty of meat and buns."

Arturo looked at his wife seeking guidance.

Observing the items on the coffee table, Aurelia offered, "I can bring potato chips and napkins."

"I have more beer. I'll get it now." Arturo confirmed.

As the couple walked back to their trailer, Jamie said teasingly, "You're not such a bad guy after all." And then holding up a beer bottle, he added, "That was a darned nice thing you did for Arturo."

"I'm just glad there'll be a competent mechanic working on my car when I take it in."

Still grinning Jamie said, "I don't care what anyone else says, for an older gentleman, you're okay."

Arturo returned with a cooler of ice and a six-pack of beer. Aurelia followed with a bag of potato chips, a plate of vegetables and napkins. Arturo returned to his trailer and reappeared with two more lawn chairs.

The familiar crunching of gravel was followed by Darell's boyish voice. "Hey mister, was that the best your car has ever been washed, or what!" Darell and his brother got off their bikes and walked over to the cookout.

"Yep, like I said, you boys are real pros."

Jamie, still in his inclusive mode, asked the two brothers, "We don't have any more hamburger meat, but we've got some wieners. You boys want a dog?"

Darell immediately answered, "Heck yeah. Why not!"

Richie mumbled, "You idiot, we just had dinner."

"Yeah, but we didn't have dogs. Get with the program."

Jamie looked at the boys and ordered briskly, "Run over to my place and get the package of wieners out of the 'fridge and get a couple of Cokes. Oh yeah, while you're there, bring the plate of hamburger patties. They're also in the 'fridge. Okay?"

The breeze was refreshing as the early evening shadows made their way across Ridgetop. The group ate their hamburgers and hot dogs and discussed topics ranging from bicycles to electronic fuel injection systems.

There had been modest foot traffic on the gravel road during the impromptu cookout, but Boyd's attention was drawn to two individuals approaching the cottonwood tree. As they moved closer, Boyd recognized Lester, who was carrying a small paper sack under his arm. Frank was at his side.

Lester was the first to speak as he handed the paper sack to Boyd. "Say, man, want you to know that we're a couple of dumb shits and we don't have nothin' against your cat."

Frank chimed in, "Yeah, sometimes we're dumber than stumps. Didn't mean no harm."

Boyd carefully opened the sack and saw the ten or twelve small cans of Friskies cat food.

Boyd's face showed no emotion as he replied evenly, "Okay." Looking at Jamie, he asked, "What do you think, partner?"

"Looks like Rosie will be well fed for a while." And then addressing Lester and Frank, he added, "It's a good thing when someone admits a mistake."

Lester relaxed for the first time since arriving. "Like I said, we're dumber than shit, but we don't have anything against animals. We're not like that."

Arturo and Aurelia and the two boys sat quietly during the exchange. After Lester and Frank left, Darell whispered, "You two guys are like Wyatt Earp and Doc Holiday. You're bringing law and order to Ridgetop!"

Shrugging, Boyd said, "I guess so. And speaking of law and order, it's getting late and you boys better be getting home. There may be more cars to wash tomorrow. And, oh yeah, I have another money making opportunity for you. I'm leaving on a four day trip this Friday. Could you boys feed the cat while I'm gone?"

Richie was first to speak. "Heck yeah!"

"Good. Come by tomorrow afternoon around four or so and I'll show you where I keep the cat food. OK?"

Darell was pumped. "We'll be here bright eyed and cushy tailed."

"Bushy tailed, you idiot." Richie got in the last word.

Aurelia had made several trips during the past hour to check on her baby. Finally, after saying her goodbyes, she grasped Arturo's arm and led him back to their trailer. Boyd and Jamie put the remains of the party in two paper sacks and placed the garbage in the trash container.

The glow from the coals had long since disappeared as the two friends reclined in the lawn chairs. The street lights, with their familiar soft buzz, arrived to illuminate the nighttime tempo of the trailer park.

Leaning back with his hands folded behind his head, Boyd reflected, "What did you make of Lester and Frank showing up with the cat food?"

"I was as surprised as you. I was even more surprised by the apology from those two bad boys."

"You know, this will sound odd, but my short eight day stay at Ridgetop has opened my eyes to a number of things...things that any half-intelligent person should have seen anyway. It's too easy to judge people by their looks, where they live, their job, their perceived socio-economic status and especially first impressions. Take the cowboy at the bar in Christina's. We'd both been drinking and my first impression of him was not too good. It ended with him on the sidewalk. If I'd really got to know him under different circumstances, I might have even liked him. He evidently won that big belt buckle in a rodeo, and you have to be a dedicated, tough son-of-a-gun to ride a bull or wrestle a steer. And I imagine he's a true friend to those folks he was with."

Jamie cocked his head and spoke slowly. "Ahh, all that cowboy needs is to be slapped down a couple of times a day to remind him of his manners. I'd be happy to take on that responsibility."

Boyd went on. "Take Aurelia and Arturo, salt of the earth. If Arturo had been able to get a college degree, along with his work ethic, he'd be running his own company today. Get what I'm trying to say?"

Hesitating for a second, Jamie said, "I suppose it takes a lot of patience to get to know and understand someone." A small grin curled his lips as he added, "What about Frank and Lester? As I think about them, I can't decide if they were really apologizing for being assholes, or whether they were campaigning to get on the board of PETA. And, of course, there are no excuses for the waiter in Cancun."

"You're right. I'm just saying, I've been prone to a lot of over-generalizations, but the waiter in Cancun is not one of them! Oh yeah, I Fedexed the tattoo equipment to Cancun this morning. It'll be there when we arrive Friday."

"Speaking of Cancun, I picked up my tickets today, and as I mentioned, I have the sleepy time stuff and a diabetes bag. I'm good to go."

"Excellent. I'll print out my tickets at home tomorrow." Pausing for a moment, he continued, "I've been thinking about the plan specifics over the past several days and I've come to the conclusion that we need to make contact with the waiter on Sunday. It's not ideal, but due to timing issues, I think it's best."

"It's good for me."

"Will you be here tomorrow evening, or will you be out with Amber?"

"Amber has to be at work at five tomorrow, so we decided to meet for lunch. To answer your question, I should be home from work no later than six."

"Good. We can go over the entire plan one last time."

The cat emerged from under the steps of the doublewide, stretched and casually made her way to Boyd's lawn chair.

Jamie just shook his head.

CHAPTER 30

Cancun, Mexico...June 2nd

It was 1:15a.m.when Hector and Estralita left the apartment. Ruben estimated Hector would be back within thirty minutes to get the DVDs that needed to be copied. Entering the bedroom closet, he stretched to reach the cardboard shoe box on the top shelf containing the stack of video recordings. He took them to the couch in the living room and started sorting through the Memorex mini-DVD-R discs. Ruben was convinced that obtaining the Sony camcorder was a pure stroke of brilliance. He'd bought the equipment for two hundred dollars from a hotel employee who had stolen it from a guest. The hotel employee assured him a new camcorder like this one would cost at least two thousand dollars. The low light illumination feature tickled Ruben's perverted imagination.

Ruben returned to the closet and removed the small disc containing the Senor Diaz debacle from the camcorder. Diaz had only been with Estralita a few minutes, but there was probably enough activity to blackmail him.

Viewing the recent video, Ruben could see Diaz fondling Estralita's breasts and moving his hand down her stomach. The manner in which Diaz jumped from the bed and bounced off the wall when Estralita screamed brought a smile to Ruben's lips. He should charge Diaz fifty thousand instead of the thirty-five thousand the other clients would be paying. This was an embarrassing moment for the timid fellow.

Oh well, no need to get greedy at this point, thirty-five thousand will be enough.

Ruben continued looking at the stack of DVDs in their plastic holders. After each encounter he had used a fine-point black magic marker to print the clients' names, the names of their companies, and the dates the events had taken place. He figured the better the documentation, the bigger the intimidation factor...and the more likely these guys would pay.

Senor Constanzo, the bank president, and Chief Salazar had each been involved three times. Pedro Gallegas, the trucking firm magnate, had visited the apartment twice, as had Mr. Ramos, the dentist. Ruben decided to copy one DVD per client. The clients would know there were other video copies and that should keep them in line.

The labels consisted of Ruben's own form of shorthand... **CONSTANZO, FIRST CANCUN BANK, 1-20-16...GALLEGAS, ACE TRUCKING, 1-28-16...RAMOS, FAMILY DENISTRY, 2-10-16...SALAZAR, POLICE CHIEF, 5-28-16.**

Ruben marked his final plastic holder...**DIAZ, CANCUN REALTY, 6-1-16.** There were two other DVDs in the stack, but they were not blackmail material. One was of Hector and Ruben with a young lady, which was labeled **RUB & HEC...IOWA 11-15-15.** This was the first experiment with Uncle Emilio's drugs. Ruben and Hector had filmed each other with a young lady from somewhere in Iowa.

The other was labeled **UNCLE EMILIO, FARMACIA DEL AHORRO, & RUBEN...DALLAS 12-26-15.**

Ruben had an excellent memory and knew exactly which DVD to select for each client. These guys were going to have a stroke when they saw the way they treated the drugged out gringo girls. The extortion note alone would freak them out, but if they took the time to actually look at the video, they would gladly pay the thirty-five thousand to get off the hook.

Hell, who knows...I may keep all the copies and come back in a couple of years and do it all over again! I'm the man!

Ruben selected the five videos to be copied and placed the rest in the shoe box. After placing the shoe box back on the closet shelf, he locked the closet door and went into the kitchen, where he carefully printed the names and addresses of the clients on the envelopes. Above each clients name was a large headline...**PRIVATE.   TO BE OPENED ONLY BY:** He then placed the appropriate DVD in each of the envelopes.

Finishing with the DVDs, he picked up the sack containing the last of the stale doughnuts, leaned back in his chair, and breathed a sigh of relief.

———

Estralita stumbled her way from Ruben's back door to Hector's motor-cycle. Even though it was the middle of the night, the temperature was near eighty and a warm breeze danced through her long black hair.

Hector was concerned, but not surprised, at Estralita's response to what had just happened. "Hey, we're going to make some money off the guy to-night. It wasn't my idea, I want you to know that, but we'll get some bucks. Okay?" Hector figured money could conquer any and all obstacles.

"Cocksucker." Estralita positioned herself behind Hector on the motorcycle and placed her arms around his waist.

"Why don't I take you home and we can get your car in the Turtle parking lot in the morning. Don't think you should be driving right now. Besides, I need to take some videos to your apartment late tomor-row morning. Okay?" Hector continued to use the "okay" question, hoping Estralita would see the light and respond with a positive answer.

No such luck.

"Jerk-off!" Estralita blurted as she slid off the back of the motorcycle and began vomiting.

Hector shook his head and watched. "Need some help?"

Wiping her mouth with the back of her hand, Estralita replied weakly, "This is all your fault, asshole. You don't have any balls, they're in Ruben's back pocket."

"Bullshit! I'm my own man. Now get on and let's get you home."

———

Ruben was finishing the last of the doughnuts when Hector walked through the back door.

"Was she pissed?"

Hector answered with a sullen, "Yes."

Pointing to the five DVDs on the kitchen table, Ruben said, "Here are the ones we need to copy. You know, three copies of each. Do you think it'll be okay to leave one set of the copies at Estralita's?"

"Yeah, but why leave them with her since she's not going with us to Nicaragua?"

"Just for insurance. I really don't give a damn what she does with them later. We'll be long gone."

Hector still had a pleading tone to his voice. "Are you sure we can't take her with us? She's been a big help with all this stuff. If it wasn't for her, we wouldn't have these videos."

"Fuck no! How many times do I have to tell you, no fucking way! We're going to split the money between us and buy a bar. Get over the god dammed heroin addict and get on board!"

"Okay, okay. I get it. Just trying to do what's right."

Calming down, Ruben uttered, "Since it's almost 2:00, I think you should sleep on my couch. You can get the copies made first thing in the morning. What kind of place are you taking the DVDs to?"

"They sell computers and shit. You know, they convert tapes to DVDs, stuff like that."

"What time do they open?"

"I called a guy I know who works there and he'll be there no later than eight-thirty. He said it won't take long to copy a few DVDs. Man, I told you I was on top of it!" Hector was mildly agitated.

"Okay, just making sure we don't have any problems."

"Also, I'm getting my messenger shirt tomorrow." Looking at his watch, Hector added, "Well, since it's almost 2:00a.m., I guess I'm getting the shirt today."

Feeling better about Hector's attitude, Ruben said, "Everything will look better when the sun comes up." And then placing his hand on Hector's shoulder, he added, "We're almost there, my friend."

CHAPTER 31

Ridgetop Mobile Estates...June 3rd...Dallas, Texas
Boyd awakened from a dream Thursday morning. He had been dreaming of sleeping in his own spacious, comfortable bed at home. He was alone in the dream, but the feeling of being in the king-sized bed was extremely satisfying. He rolled over and his knee hit the side of the wall in the cramped doublewide bedroom. Opening his eyes, he was ambivalent, both depressed and elated at the same time. Depressed because he was in a doublewide trailer, and elated because his mental distress over the Cancun incident was rapidly coming to a head.

After putting on a pair of shorts and a tee shirt, Boyd walked into the kitchen and started a pot of coffee. The scratching on the front door reminded him of his new responsibility...the cat. Rosie was waiting on the top step, her multi-colored fur highlighted by the fragments of morning light filtering through the cottonwood tree.

"Well, I see you made it through another night without getting into any more trouble." Boyd was becoming more comfortable talking to a cat. The morning elation continued.

After feeding Rosie, Boyd stood on his front step with a cup of coffee. The sky was clear, the air was clean and the June humidity was bearable. Two pickup trucks and a motorcycle made their way down the gravel street. A teenager with a Dallas Cowboys cap turned backward and a phone pressed to his ear passed from the opposite direction. Boyd recognized him as the same youngster he'd seen when he rented the doublewide.

A lot has happened in the past eight days.

There were several things he needed to take care of before leaving on the trip. He could print out the boarding passes at home. They were available to be printed twenty-four hours in advance of departure, so after 1:00p.m. today would work. This would save a few minutes of standing in line at the airport. He also needed to stop at his bank, which was not far from his home, and get several hundred dollars in cash. The two brothers would be there at 4:00 for their cat feeding instructions, and then he and Jamie would get together after 6:00 to go over the plan one final time before leaving.

There was one other person Boyd wanted to see today...Gloria, the red headed clerk at the All-In-One. He had not heard any additional news regarding Roscoe since his arrest, and the person with the news would be Gloria. He needed to buy a TV dinner for lunch anyway.

After a bowl of cereal and two pieces of toast, Boyd coerced Rosie out the door and headed for the strip-shopping center. It was the beginning of a beautiful spring day. No clouds, no wind, just sunshine. The usual sounds of the trailer park accompanied Boyd down the gravel road.

Arriving at the All-In-One, Boyd could see that Gloria was immersed in an animated conversation with two male customers. She was expressing her opinion on whether or not the highway in front of the shopping center should be widened. Boyd found the frozen dinner case and browsed through the limited selection of cuisine. He grinned as he listened to Gloria and the two men talking about the unusual amount of rain over the past week.

"Hell, it sounded like a cow pissing in a wash tub!" This being the observation from one of the men.

The other individual corrected him. "No, no…it's supposed to be a cow pissing on a flat rock. Get your sayings right!"

"Now where would a cow find a flat rock? Even if it did, why would it want to piss on it?"

Gloria's laughter filled the convenience store. The two men were leaving as Boyd approached the counter.

"Well, good to see you again, young man." Gloria appeared to be in a good mood.

"Nice to see you as well," Boyd said as he placed his frozen dinner on the counter.

"Guess you heard the police arrested the shit out of Roscoe and his prostitution ring over at the old church."

"Yep, heard about that."

"The little prick made bail yesterday. Some relative got him out. Probably another low-life drug dealer like Roscoe. Hope they all go to prison for twenty years."

Lowering her voice to a raspy whisper, even though there were no other customers in the store, Gloria confided, "You know, it was me that dropped the dime on Roscoe. The police cuffed Roscoe and a couple of other guys and hauled 'em off on Monday. The cocksuckers got what they deserved."

Gloria's vocabulary was somewhat limited, but it was descriptive and to the point.

"Looks like it."

Boyd put a five-dollar bill on the counter, got his change and walked back to the doublewide. The cat was waiting for him on the steps.

It was two hours until lunch, so Boyd got his Nelson DeMille book and parked himself on the couch. Rosie curled up beside him.

It was a little after noon when he finally looked up. He had been totally immersed in the book. After standing and stretching his arms, he walked out to the front steps. Rosie followed him out, quickly disappearing around the corner of the trailer. A slight breeze kicked up causing the leaves on the cottonwood tree to make a quiet, whispering noise.

Time for the TV dinner.

———

It was after 1:00 when Boyd finished lunch. The next item on today's to-do list was to check on his Dallas residence and to print out his boarding passes.

During the drive home, Boyd had time to reflect on the upcoming trip and the planned activities in Cancun. Many decisions, once reached, have areas of gray, and this one was no exception. Boyd subconsciously knew his Cancun decision had as much gray area as pure black and white.

Some not-so-pleasant issues could arise from this little venture. What if the waiter has a gun, what if something should happen to Jamie, what if we get arrested by the police and put in a Mexican jail? What if...what if.

Supposing I cancel the whole trip right now at the last minute. How long will it take me to get over what happened to my daughter, to my marriage? How many other women has this waiter raped? How many more lives will he ruin? Will he ever get what he deserves?

The internal struggle continued. The thoughts filled his mind. The thoughts came and the thoughts went, but the final thought was, *yes, he'll get at least some of what he deserves. And he'll get it soon! Goddamnit, quit vacillating, get on with it!*

As he parked his car in the driveway, Boyd sighed and sat still for a few seconds. He loved his home, as well as this neighborhood. More than anything else, he loved his family. It was more than a little depressing to arrive at an empty house and to think about his uncertain future.

Boyd printed his boarding passes and then walked throughout the house to ensure everything was in order. He went out the back door onto the patio and surveyed the large expanse of yard and the giant oak trees surrounding the house.

I'll be back and everything is going to return to normal. This is a promise!

———

The short trip to the bank and the drive back to Ridgetop were stress-free. The lingering doubts, for some reason, had been left behind and forgotten. It was all business from here on.

Richie and Darell were sitting on the front steps of the doublewide when Boyd arrived. He parked, and joined the brothers on the steps.

Looking at his watch, he said, "You're thirty minutes early. That's a good trait in a person. Show up early and be prepared."

The boys weren't ready for grown-up philosophy and almost in unison responded with, "Uh huh."

Boyd handed Richie a key and said, "This unlocks both doors. Come on in and I'll show you where I keep the cat food...and *don't* be inviting all your friends over for a big party while I'm gone."

The boys laughed. They understood a joke when they heard one.

Boyd showed the boys where he kept both the dry and canned cat food and explained the twice-a-day feeding schedule for Rosie.

"If it's raining, you can let her in, but you'll have to be sure and let her out within a few hours...okay?"

"She'll be the happiest, best fed cat at Ridgetop." Richie was looking forward to the new responsibilities.

"I'm leaving tomorrow morning, so you can take over tomorrow afternoon. I'll be back next Monday, but you can plan on feeding her twice that day."

Darell was first to respond. "We'll do a good job. We never don't."

After the boys left, Boyd picked up a lawn chair and sat next to the cottonwood tree, beer in one hand and the Nelson DeMille in the other.

Jamie would be returning from work in an hour or so and they could go over the plan one last time.

Boyd had finished three more chapters when he heard the sound of footsteps on the gravel. He glanced up and saw three individuals approaching...one of them was Roscoe. On his right were two larger men. It wasn't unusual to see three people walking together, but for some reason the peculiar visual effect of these three was noticeable.

The bald, bearded fellow on the far right was at least six-four and had an angry look about him. The long-haired, younger man next to him was close to six-feet tall and had a huge barrel-chest. Roscoe, on the other hand, was much shorter and skinnier than the other two.

The late afternoon sun provided the last element needed to portray the three men as a stair-step graph in a business presentation. Boyd had no idea how this picture formed in his mind, but there it was.

The three men were about ten yards from the cottonwood tree when Jamie's SUV rolled slowly down the street. He waved at Boyd as he continued toward his parking space.

"Remember me?" Roscoe was the first to speak in a high pitched, surly tone.

Boyd slightly cocked his head and responded with a single, "Yep."

"Me and the boys just had a friendly chat with the red headed bitch at the store over there and she says you're the one that ratted us out to the police."

"Is that right." It was more of a statement than a question as Boyd continued to sit in the lawn chair.

"All you need to do is slap 'em around a little and them women will give ya what you want to know." Roscoe appeared to be gaining confidence.

"Hey boys. What's going on?" Jamie approached from behind Boyd's chair, smiling as he spoke.

Roscoe looked at his two friends and proclaimed, "This here one used to be some kind of wrestler, so be careful."

Boyd casually stood up and looked down at Roscoe as he spoke, "You have anything else you want to complain about?"

Roscoe's entire body seemed to involuntarily rock back as he ordered briskly, "Git 'em, boys!"

Jamie was now standing next to Boyd, facing the larger man with the bald head. It was this person who made the first mistake by throwing a round-house right hand in Jamie's direction. It was almost as if Jamie ducked and counter punched before the big man's arm had left his side. If this had been a Friday night fight on ESPN, the slow motion replay would have shown Jamie's right fist hitting the man's solar plexus, digging in, and then retracting. The solar plexus contains a complex system of nerves and arteries that when hit can cause severe pain, maybe vomiting and sometimes diarrhea. The big man immediately experienced all three.

The barrel-chested character was in the process of taking a step toward Boyd when he saw his friend drop to his knees. He immediately took a step back, his big body crashing into Roscoe. He raised both arms with his palms waving back and forth. He was either very astute, or perhaps very cowardly and needed overwhelming odds before entering into an altercation.

The big man on the ground was making gasping sounds as his body curled into a fetal position. He had thrown up on himself and other bodily functions were happening involuntarily.

"Now Roscoe, you dumb shit, see what you caused?" Jamie was as calm as when he first arrived.

Boyd said firmly, "Why don't you boys move on. I really don't want to see you around here again. Understand?"

Roscoe had a stunned look on his face and could only shake his head up and down.

The big man was able to stand with the help of his friend and the three of them made their way back down the street.

"Thanks, how about a Dickel?" Boyd knew how to end a street fight.

"Heck of an idea. I stopped on the way from the hospital and bought some fried chicken. Let's eat, drink and talk about tomorrow's trip."

———

The two friends met a few minutes later under the cottonwood tree. Jamie brought the container of fried chicken and a lawn chair and Boyd brought the bottle of George Dickel and two glasses filled with ice.

"Okay, I'm a believer in your cage fighting training and capabilities! It was unbelievable what you did to that big boy!" Boyd was sincere in his analysis of the earlier scuffle.

"I owed you a favor for what you did to the cowboy with the belt buckle."

Grinning and slowly shaking his head Boyd reflected, "The last time I was in a fight was in high school…and that was at football practice. You know, it wasn't really a fight, more like rolling around on the grass with your hand on someone's face mask. And now, in barely over a week, I've either been in a fight or standing next to one. Explain that."

"Well, you touched on it the other day." Pouring himself a drink, Jamie mused, "There are a lot of really good people living here, but there are enough bad apples in the barrel to ruin it for everyone else. The same thing happens with our culture. A small segment of any group can define the reputation of the entire organization."

Boyd was continually impressed with Jamie's logic and intellect… not to mention his physical capabilities.

"I hear you." Boyd leaned back in his lawn chair and sipped his drink.

The street in front of the doublewide was mostly quiet, the air warm and humid. The rains over the past week had invited the mosquitoes to the small dinner party. No automobile sounds, only distant barking and the hum of the evening crickets.

The bucket of chicken was almost empty as the two friends ate, sipped and made small talk.

"Before we get devoured by these little critters, let's quickly go over the plan one more time. Okay?" Boyd was back to business.

"I'm ready."

"Okay, let's both take our cars to the airport tomorrow. You leave on Delta at 12:00 noon and I leave on American at 12:54. You have your tickets and boarding passes and I printed mine out today."

"Check."

"I arrive in Cancun at 3:55 tomorrow afternoon, and since you go through Atlanta, you'll get there at 5:20. I'll rent a car and you can take a taxi. We're staying at the Casa Maya Hotel in the Hotel Zone. About thirty minutes or so from the airport."

"I have that information written down. Sounds good to me."

"You have the diabetes bag with the stuff in it." Boyd knew Jamie had taken care of this item, but he mentioned it anyway.

"Got it."

"I shipped the tattoo equipment to a FedEx store near the Hotel Zone. It'll be there when we arrive. Only need to pick it up. Also, we can get rubber gloves and a few other items at a drug store."

"Right."

"One other thing. Remember me telling you about Miguel Burbano, the fellow I sent to Cancun to get all the information about the waiter?"

"Yep."

"Well, I talked to him this past weekend and sent him back to Cancun to do a little advance work. He arrives this morning and said he would call if anything negative turns up. He's going to meet us tomorrow evening at the hotel and give us an update. He'll be leaving Cancun Saturday morning."

"You're one thorough man." Jamie continued to be amazed at Boyd's planning and execution abilities.

"Try to be." Standing and stretching, Boyd added, "Don't know about you, but I think I'll turn in early tonight. Thanks again for the chicken and the short MMA exhibition."

"You're welcome. I'm just full of surprises."

The street lights were humming, the dogs kept barking...another typical Thursday night at Ridgetop.

CHAPTER 32

Cancun, Mexico...Wednesday, June 2nd

Ruben awakened at precisely at 8:00a.m. No alarm clock, just nerves. This was the kick-off day. The day he had been waiting for all his life. This was the day he would be on his way to becoming a very rich man... not just good looking and charming, but rich.

Hector was sound asleep on the couch, facing the wall, when Ruben walked into the living room.

"Hey, get up. Time to get started."

Slowly turning his head, Hector growled, "I just went to sleep. What time is it?"

"After eight. You need to be at the DVD copying place in less than an hour. Okay!"

"Do you have anything to eat?"

"No. Get something on the way, go hungry, whatever. Just be back here with the copies as soon as possible. This is one assignment you can't screw up. Bring the copies back here before you get your messenger shirt."

"Okay, okay, I'm going! Oh yeah, I forgot to ask. Are you working tonight? When are you quitting your job on the 'Fish?"

"My last voyage on the Devilfish will be Saturday night. I'll be getting two weeks pay. Can't pass up that much cash."

Hector tried to focus his exhausted mind. "But aren't you worried about some of the clients spotting you? Shouldn't we be keeping in the weeds, you know, staying out of sight?"

"Not a problem. These client assholes won't be taking a trip on the Devilfish. They'll be worried sick about the letter and the DVDs they just received. Stay cool my friend, I've got it under control."

"What about Salazar?"

Ruben was starting to lose patience with Hector's questioning tone. Speaking slowly, he explained, "Salazar doesn't get his letter until Monday. Remember? And like I already told you, the other clients don't know about each other, much less Salazar. Go get the copies!"

"Just hope you know what you're doing."

———

Hector was tired, hungry and troubled. He wasn't troubled by the early morning traffic, not by the excessive street pollution, but by the thought of Estralita being cut out of the game. She had been the one who took the risk of putting the drugs in the victim's drinks. Plus, she was great in bed. Something about leaving her behind was just not right. Everything was wrong about this part of the plan.

His motorcycle wormed its way through the maze of cars, trucks and busses while a warm wind blew across Hector's convex sunglasses and his face. The only positive aspect of the morning was the proximity of the video store to Estralita's apartment. He could get the copies made, drop off one set with her, and then return the rest of them to Ruben. He figured he could get the messenger shirt later today, didn't need it until Friday anyway.

No problema!

Hector had always taken Estralita for granted. She was always there when needed and now she was about to be out of his life forever. What was this feeling? Was he turning soft? He'd always considered himself to be tough as nails, not some weak-sister bitch.

Concentrate on the job, don't screw it up. Ruben knows what's right.

Hector didn't remember the name of the video store, but he knew exactly where it was located. He pulled into the asphalt parking lot in front of Digital Equipo at 8:35 and sure enough the *ABIERTO* sign was flashing red. He slid down the kickstand on his Harley, removed his sunglasses and walked to the front door, his bald head glistening in the sun. He was on a mission and time was of the essence.

————

It had taken exactly twenty minutes to make three copies each of the five DVDs. Hector's friend had accepted the twenty-dollar bill and smiled. He had seen bits and pieces of the videos, but remained silent during the copying process. Friends help out friends.

Arriving at Estralita's apartment, Hector knocked lightly, waited a few seconds and then followed with three hard knuckle blows to the upper center of the door. He waited patiently with one hand in his pocket and the other holding the DVD copies.

The door opened a few inches, making a dull thud against the security chain.

"Hey, let me in," Hector whispered, trying to soften his voice into a pleading tone.

Dressed in the same wrinkled clothes she had been wearing when Hector last saw her, Estralita whispered in a barely audible voice, "What do you want?"

"Let me in. We need to talk, okay?"

The door opened and Hector immediately gave Estralita a hug. "Sit down. Let's talk about it."

"You drugged me, asshole." Estralita was unusually subdued, which added to Hector's anguish.

"It was all Ruben's idea. Okay? I'll make it right." There was a catch in Hector's voice which disturbed him. This feeling in his throat was new to him. He'd been in fights as a child, nose bloodied, but never cried or choked on his own words.

"Sure, you'll make it right!"

"Before me and Ruben leave, I'll give you the entire payment we were supposed to get from the guy last night." His grammar was bad, but not nearly as bad as the comment he let slip from somewhere in his tired, depleted mind.

Estralita let Hector's last comment soak in and then sobbed, "Leave! What do you mean leave?"

Hector's head slowly fell forward and for several seconds he couldn't think of anything to say. Finally, again in a whisper, he said, "Estralita, I'm sorry." This was one of the few times he actually used her first name and one of the few times in his entire life he told anyone he was sorry. He had called her bitch and a few other obscene names, but not by her actual name. "Ruben wants to go to Nicaragua, and we're leaving next week. I wanted to take you. Believe me, I did."

Estralita slowly shook her head from side to side and started sobbing. Hector expected a screaming, clawing fit, but not this. He felt like someone had stabbed him in the chest with an ice pick.

Handing Estralita the five DVD copies, he stammered, "Hold on to these copies. We'll be getting the payments from the clients on Friday. I promise I'll talk to Ruben and see about getting you some of it. Okay?"

Estralita took the DVDs and stood staring at Hector, tears running down her face. Silent.

"I'll get back to you soon. We'll take care of you." Hector needed to get out of the apartment. This kind of conversation was not in his comfort zone.

He had gone no more than a block when he remembered he was supposed to take Estralita back to her car in the Blue Turtle parking lot.

Shit, I forgot about taking her to her car. This has been a fucked up morning. I'll get her later. No way I can tell Ruben about how I screwed up and told her about us leaving next week. He won't give her any cash. I'll string her along and then be gone. Need to get her out of my head. There'll be other babes in Nicaragua.

But…he couldn't get her out of his head.

———

It was 9:55a.m. when Hector walked through the door to Ruben's apartment. Ruben emerged from the bedroom, shirt off, towel in his hand.

"Did you get the copies?"

"I told you I would be here by ten, and here I am. *Early.*" Hector handed Ruben two sets of the copies.

"What about the DVD copies we're going to leave with Estralita for insurance? When are you going to do that?"

"I dropped them off at her apartment on the way here. It's done."

"Was she still pissed about last night?"

"No," Hector lied. "She's okay."

"What about the messenger shirt? Did you get that?"

"Later today. I don't even need it until Friday." With a sarcastic tone he added, "Let's see now…that's about three days from now. What's with all the questions!"

Ruben calmly stated, "No harm in getting this stuff done in advance. No screw ups. Remember?"

"Got it."

"I'll put the DVDs and letters in the client's envelopes and take them to the messenger service right away. We're off and running. Are you as excited as I am?"

Hector quietly mumbled, "Nicaraguan babes."

———

A bright red sign indicated **CANCUN MESSENGER** was located at 12222 Avenida Tulum. Ruben had stopped at Kinkos on the way and quickly typed and made a copy of the extortion note addressed to Senor Diaz. In addition, he purchased one more manila envelope. It had been a short drive from Kinkos to the messenger service and Ruben entered the store in an upbeat mood. Several bicycles and motor scooters were parked on the sidewalk near the front door.

"Good morning." Ruben flashed one of his most charismatic smiles, not only because of his near manic condition, but also due to the attractive young lady behind the desk.

"Welcome to Cancun Messenger." Not only was she pretty, she had a pleasant demeanor.

"I spoke with a fellow here yesterday about the delivery of four envelopes. He said to be here by noon and they would all be delivered by 4:00p.m. today. Here I am."

Reaching for the manila envelopes in Ruben's out-stretched hand, she began her canned response. "Not a problem. We're..."

"I know…always on time." Ruben was still smiling. Not even a corn-ball slogan could interfere with the euphoria he was experiencing. He was on his way to becoming a wealthy man.

The clerk smiled, tilted her head and said, "You're pretty quick."

Ruben was back to business. "The addresses are printed on each of the envelopes. Can you ensure me they will be delivered by 4:00? And don't tell me you're always on time."

Still smiling, she nodded, "They'll get there."

After paying the young lady, Ruben returned to his SUV and sat for a moment. He'd left the windows up and the temperature inside the vehicle was almost unbearable. He immediately started to sweat, but was surprised that he was also shaking.

———

Hector, for the second time that morning, was knocking on Estralita's door. He kept repeating over and over in his mind the term "Nicaraguan babes", but his real concern was with Estralita.

What's wrong with me? What the fuck is wrong with me!

The door opened and Estralita said, "Decided to come back for me, huh?"

Her long black hair had been combed and she was dressed in red shorts with a white halter top. No tears. She was all business.

"I came back to take you to your car. Hey, you look all cleaned up." No one ever accused Hector of being a silver-tongued devil.

"Let's go." Still, not the slightest hint of emotion in her voice.

The ride to the Blue Turtle parking lot on Hector's Harley took only a few minutes. No words were exchanged on the trip.

Estralita got off the motorcycle, walked to her car and casually looked back at Hector, who was staring at her. A slight smile parted her lips as she got in the Pontiac and closed the door.

CHAPTER 33

Cancun, Mexico...Wednesday, June 2nd

Ruben was in a quandary as where to go or what to do after he left the messenger service. His stomach was doing flips and he felt slightly nauseous. He had briefly thought about putting some moves on the young lady at the counter, but his physical system was threatening a complete shutdown.

Even the richest and most powerful men in the world get nervous on occasion. Don't they?

Sometimes to rationalize is to not fully face reality, but rationalization was a huge part of Ruben's makeup. It made a life of immorality, lying and deceit much more bearable.

Screw nervousness, I'm on my way to the top. I'll be calm when I fucking well feel like it!

After starting his Ford Explorer and turning on the air conditioner, Ruben dialed Hector on his cell phone.

"What." The abrupt greeting surprised Ruben.

"Where are you?"

"I'm in the Turtle parking lot. I just took Estralita back to her car."

"Back to her car! Where have you been?"

"Look, I don't need a bunch of questions, okay! I took her straight home last night because we drugged her. Remember! She needed a ride back to her car this morning. Okay?"

Ruben backed down a notch and said, "My friend, we both need to settle down. Our new life is about to begin. Want to meet for lunch at the Blue Gecko Cantina? You know, it's across the street from the Grand Oasis Hotel on Boulevard Kukulcan."

Hesitating for a moment, Hector calmly said, "Sure, I know where it is." After another brief pause, he continued, "Why do so many bars and businesses have the word blue in their name?"

Thank God, he's back to his normal, corny self!

"I don't know. Look it up on Google. See you in five."

———

Estralita sat in her car for a few minutes before getting out and vomiting in the parking lot. She had no idea where the contents of her stomach were coming from, since she hadn't eaten in at least a day. She wiped her mouth with the back of her arm and got back into the car.

A plan was percolating in her mind. A plan to get back at Ruben and Hector, but now was not the time. She just needed to get back to her apartment and curl up in a fetal position. She was feeling like an abandoned child, which in reality she had been...and now, she was again.

———

Ruben arrived at the Blue Gecko parking lot at the same time as Hector. As they sat at the bar facing the street, Ruben recognized the plump waitress, writing pad in hand.

"What can I get you boys?"

Ruben was first to speak. "Still have the green chili pork tacos?" Without waiting for a yes or no, he continued, "I'll take two."

"We still have them."

Studying the menu board, Hector ordered without making eye contact with the waitress, "Fiery fish tacos. Two of 'em."

"Want anything to drink? You're going to need something to put out the fire."

"Yeah, bring us both a Tecate." Ruben displayed his leadership role.

After the waitress left, Ruben expressed his entrepreneurial opinion. "We're not going to have any fat bitches working for us in Nicaragua! They're going to be beautiful and they're going to have big tits. Maybe topless. What do you think?"

"Count me in."

"Okay my friend, the shit is about to hit the fan. Not with us, but with the clients. The envelopes with the DVDs and the letters will be delivered today by 4:00p.m. These guys will be scrambling to get their thirty-five thousand rounded up… and it will all be coming our way. Are you as pumped as I am?"

"Sure."

"What's the matter? You don't sound very excited."

Hector heisted and then said, "I'm excited. Just tired, I guess."

"Have you picked up the messenger shirt yet?"

"I'll get it this afternoon after we eat. Not a problem."

The waitress returned with two plates of tacos and two beers, all on one large tray. "Enjoy."

Chewing a large bite of fiery fish taco, Hector stated, "So, you're going to work tonight on the 'Fish."

After swallowing some Tecate, Ruben answered with a series of short, staccato sentences, "Told you, I'm working through Saturday. Get two weeks pay. Too much to leave behind. Besides, the season is about over and the gringo crowds are getting smaller and smaller. Makes it easy on me."

Taking a bite of his taco, he lectured on with his mouth half full, "Since the clients have never seen you, and since you're picking up the payments on Friday, it's best if we're not seen together for the next two days. We can keep in touch by phone."

"Works for me."

"A couple of other things. Do you have a map of downtown Cancun?"

"Yeah, in my apartment."

Removing a piece of paper from his back pocket, Ruben said, "Here are the addresses of the clients. I've numbered them one, two, three and four. That's the order in which you need to pick up the cash payments on Friday. *Comprende?*"

"Got it, dude. That's the shortest and quickest distances, huh?"

Ignoring the obvious question, Ruben added, "Mark the numbers on your map...one, two, three and four."

"Still got it. Will do. Over and out."

"Goddamn it!" Ruben exclaimed in a loud whisper. He was nervous and it was showing. Looking around and making sure no one could hear their conversation, he looked directly at Hector and lowered his voice. "We've got to be serious about this. It's our entire future and more importantly...it could be our lives. You have to pay close attention. Okay?"

Hector was not accustomed to Ruben being this upset with him. They had been friends and running mates forever. He knew Ruben was the brains of the team, but he also knew he was a full partner in all of their pursuits and schemes.

"Okay, okay. Sorry, man. I'm with you and I'll be sure and put the addresses on the map. I won't fuck it up."

Calming down, Ruben said, "I know you will my friend. As you can see, I'm a little jumpy."

"Me too."

"Listen carefully. The clients will think you're only a messenger and won't suspect you know anything about what's going on. If they ask you where you're taking the envelope they give you, tell them you're supposed to call the office and get further directions when you get on your motorcycle. They'll be way too scared to try and follow you. Besides, it'll be easy for you to get lost in the Friday afternoon rush hour traffic and make it to the next pick-up."

"Good plan."

"Last thing. Let's meet at the lobby bar in the Krystal Cancun after you've made the final pick-up. You should be finished before 5:00p.m. Just make absolutely sure no one is following you. Okay?"

"I'll be there."

Ruben made a fist with his right hand and extended it to Hector. "We're going to be rich. Very, very rich."

Completing the fist bump, Hector said, "Never a doubt."

They continued to eat in silence. Everything was coming together, but something just didn't feel right.

CHAPTER 34

Cancun, Mexico…Thursday, June 3rd
It was mid-morning and Ruben had only slept sporadically. His pulse rate was nearing red alert as he sat down at his kitchen table. Fortunately, he had picked up a box of sweet rolls and a carton of milk yesterday after leaving the Blue Gecko. As he'd predicted, the Devilfish cruise was only half-full last night and was generally boring. Carmen, the blender bitch, was absent from the cruise for the second straight night. This was somewhat of a relief for Ruben, although he wondered what was wrong with her and when she would return.

Christ, I have to go through this again for the next three days. Saturday can't come soon enough!

He'd gone straight to his apartment after leaving the cruise, slowly driving through the apartment parking lot until he felt assured no one was there trying to ambush him.

Now, he not only had Carmen's boyfriend to worry about, but also the four clients. Did they receive the letters and DVDs yesterday? Surely the messenger service would have called if they had not been able to deliver any of them. No call.

Fuck the clients, fuck Carmen's boyfriend. Chief Salazar is the only possible threat and I'm ten times smarter than he is. I just need to call

Hector and make sure he's organized and prepared for the pick-ups tomorrow afternoon.

The use of everyday logic had always been one of his strengths, or at least he thought this to be the case. And logically, all four of the clients who received the letters and DVDs yesterday were terrified and too busy trying to come up with the thirty-five thousand to focus on him.

Still, Ruben was as anxious as he had ever been in his life.

Maybe I should move out of this apartment right now. What if one of the clients goes nuts and buys a gun and comes after me? What about Uncle Emilio? No, he's not a problem. He's in Mexico City with his bitch until Friday night. Be cool! I'll move out Monday morning before the letter gets to Chief Salazar. He's the only one to worry about.

At precisely the same time as Ruben was taking the first bite of his sweet roll, Miguel Burbano was landing at the Cancun International Airport on his early morning flight from Dallas. The flight landed ten minutes early. Miguel slept most of the way, was rested and was looking forward to his assignment as a forward observer.

———

Estralita was still sick and could not keep anything in her stomach. She was currently in her apartment, where she had been for the past forty-eight hours, eating saltine crackers and drinking tap water. Her head hurt, her stomach hurt and most importantly…her feelings were shattered. In her mind, she knew what she had to do, it was just a matter of getting her body to cooperate.

After showering and shampooing her hair, she walked into the kitchen, wearing only a pair of black panties. She felt better, but her stomach was still a mess. At her kitchen table, she ate two pieces of white bread and three more saltine crackers. She got up, walked to the sink and placed her hands on the edge of the counter. This was the first time in two days she didn't feel as if she was going to vomit. Head down, she tried to clear her mind and think.

Copies of the DVDs were in her possession...and Police Chief Salazar would soon be viewing the one in which he was the leading character. Hector had told her the clients would be making their payoffs on Friday, so she assumed Chief Salazar would be paying on the same day. She needed to get Salazar's DVD to him today. This would give him time to prepare and then do whatever he wanted to Hector and Ruben.

The stories about Salazar painted him as a brutal man. The consequences would be swift and painful, if not fatal, for Hector and Ruben. In her own way, Estralita had considered them her family...the family she never had. She knew they took advantage of her, but they were her family. How could they abandon her like this!

She removed the five DVDs from a kitchen drawer and sorted through them. She looked at the one labeled **SALAZAR, POLICE CHIEF, 5-28-16.** In the same drawer she found a small envelope and a red ballpoint pen. She carefully wrote his name on both sides of the envelope and then, in large block letters, she printed above his name... **VERY IMPORTANT.** She circled the words **VERY IMPORTANT,** again in red. She didn't bother putting a note in the envelope with the DVDs. Instead, she would hand it to Salazar and explain Ruben and Hector's plan.

After dressing, Estralita began the drive to One Police Headquarters. It was a little after noon and the traffic was congested. The air conditioner in the Pontiac was out of Freon and the exhaust fumes and other pollution coming through the open windows didn't help her stomach.

One Police Headquarters was located in the center of downtown Cancun in the Benito Juarez Building, also known as City Hall. It consisted of two stories with pink columns adorning the outside. A faux third-floor occupied the center of the structure with a large red, gold and blue mural depicting the sun, sand and ocean. The architecture and coloring of the building reflected the glamour of this city with close to 650,000 residents.

Estralita was able to park within a hundred yards of the entrance which was guarded by ten or so *policias*, all but two dressed in dark pants and white short sleeved shirts with emblems on the sleeves. The rest were wearing military fatigues and carrying assult rifles. An armored vehicle and several black and white motorcycles were parked in a reserved area directly in front of the building.

She could feel the stares of several of the men as she walked through the plaza toward the front doors. They were absolutely quiet, but she could sense their eyes on her body.

If I had a video player, I would stop and let all of them see their Police Chief with his pants down!

Entering the swinging double doors, Estralita proceeded to the front desk which was occupied by a fortyish woman also wearing dark pants and a white shirt.

Estralita was nervous and it showed in the high pitched, *agudo* sound of her voice. "I need to see Police Chief Salazar."

"Do you have to have an appointment?" The question was curt.

Estralita's stomach was in knots as she pleaded, "No, but I have something very important for him to see." Holding up the envelope containing the DVD she added, "He'll want to see it."

The unrelenting duty officer was firm. "Have to have an appointment. Give me the thing you want him to see."

Feeling the need to purge her stomach once again, Estralita handed the envelope to the officer and hurried toward the swinging doors.

The officer looked at the envelope, tried to feel its contents and dropped it in a basket marked **MAIL** behind the desk.

———

Fuming, Hector stood at the counter of Uniform Fitness. He had visited the store yesterday, after lunch with Ruben, and was told it would take a couple of hours to get the patch he wanted sewed on the messenger shirt. He'd returned two hours later only to be told it would not be ready until today.

Uniform Fitness. What a stupid name. Sounds like a health club.

"May I be of assistance?" The polite question was asked by a young lady, not the one who had waited on Hector the day before.

"Yeah, I've got a shirt to pick up that was supposed to have been ready yesterday, but some asshole couldn't get it ready!" Hector was relentless in expressing his displeasure.

"Name, please."

"I don't know what his fucking name was, but I do know he should be fired!"

Remaining calm in the otherwise stormy situation, the young lady replied, "No, I don't need to know his name, I need your name."

"Hector."

"What is your last name?"

"Acosta! My last name is Acosta! Do you want the name of my best friend when I was in the second grade, my dog's name? Christ, this could take the rest of my life and I only needed a name on a shirt!"

"Just a minute."

Returning with the shirt, the lady sheepishly said, "That will be twelve dollars."

Looking at the light gray shirt with a **JIFFY FLASH SERVICE** patch sewn over the pocket on the right side, Hector carried on, "You should have to pay me for all the time I've been waiting."

Reluctantly, he handed over the twelve dollars. As he picked up the shirt, he threw one more verbal jab. "By the way, I don't have a dog."

———

Miguel Burbano was in his rental car and on his way to the Hotel Zone. The most trying part of any trip to Cancun is getting from the luggage carousel to the mode of transportation. He stood in the Customs line for at least an hour.

Tourists are warned not to rent cars in the city due to crooked traffic cops. It seems tourists are stopped for any and all reasons and subtly asked for cash bribes. This did not concern Miguel.

It was only seven or eight miles to the hotel, but Miguel knew it would take at least thirty minutes due to the traffic and road conditions.

He was staying at the Aquamarina Beach Hotel on Boulevard Kukulcan, moderately priced and conveniently located for what he needed to accomplish.

He had reviewed the notes from his previous trip and had mentally prepared a list of activities for Thursday, the day he arrived in Cancun: First, ensure that Ruben Repeza is still living in his apartment. Second, follow him Thursday afternoon and make sure he still works on the Devilfish. Third, follow him from the end of the Devilfish cruise to his home, or wherever he goes. Fourth, monitor his activities during the day Friday until he reports back for work on the Devilfish and last, and most important, break into his apartment and check it out.

Miguel knew the last item would be the most difficult and risky. But then, his friends, associates and clients had not named him *The Shadow* without good reason.

Several years ago, he had been hired by three members of a prestigious country club in Dallas. A fairly new member who had recently joined their golf foursome was suspected of being a cheat in their high-dollar game. Miguel rolled his eyes when he heard their request: follow the new fellow on the golf course during one of their rounds and report any rules violations.

Miguel was able to video three instances of the new member cheating while in the trees and near out-of-bound stakes. He put the video on a DVD with titles and presented it to the three golfers a day later. They reportedly told all their friends they never once saw Miguel during the round and had no idea of how he accomplished his task. *The Shadow* emerged in Dallas.

It was after 2:00 by the time Miguel checked in at the hotel and finished lunch. The drive to Ruben's apartment took less than fifteen minutes. Miguel parked under a car port four spaces away from Ruben's Ford Explorer. The license plate number matched his notes. The occupant of this particular parking space was probably at work, so Miguel assumed he had a couple of hours before anyone returned. He could clearly see the back door of Ruben's apartment from this vantage point.

Even with all four windows of the rental car rolled down, the heat was intense. Miguel was five-seven and only weighed one hundred forty-five pounds. He had very little body fat, but he felt as if what little he did have was being melted away. He was dressed in black and white checkered shorts and a colorful tee shirt in order to fit in with the locals. In this respect, he was indeed a shadow. Unfortunately, this shadow was sitting in a very hot car.

While it was hot and humid in Dallas this time of year, for some reason the ninety-degree temperature and the eighty-five-degree humidity in Cancun was extremely oppressive. The golf shirt, soaked in sweat, was clinging to Miguel's back.

Finally, in desperation, he got out of the car, walked around to the passenger side and stood in the shade hoping for at least a slight breeze. The breeze didn't materialize, but at least he was no longer stuck to the seat of his car.

He mentally reviewed the notes from his last trip and once again surveyed the apartment building. There were fourteen back doors facing this section of the parking lot, fourteen carports and fourteen sidewalks from each of the carports to the back doors. The parking lot continued around the left side of the building, where the main lobby was located. The other side of the building mirrored this one, the same number of parking spaces and the same number of back doors. A hallway down the middle of the complex, from the lobby to an emergency back door, separated the twenty-eight units.

At 3:45, Ruben emerged from his apartment and hurried to his car, a stressed look on his face. Miguel was pleased to see that Ruben was still present and accounted for.

It was not difficult following Ruben to the Playa Langosta pier parking lot. Traffic was heavy, but Miguel knew where his target was going. Satisfied that Ruben was on his way to work on the Devilfish, Miguel exited the parking area and returned to the apartment complex.

———

It was 4:15 in the afternoon and Hector was sitting in a local dive bar near his apartment working on his fourth beer. He was still stewing over the way Estralita was being treated. The smug look she had given him when she was getting in her car at the Blue Turtle bothered him…a lot. Surely she wouldn't blow the whistle on them. Would she?

There comes a time in a man's life when he needs to make a command decision. And the time was now for Hector.

Fuck Ruben! I'm going to get a thousand dollars from our stash in Ruben's closet and give it to Estralita. That'll keep her supplied with drugs and happy as a clam. Ruben will thank me. I'll give it to her tomorrow evening.

———

Miguel was curious about the layout of the apartment building and the parking options. This time, he parked at the back of the building, near the emergency exit, and walked around the complex to Ruben's kitchen door. He had a professional set of lock picking tools at his office in Dallas, including a tension wrench and a pick, but he didn't want to risk taking them through Customs in Mexico. Instead, he took a small Allen wrench and a paper clip from his pocket. He straightened the paper clip and then bent it into an L shape. He used his car key to make several indentions in the longest segment. Placing the Allen wrench in the bottom of the door lock, he inserted the paper clip above it and scrubbed it rapidly back and forth. Seven seconds later Miguel closed the door behind him, locked it and turned on the light. He was met by an unpleasant musty smell.

Several sheets of paper were strewn about on the kitchen table. Picking one up, Miguel read the extortion note to Police Chief Salazar. He noticed four other extortion notes with different names on each of them, but with identical instructions. He focused his smart phone on each of the letters. Leaving the papers where he found them, he walked to the living area and took notice of the DVD player on the end table. In the bedroom, he turned on the light and stopped at the closet door. The flap on the bullfighter picture was slightly protruding. Miguel tried the closet door, but discovering it was locked, lifted the flap and attempted to look inside the closet. Taking a small flashlight from his pocket, he looked through the opening and the light immediately reflected on the lens of a video camera. Just as he reached for his Allen wrench and paper clip, he heard someone unlocking the back door. In seconds, *the Shadow* was at the door that opened to the central hallway.

———

The back door of Ruben's apartment opened, and the living room door leading to the hallway closed almost simultaneously. Hector entered the kitchen, glanced at the extortion letters on the table and continued to the bedroom closet. He and Ruben had constructed the secret space under the carpet several months ago. He shoved aside the boxes stacked in the corner and removed the piece of carpet attached to the plywood. The sight of so much cash in the metal box caused Hector to involuntarily exhale. Removing exactly one thousand dollars, he replaced the box in the small compartment.

This is the right thing to do. Ruben will agree!

———

At 11:45p.m. Ruben arrived at his apartment after another boring night on the Devilfish. The cruise was not well attended. Less than half of the normal crowd was on the boat and they weren't overly exciting. Not a single person had thrown up.

A rumor was circulating among the crew that the Devilfish, as of next weekend, would cease operations for the summer. Ruben didn't care. What gave him some relief though, was the fact Carmen had quit her job as bartender on the 'Fish.

I hope she and her boyfriend have moved out of the city. No, out of the country.

Ruben hadn't noticed the headlights that followed him home. He was tired. Too tired to even call Hector and double check on his preparedness for tomorrow.

I'll call him tomorrow morning.

———

The envelope containing Chief Salazar's personal DVD had been in his in-box most of the day. The **VERY IMPORTANT** written in large, red block letters was buried under a stack of other letters and manila folders. The word **VERY** extended from near the bottom of the pile, but the word **IMPORTANT** remained hidden.

307

CHAPTER 35

Dallas...Friday, June 4th

Boyd felt wide awake and alive when he walked into the kitchen of the doublewide Friday morning. It wasn't because of a sound night's sleep, it was because of the adrenaline rush. He kept rationalizing to himself that after the next few days everything was going to be okay. Back to business as usual.

The morning sun made its presence known, but just barely. He opened the front door and as he expected the cat was not there.

Too early for the night roamer, not too early for coffee.

Boyd stood in front of his Keurig trying to will it to hurry up and indicate it was **Ready To Brew**. Two minutes later he was sitting on the couch drinking coffee and checking out the news on his iPhone. As usual, the national, as well as the local news, tended to depress, not uplift. The only news worthy of a chuckle occurred when CNN had several of its on-site reporters standing knee-deep in water, mud or some type of sludge.

The plan was to leave for the airport at 9:15 this morning. Since he was already packed, there was a little over an hour to feed the cat, shave and shower. He was surprised when he opened the front door for the second time that morning. Rosie was sitting patiently on the top step along with the two brothers.

"Good morning, boys. I thought you were going to start your feeding duties this afternoon."

Richie stood and looked at Boyd. "We're getting a jump on this job. We want to see firsthand how you feed this here cat."

Darell added, "Yeah."

Cocking his head to one side and squinting, Boyd said, "You fellows looking for a raise already? Come on in and I'll show you how an expert does it."

After the feeding task was completed, Richie remarked, "We're on top of it."

Darell enthusiastically said, "Ditto."

With a stern look that didn't fool the brothers, Boyd teased, "And like I said yesterday, don't be having any wild parties here while I'm gone."

Darell rolled his eyes. "We're only kids!"

———

Boyd tried to analyze his state of mind as he drove to the Dallas-Fort Worth International Airport. He was relaxed, but edgy. As he continued to think about it, he decided he was somewhere between satisfied and strained. He knew he was ready to full-out execute the plan, whatever the feelings. Time to bring this dilemma to a conclusion.

His flight was scheduled to leave at 12:54p.m. on American. Boyd knew he should be at the airport at least two hours in advance for an international trip. He was going to arrive three hours early, no way was he going to miss this flight! It seemed as if it had taken forever to go through the boarding process during his last trip to Cancun. He had since seen a report on one of the local TV stations regarding the incredible wait times and frustrations of international travelers coming and going through DFW.

He recalled a humorous quip from a prominent New York City venture capitalist during his first trip to Dallas:

I've always wanted to come to Dallas in the worst way. So I did...through DFW!

The next decision of the day was where to park. He had the option of parking in terminal parking for twenty-two dollars per day or in long term parking for nine dollars each day. It was a quick decision to pay the extra fifty-two dollars for the four-day period. Being early for a flight out of DFW was a good thing.

Boyd pulled his carry-on bag behind him as he exited the parking garage and entered the international terminal. He was wearing dark shorts with a Hawaiian print shirt and a pair of Dockers.

The check-in process was relatively quick, but as he neared the security screening entrance, Boyd could see several lines winding around the huge area like a slow moving lava flow. He estimated a crowd of close to a hundred men, women and children standing or sitting in the various lines. Although there was a sampling of excited tourists leaving on their first international trip or a return trip to a favorite vacation destination, discontent prevailed in the lines. Most of the comments Boyd could hear had something to do with bad backs, edema of the legs, rude and officious security staff or the fear of missing a flight. Boyd remained calm. Forty-five minutes later at the departure gate he was still calm.

The mood in the departure area was somewhat lighter than it had been in the security line. The lure of the Caribbean, white beaches and rum drinks had taken hold. Boyd guessed the average age of the crowd to be less than thirty. There was a smattering of couples with young children, most of whom could be heard above the clamor of the vacation bound travelers. The boarding process was less than an hour away and the "people-watching" made the time fly. Even though there was ample space available in First Class when Boyd booked his flight, he had decided to remain as low profile as possible and fly coach.

A couple already occupied the window and middle seats when he eased into his aisle seat. The twenty-something fellow sitting by the window leaned over and said, "Hey man, where're you staying in 'Cun?"

By the glazed look in the young man's eyes, Boyd could tell he had been either drinking or smoking something significant. "Casa Maya Hotel. How about you?"

The young lady, who had been quiet up until now, slowly slurred, "My parents have a time-share. We're really going to raise hell. Want to come see us?"

With a slight grin, Boyd said, "I'll have to pass. Just going for a restful vacation."

The captain's voice came through the speaker system and informed the passengers of a slight delay in takeoff due to getting some sort of paperwork signed by maintenance. He assured everyone they would leave as soon as possible.

The couple slid closer together and both were asleep before the boarding process was complete.

As the plane lifted off, Boyd leaned back in his seat, looked at his watch and estimated the plane would arrive in Cancun about thirty-five minutes late. He closed his eyes and tried to fight off the memories flooding his mind. The memories of his family trip to Cancun five and a half months earlier:

His wife, Sally, was sitting in the window seat and Jenny, his daughter was sitting between them.

"Hey, Dad, are we going to parasail while we're in Cancun?"

"No, too dangerous."

"How about renting jet skis in the lagoon behind the hotel?"

"No, too polluted and dangerous."

"How about eating papaya every morning for breakfast?"

"No, too dangerous."

"What!"

"Just kidding about the papaya."

Listening to the conversation, Sally rolled her eyes. It was a close knit family and they all enjoyed each other's company. Boyd worked long hours and spent too much time away from home due to business travel. This was a well deserved vacation.

The one thing Boyd enjoyed most about flying was the takeoff. The roar of the engines as the plane started down the runway, the liftoff and then the serenity that came with leveling off at over thirty thousand feet. His serenity was interrupted by more memories of the events that occurred five and a half months ago.

The last night of the vacation entailed a booze cruise…the Caribbean Pirate Booze Cruise. The waiter's name was Ruben, a very nice looking, polite young man who seemed to have taken it upon himself to satisfy every need of the Tanner family. He, along with the rest of the male waiters on the boat, was shirtless and wore baby blue beach pants and sandals. He had a well proportioned body and jokingly compared his biceps with Boyd's, even though Boyd's were substantially larger. His movie star smile and engaging personality charmed all members of the family.

As the cruise neared the Playa Langosta pier on the return trip, Boyd's daughter, Jenny, excitedly asked her parents, "Ruben wants me to go with him and some of his friends to a beachside bar when we dock. Okay? Please!"

Looking at Sally, Boyd acquiesced, "Okay with me. How about you, babe?"

"It's late and I don't think it's necessary to go to a bar this late."

"Please, Mom, I won't have much to drink and I promise not to be gone too long."

"I don't think so."

Boyd said quietly, "Oh, come on. It'll be okay. It's our last night here."

Sally shrugged, knowing she was outnumbered.

Three items were tugging as his senses as he nodded off…making amends with his wife Sally, taking care of his friend Jamie and carrying out the sentence on the waiter.

CHAPTER 36

Cancun, Mexico...Friday, June 4th

Another sleepless night. And to make matters worse, he had no appetite this morning. Ruben looked in the mirror and was sure he was losing weight and muscle mass. The thought crossed his mind that he could be losing hair.

What if my teeth fall out and I go blind! Stop it! It'll all be better this afternoon when we get the money from the clients. Quit worrying!

He made an executive decision on the spot. Picking up his cell phone, he called the Cruise Manager for the Devilfish.

Speaking in a slow, sickly voice, Ruben uttered, "Antonio, this is Ruben Repeza. I've got a serious stomach problem and I won't be able to make the Devilfish cruise this evening. Don't want to infect anyone else. I'm sure I can kick it today and be there tomorrow. Okay?"

"That's disappointing to hear, but I'll try to get a sub."

"Thanks, pal. I'll be there tomorrow for sure."

Ruben's next call was to Hector. He had used the speed dial-feature for this number since purchasing his first cell phone many years ago. He

314

was not sure he could use the dial pad to call Hector, since he couldn't even remember the number anymore.

Hector answered the phone with his usual surly attitude. "Yes, this is Hector. Yes, I marked the locations on the map. Yes, I will not fuck it up."

"Glad to hear you're in such a good mood."

"I'm always in a good mood. Sometimes life pisses me off."

Ruben was relieved to hear Hector's smart-ass comments. He was evidently in a decent frame of mind...considering what was going down today.

"Let's meet for lunch and go over the pick-up schedule one more time. It'll help calm both of us down."

"I thought you didn't want us to be seen together."

"Changed my mind. I'm not worried about the sorry-ass clients. They'll do exactly what the letter tells them to do. I just need to discuss things with you one last time."

"Where do you want to meet? And you're paying for lunch."

"I think we've had this discussion before. Seems to me, I always pay for lunch. Let's meet at the restaurant just off the lobby in the Krystal Cancun." Hesitating for a moment, he continued, "I think it's called the Las Velas. Same place we'll meet this afternoon when you're finished with the pick-ups. Make it high noon. I need to stand in the shower for a while. Okay?"

"Why do you want to go to the Krystal? It's big and it cost more than a lot of other places we could go."

"There will only be gringo tourists there. Besides, I like the food and the good looking babes that hang out at the bar."

"I'll be there."

———

It was 11:45a.m. and Miguel Burbano had been sitting in his car for three hours in the parking lot at Ruben's apartment. Before parking, Miguel had circled the apartment complex and took mental notes of the general layout, the parking areas and the surrounding buildings.

The one-story apartment building was located just off Avenida Nizuc, near both the Hotel Zone and downtown Cancun. It was in a low income residential area, but the building's appearance was above average, despite the location. There was ample parking and most of the occupants had been treated to covered parking spaces, which was unusual in this part of the city.

Whoever said a private investigator's job was never a private investigator. Miguel was bored out of his mind and once again his shirt was sticking to both his back and the back of the seat. A number of residents left for work throughout the morning causing Miguel to move his car several times in order to remain as anonymous as possible. He was now parked four spaces from Ruben's Ford Explorer.

Miguel had waited for the Devilfish to return from Isla Mujeres the previous night and then followed Ruben back to his apartment. The lights in the apartment went off at midnight. Miguel waited in the parking lot for another fifteen minutes and then drove back to his hotel. It had been a long day.

And this was turning into another long day unless Ruben appeared soon. Fortunately, Miguel brought four bottles of water he had purchased from the nearby OXXO convenience store. Only one bottle remained unopened. Unfortunately, he had skipped breakfast because he was afraid of losing track of Ruben this morning. He was now hot, hungry and bored.

His persistence was rewarded when he saw the back door to Ruben's apartment open. Ruben locked the door and walked to his Explorer. Miguel slid down in his seat and waited for the SUV to pull out of the parking space.

Traffic was heavy as they exited Avenida Nizuc onto Highway 307, but Miguel had no problem keeping Ruben in sight. As soon as they turned onto Avenida Kukulcan, the hotels and condominiums on the left stretched as far as one could see and the lagoon on the right came into view. Occasionally, the lagoon would disappear from site and an everglades scene would appear. Miguel had heard numerous stories regarding the polluted waters of the lagoons. According to many sources, the tourist industry was responsible for putting undue stress on the infrastructure and caused hotel waste water to be dumped into the lagoons. Whatever the case, the view was spectacular. He could see numerous water craft already on the water, both small speed-boats and jet skis.

The Explorer eventually made a u-turn at a *retorno* sign and passed an area of restaurants, bars and nightclubs. Carlos & Charlies, Coco Bongo, Senor Frogs and other nighttime establishments lined both sides of the street. A block later, a driveway appeared on the right leading to the Krystal Cancun Hotel. The eight story cream colored behemoth was introduced by a long portico with the name of the hotel boldly displayed on its side. Miguel observed the SUV stop in front of the main entrance to the hotel. He parked a couple of spaces behind Ruben and watched him take a valet ticket from the attendant.

Miguel got out of his rental car, received his ticket and could see Ruben entering the hotel lobby.

Following a safe distance behind his target, Miguel couldn't keep from being impressed at the hotel entrance: the tall columns, the numerous areca palms and the wide steps leading up to multiple, swinging glass doors. Several couples and families were either entering or exiting the hotel as Miguel reached the first step. He temporarily lost sight of Ruben, but as he walked through the doors, he spotted him ascending another set of stairs about halfway through the lobby on the left.

Miguel's appreciation of the architecture and decoration of the hotel lobby briefly flowed through his thoughts. The white marble flooring and the matching white ceiling were eye- catching as was the white tread, offset by the gray risers on the staircase. The entire interior soared, with noticeable curves. Few flat walls or right angles seemed to exist. His attention returned to the task at hand as he reached the top of the staircase and saw Ruben and another man waiting at the reception station in front of the Las Velas restaurant.

Miguel half-turned his back to the restaurant entrance and pretended to be interested in a small sculpture sitting on a table. He immediately recognized the young man standing next to Ruben...the shaved head, the facial hair. This was Ruben's serious-looking running-mate he had observed on his previous trip to Cancun. They'd been drinking together at the Blue Turtle.

The twosome followed a young lady to a table and Miguel leisurely ambled over to the hostess stand.

The hostess, dressed in a short, black skirt, returned momentarily and smiled broadly. "May I seat you, *senor*?"

Pointing in the general direction of Ruben and his friend, Miguel replied, "Yes, somewhere in that area, please."

The interior of the restaurant had a comfortable feel, with yellow seat cushions and red, white and green table cloths. Floor to ceiling glass windows lined the back wall and provided an impressive view of one of the hotel's swimming pools as well as the deep blue waters of the Caribbean which lay beyond.

Miguel was seated near his prey. At least three-quarters of the tables in the restaurant were occupied, and no one seemed to notice one more patron.

Miguel couldn't hear the conversation, but he could keep track of Ruben and his wingman out of the corner of his eye.

———

"Damn, this shrimp is good." Ruben had temporarily forgotten about the importance of this day and was concentrating on his lunch.

"For sure!" Hector could barely talk since his mouth was full of the same delicacy. After swallowing, he added, " Just to ease your mind, I have the map with the numbers on it, which I don't even need. All four of the businesses are located in or near the downtown area and it won't take long to make all four pick-ups."

"Are you sure you can get lost in the Friday afternoon traffic after each pick-up?" An element of concern had returned to Ruben's voice.

"Hey, what do I look like…new!"

"Just as long as you're sure. That's all I want to hear."

"I'm sure. Not a problem."

"Where are you going to keep the envelopes with the money in them? You don't have saddlebags on your…ahh… Harley, do you?"

"Thanks for calling it a Harley. That's a first. And no, I don't have any saddlebag stuff. I looked at buying something to carry my shit in at a Harley store and they all cost over six hundred bucks. So, being the genius I am, I bought an Army backpack for thirty-nine ninety-five. Smart, huh?"

It was also a first for Ruben to be impressed with Hector's logic. But, most importantly, he was glad to see Hector had thought far enough ahead to at least have a backpack.

"Where's your messenger shirt?"

"At my apartment. I'll go put it on after I leave here. It's on the way."

"Okay, good. Just remember, the clients don't know you and have never seen you. The letter they received says you don't know the contents of the envelope they'll be giving you and that you'll be receiving instructions after you leave their office. Remember, the envelope will be addressed to Repeza Enterprises. No matter what happens, act innocent and uninformed. It'll go smoothly. Okay?"

An unusual calmness came over Hector as he said quietly, "We're about to be rich, aren't we?"

"Yes, indeed, we're about to be rich."

———

Miguel had a decision to make as Hector stood and walked away from the table. He knew from the extortion letters he had seen in Ruben's apartment that a messenger was going to pick up the cash payments today between 2:00 and 4:00. It was a little past 2:00 and he deduced Ruben's friend with the shaved head was going to be the messenger. Since Ruben was the object of the investigation, he decided to stick with him. He watched Ruben pay the waitress, then walk over to the bar and take a seat. It was time for Miguel, aka the Shadow, to earn his keep. This time it would not be in the shadows.

Miguel mentally took note of the bar area's twelve bar stools and five small tables, all facing the large plate glass windows. The view was breathtaking. A couple was seated at one end of the bar and Ruben had taken a seat towards the other end. Miguel casually walked to the bar and sat down. Two bar stools separated him from Ruben.

After ordering a Negra Modelo, Miguel looked over at Ruben, raised his bottle and said in a friendly way, "Here's to the good life."

Somewhat surprised, Ruben held up a glass of tequila over ice. "And it's about to get better."

"I like positive people and you sound like one. I just flew in from Mexico City for a little vacation. How about you?"

Draining his glass, Ruben smiled and lied. "Live here full time, but may be moving to Central America after a couple of big investments come through."

Sometimes it's impossible for a narcissist to answer a question without either embellishing it or outright lying. Under the influence of alcohol, a hardcore narcissist can weave a tall tale, especially to a total stranger.

And Miguel was a master at subtle interrogation. "Real estate?"

"Yeah, apartment buildings and cruise ships. I've been working on an adult cruise here in Cancun for a while. You know, more like consulting. Learning the basics of the cruise ship business. I may buy the ship in a month or so. Closing on a big apartment building real estate deal this afternoon."

"No kidding. Sounds exciting. Speaking of excitement, how difficult is it to find good looking women around here?"

Ruben wasn't wearing a wrist watch and was continually looking at the clock above the bar.

"Depends on how much time you have, you know. Lots of gringo babes at the bars around here and, of course, there's *Yucatan Escolta* about a half-mile from here."

"Humm, haven't heard of that one. Is it a bar?"

"Well, not exactly. You can get massages, escorts…anything you want for a price. In-call or out-call."

This was the first true and accurate statement Ruben had made during the conversation.

Unenthusiastically, Ruben asked, "What do you do in Mexico City?" He was ever so slightly starting to slur his words.

"I'm a movie producer. Find scripts, raise capital, bring together the resources for the production of movies."

Ruben sat straight up on the bar stool. This was a topic any narcissist would have an interest in exploring.

Waving his hand at the bartender and pointing at both his and Miguel's drinks, he implored, "Tell me more."

"I've been lucky in my career. One of the big hits I produced was *La Misma Luna* and I've worked with Salma Hayek, Demian Bichir, Inarritu and others." Miguel had used this line in previous cases and was very familiar with the Mexican movie industry.

"Hey, man, I'm not working tonight and tomorrow night is my last night on the adult cruise I mentioned. Want to come aboard and check out the chicks? I can get you on for free." Ruben drained most of his drink.

"I appreciate the offer, but I'm leaving tomorrow and headed back to Mexico City. I'll need to do my thing tonight."

Ruben enunciated as best he could, "Hang on for another hour or so and I know what we can do tonight."

Ruben waved at the bartender and again glanced at the clock above the bar. It was 3:10 and the train had pulled out of the station.

CHAPTER 37

Cancun, Mexico...Friday, June 4th
The two individuals sitting next to Boyd were still asleep when the plane landed and raced down the runway, soon followed by the roar of reverse thrusting engines slowing it to a taxiing pace at the Cancun International Airport. It was 4:30p.m., almost thirty-five minutes late. With over nineteen million passengers passing through the airport each year, Boyd didn't think these two would adversely impact the statistics if they stayed on the plane for the return trip to Dallas.

After the plane parked at the gate, Boyd stood, stretched, and waited to deplane. He changed the settings on his phone to "international roaming" for which he was paying thirty dollars a month, and checked for messages. He folded the two forms he had filled out on the flight, one for customs and the other for immigration, and stuck them in his waist band while he removed his carry-on suitcase from the overhead bin.

Since he was seated midway in the plane, the de-boarding process seemed excruciatingly long. He assumed it was because he was anxious to continue with the primary purpose of the trip.

Need to relax and get ready for the grueling process of the customs check and the car rental.

The noise was extreme in the airport. The mass of humanity in Terminal 3 was loud and excited, a shrillness of joy and frustration, a controlled bedlam reverberating off the walls and the ceiling making his ears ring. Boyd wondered if the excitement was about arriving or if it was about departing.

The first line was for the immigration check. Boyd knew from his extensive overseas travel about potential problems with passport expiration dates. His passport didn't expire for a little over a year, so that was not a problem. The line moved more quickly than Boyd expected and within fifteen minutes he had been given a thirty-day Mexican Tourist Permit. He was instructed by an immigration official to keep the permit with his passport and to have it when he returned to the airport.

The lines for the Customs stations appeared to be long, but seemed to be steadily moving forward. Boyd had nothing to declare so he joined a line and watched his bag pass through an electronic scanner. He was then instructed to press a button that activated a random traffic light. A green light meant you passed through and a red light indicated your luggage would be searched. Boyd learned from his previous trip to Cancun that you had a one-in-ten chance of getting the red light. Even though he had nothing to hide, he was relieved when he saw the color green.

Exiting the Customs area through sliding glass doors, Boyd was instantly met by a hoard of timeshare peddlers and individuals claiming to have the fastest and cheapest mode of transportation to anywhere in Cancun. He knew from his last trip to keep his head pointed forward and to ignore the desperate sharks.

The rental car experience had been stress-free and Boyd was pleasantly surprised to be in his Chevy Sonic after having arrived only forty-five minutes earlier. The car was full of gas and fully insured, the air conditioning system was on full blast, the directions the rental car company supplied were simple and straight forward. So far, so good.

Even though the air temperature was eighty-eight degrees, the tropical humidity was oppressive. The palm trees along Highway 307 were lazy and almost dead-still. The partly cloudy sky suggested the possibility of rain.

———

Jamie's Delta flight was making the final approach to the Cancun International Airport, right on time. He looked out the window and saw nothing but trees and green foliage. It looked as if the plane was going to land in a jungle, but suddenly the runway appeared.

The flight had been uneventful and Jamie was able to snooze for about an hour. The middle seat next to him had been vacant and the young lady in the aisle seat had been preoccupied with her cell phone most of the trip. Jamie assumed it was on airplane mode, since the plane hadn't crashed.

This was the first time he had been to Cancun. He was excited to be on this trip, not so much because it was an all-expenses-paid vacation to a Caribbean resort area, but because he would be able to assist his new friend in this adventure. Although he knew there was some amount of risk involved, this was not an issue...not an issue at all. He had never admired anyone as much as he admired and respected Boyd. The minute he saw Boyd put the cowboy on the sidewalk, he knew he had found a friend for life. Not because Boyd was mean or strong or anything like that, but because Boyd was the most driven, focused, decent person he had ever met. He would stand with Boyd under any and all circumstances.

Terminal 3 was buzzing with activity. Jamie pulled his carry-on bag behind him as he made his way to the immigration line. He presented his passport and received his Mexican Tourist Permit in short order.

Jamie's main concern regarded the Customs check, since the seco-barbital sodium vials were in his diabetic kit. There were six lines that seemed to be moving at a fairly fast pace. After his bag passed through a scanner, he handed an official, who happened to be an older woman, his Customs form which showed nothing to declare. The Customs agent studied the form and then looked at Jamie. With a slight frown, she nodded at the traffic light button, which was clearly labeled. Jamie had read an Internet information site regarding the Cancun airport and knew what to expect.

Unfortunately, the red light appeared and with it the requirement of having his baggage searched.

The dour agent pulled Jamie aside and asked him to open the bag. She sorted through the clothing items and observed the diabetes kit. She unzipped the black kit, glanced at the contents, including the three needles, and closed it. Next, she felt the top and sides of the bag, apparently looking for secret pockets. Finally, she motioned Jamie toward a set of sliding glass doors at the far end of the Customs area.

Relieved, Jamie emerged outside and was met by a loud, chattering group of porters, van drivers, travel reps and sales people handing out vouchers and brochures. Seeing a taxi stand straight ahead, he spoke in Spanish to a driver standing by his yellow and red vehicle. A few minutes later, he was on his way to the Casa Maya Hotel.

CHAPTER 38

Cancun, Mexico…Friday, June 4th
Hector changed into his new Jiffy Flash Service messenger shirt, slipped on his backpack and mounted his Harley, which was parked next to the steps of his apartment. It was 2:45p.m. and he planned on having a quick drink at a local dive bar near his apartment before starting the extortion pick-ups. He told himself he didn't drink for courage, he drank to relax.

The bar, appropriately enough, was named The Dive Bar. It was so dim inside, Hector had to feel his way to a bar-stool.

The bartender, an elderly man with a permanent scowl, looked at Hector and mumbled, "What's for you?"

"Shot of your best tequila."

As his eyes adjusted to the darkness, Hector looked around, not surprised that the entire bar was empty due to its limited seating and poor service. This was not a problem for Hector. He just needed to calm himself and prepare for this afternoon's activities. He and Ruben were about to be rich and own a bar on the beach.

It's going to be a hell of a lot nicer than this pit.

Tipping back the shot, he asked the bartender for one more...and then the thoughts regarding Estralita resurfaced. He knew it was useless talking to Ruben about her. She had pissed him off and would not be going to Nicaragua with them.

I'll see her tonight and give her the thousand dollars I got out of Ruben's apartment. She at least deserves that much.

After paying for his two tequila shots, Hector was back on his motorcycle with 3310 La Costa as his destination. He had memorized the locations of all four clients and knew exactly where he was going. Three of the businesses were within a few blocks of each other, and the fourth was the Ace Trucking Company which was only six or eight blocks away from the others. Senor Diaz, who owned Cancun Realty, was the first pickup and Hector had chosen him because he was such a wimp.

The video shows him almost jumping through the wall when Estralita screamed. Total Pussy!

The real estate business was located in a well kept, small strip center. There were six other businesses facing the street and all had facades painted in brown, blue or light red colors. Security bars covered most of the windows and doors.

It was 3:30p.m. when Hector walked through the door of Cancun Realty. Several desks were in an open area, with two occupied by females and one by an older man.

"How can we help you?" asked the male.

"I'm here to pick up an article from Senor Diaz." Hector was very pleased with his use of the word *article*.

A door at the back of the bullpen area opened and Senor Diaz appeared. He nervously surveyed the office and motioned to Hector.

As Hector entered the office, Senor Diaz closed the door and walked to the desk in the spacious room.

Trying to act calm, Senor Diaz, glanced at Hector, then the floor and then back at Hector. "You're here to pick up an envelope?"

"Yes, sir. I understand it's to be delivered to Repeza Enterprises." This may have been the first time Hector had ever called anyone "sir".

I can't believe I called him sir. He looks like he's about to piss himself.

"Where are you taking...." Diaz didn't complete the sentence, but instead reached into a desk drawer and produced a manila envelope.

Handing the parcel to Hector, Diaz simply said, "Take it."

"Thank you, sir."

No one seemed to notice Hector as he strutted through the office area to the front door, massaging the envelope and its contents. As he reached his motorcycle, he placed the envelope in his backpack. His hand started shaking as he realized what had just happened. He and Ruben were suddenly thirty-five thousand dollars richer.

Holy shit...thirty-five thousand! Did the wimp put the entire amount in the envelope? How thick is that much cash?

Hector was too excited to figure out how many bills it would take to make up thirty-five thousand. Did it consist of all hundred dollar bills or was it a mixture of various denominations? Off the top of his head, he couldn't figure how many hundred dollar bills it would take to make up thirty-five thousand, but he was sure it was a lot.

Damn, that was easy. The First Cancun Bank and Senor Constanzo are two blocks straight ahead and one block to the left.

The traffic was light as he pulled out of the parking lot and back onto La Costa.

No need to worry about being followed. Diaz is probably hiding behind his desk.

Turning left on Puertos, Hector could see the two story bank building ahead on the right side of the street. Parking was available in front of the white structure and on one side. Hector parked his motorcycle in a *20-minute* space and looked around the parking area as he knew James Bond would do.

Six or seven other cars, but nothing suspicious.

Hector entered the thick, plate-glass swinging door and surveyed the interior of the bank. Three tellers in their cages, one lady sitting at a desk on the right, two offices behind the desk and a security guard standing nearby on the left. Five customers were busy at the cages or on their way out of the bank.

Approaching the desk, Hector smiled and stated, "I'm here to pick up a package from Senor Constanzo."

The lady behind the desk looked up without speaking and pointed to the center office.

Hector walked toward the office and recalled videoing Senor Constanzo both times he visited Ruben's apartment. He was a conceited pretty-boy who tried to act smooth and important. His carefully coiffed hair and his fake smile, even when he was raping a knocked out gringo girl, made Hector frown and shake his head in disgust. Not from the rape itself, but because the guy thought he was so perfect.

Picking up this asshole's payment will be totally satisfying.

The office door was closed and Hector knocked politely.

"Come in!" The invitation was loud and abrupt.

Entering the office, Hector said innocently, "I'm here to pick up a parcel addressed to Repeza Enterprises."

"Who sent you?"

"My boss at Jiffy Flash."

"What's his name?"

"Ahh, Ricardo."

"Where're you taking it?"

"The parcel?"

"Of course...the parcel!" Constanzo was visibly irritated.

"Not sure, sir. I'm supposed to call in after I leave here. It seems like an unusual way to do business, but I only follow instructions."

Handing a manila envelope to Hector, Constanzo made a parting comment: "Take it and get out of my sight!"

"Yes, sir."

Carrying the envelope in both hands, Hector felt the contents and determined it was about as thick as the first envelope he had picked up a few minutes earlier. He stopped at his motorcycle and placed the envelope in the backpack.

Mother of Jesus, we're twice as rich as we were just a little while ago!

Slipping his arms through the straps, he mounted his bike and sped out of the parking lot. There was something about Constanzo's actions that bothered Hector. He seemed to be taking out his rage on an innocent delivery boy.

Total asshole!

Senor Ramos's Family Dentistry was next. Hector could have backtracked on Puertos and reached 2721 Bocapaila in less than five minutes, but due to his concern about Constanzo, he decided to go back into his James Bond mode.

He turned left on Puertos and then made a quick right on Avenida Kabah, one of the most congested streets in the downtown area. This was near the intersection in which the kidnapped girl from the orphanage jumped out of the car. This no longer bothered Hector. He and Ruben were now two steps closer to *Easy Street*.

He gunned the Harley and managed to maneuver himself to the far left lane of the three lane thoroughfare. After a block, he looked back over his right shoulder and moved once again into the right lane.

No way could anyone be following me. Too smart. Too fast.

Hector turned right on Bocapaila and started looking for the 2721 address. He saw a light blue, one story building with Family Dentistry displayed on both the side and the front before he noticed the address.

I'll soon be three times richer than I was when I started this trip.

The stand-alone building was situated close to the street. As Hector pulled into the narrow parking lot, he noticed several other cars in the lot, so he parked his bike next to the building and walked around to the front entrance, his backpack firmly in place. The sun was taking advantage of the partly cloudy sky and caused the backpack to stick to Hector's shirt and the shirt to stick to his back.

It's all worth it.

The waiting room was empty, as was the reception desk. The minute Hector entered the door Senor Ramos appeared from one of the rooms lining the far wall. He carried a manila envelope in his hand.

"Are you the messenger?"

Hector was starting to feel cocky and a little superior.

"Well, I'm a messenger. Don't know if I'm *the* messenger." He put emphasis on the word *the*.

"Are you here to pick up the Repeza envelope?"

Pointing to the name on his shirt, Hector responded, "Yep, Jiffy Flash here to pick up the Repeza parcel." He loved the word... parcel.

"Do you know Repeza?" Ramos's tone was quiet and even.

"Nope, I only work for Jiffy Flash. Don't know any of the clients." The word *client* had a double meaning for Hector, but it obviously didn't register with Senor Ramos.

A visual of the dentist flashed across Hector's mind. He was the polar opposite of Constanzo… short, fat with thick glasses. He spent more time looking at the unconscious girls' naked bodies than he did messing with them.

Kind of a pervert. I'm surprised he didn't check their teeth for cavities.

A patient, wearing a paper gown over his clothes, emerged from the same room as Ramos and made a coughing sound. With a look of surrender, Ramos handed the envelope to Hector.

Hector's confidence was at the highest level since the pick-ups began. He started to involuntarily giggle as he got back on the Harley. The last rube on the list was going to be the easiest. Senor Gallegas, the owner of Ace Trucking, was even less intimidating than Senor Diaz, the realtor. This was the client who had a premature ejaculation while he was taking off the girl's bra. It was the most interesting video of them all. He and Ruben had viewed it many times.

It only took a few minutes for Hector to turn onto Avenida Chichen Itza, another three-lane thoroughfare crowded with the Friday afternoon traffic. He knew there was absolutely no way anyone could be following him. In five minutes, he came to a traffic circle and made his way onto Palenque. He knew the trucking company was close to Highway 180 and soon saw it on the right side of the street.

There were several buildings and warehouses on the property, but a brown, one-story building seemed to house the main offices. Numerous eighteen-wheeler trucks and trailers were parked randomly around the warehouses.

Hector parked his motorcycle directly in front of the one-story. The door opened and who should appear but Senor Gallegas.

He must have been looking through one of the windows. What a jerk off!

Senor Gallegas was tall, skinny and mostly bald. He was a man of few words.

"Do you work for Repeza?"

"No sir, I work for Jiffy Flash. Don't know Repeza. We're just a messenger service." Hector was getting better and better at selling his innocence.

"I'll be talking to Emilio! This is not over."

"Who's that?" Hector was proud of his quick response.

Gallegas hesitated for a moment, studying Hector and then removed an envelope from his back waistband.

Hector put the envelope in his backpack, got on his bike and tried to multiply thirty-five thousand times four. He had made this small fortune in just over an hour. He was thrilled, elated, fulfilled.

———

It was almost 5:00p.m. on Friday and Chief Salazar was not in a good mood. Rumors were circulating about an investigation into the Cancun criminal justice system, especially the police force of which he was the head. The Mexican government was attempting to stop corruption in all of its major cities. The resort cities of Cancun and Puerto Vallarta were at the top of the list, and this was troublesome to Salazar.

The Chief had his fingers in a number of questionable pies: traffic-stop bribes, drunk and disorderly bribes, business protection bribes and the most problematic…accepting payoffs from known drug cartels in the Cancun area. The natives were restless, especially the natives reporting directly to Salazar. Spending time in a Mexican prison was something a police official feared.

He looked at his in-box as he walked toward the door. It was stacked high with envelopes, letters, reports and flyers. Hesitating, he picked up the top item, glanced at it and threw it back on the pile.

No fucking way I'm going to mess with all this stuff now. I'll come back tomorrow morning. Right now I need food and drink!

The manila envelope with the word **VERY**, in red block letters, still extended from near the bottom of Salazar's in-box, but the word **IMPORTANT** still remained hidden.

CHAPTER 39

Cancun...Friday, June 4th

Thirty minutes after leaving the airport, Boyd turned right onto Boulevard Kukulcan. It started as a six lane thoroughfare, three lanes on each side of a median filled with lush green vegetation and palm trees.

He was amazed at the sheer beauty of the roadway, the median and the view on both sides. Mexican officials had obviously paid close attention to the appearance and maintenance of this cash-cow resort section of Cancun.

He remembered from his visit of a few months ago the stories regarding the Nicupte lagoon on the right. Some environmentalists referred to it as the "Nicupte Sewer", but nonetheless, it provided a stunning sight.

A mile later the six-story white towers of the Casa Maya Hotel appeared on the left. Flags from seven countries flew from the top of the bright blue portico protecting the entrance to the hotel.

The extravagant service began as Boyd took his parking pass from the attendant. This would be another twelve to fifteen dollars a day hidden charge over and above the quoted daily room rate. This did not bother Boyd in the least. He was prepared for the extra expenses associated with parking, tipping, the honor bar in his room, Wi-Fi, television movies and a host of other surprises that come with vacation travel. He was on a mission and being cost conscious was not part of the plan.

Even though he was in the shade of the portico, Boyd could feel the sweat starting to form on his brow. His car thermometer had displayed eighty-eight degrees only thirty minutes ago, but the heat and humidity seemed to be working overtime now.

Hello, Cancun in June.

Boyd walked into the spacious hotel lobby and observed the opulent surroundings and décor. The upbeat, excited chatter of the individuals milling about was somehow comforting. The chairs and couches in the center of the lobby were occupied by vacationers looking at maps, restaurant guides and other types of advertisements. Children, and some adults, were dressed for a late afternoon on the beach.

La Buena Pinta, the lobby bar, was on the left side of the lobby across from the check-in desk. A casual looking restaurant was adjacent to the bar and already had a few patrons at this time of day.

Three clerks were busy with customers and the fourth, a friendly male clerk, assisted with Boyd's check-in. He assured Boyd that his fifth-story room had an ocean view, a king-size bed and was indeed fit for a king. The clerk then took Boyd on a verbal tour of the hotel: the private beach, three restaurants, a swim-up bar at one of the three pools, the night shows and the daily activities programs. Boyd declined the offer to make reservations for any of the night shows and walked over to the lobby bar, pulling his carry-on suitcase behind him.

Seating himself at the bar, he asked, "Do you serve George Dickel?"

The dark haired young lady behind the tiki themed bar tilted her head and responded with another question, "Is that a brand of rum?"

"No ma'am, it's a Tennessee sipping whiskey."

"We have Jack Daniels. Will that be okay?"

"Sure. On the rocks."

The bar area was bustling with young adults, all in vacation mode. He judged the average age to be somewhere between twenty and thirty.

I may be old…but not out. Yet.

The bartender returned with his drink and Boyd asked, "I really like the décor in here. What exactly does *La Buena Pinta* mean?"

"Well, it's kind of a play on words. If something is *tiene buena pinta*, it means that it 'looks good'. Since *pinta* is the Spanish word for pint and *buena* is the Spanish word for good, a more literal translation would be 'good pint.' Get it? Pint of beer."

"Got it," Boyd said, smiling and poking at the ice cubes in his glass.

Glancing at his watch, Boyd saw that it was almost 6:00. Since Jamie's plane had been scheduled to land at 5:20, he assumed Jamie would make it to the hotel within the hour. He was taking a taxi, so that would cut some of the travel time. Miguel Burbano would be arriving in the lobby at 8:00p.m. and had been instructed to call Boyd's cell number.

Might as well wait for Jamie here and then we can go up to our rooms together. It's not as if we can't be seen together. The main thing is that the airline travel and hotel check-in are separate.

Boyd looked around the bar at the tiki theme. He knew from his business travel to the South Pacific that in Polynesian mythology tiki meant the "first man on earth."

This is southern Mexico. Close enough.

The bamboo siding on the bar and the bamboo chairs were only the beginning of the tiki theme in the lounge area. Lush green foliage hung from the ceiling and walls. A large painting of an erupting volcano was prominent at one end of the bar. Well placed red and blue lights added to the atmosphere. The view from the large plate glass windows across from the bar was even more spectacular than the desk clerk had described: swimming pools, a white sand beach and then the turquoise waters of the Caribbean as far as one could see. Boyd fully appreciated the view and the atmosphere even though dark feelings about Cancun still lingered based on his previous visit.

"How about another Jack Daniels?" The experienced bartender was on top of her game. Even though there were several other patrons seated at the bar, all of them felt as if they were getting personalized service.

"Sounds good. Say, how far is the Playa Langosta Pier from here?"

"Only about a five-minute walk."

"Thanks. Oh, is the Blue Turtle Bar near there?"

"Also close. The Turtle is another few minutes past the pier. Plan to go there?"

"A friend of mine said the pier is a good place to see some interesting boats and the Blue Turtle is a popular beach-side bar."

"Right on both counts."

On one hand, the sights, sounds and relaxed atmosphere of this resort paradise created a sense of calm in Boyd's rational mind. The flip side of the same equation brought back the vivid memories of his last trip to Cancun and the events that followed. He had received the call from Sally on Wednesday afternoon, a day he will never forget.

"Hey babe, what's going on?"

His wife's quiet sobbing told him it was not good news. "I'm at the Richardson Medical Center. You need to get here as soon as possible."

"What happened! Are you okay!"

"It's not me, it's Jenny. She...she...had a miscarriage."

The shock jolted through Boyd's body like an electrical charge. He involuntarily shook his head and couldn't speak for several seconds.

"What room are you in?"

"Three twenty-five."

Boyd arrived at the hospital and went directly to the room. Sally was waiting in the hall with a stricken look on her face.

"She was raped in Cancun the last night we were there. She says she wasn't sure what happened or how it happened. She must have been drugged."

"Why didn't she tell us?"

"She was scared, unsure, ashamed... I don't know."

A few days later, Boyd talked to Jenny on two separate occasions and came away completely convinced that she had been drugged and raped the last night of their Cancun vacation. Sally came away convinced that this was the result of permissive parenting on his part.

Boyd wasn't concerned about the effects of the "revenge paradox" anymore, not even the risk factor associated with this trip. He had developed a more complete understanding of his true inner self. The things that make him tick. He couldn't put a label on it, he couldn't describe it in a written report and he certainly couldn't verbalize it in a cogent way.

His feelings and actions of the past few days, actually the past few months, hinted at his real being. He was the sum of all his experiences. He had evolved to this stage over a long period of time and he was prepared to live with it.

I am who I am. Can't change.

CHAPTER 40

Cancun…Friday, June 4th

It wasn't often that Ruben got drunk. Getting drunk on alcohol was one thing, but Ruben was also drunk on greed, power and the distinct possibility of being in the movies. Or at least he thought he might get a chance to be in the movies.

Ruben again looked at the clock and his somewhat clouded mind determined it was almost 5:00p.m.

Traffic. Lots of traffic on Friday afternoon. He'll be here soon.

Summoning the bartender, Ruben ordered his fifth drink of the afternoon, another tequila-on-the-rocks.

"Okay, so you really think the movie business is not out of the question for me?"

Miguel took a sip of his third beer and assured him, "Not at all. As we discussed, there are many opportunities to invest in new movie ventures, and in your case, maybe even to become an actor. It's not easy, but you certainly have the *it* factor. Good looks and on-screen charisma are critical to an acting career and you have that in spades."

"Humm. Never really thought about that before, but it makes sense."

"I've met many actors and have referred several novices to the studios. You would be the closest to a sure thing I've ever seen." Miguel was pouring it on and Ruben was drunk enough to be extremely gullible. "I'm currently producing a film in which you might be able to get a small part. Good way to get your feet wet."

"Really!"

"Yes, indeed. Say, you mentioned you may be moving to Central America. When are you leaving and how will I be able to get in contact with you?"

"I'm leaving for Nicaragua this coming Wednesday. Let's trade cell numbers so we can stay in touch." Ruben's mind was working overtime and he was rushing his words.

Getting a pen from the bartender, Miguel wrote a series of numbers on a napkin. Handing it to Ruben, he pointed at the numbers and said, "Since you'll be calling from outside Mexico, dial the country code followed by a one and then the area code and then my number. Okay?"

Handing the pen and another napkin to Ruben, he added, "Here, give me your number. We'll make contact within the next two weeks, one way or the other."

Ruben scribbled his cell number on the napkin and returned it to Miguel, not even trying to hide his drunken grin. He glanced at the entrance to the bar and immediately stood, rattling his stool against the bar. Hector was standing there with his backpack in his hand and the biggest smile Ruben had ever seen.

"Back in a minute."

Miguel could see Ruben and Hector talking briefly and then hugging. They danced around, still hugging like long lost friends. With his back to the bar, Ruben took something from the bag and studied the contents.

Ruben was talking to Hector and looking at Miguel as they approached the bar.

Slurring every word, Ruben said, "This is my business associate, Hector Acosta. We closed today on that real estate deal I mentioned."

Satisfied that Hector was on board, he looked again at Miguel and said quizzingly, "Say, we've been drinking all afternoon and I don't even know your name. I'm Ruben, what's yours?"

"Renaldo. Renaldo Del Toro. Glad to meet you both."

Ruben was both drunk and giddy. He flashed his best movie star smile at Miguel and then waved at the bartender, trying to get his attention.

"Hector, my friend, if that goddamn bartender ever shows up, get a drink. Need to use my phone."

Ruben fumbled with his phone for a couple of minutes and finally came up with the number he wanted to call. After listening for a couple of seconds, he firmly commanded, "I need three of your best-looking girls. Right away."

After listening to the reply, he clarified, "I don't care what they cost. I want the top of the line. Young, beautiful and willing. Okay?"

Looking at Miguel, again with his best Ryan Gosling grin, he resumed his phone conversation, "Fine, no problem. We're sitting at the bar in the Krystal Cancun Hotel. You know, only a few blocks from where you're located. Have them meet us here. Got it?"

As Hector stirred his drink, he asked, "Who was that?"

"*Yucatan Escolta.* Tonight we party! Right, Renaldo?"

Raising his beer bottle, Miguel agreed enthusiastically. "Tonight we party."

———

The girls arrived within forty-five minutes. Ruben introduced himself and asked for their names. After a short amount of deliberation, he chose one for himself and assigned the other two "escorts" to Miguel and Hector.

All three ladies wore copious amounts of makeup and were dressed provocatively. Staying seated, Hector took Contessa's hand and immediately started telling her about the feedlot he owned. Raven stood behind Miguel and began massaging his neck and shoulders. Bambi, the long haired, long-legged bleached blonde, collected the up-front cash from Ruben and gently kissed him on the cheek.

"You're the luckiest babes in Cancun, for sure. We're in the movie business, investments and all kinds of cool stuff. Really, you're really lucky!" Not only was Ruben drunk, he was having more and more trouble putting together a coherent sentence.

Bambi, in her sexiest voice, replied, "Well, we get to be lucky for three hours, and so do you. That's how long you paid for."

Hector did his best to catch up on the drinking and celebrating. Less than an hour had passed since he arrived at the bar, and he had already drained three drinks and was ordering another for himself and one for Contessa.

Speaking loudly to the bartender, Hector bellowed, "Make 'em stiff." And then turning to Contessa, he explained, "Get it. Make 'em stiff? You know, like stiff."

Contessa, doing her best to get into the spirit of the evening, said evenly, "I like stiff."

Making sure the backpack was still between his feet, Hector grabbed Ruben's arm and said loudly, "Hey, my babe likes stiff!"

All the tables in the lounge area were filled and only two bar stools remained vacant. A couple at a nearby table got up and slowly walked toward the main lobby, staring at the raucous celebration occurring at the bar. Hector noticed the annoyed looks on their faces and stood up.

Ruben put his hand on Hector's arm and mumbled, "We're rich. Fuck 'em."

Contessa, who had been standing since arriving at the bar, leaned closer to Hector and gently bit his earlobe. "It's okay baby. Just stay stiff."

The drinks kept coming and Ruben and Hector continued their intimate conversations with their two ladies. Patrons at nearby tables were either amused or repulsed by the scene.

Miguel was still nursing his third beer and quizzing Raven about her background and her job at the *Yucatan Escolta*. She seemed to be open and honest about her profession, although not particularly proud of it. Miguel always went out of his way to gather "facts and contacts."

Miguel had given Raven his seat and was now standing behind her. He said to Ruben cordially, "Raven and I are going over to my hotel. Remember what we discussed. And what do I owe you for this evening?"

Ruben struggled with the answer. "Nothing. Not a thing. Call me and I'll come see you in Mexico City. You can repay me there."

"I will, for sure. You and Hector take it easy."

Hector fist-bumped Miguel and returned to his discussion with Contessa, his feet still firmly planted on his backpack.

Miguel took Raven by the arm and walked out of the lounge into the lobby. Handing her a one-hundred-dollar bill, he said, "Enjoyed talking to you. Just out of curiosity, what's your real name, and where are you from?"

"Diane. I grew up in Scottsdale, Arizona."

"You seem honest and straight forward. I like that. Have a good life."

"But...but."

"Take a couple of hours off."

———

Boyd was deep in thought at the tiki bar when a young man quietly sat down next to him and spoke to the bartender, "I'll have a George Dickel on the rocks."

The dark haired bartender cocked her head in surprise. "You've got to be kidding me! That's the second order for that particular whiskey I've had in the past hour!"

Boyd, with a big smile, turned and addressed Jamie. "Good to see you partner. Got in early, huh?"

"Oh, so you know each other. I thought I had just observed the most unbelievable coincidence ever!"

Still smiling, Boyd said, "Give him a Jack Daniels and put it on my tab."

"Yeah, the plane landed twenty minutes early. Pretty amazing."

Boyd and Jamie engaged in small talk for a while and as their drinks were almost finished, Boyd said in a low voice, "Let's get settled in our rooms and then meet in the lobby at a few minutes before eight. Miguel will be here by then."

———

Boyd exited the elevator and spotted Jamie looking at the view from a nearby window. As they walked through the lobby, they saw Miguel Burbano sitting in a hotel chair.

Miguel rose as the two approached and was the first to speak. "We meet again. Slightly different environment."

"Indeed it is. Miguel, this is Jamie Rodriguez, a good friend of mine."

After Miguel and Jamie had exchanged pleasantries, Boyd looked around the lobby and was comfortable no one else was close enough to hear their conversation.

"Miguel, anything of interest turn up during your brief visit?"

"I think you'll be pleased. I've been drinking with Ruben Repeza and his bozo friend, Hector, for the last few hours. Let me catch you up on my findings of the past three days."

Boyd's eyes widened when Miguel mentioned he had been drinking with Ruben and Hector.

Damn, this guy is good!

"I'll try to succinctly verbalize my short stay. And, if you want, I'll type up a report for you."

"No need for a written report this time."

"Okay, my first goal was, of course, to be sure that Ruben was still here and working on the cruise boat. I followed him to the boat Wednesday afternoon and then doubled back and let myself into his apartment for a look-see. He left me a nice present on his kitchen table."

Jamie grinned and nodded his head in approval.

Miguel took his phone out of his pocket and found the pictures he had taken of the extortion letters.

He handed his phone to Boyd and instructed, "Look at this letter to a Senor Diaz. There are three more just like it and then a fifth which I'll show you in a minute."

Boyd read the letter and handed the phone to Jamie.

Slowly shaking his head, Boyd hissed, "I think I see where this is going. Very troubling."

"Holy shit," was Jamie's only reply.

"And you say there's a fifth letter?"

Taking his phone from Jamie, Miguel clicked on the picture of the extortion note to Police Chief Salazar.

Before handing the phone to Boyd, Miguel explained, "The first four extortion letters are all just alike and delivered Wednesday afternoon. Since Ruben was on the cruise boat, it must have been his buddy, Hector, who delivered them. As you can see, the demand letters totaled one hundred forty big ones!"

"It seems unbelievable they think they can pull this off!" Boyd's sensibilities were rattled. "How did they manage to video these guys?"

"Simple. They have a video camera in the bedroom closet. Ruben's buddy must have been doing the video work. I almost got a look at the closet, but I was interrupted and had to make a quick exit from the apartment."

Boyd pressed on. "By the way, someone named Emilio is mentioned in the letter. Who's he?"

"Glad you asked. As you noticed, Emilio appears to be associated with a *farmacia*, so I started calling all the pharmacies in the hotel zone and the downtown area. I got a hit on the fifth call. Pure luck. Emilio Repeza is the owner of a *farmacia* on Avenida Coba near downtown. Could be Ruben's father, uncle, brother, cousin or whatever. Not sure about his connection to this whole thing."

"My man…you are thorough!" Jamie's respect for Miguel continued to grow.

Handing the phone to Boyd again, Miguel continued, "Now, look at this letter."

Boyd read the letter and exclaimed, "No way! They're going to extort a hundred thousand dollars from the Cancun Chief of Police!"

"Appears so." Miguel was all business.

Shaking his head, Boyd handed the phone to Jamie.

Jamie read the note and slowly nodded. "It would be interesting to see those DVDs. For some reason, I'm having trouble wrapping my head around all this."

Miguel retrieved his phone from Jamie and continued. "Now, I'm certain they've succeeded in shaking down the first four individuals. I followed Ruben this afternoon to the bar in the Krystal Cancun Hotel and later introduced myself to him. He thinks I'm a movie producer from Mexico City…but that's a story for another time. Anyway, we both had several drinks and later Hector showed up with a backpack, which I believe was full of cash he had picked up today. They high-fived, hugged and carried on like a couple of excited teenagers. This led to Ruben paying for three escorts to meet us at the bar…but that's another story for another time."

Boyd had been listening intently and with a hint of a grin said, "Sounds as if you had a full afternoon."

Without missing a beat, Miguel plowed on. "I have a number of facts that will interest you. Ruben's final trip on the Devilfish will be tomorrow night. He offered me a free ride if I was going to be in town. He mentioned that he and Hector were moving to Nicaragua this Wednesday, and I assume they'll be hauling ass after they pick up the hundred thousand mentioned in the last extortion letter. That's a sure thing since this is a police chief they're trying to extort."

With his thumb and forefinger on his chin, Boyd said as much to himself as to Miguel, "How can they get away with this?"

Tilting his head, Miguel replied, "Now, I haven't asked and I don't want to know why you want this information about Mr. Repeza, but here's some more salient information."

Boyd raised his eyebrows and gently pressed his lips together. He had never mentioned the purpose of his trip to Miguel or the reason the information had been requested. However, he was sure Miguel could read between the lines and figure out what was going on.

Miguel continued. "Since the letter and DVD will be delivered to the police chief on Monday, I'd bet my bottom dollar Ruben will be vacating his apartment by sometime on Sunday, maybe early Monday morning at the latest. He doesn't seem concerned about the other four guys."

"Makes sense." Jamie had been listening intently.

Boyd leaned back on the couch and whispered, "Yep."

"This is just a guess, but I have a feeling Ruben, his friend and the two escorts will end up at his apartment tonight. How long the party will last, I don't know. So, again just a guess, but Ruben will probably stay at his apartment for the next two, maybe three nights before leaving Cancun for good."

"Miguel, this is more information than I hoped for," said Boyd in a sincere tone. "You're truly a professional and I can't tell you how much this is appreciated."

"I'd be happy to stay over another night or two if you prefer."

"No, you've been of tremendous assistance. Go ahead and take your flight back to Dallas in the morning. I'll talk with you next week."

Handing Boyd a folded sheet of paper, Miguel said, "I won't send you a written report, but at least let me give you this. It includes the address and directions to Ruben's apartment from here, the layout of the parking area at the apartment, a description of his SUV, the address of the *farmacia* we discussed and a description of Hector, Ruben's running mate. Also, Hector rides a Harley Davidson motorcycle, which may or may not be parked somewhere in the parking lot."

Unfolding the piece of paper, Boyd studied it for a moment.

"Ahh, one other thing about the apartment building." Miguel felt obligated to impart as much information as possible. "Based on my visits to this apartment complex, let me point out something." He pointed to the detailed drawing. "Ruben only uses the covered parking space behind his apartment, which is only about fifteen steps from his kitchen door. Now look at the other side of the building. It has no covered parking, but there is ample space to park."

Boyd nodded.

Miguel continued with a sly look. "Ruben's apartment has a door in the living room that opens into a central hallway." Again pointing at a detail on the drawing, he said, "The hallway is about forty yards long and leads to a door that opens out to the parking area on the other side of the complex." Hesitating, and then looking directly at Boyd, he finished. "If I were going to Ruben's apartment, I would park on the far side of the building and walk around to the kitchen door entrance. As you can see, his apartment number is sixty-one."

Boyd smiled as if to acknowledge Miguel's understanding of the situation.

Standing, Miguel extended his hand to Boyd. "It's been a pleasure working with you." Turning to Jamie, he said, "Nice to have met you, Jamie."

With a look of respect, Jamie said, with a big grin, "Same. Absolutely the same. And, just out of curiosity, how long did it take you to pick the lock on Ruben's back door?"

Miguel responded good-humoredly, "Hate to give away company secrets, but I would say it took…ahh…eight to ten seconds… tops. Think you can beat that?"

Jamie shrugged and smiled.

CHAPTER 41

Cancun...Friday, June 4th

Ruben leaned over, putting his arm around Hector's shoulder, and spoke in a loud whisper, "Okay, tell me about it." He was shaking with excitement.

Bambi and Contessa were talking to the bartender trying to determine their next free drink of choice.

"Easy as pie. I'll have to say, you're a fucking genius! Not a hitch. All four of those pussies were pussies. How many times did I say pussies? Whatever." Hector was seriously drunk.

"You mean they just handed over the cash with no problems!" It was more a statement of astonishment than a question.

"I didn't stop and count it after each pickup; however, I could tell from the look on every one of their goddamn faces... it's all there!" This was the most perfectly constructed sentence Hector had put together in the past hour.

"You mean they all handed it over without any shit! Even Senor Constanzo? I figured he would be kicking and screaming."

"He was an asshole, but he gave it up like all the rest. Once a pussy, always a pussy. Right?"

"I just can't believe it went so smoothly. Can't believe it! And you're sure no one followed you?"

"Fuck no. I'm slicker than shit and smell twice as good." Hector was losing control of his cool sayings.

Ruben mumbled, "We did it."

Hector looked down at the backpack between his feet and added, "We're so fucking rich. We are rich motherfuckers. Right?" There was a direct correlation between the amount of alcohol Hector consumed and the curse words he used in a sentence.

Ruben removed his arm from Hector's shoulder and yelled at the top of his lungs, "Finally, we did it! Finally, we did it!"

The bar had become filled almost to capacity with Friday evening patrons. At Ruben's outburst, heads turned.

The bartender leaned over the bar and said softly to Ruben, "Sir, I think it's time you paid up and moved on. I've been getting complaints about you and your friends."

Too drunk to be insulted, Ruben mumbled, "You know, me and my friends were about to just get ready to leave right now…probably."

Hector chimed in, "Pussies."

"What do you think, Bambi? I think it's time all four of us go to my apartment, you think?" Ruben was in charge even when totally inebriated.

Bambi whispered into Ruben's ear as he was paying for the afternoon's drinking spree, "You're about out of time. Want to sign up for two more hours?"

A little too loud, Ruben said, "What the...you got a meter up your ass! Damn sure. I'll pay you when we get to my place. Okay?"

A young couple sitting next to Ruben looked at each other and silently shook their heads in disgust.

Hector had a momentary thought about Estralita. They hadn't talked since he accidentally mentioned that he and Ruben were leaving Cancun without her.

I'll take her the thousand dollars tonight after we finish with these two bitches. Maybe tomorrow morning. Whatever.

Ruben was still in command as he blurted out orders. "Okay, the girls ride with me to the apartment and Hector can take his Harley." He had a stupid grin on his face and repeated, *"Harley."*

Hector matched the grin, and said, "I'll take the Harley and the backpack and follow you there. See you shortly." Pressing against Contessa, he softly murmured, "I'll stay stiff."

———

Hector walked into the kitchen just as Ruben was pouring tequila shots for the foursome. It was now almost 9:00p.m. and the two escorts had drunk more than their fair share of alcohol that afternoon.

Handing out the shots, Ruben held up his shot glass and proposed what he considered a toast, "Here's to the two luckiest women in Cancun.

You get the honors, I mean honor, of being with me and my friend, whose both of us richer than shit. Or something like that."

"Fucking right." Hector tipped his glass as best he could and half of the contents trickled down his chin into his goatee. He was still wearing the backpack as he walked into the bedroom and closed the door. Using his key, he opened the closet door and placed the backpack on the floor.

Walking back into the kitchen, he motioned to Ruben who was standing behind Bambi with his hands around her waist.

"Come here, bro. You need to see what's in my thirty-nine-dollar backpack." Hector pointed toward the bedroom while wobbling his head back and forth like a small child.

Nodding in understanding, Ruben said, "I'll do it." Walking into the bedroom, he added, "We're so goddamn rich I can't believe it!"

"We're more richer than a big pile of money." Hector's vocabulary was on a downhill slide.

Ruben took one of the envelopes from the bag and retrieved several hundred dollar bills. In a surprisingly well thought out bit of logic, he stated, "Yes, we are rich, my brother. The amount of money we're paying these whores tonight would feed a poor family of four for three or four months."

"Fuck the poor family and all their babies, we earned our riches." The logic of life continued to elude Hector.

Contessa finished her tequila shot and placed the glass on the counter. She turned around, reached for a chair and projectile vomited all over her arm and the kitchen table. Bambi grabbed a towel from the counter and wiped at Contessa's face.

Hector viewed the sight from the bedroom door and hollered, "Goddamn, woman! Where am I going to sit to eat my cereal in the morning? This is what I get for hanging around with a bunch of pussies!" His new favorite word.

He walked over to Contessa, who was still leaning over the table, and grasped her in an awkward Heimlich maneuver. Lifting her off the floor, she vomited again. This time on her leg and on Hector's shoes.

Hector was too drunk to care about the collateral damage. Instead he declared, "I'm going to fuck you like a runaway stallion. Get ready, bitch." Hector obviously didn't know the difference between a stallion and a mare...or at this point he didn't care.

Ruben walked into the kitchen and was too drunk and too exhilarated from the day's adventures to care about the vomit or anything else happening in his apartment. He was on his way to self-actualization.

Hector led Contessa to the couch and started removing her blouse.

Ruben took Bambi by the hand and staggered toward the bedroom. "Come on babe, it's time to feed the poor."

———

"Miguel is amazing. How did he accomplish so much in such a short period of time?" Jamie had become a big fan of Miguel Burbano.

Boyd and Jamie were still sitting in the lobby of the Casa Maya Hotel after Miguel had gone.

361

Deep in thought, Boyd said, "He's good. Here are my thoughts as how to proceed. See if you agree." Boyd was comfortable with bringing Jamie more and more into the plan.

"Let's hear it."

"First of all, I need to pick up the tattoo equipment from the FedEx store tomorrow morning. They open at 8:00. Then I need to acquire a few items…duct tape, shaving equipment, latex gloves and a magic marker."

"There should be plenty of pharmacies and supermarkets in the downtown area, maybe around the hotel zone," Jamie said, thinking out loud.

Boyd raised his eyebrows and tilted his head. "Actually, there's a Walmart not far from here. It's just off Calle Mayapan near downtown. We went there on our previous trip and bought a case of bottled water. They should have everything I need, plus, it's only five or ten minutes from the FedEx location."

"How do you know all this stuff?"

"Simple. Internet maps. I chose the FedEx location based on where we're staying."

"Excellent." Jamie just shook his head in admiration for Boyd's attention to detail.

"Okay, based on what Miguel said, Ruben and his buddy have successfully extorted four individuals and have one to go…the big fish. Also, Miguel thinks Ruben will be staying in his apartment for two, maybe three more days. And for some reason, Ruben will be working on his cruise boat tomorrow night. Can't quite figure that one."

Jamie leaned closer to Boyd and said, "These two guys either have big brass balls or else they're totally stupid."

"Yep. It seems to be working though. Whatever it is."

"I'm going with stupid. Humm, sounds like something on a tee shirt."

It was a typical Friday night. The hotel lobby was busy with tourists busily checking in at the front desk, looking at advertisements on the walls and wandering toward the lobby bar determining where to go and what to do. The possibilities were endless.

Boyd was deep in concentration and then said quietly, "The plan was to culminate this visit day after tomorrow, on Sunday. Now, I'm starting to wonder if that might be a day too late. What do you think?"

Hesitating for a second, Jamie suggested, "I realize you've put considerable thought into this little venture. After listening to Miguel's report, I feel we should look for the first opportunity that presents itself... starting the minute you get the tattoo equipment and the other supplies. Tomorrow morning. Tomorrow afternoon. Tomorrow night when he returns from his boat trip. First opportunity."

"I agree. I'd prefer Sunday, but the first opportunity that presents itself seems to be the most practical, assuming all the conditions are right."

"Okay, okay...let's think this through." Jamie was trying to apply logic to the situation. "They are with a couple of escorts tonight, who probably charge by the hour. They may or may not be spending the night at Ruben's apartment. His friend, what's his name, Hector, may also be spending the night. But no matter what, all of them will likely be leaving sometime tomorrow morning. Right?"

"I'm with you." Boyd slowly nodded in agreement.

Jamie continued his line of reasoning, saying, "We should be finished with our errands at the FedEx store and Walmart by around ten o'clock. We could drive to Ruben's apartment complex and see what's going on."

Looking at his watch, Boyd said, "Good plan. Now, since I'm an old man, I need to get some shut eye. It's been a long week. How about we meet for breakfast at the restaurant by the pool at seven-fifteen?"

"Even though I'm fifty or sixty years younger than you, I totally agree. Bedtime it is."

———

It was 11:00p.m. when Ruben walked out of the bedroom, sans clothes, proud of his body and unashamed of revealing it to Hector and Contessa, who were entangled on the couch, totally nude.

Bambi entered the room, also naked, and sleepy-eyed. In a matter-of-fact business-like tone, she said, "We've got to get back to work. The night is young. Take us back to our car at the hotel."

Shaking Hector, Ruben said, "Get up big boy. You've got one more errand tonight."

Hector groggily complained, "Don't think they'll both fit on my Harley."

"Take my SUV. Hurry, before they charge us for another hour. Then come back and spend the night here."

Immediately alert, Hector stood and loudly proclaimed, "Goddamn, we're richer than a couple of motherfuckers. Right!"

———

Estralita walked into her living room, carrying a towel in one hand and a syringe in the other. She placed the towel on a short, thread-bare couch and the syringe on an end table. She went slowly, deliberately to the kitchen, which was essentially part of the living space, and took a bottle of pills from a cabinet above the sink. The label on the bottle indicated the brand name, the dosage and the name of the pharmacy from which it was purchased... Oxy IR, 20 milligrams and Farmacias del Barato, Uncle Emilio's pharmacy. The IR indicated "immediate release" and the caution that came with the bottle indicated no more than one pill in a six-hour period.

She swallowed two pills without water and walked back to the couch. She took off her shorts, panties and bra and reclined on the towel. It only took five minutes for the warm feeling to arrive, followed by a complete sense of euphoria. However, her thoughts were not on the floating feeling she was experiencing, but instead on Hector and Ruben. She considered them family, the family she never had... friends, lovers, pals. They were a team. Hector was special and she thought he would always be there for her, but instead he planned to leave Cancun without her. And now they were probably going to die at the hands of Chief Salazar. Maybe they were already dead.

With barely the strength or concentration to reach over her shoulder, she felt for the syringe on the end table. It contained Mexican Brown heroin she had mashed and mixed in cold water. Estralita had tried this drug several times in the past and didn't believe she was addicted. The first time she used it, she felt free, totally free of the world and all its problems. That's the feeling she needed now.

She could see Hector's image as she pumped her fist and injected the liquid into a barely visible vein in her arm. He was shaking his head and screaming something she couldn't hear. Then he smiled and walked away.

Instead of feeling free, this time Estralita felt as if she were trapped in a cage, her thoughts strangled. Her breathing became shallow, followed by muscle spasms in her abdomen and her legs. She tried to focus on the image of Hector, but he was gone. An uncontrollable seizure gripped her entire body and then she relaxed. Her dilated pupils announced the end to her journey.

CHAPTER 42

Cancun...Saturday, June 5th

Boyd opened the drapes in his sixth floor room and was met by a beautiful day and a panoramic view of the Caribbean...or perhaps it was the Gulf of Mexico.

Caribbean or Gulf? What the heck.

During his previous visit to Cancun, he and his family had been staying at the Riu Palace Hotel on the northeastern point of the Hotel Zone. One day at the beach, another guest pointed to the northeast and stated that the waters of the Caribbean and the Gulf mixed together there. Later looking on a map, Boyd could see how the argument could be made; however, all subsequent documentation pointed to Cancun being on the Caribbean Sea.

Boyd slid open the window as far as it would go. The sun had barely made its presence known in the east and the early morning breeze was badgering the palms. It was nearing 7:00 and almost time to meet Jamie for breakfast, but he was having trouble blocking out memories from over five months ago.

Time to brush my teeth and get on with life.

Boyd spotted Jamie standing at the entrance to the restaurant as he walked down the steps and maneuvered his way around one of the swimming pools. There was no one swimming or sunbathing at this time of morning, although there appeared to be several couples already taking part in the breakfast buffet. The palapa styled restaurant was open and airy with a spacious buffet line.

"Hey, did you have any trouble getting to sleep?" Jamie was in his usual good mood.

"Let me tell you, there's no comparison between the bed I slept in last night and the bed in the doublewide. This one felt twice as long, twice as wide and ten times more comfortable! When I slid between the sheets, it was like lowering a box in the ground. To more fully answer your question, no, I did not have a problem getting to sleep. How about you?"

Jamie tried to be serious. "It was too darn quiet. I'm used to barking dogs, screaming kids and bumps in the night."

Boyd chuckled. "We'll see about getting you a room closer to the street."

A young man asked to see their key cards and then escorted them to a table at the edge of the seating area. The ever-present Caribbean still in view.

After they ordered coffee, Boyd pointed toward the buffet line and suggested, "Well, let's start the day the right way...with a plate of papaya, scrambled eggs and bacon."

"Lead the way."

Small talk dominated the breakfast conversation. Plans had been made and the mission was clear. Time to execute.

Finishing his second cup of coffee, Boyd asked, "Okay, partner, ready to get on with it?"

"You know I am." Jamie had a determined look on his face.

It was 8:15 when Boyd tipped the car attendant and got behind the wheel of the rental car. He knew exactly where he was going since he had studied the map of the hotel zone and the downtown section of Cancun.

Fifteen minutes later Boyd turned left off Avenida Uxmal and the familiar blue and white FedEx sign signaled the first destination of the morning. The store was situated in the middle of a small strip-shopping center, a ladies' cosmetics store on one side and a vacant space on the other.

"Wait here. This won't take long." Boyd observed the empty parking spaces in the lot. "Looks as if we're the only customers at this early hour."

As he entered the glass door, Boyd noticed the exterior room of the store was approximately twenty feet wide and ten feet deep. The counter was unattended and littered with paperwork, various instructional materials and several empty coffee cups.

A short male clerk appeared from the door leading to the back room and politely asked, "Senor, may I be of service?"

"Yes, my name is Boyd Tanner and I have a package to pick up." Handing the clerk his drivers license and the receipt from the Dallas FedEx, he added, "It was shipped from a FedEx location in Dallas, Texas and was supposed to have arrived yesterday."

"One moment, please."

The clerk disappeared for a short time and returned with the ten-pound package.

"That will be one hundred ninety-seven dollars."

Boyd gave the clerk two, hundred dollar bills, received his change and carried his package back to the car.

"That was fast." Jamie was surprised at the speed of the transaction.

Boyd carefully placed the box of tattoo equipment in the back seat of the car. Looking over the seat at Jamie, he said, "Occasionally things go as planned. Look at the map and guide me to the next stop." Boyd was already focused on the supplies he needed from the Walmart, located just off Calle Mayapan.

The conflicting views on Avenida Xcaret caught Boyd's attention. A confusing mix of well-maintained roads along with stretches of potholes. Lax, if not completely absent zoning laws, resulted in low income housing situated next door to restaurants, flower shops and hotels. The pedestrians, bicycles and delivery trucks kept the traffic at a relatively slow pace.

It was almost 9:00 when Boyd parked in the huge parking lot of the Cancun Walmart. Customers were filtering between the rows of cars like the gentle waves of the Caribbean. The flow was headed toward the unmistakable yellow spokes of the Walmart sign glistening in the early morning sun.

Jamie surveyed the parking lot and exclaimed, "Walmart! A Walmart in Cancun! What is the world coming to? Okay, what all do we need to pick up?"

"Duct tape, single edge razor blades, latex gloves and a black magic marker. Oh yeah, we should probably get a case of bottled water." Boyd was thinking ahead.

Opening the car door, Jamie said, "Will we need any, ahh, clothes-line rope?"

"Don't think so. The duct tape will be adequate."

Jamie was also thinking ahead, "Just a thought, but how about we get a couple of caps. You know, baseball, golf or whatever."

"Excellent idea. You get the duct tape and latex gloves and I'll get the rest. Then let's meet in the sporting goods section."

"That'll work."

They walked through the entrance and looked at a *Departamentos* map with the various sections of the store designated.

As they started to walk in different directions, Jamie said, "See you in sporting goods."

Twenty minutes later, Boyd found Jamie in the golf equipment area of the store trying on caps. Jamie was looking at his reflection in a small mirror on one of the display stands. He was trying on a white Calloway golf cap and holding a black one in his hand.

Pulling the cap down over his eyes, Jamie said in jest, "I'm pretty sure I could break seventy wearing this one."

Boyd cocked his head and retorted, "Yeah, after about three holes. What brand is the one in your hand?"

"Srixon. Want to try it?"

Picking up the twenty-four bottle case of water by the plastic wrapping, Boyd concurred, "Looks good enough to me. Here, give me the hats and gloves and you take the duct tape. Let's check out at different registers."

"See you back at the car."

It was 9:30 when the rental car slowly made its way through the Walmart parking lot onto Calle Mayapan. Jamie was back on the job looking at Boyd's map of Cancun and giving directions. Ruben Repeza's apartment complex was only ten minutes away.

As Boyd turned onto Avenida Xcaret, he uttered, "First opportunity."

Jamie looked up from the map and repeated, "First opportunity."

———

It was painful when Hector rolled over and sat up on the couch. He had planned to sleep until at least noon today, but something besides the alcohol had caused a fitful night's sleep. He knew what it was...Estralita. They had discarded her as if she had never even existed in their lives. He felt guilty...very guilty. At the very least, he would give her the thousand dollars he had taken from Ruben's stash. They could afford it now.

He slipped on a shirt and shorts and walked to the bedroom door, opening it a few inches. He could see Ruben stretched out with a pillow over his head.

How many bitches have been screwed on that bed!

Hector felt a little lightheaded as he walked toward his Harley in the parking lot. Checking to make sure the wad of cash was still in his pocket, he decided to go to Estralita's apartment after satisfying the craving in his stomach. He was hung over and hungry, but that was minor in the scheme of things. He was close to having more money than he could ever spend.

Even though it was out of the way to Estralita's apartment, Hector decided to go to Avenida Yaxchilan. This avenue was known as a paradise for nightlife lovers, the street that never sleeps. Bars, nightclubs and restaurants were open most of the day and night.

Hector initially met Estralita in one of the clubs on this very street. In the early morning they ate breakfast at *Pescaditos* and then went to her apartment and engaged in sex for the next several hours. He often thought of that night.

She'll be impressed and will totally forgive me when I tell her where I went for breakfast!

Pescaditos was located in a unique setting. Several Eastern Rosebuds lined the street in front of the restaurant, their trunks small, their leaves large. A two-foot stone wall held in a variety of crawling, green plants and smaller trees. Green lattice work on both sides of the outdoor patio guarded the blue plastic tables and chairs.

Most of the tables were occupied, so Hector chose a table in the center of the patio and looked at the menu on the wall. He mentally decided on two pieces of *pescaditos* and a plate of chili rellenos.

Fish and chili rellenos will make my stomach feel better. I think.

The morning was sunny and breezy, not too hot, not too cold, just perfect. Eventually a waiter took his order and Hector cautiously checked-out the other patrons. Most appeared to be vacationing couples, a few children and a few locals.

No clients, thank God.

Hector noticed one couple at the next table with a pitcher of margaritas and almost had a gag reflex.

I'm not going to drink again for...for several hours. Absolutely not this morning!

As Hector consumed the meal, his thoughts returned to the previous day and the way it culminated at Ruben's apartment. His hangover and stomach distress disappeared the instant he thought about the extortion pick-ups and the backpack full of cash.

He sat at the table and couldn't contain a wide smile, even though his mouth was full of chili rellenos, when he thought about the hooker... no she was an escort. He'd only managed three ejaculations, but it was nothing to be embarrassed about. It had been a stressful day at the office, and after all, he was extremely drunk from celebrating by the time they made it to the couch. Three times was a long way from his all-time record, but under the circumstances it was acceptable.

It was 10:45 by the time Hector arrived at Estralita's apartment. He had a key, but logic told him to be on his best behavior and to lightly knock on the door, not just barge in.

He tried the light knock and then resorted to a medium knock and finally to his usual fist pounding approach. He waited, but still no response.

Maybe she went out for lunch. What the fuck, I'll let myself in and wait for her.

He unlocked the door and walked in to the worst surprise of his young life. He looked at the odd colored, motionless, nude body on the couch and immediately knew something was wrong.

Dead wrong.

Leaving the front door open, he slowly approached the couch. Estralita's vacant eyes confirmed his initial fears. He turned his head toward the front door and up-chucked his fish, chili rellenos and what remained of last night's tequila. He turned back to the strangely pale body on the couch and threw up again.

I'm as big a pussy as the whore I was with last night.

Wiping his mouth on his sleeve, he looked around the living room and tried to regain his composure. He tugged at the blanket, pulling it from under Estralita's body, and covered her as best he could. Her face was still showing, so he pulled the blanket over her head.

Tears were forming in Hector's eyes, but he was sure it was from throwing up so violently. After all, it had been a rough couple of days.

Where would she keep the DVDs? I need to get them out of her apartment.

He spent the next ten minutes going through drawers in the bedroom, under the couch and in the pantry. Nothing. Finally, he found what he was looking for in a kitchen drawer.

Almost as an afterthought, he fanned out the DVDs in his hands and noticed there were only four...not five. He quickly determined the missing DVD was the one containing Salazar's exploits.

What the….! Need to get back to Ruben's apartment and see what to do about this.

He stopped at the door and turned for a last look at Estralita. Tears were now streaming down Hector's face. He lowered his head and choked back a groan.

A real man doesn't do this. Fuck!

CHAPTER 43

Cancun...Saturday, June 5th
It was 9:45 when Boyd and Jamie arrived at the driveway leading to Ruben's apartment building. Jamie was intently studying the drawing Miguel Burbano provided. They had discussed during the short trip what they planned to do after arriving.

"Okay, turn to the left as we approach the covered parking spaces," Jamie directed. "According to the drawing Miguel gave us, it appears that Ruben's apartment is the second one on the right...number sixty-one. As Miguel suggested, left will take us to the other side of the building and we can walk around to here. Okay?"

"That's what Miguel recommended, so let's do it. Do you see a Harley in the parking lot?"

"Nope. There may be one, but I don't see it."

Boyd continued around the building and parked in a vacant, unmarked space. He removed the tattoo bag from the car and Jamie took the diabetic kit along with the plastic sack containing their Walmart supplies.

Pointing, Jamie said, "There's the door to the hallway. Let's walk around the building. Okay?"

"I'm right behind you."

They put on their sun-glasses and pulled down the bills of their caps as they started the short trek to number sixty-one.

There was something about the atmosphere of this section of Cancun that reminded Boyd of Ridgetop. Even at this time of morning, a number of children were playing in their small yards, on their steps, or in the street. He assumed the sound of dogs barking, squealing voices and music playing must be a staple of any apartment complex or trailer park.

As they rounded the corner, the first apartment number coming into view was sixty. Jamie pointed straight ahead. Both men surveyed the parking lot in front of them.

"There's Ruben's SUV," Jamie whispered. "And there's lucky number sixty-one."

As discussed, Boyd stood behind the SUV as Jamie approached Ruben's back door. Sweat trickled down the side of his face even though he was in the shade of the carport. He was only yards away from the person he had been obsessing about for months, the pervert who had raped his daughter.

The plan they had discussed in the car was for Jamie to knock on the door and determine if they should proceed or come back at a later time. Boyd was inclined to kick in the door and beat the living hell out of anyone in the house. But he knew better.

One of the things setting him apart from his peers in the business world had been his ability to perform under the most stressful of circumstances. There had been instances when everything seemed to be falling apart around his start-up company and panic prevailed among the employees and the investors, but the more unpredictable the situation, the more in control he seemed to be. It was like waiting for the opening kickoff in a big game. He was calm, even though it was an uneasy calm.

Jamie knocked...waited a few seconds...knocked again. A small window with a tattered shade was centered head-high in the door. Just as he was about to knock a third time, someone pulled back the shade a few inches and opened the door. Ruben appeared in his underwear.

"Do you know what time it is?" Ruben was rubbing his eyes and seemed confused to see a total stranger so early in the morning.

"Is the lady of the house in?" Holding up the diabetic kit and the plastic bag, he explained. "She's won several prizes."

"There's no fucking lady in this house!" Ruben didn't like to be awakened before noon...by anyone.

Jamie moved lightning fast. Dropping his diabetic kit and the plastic bag on the floor, he pushed Ruben back into the kitchen with his left hand and was instantly behind him with his right arm around his throat. He executed the rear naked choke as hard as he possibly could without breaking Ruben's neck. Ruben kicked and tried to move his shoulders, but within fifteen seconds he slumped and became completely still.

Boyd entered the door, locked it and picked up the diabetic kit. He stood over Ruben, glaring down at him, barely able to contain his emotions. He handed the kit to Jamie, struggling to regain his composure. "I'll check out the bedroom."

Boyd returned from the bedroom and carefully opened the door to the hallway, looking both ways. Walking back into the kitchen, he reported, "Appears we're alone."

Jamie had already removed one of the syringes from the kit, removed the plastic cap, and had the needle pointed toward the ceiling. Pumping it twice, a barely detectable spray of liquid appeared. Jamie was experienced in administering secobarbital sodium shots, although the patients were usually awake when the shots were being given.

"Here, stretch out his arm and hold on," said Jamie. Now he was directing Boyd.

Ruben moaned and began to move as Jamie made the injection. Ruben's eyes were still open and he momentarily looked directly at Boyd. Within seconds, his body relaxed and he slipped into the same blackness in which he had taken scores of young, unsuspecting women.

"Finally," Boyd uttered as he took Ruben's feet and dragged him to the kitchen table.

Jamie grasped Ruben's wrists and they lifted him on top of the table, face up. Boyd reached into the plastic bag and dumped the contents on the kitchen counter. Removing his cap and sun glasses, he slipped on a pair of the latex gloves and handed the other pair to Jamie. The remaining contents were scattered on the counter.

Boyd removed the cellophane from one of the duct tape rolls and pulled out a two foot segment while Jamie watched. He wrapped it around one of Ruben's ankles and then extended it further and wrapped it around a table leg. He repeated the procedure again with the other ankle. With Ruben's legs firmly attached to the table, he attached both of Ruben's arms to the other two table legs in the same manner. Ruben was spread-eagled on the table and there was duct tape to spare.

Boyd sat down in one of the kitchen chairs, removed the tattoo equipment and the extension cord from the leather carry-bag and placed all the items on the floor in front of him. Without speaking, he nodded toward a wall socket near the sink and handed Jamie the extension cord.

As he examined the tattoo machine and the accessories, Boyd looked at Ruben lying on the table, wearing only his underwear, and then looked at the packet of single-edged razor blades on the counter. He tried to maintain his focus, but thoughts of the recent past came in flashes.

We need to spend some time apart! This never would have happened if only you had listened to me that night. See what it caused! Our daughter was raped because you talked me into letting her go out with someone we didn't even know! I'm leaving day after tomorrow for Europe. I don't know if I can get over this.

Remembering what the tattoo artist in Dallas told him, Boyd first assembled the grip by attaching the barrel with the electromagnetic coils to the frame. He was told to wash his hands with antibacterial soap before handling these items.

Think I'll skip that step.

He proceeded with the rest of the grip assembly and then inserted a needle through the plastic tube in the barrel. After tightening several screws with his fingers, he plugged the foot pedal and the gun into the power supply with the appropriate cables.

His last step was to open the Black Onyx ink bottle and set it on the counter. The tattoo artist had insisted that getting the ink into the gun reservoir was an easy step. He picked up the tattoo gun and placed the tip of the needle in the black ink. He then pressed the foot pedal three times and saw the ink level in the bottle drop somewhat.

Boyd tore the plastic enclosing the two black magic markers and removed the tip from one of them. He stood over Ruben's chest and very carefully printed in approximately three inch letters the word **CUNT**. The letters extended in an arc between Ruben's nipples.

Jamie stood on the other side of the table and watched as Boyd attached the power supply cord to the extension cord. He was amazed at what can be accomplished in such a short period of time.

Feeling as if he should be doing something productive, Jamie went to the kitchen door and slid open the window shade.

"The coast seems to be clear. I'll keep an eye out for visitors."

Boyd was surprised that he wasn't more excited, more nervous, more something. He stared at Ruben's chest and then at his face. This was the waiter who told Boyd and his family about his college plans, the charismatic person who totally convinced Boyd as to his good intentions and trustworthiness. This was the person who drugged and raped his daughter. He glanced again at the razor blades on the counter. This was the person who was going to pay.

Jamie listened as the humming noise increased as Boyd adjusted the dial on the power supply. The little screen indicated the voltage rate was at ten. Boyd's hand appeared steady as he placed the tip of the needle at the top of the C. The time had come.

Remembering what Miguel said about the bedroom closet and the possibility of a video camera being located there, Jamie decided to check it out. First, he peeked again through the window in the kitchen door and then headed for the bedroom.

He lifted the flap on the bullfighter picture and saw what appeared to be a camera lens. He tried the door-knob and as he suspected, it was locked. Stepping back, he took his wallet from his back pocket and removed his Visa card.

This is not going to be much of a challenge.

Jamie inserted the credit card into the vertical crack between the door and the doorjamb. He tilted the flexible card toward the door handle and pushed it into the crack as far as possible. The last move was to bend the card away from the handle and push on the door at the same time. This forced the bolt back into the door and in a matter of seconds Jamie was admiring his handiwork.

Even Miguel, the Shadow, couldn't beat that time. Can't wait until I see him again!

Jamie tried a light-switch inside the closet and was rewarded with a dim glow from a red light bulb. The light was adequate to see the video camera on its tripod and a backpack on the floor. Jamie opened the backpack and his head jerked back when he saw the stacks of money. He stood and looked at the shelf above his head which contained an open shoebox. Lifting it off the shelf, the red light reflected the plastic holders containing the DVDs.

As he walked into the kitchen with the backpack slung over his shoulder and the shoebox in his hands, he asked Boyd, "What letter are you on?"

"Finishing up the N."

"Damn, you're fast."

"I'll go over all the letters again to make them wider. Quality is not a huge priority, just as long as it's readable."

The steady hum of the power supply and the oscillating needle in the gun created a soothing white noise in the kitchen. Jamie sat the box of DVDs and the backpack on the couch and again went to the door and looked through the narrow opening between the shade and the window.

"Still no problem." Pointing at the shoe box and the backpack Jamie added, "When you get a chance, look at all the loot."

Having noticed the DVD player on the end table, Jamie took a seat on the couch. The writing on the plastic holder that initially caught his attention was labeled **UNCLE EMILIO, FARMACIA DEL AHORRO, & RUBEN...DALLAS 12-26-15.**

Jamie narrowed his eyes and frowned. The name of the city and the date brought the shocking realization of what might possibly be on the video. Looking at Boyd, who was still at work with the tattoo machine, he removed the DVD from the plastic holder and inserted it into the player.

The image of an older, grey haired man on top of a young woman with her legs spread apart was sickening to Jamie. The camera zoomed in on the face of the man as he got up from the bed and then went black for several seconds. The video continued with a shot of Ruben looking at the camera and smiling one of his most radiant smiles before taking his turn with the girl. A close up shot of the victim's face ended the spectacle.

Jamie lowered his head, covering his face with his hands. He sat still for a few seconds and then glanced over at Boyd again before removing the DVD. He placed the DVD back in the plastic case and slid it into the front pocket of his shorts.

The next DVD he viewed was labeled **SALAZAR, POLICE CHIEF, 5-28-16.** It was also a disgusting example of humanity at its worst. Jamie couldn't believe what he was seeing.

384

Boyd, in the meantime, had finished his tattoo work on Ruben's chest. This would be a permanent reminder for Ruben. This is what happens when the dark side takes over one's logical thought process.

Boyd laid the tattoo gun on the counter and picked up the single-edged razor blade. He'd been thinking about this for some time and hoped he wouldn't regret it at a later date...but the decision had been made. In one's lifetime, a few decisions can make or break reputations and peace of mind. This was one of them.

He easily sliced through the duct tape holding Ruben's ankles to the table legs and then did the same to the tape on his wrists. Ruben would be a free man when he woke up. Free to go back into the world, all body parts intact. Hopefully the reminder on his chest would guide him in a different direction.

"Anything of interest?" Boyd said approaching the couch.

"First of all, look at what's in the backpack."

"Damn! Miguel was correct. These guys did some serious extorting!" Boyd took several stacks of cash in his hand and then returned them to the backpack.

Jamie wasn't sure how to proceed, so he said quietly, "Not sure you want to see this, but here's an example of what these assholes have been doing."

"Let me see."

Jamie pushed PLAY on the DVD player and Boyd witnessed Salazar performing unspeakable acts on an unconscious victim. The last image was a close-up of the young lady's face.

"How many DVDs are there?" Boyd was visibly upset.

Pointing at the shoebox, Jamie responded, "Here they all are."

"No others?" Boyd shuffled through the stack of DVDs.

"Nope. This is it." It wasn't the truth, but it was all Jamie could think to say on the spur of the moment. "I think we should take them with us. Are you finished with your work?"

Boyd hesitated and his sense of calm started morphing into a sense of quiet rage. "You know, I actually thought I was through, but I guess not."

Boyd went back to the table and in less than fifteen minutes had tattooed **CUNT** in one-inch letters across Ruben's forehead.

Boyd's task was completed. He stated evenly, "Okay, partner, let's clean up and leave. I'll pack the tattoo equipment and you can put the rest of the stuff, including the DVDs, in the plastic bag. Be sure and bring the backpack. We'll have to decide what to do with all this."

Jamie said firmly, "On it."

CHAPTER 44

Cancun...Saturday, June 5th
Chief Salazar arrived at his office in the Benito Juarez Building promptly at 10:00a.m. If nothing else, the Chief was punctual. Captain Rohan, as requested, was there to discuss the cover-up needed for the upcoming corruption investigation.

Salazar was seated on the front edge of his desk when Rohan entered. "Where are we on this?"

The Chief was a man of few words and all of his subordinates knew it.

"I talked to all of our suppliers and distributors yesterday and they won't be a problem." With an effusive smile, he added, "Same with the white powder chemist. He won't be talking to anyone for quite a while."

"Good man." Salazar was listening, but thumbing through the pile of papers in his in-box, when something caught his attention.

The end of a small envelope was sticking out near the bottom of the pile. The words **VERY IMPORTANT** were written in red ink. Everyone thought their problems were important and the Chief essentially didn't care; however, the two words being circled in red piqued his curiosity.

Captain Rohan stood silently while Salazar pulled the envelope from the stack and studied the printed words. Salazar could feel the small disc, separated from his fingers by only a thin layer of paper.

Salazar ripped open the envelope and removed the DV D. For some reason he thought there would also be a note or letter, but nothing, just the DVD with his name and a date.

Holding up the disc, he quizzically asked the captain, "What do you think we have here?"

Knowing it was a rhetorical question, Rohan said, "I'll bring in a DVD player." He knew the answer to the question he was about to ask, but he asked anyway, "Or we can go next door to the audio visual room."

"Bring it. Now!"

Salazar was still sitting on the edge of his desk when Rohan returned a few minutes later, a DVD player and extension cord cradled in his arms.

Salazar inserted the DVD as soon as Rohan plugged in the equipment and both men sat in the two chairs facing his desk.

The first image on the screen was of a young lady lying on a bed wearing a white tank top and a short skirt with blue and green floral patterns. The skirt was pulled over her thighs and her tanned legs were spread apart.

Salazar's eyes narrowed as he began to recognize what he was watching. He panicked as the video camera showed a close up of his face. It wasn't just the fact his face was in the movie, it was the look on his face and what he was doing...licking his lips.

"What the …" He looked at Rohan as if it was entirely his fault. "Turn the goddamned thing off!"

Ironically enough, Salazar had told Rohan, his most trusted employee, about the "rape ring" as he liked to think of it. He'd planned to let the captain participate.

Salazar knew all too well what happened next in the video. He removed his thick, black-framed glasses and put his hands on his forehead. This was a huge surprise and he was trying to understand what was going on. Once again, he looked at the wadded up envelope. Still no note or explanation.

Confusion quickly turned into rage as he thought of Emilio Repeza, the coordinator of the secret program. For some reason, Salazar never liked or completely trusted Repeza or his nephew. They both thought of themselves as handsome and suave. Now, just when Salazar was about to be under investigation for various drug and corruption charges, this happens.

Smug assholes! What do they want? Money? Or do they only want to make fun of my sex habits and my face? Makes no difference. They'll pay. Right now!

Salazar reached into his top desk drawer and removed his new Glock 26, which had been designed for concealed carry. He checked to make sure the ten-round clip was full, placed it in his pants pocket and then looked up at Rohan.

"Got your weapon?"

Rohan patted the holstered pistol on his belt and quickly replied, "Yes sir."

Rohan also carried a Glock, but his was an older version Glock 17 with an eight-round magazine containing 9x19 parabellum metal-jacketed, hollow points.

It didn't take long to get to Emilio's *farmacia*. Salazar was in the passenger seat of the police vehicle and his rage was growing by the minute. He had given Rohan instructions on how to proceed.

How did they make that video? Had to be someone in the closet! Maybe Emilio!

It was 10:40a.m. when Salazar and Rohan entered the open doors of *Farmacia del Barato*. The store appeared to be empty except for Emilio who was studying a document on the counter. He casually looked up and did a double take when he saw Salazar and Rohan storming into the store.

"*Giliplollas malvivientes!*" There was never any doubt as to how Salazar felt about a particular situation.

Raising his open hands, Emilio responded in complete fear and bewilderment, "What's wrong!"

The door to the office behind the counter opened and Azahara, Emilio's assistant, appeared with several glass containers in her arms. She seemed startled by the loud voices.

Salazar glanced at Rohan and then turned back to Emilio. "You think it was smart to video me at the apartment? Huh? You think it was smart!"

Emilio was still in partial shock with his arms extended and palms open when he heard the explosion from Rohan's pistol. He went into total shock when he saw the back of Azahara's head come apart and splatter on the shelf behind her, the containers she had been carrying shattering on the counter and the floor. The small hole in her forehead was overshadowed by the exit wound in the back of her head. Emilio's knees went weak as he saw Azahara's body slam into the shelf and fall to the floor.

"No one makes videos of me. Understand!"

Emilio was pale as a sheet and managed a high pitched plea. "It must have been my nephew, Ruben. It had to have been him. I am innocent. Please...."

Salazar had already removed his Glock from his pocket and was pointing it at Emilio.

Standing close to the counter, Salazar motioned with his finger and demanded, "Come here!"

Emilio fully expected to be slapped in the face or, even worse, hit in the head with the butt of Salazar's pistol. He knew of Salazar's reputation, but this was ridiculous. What had happened? His confusion morphed into pure terror. As he followed instructions and leaned forward on the counter, Salazar grabbed a handful of his shirt.

Salazar hollered, "No one! No one!"

Emilio started to beg for his life, but that was a mistake. Salazar jammed the gun into his mouth and pulled the trigger. Spittle, blood and part of Emilio's tongue blew back on Salazar's hand.

The force of the bullet caused Emilio's body to stand up straight and then to crumple in a heap behind the counter. Emilio was no longer a partner in the "rape ring."

Salazar shook most of the matter off his hand and wiped the remainder on his pant leg. He reached into a glass jar on the counter full of various colors of hard candy, taking his time to pick out two of them.

Holding his hand out to Rohan, he calmly said, "Want one of these?"

CHAPTER 45

Cancun...Saturday, June 5th

It was a troubled ride for Hector between Estralita's apartment and Ruben's parking lot. He felt hollow inside and was afraid he was going to throw up again during the trip. On top of his guilt and misery over Estralita's death, there was one other issue.

What happened to the DVD of Salazar? It wouldn't be such a big deal if Ruben and I were already in Nicaragua or wherever we're going, but what if Salazar gets hold of it? Ruben needs to go back to the apartment with me so we can tear the hell out of it until we find it. What about her body? Goddamn it!

Hector parked his motorcycle in an empty covered parking space next to Rubens SUV. He hesitated for a few seconds trying to get his head straight, and then hurried up the sidewalk to the back door. He distinctly remembered leaving the door unlocked when he left for breakfast and was surprised when he tried to turn the knob and discovered it wouldn't open. He removed his key from his pocket and inserted it into the door lock.

Jamie glided across the kitchen floor to the door when he heard the knob jiggle. The instant he saw the bald head come through the door, he knew from Miguel's description that it must be Ruben's sidekick, Hector.

Boyd, standing at the kitchen counter, was in the process of zipping the leather case containing the tattoo equipment when he saw Jamie moving toward the door.

Hector stopped and flinched when he saw Boyd in the kitchen and Ruben's mostly naked body on the table. What he didn't see was the heel of Jamie's hand land solidly above his right jaw, causing several teeth to break and then rattle on the linoleum floor. Nor did he see or hear anything else for five minutes.

Jamie retrieved the plastic bag and removed the roll of partially-used duct tape. He quickly wrapped Hector's feet together and then wrapped the last of the tape around Hector's hands and placed them in his lap. Because of the bleeding from Hector's mouth, Jamie made the decision to lean his body upright against the wall next to the door.

Looking around the kitchen, Boyd said, "Okay, looks like we have everything...tattoo equipment, tape, gloves, blades, magic marker. Anything we forgot?"

The only thing he didn't see was the slight movement of Ruben's body on the table and the flicker of his eyelids. The half-closed eyes quickly became focused on Boyd's face. Was it a look of bewilderment... or recognition?

"Nope. I've got the backpack with the cash and the DVDs. All our supplies are in this plastic bag. Are we going back the way we came or down the hallway?"

The question was answered for them by the squealing of brakes in the parking lot. Jamie looked out the window and motioned toward the living room door that opened into the hallway.

"Two guys getting out of a police car and they may be heading this way."

Boyd opened the door and looked both ways down the hallway. He nodded to indicate the coast was clear, then he and Jamie entered the hall, quietly closing the door behind them. Ten yards away, another door opened and a young couple carrying a baby came into view. Boyd and Jamie hesitated as the man locked his door, but had trouble removing his key from the lock. Finally, extracting the key, he placed his hand on the woman's back and they walked toward the exit.

————

Ruben rolled off the kitchen table and fell on his hands and knees, smashing his head on the floor. His forehead hurt, his chest hurt and blood was trickling into his left eye. The black substance, mixed with blood, on his chest didn't register with any of his five senses. It was just painful.

Somehow, in his confusion, he had the presence of mind to go to the back door and look out the window. The sight of Police Chief Salazar standing next to a police car talking to another man caused a shockwave to shoot through his entire body. It almost shook him back to reality, but not quite. His confusion returned when he noticed Hector moaning only a few feet away.

What's he doing up against the wall with his mouth bleeding?

"Get this tape off me!" Hector spit blood as he spoke and was no more lucid than Ruben. "The girl from Dallas. Her dad!"

Hector had met Boyd when Ruben introduced them last December, standing at the end of the Devilfish pier.

The same image was in Ruben's brain, but his self-survival instinct completely took over. He took a step in Hector's direction, did an about-face and turned toward the living room door, the strands of duct tape still clinging to his wrists and ankles.

"Ruben!"

———

Salazar got out of the police cruiser and walked around to the driver's side. Leaning against the car, he spoke softly. "He lives right there, in sixty-one. This is the nephew. This is the movie maker. This is the one I am going to butcher…slowly."

Rohan, trying to be logical, while in the company of a very illogical person, commented, "Several cars parked around here. We need to be careful."

"Careful my ass! You saw the video. This asshole is going to pay."

"Maybe I should park the car away from the apartment."

Standing and looking Rohan in the eye, Salazar ordered, "Come on…now!"

Not even checking to see whether or not the door was locked, Salazar kicked the lower center of the door and it slammed open, tearing off one of the hinges and causing wood splinters to fly into the kitchen.

Glocks drawn, both men casually walked through the doorway as if they lived there.

Seeing Hector bound hand and foot, leaning against the wall, Salazar erupted, "Check the bedroom!"

Doing as commanded, Rohan checked the bedroom, bathroom and the closet.

"No one here, but the video camera is in the closet, Chief."

Walking into the bedroom, Salazar entered the closet and in one motion slung the camera and the tripod through the doorway, smashing it against the wall. He returned and stood in front of Hector who was shaking uncontrollably, still bleeding from the mouth.

Glaring at Hector, he yelled, "What are you doing here? Are you Ruben's friend?" And then it dawned on him, and he slowly muttered, "You're the video man!" His rage rekindled and burned red-hot.

This was the first time since he was four years old that Hector had wet his pants. He couldn't control his bladder and his shaking continued unabated. He knew what was coming and he wasn't pre-pared. The only excuse he could think of had little to do with his wellbeing.

"The guy from Dallas did this. He did it. Find him and he'll tell you! I saw him...I saw him."

Salazar was now pointing his Glock directly at the bridge of Hector's nose. "Where's Ruben!"

Again, the only thing Hector could think to say was, "The guy from Dallas. It was her dad!"

No sooner than the words left his mouth, a powerful, comforting, near-end-of-life experience occurred. Maybe it happened in less than a second, maybe a nanosecond. Salazar hadn't yet pulled the trigger, so it could have been a few seconds.

Researchers refer to the phenomena as the "death-bed vision" or the "departing vision." The dying have reported visions of angels, deceased loved ones or religious figures moments before passing. Often it is an image of one's mother. This was not Hector's vision.

Hector's body relaxed, the color returned to his face and a hint of a smile parted his bloodied lips. He had never been so calm, so much at peace. A vision of Estralita materialized. She was approaching him, hand extended. She was beautiful, with her long, silky hair flowing over her shoulders. He would have taken her hand, but his were still tightly wrapped in tape. He strained to hear what she was saying, but her voice was inaudible. He closed his eyes and continued to smile.

It was just as well his eyes were closed because the first bullet went through his left eye and the second bullet went through his right one. His head bounced against the wall and was followed by his entire body falling to the floor, the smile replaced by a silent scream.

"Let's tear this place apart until we find the rest of the DVDs. Move!" Salazar was back to what he did best...shouting orders to his underlings.

The next fifteen minutes resulted in the apartment being taken apart piece by piece. They found the empty shoe box, the hidden compartment in the closet floor and used condoms under the bed, but no DVDs.

Rohan had given up the search and finally said, "Where's this Ruben kid, and who was the guy from Dallas this little prick kept mentioning?" He pointed at the bloody mess on the floor.

"Don't know, but maybe he's the one who tied the fucker up and left him. Maybe he took the DVDs! Maybe he and Ruben are on their way to Dallas while we stand here with our dicks in our hands!"

Rohan was puzzled, but said anyway, "There are hundreds of visitors coming from and going to Dallas on any given day. Where do we start?"

"You're a goddamn detective. Figure it out!"

———

Boyd and Jamie reached the rental car, bags in tow. Both men continued to watch the door from which they had just exited, expecting at any moment a flood of Mexican police to come storming at them. Boyd got the keys from his pocket and tried to unlock the trunk of the car. Two keys were on the key ring and the first one didn't work. He fumbled with the keys and dropped them on the asphalt surface of the parking lot. They bounced once and ended up somewhere under the back bumper. Getting on his hands and knees, Boyd reached under the car and once again had the keys in his hand. Jamie, in the meantime, was getting fidgety while he kept an eye on the apartment door.

"This kind of stuff only happens in movies." Boyd was talking to himself.

Finally getting the trunk open, Boyd placed the tattoo equipment bag inside, followed by Jamie tossing in the backpack and the plastic bag.

Boyd drove slowly toward the corner of the apartment building, not wanting to attract any attention. Still concerned about being followed, he glanced in the rear view mirror and was puzzled by the fleeting image of a partially nude person running from the same door they had just exited.

"Humm, I think I just saw...no, it couldn't have been."

"Saw what?"

"I think I just saw Ruben running across the parking lot."

"Not possible. He's still out from the dose of secobarbital sodium I gave him." Jamie didn't sound completely convinced about his diagnosis.

Boyd shrugged and whispered, "Makes no difference. He's marked."

They continued around the narrow lane in the parking lot and just before turning up the driveway to Avenida Nizuc, both Boyd and Jamie took one last look at apartment number sixty-one. The police car was still parked directly behind Ruben's SUV.

"Uh oh." Boyd was first to notice the battered door hanging on one hinge.

Hearing the unmistakable crackle of gun shots, Boyd accelerated the rental car up the driveway.

"Turn right."

Jamie could still feel the sharp edges of the DVD holder in the pocket of his shorts.

CHAPTER 46

Cancun...Saturday, June 5th

As soon as they made the turn onto Avenida Nizuc, Boyd said, "Did we hear gunshots coming from Ruben's apartment, or what?"

"We were both a little tense at the time, so it could have been anything...but, it sounded like gunshots. Two of them."

"The door had been busted down and there was a police car parked right behind Ruben's SUV. I can speculate as to what happened, but something about the whole thing is strange." Boyd's face was a mask of confusion.

"I'm sure we're both thinking along the same lines. Somehow, the Police Chief got the extortion letter or saw the DVD and all hell broke loose. What do you think?"

"That's the only scenario that makes sense. Of course, the other question is about the two gunshots. Who, if anyone, got shot. Although the fact the door was knocked off its hinges makes me think the worst happened."

Boyd kept looking in the rear view mirror and Jamie looked back over his shoulder several times. Halfway back to the hotel, Boyd suddenly applied the brakes and made a quick turn into a driveway on the right. Surrounded by large trees and a well landscaped lawn, the white, open air structure of the *Catedral de Cancun* came into view.

Boyd turned to Jamie and suggested, "How would you feel about taking the backpack and giving it to a church official?"

"Your surprises never cease. Pop the trunk and I'll make it happen."

In less than two minutes, Jamie was back in the car. Glancing back at the church and then at Boyd, he said, "That was easy. I met a priest coming toward me as I entered the building. I simply handed him the backpack and told him it was for the poor. That was the first thing that came to mind. I turned around and left before he had a chance to open it."

Both men were quiet for the next five minutes of the trip, trying to mentally absorb the happenings of the past few hours. Up ahead on the left, the white, six story towers of the Casa Maya Hotel appeared. The flags struggled to show off their colors in the light breeze.

Finally, Jamie pressed his lips together, hesitated, and then spoke. "You'll think this is the craziest idea you've ever heard, but bear with me. What if you get out at the hotel and I go back to Ruben's apartment." It was a statement, not a question.

Jamie didn't quit there. "You've put a substantial amount of thought and planning into this whole venture, and I think you deserve to know the final outcome." He fully understood Boyd by now.

Boyd blinked, but didn't respond.

Jamie's logic was unrelenting. "Think about it. I fit in with the local population and won't be noticed one way or the other. I'll simply walk by the apartment and see what's going on. Other people will have heard the commotion and will probably be in the immediate area. If the police are swarming the apartment building, or whatever, I won't risk stopping. Okay?"

Boyd drove up the ramp and parked under the Casa Maya portico. One other car was in front of the door and its occupants were busily getting their luggage out of the trunk.

"I do like the idea, but I don't like you taking a risk. Know what I mean?"

"Like I said, I'll be extra vigilant. My cap will be on backward and I'll just be one of the boys."

"Okay. Be careful. Be very careful. One other thing. What about the items in the trunk?"

"I'm glad you still have your wits about you! You take the case of water and I'll dispose of the tattoo equipment and the plastic sack full of stuff on the way to the apartment. Not a problem."

Closing the trunk, Jamie got in the driver's seat and was gone before the attendant had finished with the car in front of them. The early afternoon traffic was much more congested than when the two friends departed that morning for the FedEx store.

There were numerous poor neighborhoods on the way to the apartment. Jamie drove down a deserted alleyway and immediately came upon two dempster-dumpsters, one overflowing and the other completely empty, leaning next to a dilapidated fence.

Jamie took a pair of latex gloves from the plastic bag and slipped them on. The first item of business was to remove the DVD holder from his pocket, take out the disc and stomp it with the heel of his shoe. The fragile DVD broke into numerous pieces and Jamie kicked most of them to the other side of the alleyway.

That DVD is gone as if it never existed, and I'm going to forget that it ever did!

Next he removed the leather tattoo bag from the trunk, unzipped it and dropped the contents into the bottom of the empty container. He took several bags of garbage from the other dumpster and threw them on top of the tattoo equipment. Finally, he tossed the plastic bag, along with the latex gloves he was wearing, on top of the garbage bags.

Ruben's apartment was only minutes away.

Jamie turned down the driveway to the apartment building. The police car was gone. The door to Ruben's apartment was still partially open, numerous strips of yellow and black police tape across the frame. As Jamie suspected, ten or twelve people, mostly teenagers, were standing around the walkway leading to the back door.

Jamie turned left and retraced the route he and Boyd had taken earlier, parking in the same spot. He hurried around the building, slowing his pace when he made the last turn, and then casually walked down the sidewalk, cap turned backward.

The first youngster Jamie encountered was standing with two other teenagers looking toward the broken door to the apartment. Several other boys and an adult were struggling for space on the top step, trying to look through the half-open door.

"What happened?"

"Dead guy in there. I saw him through the door. Blood everywhere!" The young man was excited and talking in high pitched sounds.

"How do you know he was dead?"

"I told you, blood everywhere! Two holes in his face. He's one dead dude!"

"Only one guy and he had two holes in his face?"

Pointing at one of the gawkers on the steps, the youth explained, "Yeah, my brother went under the tape and checked out the apartment. He saw the body and said it was all tied up. I ain't about to go in no death house!"

Jamie walked back to the car and drove straight to the Casa Maya.

———

Captain Rohan was sitting at his desk staring at his computer screen. Salazar wanted him to find Ruben Repeza and some guy from Dallas. The person from Dallas was someone's dad.

Seriously, he's someone's dad! The poor bastard that Salazar shot in the eyeballs squealed about the guy being someone's dad and now this. This is the most ridiculous assignment I've ever been given, even from this dumbass.

Rohan was sick and tired of looking at statistics. His computer regurgitated facts he already knew...over ninety hotels in the *Hotelera Zona* and another twenty-seven in the downtown area. Plus, there were more than five million visitors each year to Cancun.

And to top it off, there are around thirty-two thousand hotel rooms in Cancun. Thirty-two thousand! How many of the occupants came from Dallas? How many!

Exploring further, he discovered the Cancun Airport handles over nineteen million passengers a year.

But wait! How can there only be five million visitors to Cancun each year and yet over nineteen million passengers go through the airport? If each of the five million come and go through the airport, that still only accounts for ten million passengers. What happened to the other nine million! Can't believe anything on the Internet! Maybe the airport authority jacked up their numbers to get more funding.

He finally settled down and started asking himself detective like questions.

Too many hotels to contact, and besides, what if the Dallas guy is staying with a friend? Jesus! Maybe he's been staying in Ruben Repeza's apartment. Yeah, that's it. He's been staying with Repeza and now they're going back to Dallas together. They were going to blackmail Salazar and move to Dallas.

Rohan's next dilemma was to figure out how to cover all the flights leaving for Dallas. He had called four of his best men to report to work immediately, even though it was Saturday.

The clerk he assigned to check on the flights leaving for Dallas walked into his office. "Captain, there are ten nonstop flights to Dallas today and six of them departed early this morning."

"Did you check with the airlines to see if a Ruben Repeza was on any of them?"

Oh yeah, did you ask if a dad from Dallas had a seat! What a stupid assignment!

"The airlines are checking for me and I should hear back from them within the next thirty minutes."

"Also, have them check on anyone by the name of Repeza leaving on a flight during the next week."

Rohan again engaged his detective thought process and concluded Repeza was not on any of the flights that left this morning. Repeza's friend had been bound and bleeding from the mouth when he and the Chief entered the apartment. Someone had been there shortly before they arrived. No way Repeza could have been on an early morning flight. Maybe he's leaving this afternoon or within the next few days.

We've got to cover the departing flights for Dallas starting now! I'll send all four men to the airport. Repeza and his friend could be flying standby in order to keep their names off the advanced-passenger list. It's the only chance we have.

Come to think of it, Repeza and his friend are probably partying tonight at one of the hotels or at one of the clubs. I'll get the other six members of my team to come to work tonight and check out the party scene.

Calling the clerk back into his office, Rohan had one additional request.

"Write up a description of Repeza and we'll give it to all my men and to the evening patrol officers."

The confused clerk answered, "But I don't have a description."

"Get it from Salazar. Repeza was his pim…" Thinking for a second, he corrected his last statement, "I mean Chief Salazar has met Repeza in the past. He'll give you the description."

———

Boyd was sitting in the lobby on the same couch they had occupied the previous evening with Miguel Burbano. He was relieved when he saw Jamie enter the glass doors and walk toward him.

Boyd stood and was first to speak. "So, how'd it go?"

Speaking in a lowered voice, Jamie looked around the lobby and said, "Well, as we suspected, there were gunshots. Apparently, the recipient of both of them was the bald headed guy…Hector."

"Dead?"

"Apparently so."

"There could have been more shots fired after we left. As you remember, we hauled ass when we heard the first two shots." Boyd still had questions.

"I guess it's possible," Jamie said, "but the kid I spoke with at the apartment said something about his brother ducking under the police tape and looking around inside. Don't know if he looked in the bedroom, but he only saw one dead body."

"Humm." Boyd looked at the floor and rubbed the back of his neck before speaking. "This was not part of the plan."

"Makes no difference. These guys were living on borrowed time anyway."

"The more I think about it, the more certain I am that I saw Ruben running out of the back entrance to the apartment."

"Oh well, as you said, the little bastard is marked...for life."

"Yep. No question about that."

Looking around the lobby again, Jamie said wearily, "This will sound strange coming from me, but I have absolutely no appetite. How about you?"

Managing a hint of a smile, Boyd stood and looked at the bar. "I know what I would like to do, but it's too early. Let's meet here in a couple of hours."

Boyd went to his room, locked the door and closed the drapes. Other than the steady hum of the air conditioner, the room was quiet and cool. Boyd removed his shoes and placed the contents of his pockets on the bedside table.

Easing his fatigued body on top of the bedspread, too drained to digest the events of the day, he remembered something that was constantly on his mind. In the dim light, he reached for his cell phone and checked for text messages.

The bright glow of the screen gave him exactly what he expected... nothing.

————

It was 3:30 and Boyd had slept soundly for over an hour. Raising his head, he was finally able to focus his eyes on the red numerals of the bedside clock. An afternoon nap for Boyd was unusual and sleeping soundly had been difficult for the past several months.

Sitting on the edge of the bed, his first thoughts were not about Ruben or the morning's activities, but instead, he immediately thought about his wife.

She's the one who became upset. No, she became enraged over the incident with their daughter. She's the one who questioned their marriage and had gone to Europe. She's the one who needs to make the next move.

Boyd checked his phone for messages one more time and made a decision.

Sally's right to be angry and she's right to blame me. That's one decision I would like to have over…letting our daughter go out with that goddamn waiter. Time to take it like a man.

Boyd walked to the window and opened the drapes. He could see the tops of the palm trees swaying in unison with the invisible breeze. In the bright sunlight, the Caribbean sparkled an amazing aqua color with sugar white combers marching steadily ashore. Most of the beach chairs and loungers appeared to be occupied by sun-hungry tourists.

Returning to the side of his bed, Boyd picked up his cell phone and decided on a text:

Sal…I made a mistake in Cancun and I'm very sorry. I hope you'll forgive me someday. I love you. I really, really love you…Boyd

The nap, a shower and a change of clothes made Boyd feel like a new man. He opened the door to his room and on the spur of the moment had an idea. He returned to the desk and removed his cell phone from his pocket.

It only took a few minutes to discover that he could leave Cancun for Dallas tomorrow on an afternoon flight, although there would be a change-fee of two hundred dollars. It would be worth it to get back home.

He felt new and improved as he entered the *La Buena Pinta* and spotted Jamie sitting at the bar drinking a beer.

"Drinking without me, huh?"

Holding up his bottle, Jamie said, "It's only beer. I would never drink George Dickel without you."

Grinning, Boyd said, "Well, it would be difficult at this particular bar, since they don't serve Dickel."

Boyd motioned to the bartender and pointed at Jamie's beer bottle and held up one finger.

The tiki-themed lounge was busy on this Saturday afternoon. Two other couples were seated at the end of the bar and over half the tables were occupied. The painting of the volcano was still erupting.

Taking a long drink from the bottle, Jamie frowned and said, "The thought of Ruben's friend being murdered only minutes after we were in the apartment is troubling. I suppose he had it coming, but never-the-less, it's troubling."

"Like you said, he and Ruben would have gone down sooner or later. Right?"

"Right."

Picking up his Tecate the bartender had placed in front of him, Boyd raised his bottle without saying anything. Jamie did the same.

They sat in silence for a few minutes, both men staring at the bar. Jamie finally spoke. "With all that was happening today, I totally forgot about the Emilio guy Miguel Burbano mentioned. You know, the one that owns a pharmacy."

"I didn't forget about him…he just wasn't on my radar. I came here with a purpose and now it's done. In the scheme of things, I'm not sure if justice was served or not, but in my own mind I'm at peace. Look, I have the same feelings as you about someone being murdered, but again, he brought it on himself. It seems the police have far less patience than I do."

"I'm with you."

Boyd turned serious again. "Jamie, I can't tell you how much I appreciate your assistance. I don't think this would have worked out if it hadn't been for you."

"You're a true friend and I'm just glad I could help." Getting the bartender's attention and holding up two fingers, he added, "Let's have another."

Patrons continued to flow through the doors of the *La Buena Pinta*. The tables and the surface of the bar reflected the subtle red and blue lights, creating an almost surreal atmosphere.

Two women dressed in shorts and tank tops sat down at the bar, one of them next to Jamie. She had multi-colored hair, multiple eyebrow piercings, and one arm covered in tattoos. Her face may have been pretty, but it was difficult to tell due to the excessive make-up. She could have been twenty-five or she could have been forty-five.

Looking at Jamie's arms and then at his eyes, she said, "You ever had a sex-on-the-beach?" Her voice sounded younger than forty-five.

Caught off guard, Jamie stuttered, "You mean the mixed drink?"

"Sure, silly. I'm not propositioning you."

"Don't think I have."

The two newcomers started talking to each other and both began waving their hands trying to get the bartender's attention.

Boyd leaned over to Jamie and whispered, "I think you have a new fan."

Jamie whispered back, "Ahh... this reminds me of a sign I saw in the Home and Garden section of Home Depot. It said, and I quote, 'Don't Ever Plant a Ten Dollar Tree in a Four Dollar Hole'. Just saying."

Boyd lowered his head, stifling a laugh. Finally, he said, "I checked with American and found out I could return on an earlier flight tomorrow afternoon. I won't leave unless you can leave as well. What do you think? Want to check and see if Delta has room for you to do the same thing tomorrow?"

"Glad you thought of it." Jamie removed his cell phone from his pocket and began entering information. "Just a minute."

Boyd added, "There will probably be a change fee with Delta. There was with American. If you'll charge it to a credit card, of course I'll reimburse you."

Within minutes, Jamie was entering his credit card number and said, "Done deal. I leave at 4:10p.m. What's your departure time?"

Boyd took longer than Jamie to complete his transaction with American Airlines, but after a few minutes he answered, "I leave at 4:30. We can go to the airport together in the rental car."

"Modern technology!"

"Another thought. Since we missed lunch, how about we go to Senor Frogs or someplace like that and grab a burger and some nachos?"

"I think it's a good idea and I think we should take a taxi."

"Let's go."

CHAPTER 47

Cancun...Saturday, June 5th
Boulevard Kukulcan was busy with Saturday traffic. The evening sun seemed to set fire to the giant towers of the beach front hotels on the left, while the lagoon on the right was busy with boat traffic, even at this time of day.

Boyd instructed the taxi driver to take them to Senor Frogs in the Hotel Zone. Ten minutes later the taxi parked directly in front of the Forum, a shopping mall located at ground zero of Cancun's night life. A police car was parked in front of the taxi and another pulled up behind them as Boyd was paying the driver.

The taxi driver commented, "A lot of police cars here tonight. I saw several more parked near here."

Jamie looked at Boyd and shrugged. Seeing no reason for concern, Boyd paid the driver and received his change.

After exiting the taxi, they could see Carlos and Charlies in the Forum Shopping Mall and Coco Bongo, displaying the Spiderman statue, a short distance away. Across the street, the Dady'O exterior looked like a huge rock. La Vaquita, the open-air nightclub, decorated in red, black and cow print, featured scantily clad go-go girls clinging to their poles in full view of the street while spectators gawked. The weekend night seemed to stifle any inhibitions that may have existed in people on the street and in the entertainment alleys near the clubs. The evening air was heavy, the outside noise level reverberated with a steady beat and the general atmosphere cried "let's get it on."

As a matter of habit, Boyd checked his cell phone and was surprised to see a text message. He slid his finger across the screen and took a deep breath as he read it.

I had a really good talk with Jenny. She's looking only to the future. She's in a good place and is happy again. If she can put it all behind her, I can too. You and I can also…together.

Boyd read the message twice. The last work struck a deep chord… *together.* A mixture of emotions overwhelmed him. He immediately sent a text to Sally…*Yes, together.*

"Good news?" Jamie was beginning to understand Boyd's mannerisms.

"Yes. Life is coming around." The coincidence of receiving this particular text, combined with the events of the morning, was not lost on Boyd.

"Great."

Pointing across the thick flow of cars, Boyd, in an upbeat tone said, "We had lunch at Senor Frogs when we were here in December. Could be a bit more boisterous at night. Good hamburgers…if we survive the street-crossing."

And it *was* a bit more boisterous at night! The motto on the front of the building…*Saving the World from Boredom*…was only a precursor of the bedlam inside.

The two friends found seats at a huge circular bar facing the stage. They each ordered a beer and a hamburger and took turns reaching into a bowl of popcorn as a hunger stop-gap. The containers of popcorn were constantly being refilled on the tables and at the bar.

A band with a sexy lead singer was covering popular American rock and roll, disco and recent hits. The noise level in the club was bone-jarring and indescribable. The loud music of the band, a siren randomly screeching, the squeals of the women whose dresses were being blown up with CO_2 canisters and the constant hollering of the MC contributed to the absence of boredom.

Several young ladies from the audience staggered onto the stage and began dancing even though the band was in between songs. They were saved from themselves when the speaker system overflowed with the fast complicated beats and the deep bass sounds of synthesized turbulence. This brought many of the revelers to their feet and the fifty or so tables in the main area of the club became unwanted barriers separating the throng.

A waiter offered Jamie a shot of tequila straight from the bottle, which he declined. The MC interrupted the clamor and instructed the crowd to start throwing popcorn on their neighbors…and everyone complied.

Jamie exclaimed, "This is organized chaos!"

"Better yet… hedonistic chaos," Boyd said. "Guess it's good to let off steam every once in a while."

"Need to make a quick trip to the restroom." Jamie had to raise his voice even though Boyd was only two feet away. "Be right back."

The restroom was on the second level of the nightclub where people were leaning on the rail observing the mob scene below. As Jamie left the restroom, he saw a uniformed policeman asking one of the *juerguis-tas* for an ID. Another individual was being questioned by two additional policemen at the bottom of the stairs.

Jamie couldn't hear the conversations, but the word Dallas made its way through the background clutter. Boyd was taking the first bite of his hamburger when Jamie finally negotiated his way back to the bar.

Jamie placed twenty dollars beside his plate, picked up the hamburger and said with a hint of urgency, "Bring your burger with you and follow me. Could be trouble."

Several taxis were parked in the same loading strip in front of the Forum. The humid night air had only encouraged more fun seekers to this part of the *Zona Hotelera*.

Entering the taxi at the front of the line and sliding across the seat with Boyd following, Jamie simply stated, "Casa Maya Hotel."

"Got it, boss."

Speaking in a muted tone, Jamie said, "Remember the police cars when we arrived tonight? I saw several policemen in the club questioning some guys. The only word I heard was Dallas. Set off an alarm."

"Not sure how it could involve us, but the pace of Senor Frogs was a little more than I needed anyway, especially after the day we've had. Glad we brought the burgers with us."

———

The hand emerging from the large metal trash container grasped the edge and pulled up a worn, battered body. The steam from the garbage rose into the night air, adding to the smells of the neighborhood. Ruben shook off a clump of tissue paper clinging to his shoulder, climbed out of the dumpster and fell into the dirt and mud of the alley.

Ruben had run and stumbled for two blocks after fleeing his apartment building a little over ten hours ago. He'd burrowed like a *rata* in the filth and passed out. The dumpster didn't have a lid and the afternoon heat of the sun stirred the odors into a fine stew. He never fully regained his senses, even though he awakened several times. His mind had morphed into a blend of confusion and terror due to the effects of the drug and what he had experienced. He had remained in the garbage because fear overcame any desire of escape.

Still wearing only his underwear, and a borrowed garbage bag, Ruben walked another six blocks to a familiar house...his aunt's.

CHAPTER 48

Cancun...Sunday, June 6th
Returning to the table at the poolside restaurant, Boyd set down his plate from the buffet. Jamie was already seated, reading a newspaper and drinking coffee.

"I got here early with a big appetite, so I went ahead and ate." Jamie took another sip of coffee and added, "I see that you like the Mexican papaya as much as I do."

"Can't get enough."

Jamie leaned back in his chair with *the Cancun News Journal* in his hand. "Yesterday turned out pretty darn good."

Boyd finished chewing a bite of eggs and wiped his mouth with a napkin. "It was a little off-plan, but the outcome was fine. The only troubling item...is what happened to Ruben's friend. Maybe he deserved it, maybe not. It appears the justice system here is out of control."

"For sure."

"You know, I'm amazed at the big picture of this whole thing. Less than two weeks ago you and I hadn't even met. And now we're sitting together in Cancun, Mexico having breakfast. You'll never know how much I appreciate your helping me..." Exhaling, he finished the sentence, "find myself. Really."

Jamie peeked over the newspaper and said politely, "Not a problem my friend."

Jamie continued reading the paper while Boyd ate. After a couple of minutes, wide-eyed, he exclaimed, "What's this! You're not going to believe this...and you were just talking about the justice system. Remember Miguel Burbano talking about Ruben's relative...Emilio Repeza? He had something to do with a pharmacy, right?"

Jamie quoted the headline and read aloud the brief article:

FARMACIA DEL BARATO ROBBED
A robbery and double homicide occurred early Saturday morning at the Farmacia del Barato near downtown Cancun on Avenida Coba. The owner, Emilio Repeza and an unidentified employee were brutally murdered during the robbery. The police are investigating the incident and will release more information at a later date.

Boyd laid his fork on the table and thought for a moment before speaking. "This Repeza fellow, whatever his relationship to Ruben, was somehow involved in the extortion scheme since his name was in the letter to the Police Chief. Also, Miguel seemed to think the friend of Ruben's, who got shot in his apartment, was the individual who picked up the cash from the other participants. These are not just coincidences."

"Damned right! And you were also right about the justice system here being out of control." Jamie, his lips tight, was adamant.

Boyd tried to apply as much logic as possible to the situation. Leaning closer to the table, he said, "I still don't think we're at risk here. I'm certain no one saw us yesterday and we certainly couldn't be dragged into a blackmail scheme. Just no way. Which brings up another issue..."

"I know what you're about to say. The DVDs. Right?"

"They're in my room. The extortion letter indicated the DVDs would be sent to the *Cancun News Journal* unless those guys paid up. Too bad for all of them, including the Police Chief, because I'm going to get an envelope from the front desk and send them to the newspaper when we check out. I certainly don't want to go through Customs with them. Who knows what would happen."

Jamie chuckled. "Well, I'm glad we're headed back to Big D this afternoon."

"Same here. Let's be ready to leave at noon."

———

The speculation as to what happened on Saturday morning continued during the trip to the airport. Boyd dropped Jamie off at Terminal 3 before returning the rental car. He would be flying out of the same terminal, but twenty minutes later.

The lobby of the airport was only moderately busy, compared to Boyd's arrival three days ago. The first line was short and it only took a few minutes to return his Mexican Tourist Permit and to show his passport and plane ticket. The security employee closely examined the passport and then looked at Boyd before waving him on.

The next line was moving more slowly as travelers placed their bags on the conveyers and entered the metal detector.

Boyd turned in surprise when someone poked a finger in the back of his shoulder and ordered, "Step over here, please. Bring your bag."

A woman in a police uniform, as opposed to the airport security garb, motioned Boyd to the side.

"Passport, please." The policewoman was polite, but direct. Looking at the passport, she asked, "You live in Dallas. Yes?"

A million thoughts were racing through Boyd's mind. How could the fact he was from Dallas have anything to do with what was going on? Didn't Miguel Burbano give him a phone number to call about someone driving him to the Texas border?

Forget that. Way too late.

"Yes, I live in Dallas."

The policewoman was looking at a sheet of paper and was having some trouble reading the information.

She stammered, "Are you traveling with a Repeza…a Mr. Repeza?"

"No."

"Okay, you can go. We have to ask all Dallas passengers this question."

It was clear the policewoman was only going through the motions. She had been briefed on what to do this afternoon at the airport and she was half-heartedly carrying out her job. It was also clear that Captain Rohan was looking for a needle in a haystack. Except in this case he was looking at the right haystack, but for the wrong needle.

THREE WEEKS LATER

CHAPTER 49

Dallas…Saturday, June 26th

After returning from Cancun, Boyd and Jamie had rehashed their three-day trip over and over. They speculated about a number of things: Ruben's fate, the fate of his running-mate, the other Repeza at the *farmacia*, and the role of the Cancun police in the entire affair. Boyd had permanently checked-out of the Ridgetop Mobile Estates and he and Jamie had not seen each other in two weeks, although they had talked briefly on the phone.

Boyd, standing on the front steps of his home in Northwood Hills, watched as Jamie's SUV slowly made its way up the tree-lined driveway. The partly-cloudy, late afternoon sky cast both shadows and rays of light on the huge expanse of lawn and foliage. It was too hot and humid to be voluntarily standing outside, but Boyd had been looking forward to this get-together.

Jamie and Amber exited the SUV and held hands as they walked toward the steps, smiling. Jamie was carrying a wine bottle decorated with a red bow.

"Hey, old man. Good to see you again. You actually haven't changed that much." Jamie loved playing the "you're-older-than-me card."

Returning the smile, Boyd said, "Good to see you also, kid. And it's really good to see you, Amber. I still don't understand how you put up with him!"

Without verbally responding, Amber held up her left hand and showed the engagement-ring to Boyd.

Engulfing Amber in a bear hug, Boyd said, "Congratulations, you make a lovely couple...and I mean it. Jamie told me about it when I called him the other day."

Boyd shook Jamie's hand and invited them into his home.

The temperature dropped dramatically upon entering the front door. Sally met them in the family room and was introduced to the newly betrothed couple.

Sally was wearing a simple Lanz sundress with small floral print, her auburn hair cut short. She was a living example of understated beauty. "Boyd talks about you two non-stop." Pointing at the couch, she smiled and continued, "And I hear Jamie saved Rosie from a lot of terrible people."

Rosie was curled up on the center cushion of the couch looking curiously at her admirers. After staring for a moment, she licked her paw and rubbed it over her face.

Sally shook her head and confirmed what everyone already knew. "*The Rose* has pretty much taken over the house."

Boyd chimed in, "She's my trailer park cat."

"Hey, she likes me too!" Jamie playfully stated.

Ignoring them both, Sally asked Amber, "Would you like a glass of wine or something stronger?"

"Wine would be wonderful."

"I have an open bottle in the kitchen," Sally said cordially. "Follow me, because I know what these two guys are going to drink, so let's leave them to it."

The two women walked toward the kitchen and Boyd and Jamie headed for the wet bar in the game room.

Leaning against the pool table, while Boyd was behind the bar pouring two George Dickels on the rocks, Jamie uttered with genuine admiration, "Jeez, this is a fantastic house! Beats the heck out of your doublewide."

Handing Jamie a drink, Boyd had a serious moment. "We've been here for a while and it's special for us. But you know what? This will sound weird...as weird as anything you've ever heard... but I could live full time at Ridgetop or any other similar place and be just as content as living here."

Touching glasses with Boyd, Jamie said, "I know you could and that's a really unique trait."

"You mentioned on the phone that you and Amber are getting an apartment somewhere in Dallas. Right?"

"Right. Amber graduates with her marketing degree at the end of the summer, so we're looking at a few places in the city." Jamie raised his eyebrows and finished. "And something has come up that I plan to check out. Nothing will probably come of it, but it's exciting to think about. Anyway, as soon as I know more about this opportunity, we'll decide where to live."

"Tell me about the opportunity," Boyd said in an amicable tone, a completely neutral look on his face.

"Well, my department head at Parkland…just out of the blue…approached me the other day and said he wanted me to consider applying for medical school. I was shocked, to say the least. And then he said there was a new scholarship grant available."

"Sounds good to me. So what's next?"

Jamie's excitement was showing. "It's a full-ride scholarship to UT Southwestern Medical School here in Dallas and I'm applying for the grant on Monday. I'm sure there will be a ton of people applying, but I'm going to do it anyway. Unbelievable long-shot."

Boyd turned and set the bottle of bourbon back on a glass shelf, hiding the grin on his face. Holding up his glass, he toasted, "Here's to you and Amber… and here's to you having the luck of the draw in your application for the grant."

As they clinked glasses, a thought flashed through Jamie's mind: *Is it possible that Boyd…surely not. Humm.*

Dismissing the thought, Jamie turned to another topic. "How's the book coming along?"

"Surprisingly well." Boyd took a sip of his drink and went into more detail. "I've finished a very tentative outline and know generally where I'm headed."

"So give me a summary of the plot."

"Well, it involves friendship, revenge and a back story of cultural enlightenment." Boyd thought for a second and went on, "Takes place in two different locations and everything comes together at the end of the story. Sound familiar?"

Grinning, Jamie continued to probe. "Do you have a title yet?"

"Yep...*Ridgetop*."

Boyd changed the subject by saying, "I told Sally about you and I going to Cancun to research the book. I hate withholding information from her, but I'll tell her about the other details of the trip when the time is right. Sometimes withholding information is as bad as outright lying, but under the circumstances, I need to wait."

"I completely understand. I have the exact same situation with Amber. She'll understand better at a later date."

Laughter from the two ladies could be heard coming from the kitchen. The beautiful home, the atmosphere, the friends and the mood were comforting. A sense of tranquility permeated the evening.

Jamie set his glass down and took a deep breath. "This will sound a bit corny, but just sitting here in this stunning home, knowing you, and realizing what you've achieved by hard work and dedication, gives me..." he hesitated, and then completed his thought, "a feeling of motivation, inspiration."

Boyd whispered, "Reach for the feeling, my son."

EPILOGUE

Cancun, Mexico

The elderly woman walked into the small bedroom and opened the shades on both windows. The sunlight seemed to focus on the cot shoved against the wall. She noticed that the foul odor from the wounds was becoming stronger.

As she stood over the bed, Ruben made several groaning sounds and shifted first one way and then the other. The woman did not speak a word of English and had no idea what the words on her nephew's forehead and chest meant, if anything. She only knew the fever had not dropped during the weeks he had been here. The sheets, as usual, were soaked in sweat.

The four letters on his forehead were black and sank into a puffy, red discoloration around the tattoo. They actually didn't look as bad as the mess on his chest.

The inflammation between his nipples was excessive, giving the U and the N a distorted appearance. All four letters had developed pus pockets and were steadily discharging a yellowish-green liquid mixed with traces of blood. Nasty looking red streaks extended out from the tattoo site.

The woman gently placed a wet dish cloth on his forehead and whispered a prayer of healing.

Suddenly, Ruben opened his eyes wide, looking, but not seeing and uttered one word... **"TANNER."**

ACKNOWLEDGEMENTS

I would like to thank my wife, Jan, for her support and understanding during the writing of this novel (even if she winced at some of the content and language). We had a great time working together in the initial "home" edit of the book.

My sincere gratitude goes out to Mike Valentino who conducted the professional editing. He knows more about grammar, spelling, sentence structure and the unique use of words than anyone I have ever known (and I'm sorry I teased him about graduating from Harvard!).

Two close friends, Darell Choate and Richard Belmont, deserve special recognition. After reading portions of the book, their comments inspired me to "get on with it" and finish the work. Their wives, Diane and Suzanne, also read several early chapters and offered their support.

I am also grateful to other friends and relatives who read some of the early chapters and provided feedback: my daughter Ricki and her husband Ray Syufy, my son Jim and his wife Tiffany, Gaye and Miguel Burbano, Dennis and Liz McGuire, Kenneth Lokey and Pat Melton.

Jim Abelsen and Bob Campbell were both of great assistance with their words of wisdom regarding the writing process.

I appreciate the assistance and openness of Gary Garrigus at the Rocky Point Mobile Estates in Flower Mound, Texas and Ray Tiempe, Manager of the Double R Trailer Park in Desert Hot Springs, California. Also, thanks to Wyatt Johnson at Anarchy & Ink in Cathedral City, California for his comments on the art of tattooing (I promise, Wyatt, that I will come see you if I ever decided to get a *tat*).

The disappearance of Natalee Holloway in Aruba formed the basic idea behind this novel. The number of rapes that occur each year in resort locations around the world is staggering...and four or five times as many go unreported.

And finally, thanks to my taxi driver and guide in Cancun...Pacco... for his knowledge of the *Zona Hotelera*, and the downtown area of Cancun.

ABOUT THE AUTHOR

Jim Tindle lives in Southern California with his wife, Jan, and calico cat, Rosie.